BLOOD
IN SWEET
RIVER

T0201622

THE CLEVE TREWE WESTERNS
BY JOHN SHIRLEY

Axle Bust Creek

Gunmetal Mountain

Blood in Sweet River

BLOOD IN SWEET RIVER

A Cleve Trewe Western

JOHN SHIRLEY

PINNACLE BOOKS
Kensington Publishing Corp.
www.kensingtonbooks.com

PINNACLE BOOKS are published by

Kensington Publishing Corp.
900 Third Avenue
New York, NY 10022

Copyright © 2024 by John Shirley

This book is a work of fiction. Names, characters, businesses, organizations, places, events, and incidents either are the product of the author's imagination or are used fictitiously. Any resemblance to actual persons, living or dead, events, or locales is entirely coincidental.

All rights reserved. No part of this book may be reproduced in any form or by any means without the prior written consent of the Publisher, excepting brief quotes used in reviews.

To the extent that the image or images on the cover of this book depict a person or persons, such person or persons are merely models, and are not intended to portray any character or characters featured in the book.

If you purchased this book without a cover you should be aware that this book is stolen property. It was reported as "unsold and destroyed" to the Publisher and neither the Author nor the Publisher has received any payment for this "stripped book."

All Kensington titles, imprints, and distributed lines are available at special quantity discounts for bulk purchases for sales promotion, premiums, fund-raising, and educational or institutional use.

Special book excerpts or customized printings can also be created to fit specific needs. For details, write or phone the office of the Kensington Sales Manager: Kensington Publishing Corp., 900 Third Avenue, New York, NY 10022. Attn. Sales Department. Phone: 1-800-221-2647.

PINNACLE BOOKS and the Pinnacle logo Reg. U.S. Pat. & TM Off.

First Printing: September 2024
ISBN-13: 978-0-7860-4929-5
ISBN-13: 978-0-7860-4930-1 (eBook)

10 9 8 7 6 5 4 3 2 1

Printed in the United States of America

Dedicated to the memory of my aunt, Margaret Edgell

Chapter 1

San Francisco. September 1875.

A pair of jacks . . .

A queen, a king, and a seven of spades.

Clevcland Trewe was trying to decide if that pair of jacks was worth the risk of a big raise. Poker seemed on his side tonight. He'd caught some good hands. But he full well knew that luck was "fickle as a country girl hunting a rich husband," to use an expression favored by Leon Studge. Luck could turn tail with any new deal of the cards.

Still, Cleve had reasons to raise. He had a draw remaining, to improve his hand, and the man across from him at the circular table at the Montgomery Street's Gentleman's Club was fair drunk. A drunk card player could jump any old way. He might toss down his cards in disgust. He might call or raise on a whim. A drunk would just plain make the wrong decision.

But there was another reason Cleve wanted to raise—he was bored. He was full bored with poker games; he was bored with saloons, whether highfalutin saloons like this one or the sawdust and spittoon variety. He was powerful weary of San Francisco. He and Berenice had been here ten months, near nine of them waiting for the baby to come, for this was where the best physicians resided. Cleve had been able to make only the most pitifully tentative efforts to set up a ranch in Sweet River Valley. A few hundred cattle bought, kept for him near Sacramento; a discussion by mail with a man who might or might not sell Cleve the grazeland he hankered for. But the baby had come three weeks early, and it wouldn't do for him to drag Berenice and little Alice to Sweet River till both were strong and fit enough.

It was stuffy in the "gentleman's club," and Cleve tilted his Stetson back on his head and considered taking off his black coat. Under it was a white silk shirt with French cuffs, a present from Berenice. The frilled cuff was a men's fashion exhibited by the local bon vivants, and Cleve had been uneasy about it, figuring he'd resemble some decadent fop. But he'd come to prize the shirt, even if it didn't quite go with his gray Stetson, gray-and-black-striped trousers, and well-worn black riding boots.

"Mister, you going to call, raise, or toss in the hand?" asked Stogie Whitt—snarling around his stub of a cigar. A black-bearded slab of a man in a gold and scarlet waistcoat, gartered shirt sleeves, and a Homberg tilted aggressively forward, Stogie chewed on the cigar with his bared tobacco-stained teeth and stared at Cleve with piggish eyes.

Given the tone of the question, Cleve declined to answer. He laid his cards face down, picked up a handful of gold eagles, and clinked them in his palm as if to amuse himself.

"Dammit, sir!" Stogie snapped. "Call, raise, or fold! I've got a pistol in my hip pocket and I do not care to be kept waitin'!"

Cleve kept clinking the coins and yawned, glancing around the saloon, as if casually wondering who else had come in.

Three men were drinking at the bar. The bespectacled, mustachioed bartender was lighting a customer's pipe. It was Tuesday, approaching midnight. The stage's few musicians had departed an hour ago, leaving a deathly quiet. Yet the gentleman's club looked smokier and dingier than when he'd strolled in. Yellow gaslight sconces on the gold and red velvet walls threw a phlegmy light across two billiard tables, the carven-walnut back room bar, the brass statues of half-clothed Roman women boldly displaying their bosoms as they danced to either side of the mirror. The air was heavy and close, and in the cone of light over the bar the smoke seemed to arrange itself to mimic the paisley carpet.

"That's done it," said Stogie. He stood up and made to reach for the cash on the table. "You folded."

Cleve tossed the double eagles on the table. "Raise a hundred. You want to win it from me, sit down. Call or fold—but *do not touch the pot.*"

Stogie glared, nostrils flaring. Cleve was ready to deal with the matter if the gambler reached for his gun. They were not supposed to carry weapons in San Francisco, but it was a rule often flouted.

Stogie snorted and sat heavily down. "You're called!" He pushed a hundred dollars into the pot.

"I'll take a card," Cleve said, tossing down the seven of hearts.

Stogie blinked. "Just the one?"

"Just the one." His hand might improve to a pair of queens or kings, to go with his jacks, maybe even three of a kind.

He watched closely as Stogie dealt him a card. The card was a jack of spades.

Cleve pretended to ponder his cards, humming to himself and peering at them. Then he shrugged and laid them face down on the table.

"Let's shove it all," Cleve said. "I'm about ready to go on home." He pushed the rest of his money toward the center of the table.

"Ha!" Stogie said. "I call!" He flipped his cards onto the table face up. "Two aces, two tens!"

Cleve gave him a tight smile. He showed his cards. "Three of a kind." He reached out and scooped the money toward him. "It's been a pleasure."

Stogie jumped to his feet, upsetting his chair. "You've been winning all night, and I know you've got cards tucked away in that coat!" He tugged at his pistol.

Cleve put his hand in his coat for his hideaway gun, reflecting that Berenice would not be pleased to hear he got in a shooting affray.

Someone hidden by Stogie's bulk stepped up behind

the gambler. Stogie grunted as his arm was twisted behind his back. "Reaching for that gun would end with you dying, feller," said a familiar voice.

Cleve stood and blurted, *"Leon Studge!"*

"Let go of me!" Stogie bellowed.

Leon pushed Stogie away, keeping the big man's gun. "You should be thanking me, mister," Leon said. "I calculate I just saved your life." Stocky, snub-nosed, not quite forty, Leon was dressed in a blue suit and an oxblood bowler hat; his eyebrows were lofted, his brickish face lit up by his grin. Cleve noted that Leon no longer wore a badge.

Stogie spat his cigar onto the floor and spun around, his cheeks flaming red as he massaged his arm. "You like to broke my arm!"

"I didn't put so much as a bruise on your fat little arm. You know who you were about to pull a gun on?"

"I don't know his name but I know his kind!" Stogie snapped.

Leon laughed. "You mistake him! That's Cleve Trewe. Lawman of Denver and Axle Bust Creek. You might've heard something."

Stogie's mouth dropped open. The color drained out of his face. "Do you say so? Cleve Trewe?" He looked at the bartender. "That right?"

The bartender nodded. "That is indeed Mr. Trewe. And he does not have the reputation of a deceitful card-player."

"Why—I might have mistaken . . . that is, the light in

here is bad . . . perhaps I imagined . . ." He sniffed and took off his hat to Cleve. "I do apologize."

Cleve nodded impatiently. "Give him his gun, Leon, and"—He took two of the twenty-dollar gold coins up and laid them together at the edge of the table—"buy yourself a drink or two on me, Stogie. No hard feelings."

Leon handed the gun over, Stogie stowed it away, snatched up the two gold eagles, slapped on his hat, and hurried out. Leon chuckled, watching him go.

Cleve turned to Leon, so inordinately pleased to see his old friend he had to grin. "I just mailed a letter to you, yesterday, damn you!"

Leon shrugged. "Maybe it'll be forwarded on to me, but I doubt it. I quit the job in Axle kind of sudden."

Cleve laughed and the two men shook hands. "Lord, it's good to see you. Is Teresa here too?"

"She's with your wife, cooing over that baby!"

"How'd you find me in this teeming metropolis?"

"Your missus knows just where you like to gamble. I thought to hear a note of exasperation as she told me where you was likely to be."

"Oh, well, once or twice a week. I've hired a house-keeper who nannies, too, and she—wait now! Berenice is all right? There's nothing—?"

Leon was stacking Cleve's coins and greenbacks. "Berry is just dandy. She wants you back before she goes to bed. Let's have a drink and then I'll drag you home by the ear, just like she asked me to." He flicked a gold eagle to Cleve who caught it between two fingers. "Looks like you're buying, Major . . ."

They walked side by side down the wooden walk along Montgomery Street, passing through pools of gaslight. The night air was cool, as a breeze came off San Francisco Bay. Cleve could smell the brine of it. Here and there, clusters of men, and a few women, were to be seen in front of the occasional saloon or whiskey bar, each group with its own little cloud of tobacco smoke catching the streetlight gleam.

Montgomery sported some hulking blocks of buildings, four and five and six stories, interspersed with smaller wooden structures, many with a false front, that could almost have come from Dodge City. A horse and buggy clipped and clacked by; two men across the street sang an obscene song about sailors as they drunkenly swaggered along, when Leon asked, "What's this road made of? Looks red, like."

"That's crushed basalt. Does not get muddy. An old forty-niner friend of mine, Jep Cornwall, he says in the old days, the mud got so deep out here you couldn't cross the street without fear of sinking away. And one night the rain was a pure deluge, so a horse sank and smothered in the mud. After that, they laid down redwood logs and basalt over the roads."

"Is that so! Now, tell me this—what gun was you reaching for, back in that fancy saloon?"

"Forehand and Wadsworth .38 pocket gun. Based on

an old Smith and Wesson hideaway. Haven't had to fire it except at a target, as yet."

"Forehand and Wadsworth? Is that the Swamp Angel?"

"No, young 'un, that's their .41. They call this one the Bull Dog. Two-inch barrel."

"Better have that man nose-to-nose-close with a dainty gun like that."

"You're not carrying an equalizer?"

"I don't need a gun—I got two equalizers, we call 'em fists. And I got a folding knife on me."

"You are surely bold since you killed that Hortlander son of a bitch—you did it without a gun, as I recall."

"You forget, I did use a gun. The *butt* of a gun. Hammered him good with it."

Cleve winced at the thought. "Well if ever a man deserved it . . ."

Leon paused in front of a false-fronted business and looked up at the gaslit sign. "I'd carry that fine Colt you gave me here, but I'm told the local gendarmes don't like to see a man wearing his gun."

"Which is why we carry them out of sight. About half the men you see have them, tucked away somewheres. We don't all have your powerful fists."

"Now you're just taunting at me."

Cleve chuckled. "You still got that town marshal badge somewhere?"

"I got the badge as a keepsake. I told you, I resigned."

"And why?"

"Y'all don't know—I decided to come in person to tell you and Berry. I'm plain done with Axle Bust! Six weeks ago, maybe seven, Berry's brother shut the Golden Fleece. Said the mine was played out and too expensive, even if it wasn't. Floodin' on 'em all the time. Town got worried, and the laid-off men got drunk and rough and some of the old-time southern seshers— they come after Dave Kanaway, saying he was too uppity." David Kanaway was a Black businessman in the mining camp. "I knocked some heads and had to shoot a man."

"You shoot him dead?"

"He was still alive when I left. Anyway, the town council gave me a tongue-hiding over it, and I said you can kiss my Texas ass."

Cleve chuckled. "I resigned from lawing there in much the same case."

"So then, I calls on Kanaway and I says, 'Dave, how's about you sell out and go with me and Teresa, and we'll see ol' Cleve in Frisco? Dave, you know all about horses,' I says, 'and Cleve's going to need that on the ranch.'"

"Dave's here?" Cleve was much pleased. "A valuable man! Where is he?"

"Staying at some inn down by the ocean."

"Close to the water? Not down in Barbary Coast!"

"It could be."

"He could have bunked with us."

"He didn't want to put you out none."

"Why, he'd be welcome. We have a sizable suite. If he's in the 'Barbary Coast' district—that's the rough part of this burg. Have to look into it tomorrow. You bring anyone else to San Francisco? Maybe Drizzle Dan?"

"Is that what you think of me, I spend my hours with that drunk?"

"You saying you never keep company with the lushes?"

"Why, I've got to keep an eye on them is all! Got to drink with 'em to do that. But you know—Drask come along with us, too, him and his Mai. He's at the Grand. Going to hang out his shingle right here in town. They want to do something for some folks she's got out here."

"Lawyer Drask too! Berry will be pleased to see Mai." Mai Ling, a Chinese girl who'd been sold into a kind of slavery and rescued by Cleve, was now Mai Drask, the lawyer having married her. "Be good to see 'em both. Now wait—you're not staying here? You coming in with me at all?"

"Not if you don't want me to," said Leon, looking at him askance.

"I told you twice by mail, if you ever got tired of lawing, you can come in on the ranch with me. But it's going to be rough out there."

"Me raised up man and boy on a Texas ranch, you're gabbling about rough?"

Cleve laughed and clapped him on the shoulder. "I have never been gladder to see any man than I was to see you tonight, Leon!"

Seeming moved but embarrassed, Leon looked back at the sign on the false front and read it out: "*California*

Steam Artisan Well Boring and Rock Drilling Company. Lord, is that what the man says when they ask him where he works? Sure'd be a mouthful." He looked up at the gaslights on their wrought iron posts. "Pleasure to have some good lighting after Axle. I gloried in the gas lighting up in Chicago, after you let me out of Fort Slocum." Leon had been Cleve's prisoner, officially anyhow, at Fort Slocum, in the last months of the Civil War.

The Union Army had given Major Cleveland Trewe, wounded in the war's last battle, what was supposed to be light duty overseeing Confederate prisoners at Fort Slocum. Shortly after Cleve's arrival, Leon came to talk to him about conditions for the prisoners, and they worked together to get the men more food and medical care. They met again in Axle Bust, developing a close bond and mutual respect.

Leon turned to gaze up at the San Francisco hills, where the gaslights were like a diadem upon the city. "Now, that's fine. Looks like stars in the prairie night. How they get the gas out here?"

"There's a gasworks that pumps it out, sends it through the pipes. But you know every gas flame in every lamp still has to be lit, one at a time. And if the flame goes out indoors, and the gas is still on, why, people die from it."

"I heard some theaters blew up, too, just like a mine explosion." Leon yawned. "Say—that's your hotel right there!"

Cleve chuckled. "Yep, four stories of stone and iron

frame. When we first got here, Lotta Crabtree was staying in it too."

"Lotta Crabtree! 'San Francisco's darling!' I saw her dance and sing in Yuma. Did she kiss you? She is supposed to be a live one."

"Kiss me? No, Lotta Crabtree is still alive." Cleve went on with a straight face. "Berenice would have said she was sad to do it, but she'd have shot her dead for any such presumption."

Leon laughed. "I reckon not—but she'd have cut that woman with a sharp tongue. For Berenice is a lady, if there ever was one."

"You forget she shot that boss pimp in Axle. And she got pretty rough with those riders at Gunmetal Mountain . . ."

"Now that you mention it, I'd best be on my best behavior."

"You ready to enter the Monkey Block?"

"The what! I saw no apes here! 'Cept maybe that big galoot across the street, making fists at the little fella."

Cleve snorted. "That building is called the Montgomery Block—some, like Miss Crabtree, amuse themselves by calling it the Monkey Block."

"Let's go in. I'm about wore out, and I'd like one more look at that daughter of yours while she sleeps. Alice is sure the angel. How a Yankee rascal like you had anything to do with the making of her, Major Trewe, is past understanding."

They went into the big stone building, shops and cafés on the ground floor, flats up above. Cleve's mind was straying to Kanaway staying in the Barbary Coast district. Dave Kanaway could take care of himself— but the thugs in Barbary Coast did not fight fair, and once or twice a month a body washed up on the rocks near there, a man stripped of his valuables, and shot in the back . . .

Chapter 2

They breakfasted on the first floor of the Montgomery Building, at the True Café—Cleveland Trewe stoically abiding the jokes twinning his name and the café's. Cleve was in his frock coat and a white cotton shirt, for Leon had made fun of his "lady's wear" silk shirt.

But Leon surprised him by cooing over the baby in Berenice's arms even more than Teresa did.

Leon's wife, red-haired and blue-eyed Teresa, gazed on Leon with benevolent speculation, as he held the infant's tiny hand. Leon had mentioned in a letter that they were "abundantly happy," though "she's cruel strict in keeping the moons": the method of timing marital intimacy so that conception was unlikely. The look on Teresa's face, as she gazed at Alice, suggested to Cleve that she might soon set aside the calendar.

A successful dust panner and nugget digger, Teresa was petite yet voluptuous, prone to a mischievous smile, her scarlet hair tied back in a bun. She was a woman with wanderlust. A one-time partner of Nellie Cashman's, she had held her own in a number of mining camps. Like Berenice, she had a fierce streak of independence.

Berenice. He turned to gaze on her. Cleve was always drawn back to contemplating Berry. Her dark brown, gold-flecked eyes, like the golden-brown form of the gem tourmaline; the onyx pupils glittering with intelligence; the pert set to her delicate lips; the tumble of her wavy chestnut hair, contrasting with the ivory shoulders exposed in one of the daring dresses inspired by French *bateau* gowns.

"I shall have to feed Alice soon," she said. "She was too sleepy to have much interest when she first woke." The infant had her mother's eyes, and she shifted them toward Berenice at this. A toothless smile played around the infant's lips. She was well aware of the word *feed,* it seemed. Alice had been born a few weeks early, small and frail, but she had put on weight with breast-feeding; as had the breasts who fed her. *"At this stage, Cleve,"* Berry had warned him, *"you make free with my bosoms at your own risk."*

Alice was a good-natured, alert child, and Cleve was still astounded when he looked upon her, and thought, *She is mine, my own child . . .*

Cleve watched as Berry glanced around the crowded café, filled with people talking, or peering frowningly at the crabbed print of the *San Francisco Call* or *The Spirit of the Times.* She had that recurrent expression, a little puzzled, a little amused, that suggested she was surprised to find herself here—married, with a baby, in San Francisco. Mildly perplexed but not disheartened.

"How'd you come to call her Alice?" Leon asked.

"A grandma's name? In Texas, we name children after Bible folks and the elders, mostly. I've got a cousin named his boy Robert E. Lee Studge, but I don't countenance any such."

"The night before she was born, I was reading a book by a Mr. Lewis Carroll," said Berry, pouring more tea into her china cup. "The heroine is a young girl named Alice. I admire her spirit, her gumption—"

"Her willingness to crawl down a hole to see what a rabbit was up to?" Cleve suggested, grinning. When they'd traveled together from Axle Bust to points west, many a time his wife, fascinated with the intricacies of the natural world, had tried to explore an animal's lair. And she'd come riskily close to a pack of coyotes. He loved his Berenice for her free spirit, but it unnerved him sometimes. He feared her intrepid curiosity could cost her life.

"That what that Mr. Carroll's child does?" Leon asked, shaking his head. "Seems foolish!"

"The rabbit was wearing a weskit and a pocket watch," said Berry primly. "That's reason enough to investigate."

"Now I thought you read those journals of science all the day," said Leon. "I don't believe rabbits wearing pocket watches are found in burrows. I could be wrong. It's a strange ol' world."

Berry laughed; a soft, liquid laugh that always seemed to reverberate somewhere inside Cleve.

"I do read the occasional monograph," she said. "I'm reading one by Mr. T.H. Huxley: a great comparative anatomist who—like me—is largely self-taught in the ways of science. He has the advantage of his gender, and is quite influential. But I do admire him—he seems to be suggesting that *Archaeopteryx*—"

"The ark of what now?" Leon asked, blinking.

"It was a dinosaur," Cleve said. "One that had feathers."

"Just so," said Berry, reaching out to squeeze Cleve's hand. Her touch was as firm as it was soft—should that be possible?

"A dinosaur!" Leon said. "I read about them big lizards in the newspaper. Folks finding their bones and such. But lizards surely don't have feathers, Berry!"

"This one did," she averred. "It cannot be quite called a lizard. It may have been—as Mr. Huxley suspects— the ancestor of many of today's birds. Indeed, all birds may have some ancient source in dinosaurs . . ."

"Now hold on a minute—!" Leon began. "Birds aren't lizards!"

"Leon," Teresa interrupted. "Aren't you and Cleve going to see Mr. Kanaway at the docks this morning? Berry's got to feed the little one. She and I shall retire upstairs."

"Where's Ulysses, Cleve?" Leon asked, as they headed down the slight slope toward Montgomery Street, the sun over Telegraph Hill warming their backs.

"Him and Suzie are in Alameda, there's a good stable there, with a fair pasturage. We go and see them when we can. They're getting restless. But Suzie's had a foal. He looks more like Ulysses than her."

"So you're telling me you got your wife with child— and your horse got her horse with child?"

Cleve laughed. "He did! Where's your own horse?"

"Place over by the missions. Wish I had him right now." Watching a hire buggy clopping by, he added, "We could hire a buggy."

"We need the walk. Too many flapjacks."

A few couples in fineries were strolling down the sidewalk, the men in silk top hats and three-piece suits and the women in beribboned ladies' toppers and lacy walking dresses. Cleve and Leon tipped their hats to them.

Leon wore the same rumpled suit today, and he shivered as a cold wind from the sea veered between the wood frame and stone buildings. "Lord, I thought it'd be warmer here in Californy."

"We had our hot weather in high summer. But the ocean's right here and the current is never warm. You know, most early morning there's fog come rolling in off the bay. Even at this hour, down by the docks—"

"Now who the red devils is that?" Leon interrupted, as a tubby bearded man topped by a plumed top hat stepped out onto the corner up ahead. His hair and beard, black streaked with gray, poked out all unruly. He wore a gilded-buttoned blue officer's parade coat with large gilt epaulets and an old cavalry saber on his belt. He paused on the corner reached into a pants pocket and drew out a large hunk of cheese. Watching horsemen and carriages pass, he began to gnaw on the cheese.

"Some kind of foreign ship captain, I expect?" Leon suggested.

"No—he's a man of some importance around here."

"Carries a hunk of cheese in his pocket, I see."

"He lives hand to mouth. Yet that man is the Emperor, Norton the First—Imperial Sovereign of the United States. You never heard of him?"

"Believe I saw it in a newspaper once. He's the madman who thinks he's emperor?"

"I suppose he is. But he's a good fellow. Kind to children and dogs, and sometimes he publishes a declaration of plans for improving San Francisco. Many of his ideas are good ones. He was a commodities merchant here, in gold rush times, and did well—and then got himself into a pickle and lost it all and his wife too. He never recovered. He blamed the government and announced he would replace it with something better. Declared himself emperor."

"Is that all a man has to do? I'd like to declare myself King of Texas."

"He's wearing his finer hat today, I see. But he's gone to seed some, of late. Getting old and accepting too many free drinks. He lives on the kindness of San Franciscans. Most will not laugh at him and always address him as Emperor Norton, or Your Majesty. He's something of a friend of mine, and Berenice has a great affection for him—he blessed our baby, you know—and you must give him his dignity, Leon."

"I surely will."

They walked up to Norton, Cleve taking off his hat and bowing to the emperor. "Good morning, Your Majesty."

Norton swallowed a mouthful of cheese and beamed at them. "Why, Cleveland Trewe, my General of City

Forces and the Sergeant of Arms of my Court!" Norton sounded neither pompous nor facetious. He had an uncanny way of making portentous pronouncements with conviction. "And who is this gentleman?" he asked, looking on with approval as Leon doffed his hat and bowed.

"Leon Studge, sir, business partner of ol' General Trewe here. I just yesterday come to Frisco, and I do admire how you're keeping the town."

But Norton's manner abruptly changed. His eyebrows shot up, and he glowered at Leon and said, "'Frisco,' sir? *Frisco?*" He thrust his cheese into his pocket and used the same hand to fetch a scrap of parchment from his coat pocket. He handed it, in a sharply peremptory manner, to Leon.

Cleve and Leon read it—despite its being smeared with cheese grease:

> *Whoever after due and proper warning shall be heard to utter the abominable word "Frisco," which has no linguistic or other warrant, shall be deemed guilty of a High Misdemeanor, and shall pay into the Imperial Treasury as penalty the sum of twenty-five dollars.*
>
> *NORTON I., Emperor of the United States*

"Twenty-five dollars!" Leon burst out. "Cleve, surely you do not expect me to pay—"

"Sorry, Leon," Cleve said sternly, clapping on his hat. "Ignorance of the law is no excuse. Pay it over!"

"I'll be a ringtailed son of a . . ." Leon muttered,

digging into his pocket. He took a deep breath, and with marginal grace, passed a twenty and a five to the Emperor, who promptly nodded, smiled, and tucked the cash away in his coat.

"You are absolved," Norton said loftily. "You may remain in my capital city." He leaned toward Leon and added meaningfully, "In . . . *San Francisco.*"

With that, he nodded to Cleve and crossed the street to a handy bar and grill.

Leon frowned at Cleve. "You're the Sergeant of Arms of his court, are you?"

"So he tells me."

"Then you could've spoke up for me."

Cleve smiled. "And miss seeing you pay that fine over to him? Besides, any man in town will buy you a drink if you tell him you paid a fine to the emperor. You can dine out on it."

"You don't say so! Before I leave, I'll give it a test. And you know, maybe that emperor would be a sight better at running this country than your Ulysses Grant!" Cleve was a booster of President Grant, and Leon was a Texan.

"Why, Grant is a fine president."

Leon snorted. "When he's sober."

"And you are a good horseman, Leon . . . when you're sober. Come on, let's find Dave Kanaway."

Cleve and Leon could hear San Francisco Bay before they could see it. Waves soughed and seabirds screeched.

They came to the end of the street, where two big

freight wagons waited outside a warehouse. To the right was an alley that led them to a narrow, cobbled street that followed the bay. "This is one end of the Embarcadero," said Cleve.

The docks were still festooned with curls of fog, slowly disappearing in the rising warmth. Gulls gossiped and wheeled overhead. Out on the bay, the sluggish waves were like unpolished emerald, translucent green in the sunlight coming over the roofs. Fog hid the ocean horizon, and clung around the shores of Yerba Buena Island. Nearer to hand, thin smoke issued tentatively from the two iron smokestacks of a three-tier side-wheel steamship, docked on its port side to a pier about forty yards north. The engine was kept hot, but not fully stoked. On the vessel's prow was painted *The Seattle Souther.* Beyond the ornate steamer, a small forest of masts and steam chimneys announced other ships, steam and sail and hybrid. Stevedores carted freight off ships down there, and stores back aboard.

"Embarcadero, you say," Leon noted. "Spanish for where you get your boat ride, or some such."

Cleve nodded. "San Francisco belonged to Mexico before it was ours."

"Little something called the Mexican-American War come along . . ."

"You know, this land we're standing on wasn't here, not so long ago. They filled it in with sand and old ships and such."

Leon looked at the ground. "We're standing on old ships?"

"Hulks of ships. Wrecked and towed. They're buried

under us right here. What was the name of that inn Kanaway was at?"

"The *Winking Annie Hotel*—recommended by a fella he met on the train."

"Sounds like Barbary Coast. Which is up this way . . ."

They strode past the warehouses, nearly getting run down by cursing stevedores and tote carts. Gulls shrieked, and cartwheels squeaked, till they reached the mercantile part of the neighborhood at the end of Pacific Street.

Here were a few shops; boxy buildings, crowded together, one and two stories high: *Gisborne's Seagoing Supplies; Chillwell's Drugs & Medicines, Wholesale and Retail; Pacific St. Fresh Fish and Crab.* Here was a small hotel, *The Californian,* with its own restaurant; across from it was a print shop, and a store called *Hunter's Delight.*

But soon, as they strolled up Pacific, it was as if they crossed a seam into steaminess; traipsing over a line marked by a trash-strewn alley, they were suddenly in the red-light district.

It was still morning and there were no red lights showing, but two women were lolling sleepily in the windows of a brothel. The narrow, three-story building was painted blue, but weathering was making the paint crackle so it looked like a snakeskin partly shed. One of the women had an elbow on the sill, her head on one hand, her cleavage well displayed in a scant nightgown; the other, in a torn frock, was sitting in the window, smoking a pipe, drooping one pale bare leg down, swinging it lazily . . . She had a shoe dangling from her toe and now she let it drop right beside them. Was that the brothel variety of a lady dropping her kerchief?

Leon looked at the shoe and stopped to look up at her, so Cleve had to stop too. But his eyes were scanning the street, watching for Kanaway, looking for the Winking Annie Hotel.

"Hello, boys, you from Oregon?" asked the girl who'd dropped her shoe.

"Now why'd you suppose we'd be from Oregon?" Leon asked, squinting at her.

"We get a lotta boys here from Oregon. But now I hear your voice, you sound Texas."

"Well, o' course I am. I'm not a *Yankee* like this big carpetbagger here with me."

"Carpetbagger!" Cleve snorted. "And you're a cowboy hasn't pulled all the cactus needles from his britches!"

"You going to bring my shoe up to me, sweet Texas boy?" the girl asked. "You can bring your Yankee friend too."

"I'm sorry, darlin'," Leon said, gazing with interest at the girl. "We got an appointment with a feller staying at the Winking Annie. You know where that is?"

"Round the next corner, a piece. They're some snooty up there."

"Kind of early for business, isn't it?" Cleve asked her.

"Oh, we're open all night!"

"Yep, I bet y—" Leon began.

"Leon, don't say it," Cleve interrupted. "Ladies . . ." He raised his hat to them. "Good mornin' to you."

Cleve had noticed a sailor walking a little ways behind them, and he heard the girl call out, "Hey, good looking! Can you bring up my shoe for me, oh please, sweet sailor, dear?"

Cleve and Leon strode on, the street rising a little here. A wind from the bay tugged at their hats from behind. They passed a saloon. There were already a few men and women within. "Here, they call this kind of saloon a deadfall," Cleve remarked. "An unwary man with money wanders in, and some jolly ruffians, seeing the mark is flush, buy him drinks and it goes to hell from there. When the mark is too drunk to object, they take him into the alley and rob him blind." Cleve shrugged. "Sometimes he comes out of it alive, sometimes not."

"The local law don't set foot in here?"

"Of a certain they do. But in the doubtful event they find the malefactors, it's their word against the mark's. Most of these men—and a good many of the women—are part of a gang. Some of the men are Australian convicts. Some are an Italian bunch. The gangs protect their crews, even paying for lawyers."

"I read they had some fuss with a vigilance committee here. Lynched a man or two."

"That was years ago. I've talked to the city police some . . . the way they see it, if a man is fool enough to 'wander The Coast,' with the reputation of this place, then good luck to him. Officers walking a patrol here are sometimes never seen again . . ."

"You said in a letter the U.S. Marshal made you an offer. Marshal Beaman, it was."

"He offered me deputy marshal. But I've got a ranch to build, Leon."

They turned a corner and the playing of a wheezing organ drew them to look into a rickety two-story saloon. A few men sat drooped on benches, chortling and waving their liquor glasses. To one side sat a woman, playing an indecipherable tune on the old organ. Even from here, Cleve could see bullet holes in the ivy-carved facing over its pipes.

"That's a parlor organ, ain't it?" Leon asked, as they walked past the melodeon.

"They call it a melodeon around here. They're pleased to call a groggery like this one a melodeon too."

"I know a feller in Dallas plays the squeeze-box. He called *that* a melodeon."

"Now where I come from, an accordion—" Cleve broke off and stopped at a narrow alley.

Within, two men were marching a drunken preacher between them—at least the stumbling figure had a preacher's collar and black coat. But his long brown hair and beard were disheveled, his eyes wild. The man on the right of the cleric was as short and stocky as the other was tall and broad-shouldered. The big one, in a shabby frock coat, had a mouth full of crooked teeth, deep-set eyes, a jutting, razor-scraped jaw, and a plug hat. The short one had a bent stovepipe hat, handlebar mustaches, and a long woolen coat that went to his boots. He gripped a bowie knife in one hand. With the other hand, he was digging greenbacks out of the drooping minister's coat pocket.

"This part of the burg sure lives up to its reputation, don't it, Cleve?" Leon said, giving a sad laugh.

The big man turned to glare at them. "Git yer gone!" he snarled. He had an Australian accent.

"Turn that gentleman loose," Cleve said, his hand going to the hideaway gun. "Gently, I mean. Then you can go, and we'll assist him hereafter."

"The little feller can put the money back in the reverend's coat," Leon added, as if making a helpful suggestion.

"Fook yer!" thundered the big man, reaching into his coat for a gun.

Chapter 3

Cleve drew his Bulldog pistol and fired, aiming at the big man's left shoulder, for the thief had used his left hand to draw; and at the same moment, Leon fired a gun Cleve hadn't known was there. Leon's round struck the big man in the right shoulder.

Two gunshots within the flick of an eyelash of one another—and the big man staggered back, gasping with pain and letting go of the drunken minister. Stumbling, he crashed into a wooden wine cask, smashing it. A cat leaped squalling out of it and darted away.

Dropping his pistol from a nerveless left hand, the big man turned and lumbered through the side door of the saloon, cursing with pain and leaving a trail of bloodspots. The pint-sized ruffian gawped at them, his eyes big and round, then let go of the money and turned to dash into the saloon. The minister collapsed to his knees, blinking about him in confusion.

Cleve and Leon both shrugged at once.

In Leon's hand was a smoking two-shot Remington 95

pocket gun. "Now where'd you get that, Leon?" Cleve asked.

"I cannot tell a lie," Leon said solemnly. "I borrowed it off'n my darlin' wife. It's hers. Didn't want to come down here without some kind of shooter."

"It's your wife's! Oh—now isn't that *sweet!*" Cleve said, grinning at him.

"Oh, shut up and tell me why you shot him in the shoulder."

"Why kill a man when I don't have to? Figured that will discourage him for a time. Anyway, you shot him in the other shoulder."

"I was aiming at his head." He sighed. "I don't know how I missed that big ol' punkin head of his. Shall we look for the law, report the gunplay?"

"I yet hope to head out for the ranchlands, Leon. Soon's I can! I don't want to complicate matters."

"You think that big galoot will come after us, out here?"

"Shot in both shoulders? Nope! He'll be cussing in a corner somewhere."

They tucked their guns away and went to the moaning preacher. Leon picked up the money while Cleve picked up the minister.

Leon's nose wrinkled as he looked around at the trash-strewn alley. "Smells like the whole neighborhood comes here to piss."

Cleve helped the minister to the street and leaned him on a lamp post. He was a gaunt man, perhaps forty, with a long nose and a weak chin. Leon stuffed the money, at least a hundred dollars, back into the minister's coat.

"Are you . . . are you after my money too?" the minister asked, looking blearily at Leon.

"I'm puttin' your money in, not takin' it out, mister," said Leon, nettled.

"Oh! I do apologize—those men were . . . I had been playing poker, you see, and I got lucky and they saw it and they insisted on buying me drinks, to celebrate, many drinks and . . ."

"We figured," said Cleve. "There's a lot of it going around, down here. What's your name?"

"Why, I am the Reverend Oliver Blevin, sir. My head is spinning . . . that vile wine . . ."

"You know, something they do hereabouts," said Cleve, "is they take raw spirits, add a little sugar and coloring, and they tell you it's wine. It's to dodge some local law, I believe."

"Raw spirits . . ." The minister turned away and vomited in the street.

Both being former lawmen, and habitués of frontier settlements, Cleve and Leon watched impassively as the Reverend Blevin emptied his belly. When he was done, Leon said, "What say we take you to yonder coffee beanery, see if you can keep some coffee down."

Cleve reluctantly nodded. The miscreants still close by, he felt a responsibility to see Blevin to safety. "We can't take much time with it," Cleve said, giving the drunken minister his arm. "But we'll get you on a chair and served with a pot of the brew."

* * *

Soon they were seated at a wobbly table by a fly-specked window. The little beanery smelled agreeably of fried ham and black coffee. Having imbibed a half pot of coffee and a fair amount of milky porridge, the minister gave thought to his companions. "I have told you my name," he said, rubbing his aching head with one hand. He was within sight of being sober now. "I have not heard yours."

"Leon Studge." They shook hands. "This here's Cleve Trewe."

The minister sat back in his chair. "Studge and Trewe? But—I had hoped to meet you! Mr. Kanaway told me about you!"

Cleve grunted. "That's some coincidence."

"Not so much, perhaps, Mr. Trewe. You see, it happens I shared a room with Mr. Kanaway. I was told the, ah, Winking Annie was clean and not ruinous to one's pocketbook—but there was no room left in the inn. When they were turning me away, Mr. Kanaway said there was a spare cot in his room I was welcome to. He said he valued the holy word, and he asked only that I say a prayer with him. I did so, and we took to talking. He told me all about you gents. He said he was joining you to head south, to the Sierras, near the Sweet River. Now, a friend who went to seminary with me, Lawrence Moss, lives about fifty miles from Sweet River, at Kerosene Corners, and he wrote me there's, ah, a possible place for me there, as a minister of God . . ."

He closed his eyes and it might have been the pain in his head. But Cleve suspected another sort of pain. "You have seen me badly out of countenance—drunken and gambling and fallen into the clutches of two brutes any sober man would not accompany to an alley!"

"I have seen more'n one gambling, drinking minister," said Leon. "Never surprised by it."

Seeing the reverend cringe at Leon's remark, Cleve said, "'It is always hard to see the purpose in wilderness wanderings until after they are over.'"

Blevin looked at him with a sudden interest. "You quote *Pilgrim's Progress!* You are a learned man, sir?"

"Not so very much," Cleve said.

"Why now, the Major here went to West Point," Leon declared. "He traveled the world, speaks the French talk, and the Latin too!"

Cleve was amused by Leon's tendency to boast of him, with a sort of pride of ownership in his voice. "Anyhow I've been drunk and unlucky at poker in my own time," Cleve continued. "You were drunk—and lucky at it. A rarity! Maybe you're meant to do some good with that poker pot."

"I pray it is so," Blevin said, his voice hoarse. "Indeed, I was looking for a place to start my ministry afresh. Then Mr. Kanaway and I came here to this very place for a meal—and I heard talk of a poker game starting up. Well, sir, we all have our weaknesses and poker is mine. Ah—*one* of mine."

"Where was Dave Kanaway when you saw him last?" Leon asked.

"He said he was going to hear music played. My throbbing head won't give me the name of the establishment. Said it had been recommended to him. He plays violin himself, you see."

Cleve nodded. He had heard Kanaway ably play an air on the fiddle.

The Reverend Blevin took a sip of his coffee, put the tin mug down, and went on, "I never did go back to that rooming house . . . the game seemed to go on forever. I lost some and won some and lost some and won some . . . and it became hard to leave, and I was there until the game broke up this morning . . ."

"I do understand how that can happen," Cleve said feelingly. "What's the hotel keeper like, at Winking Annie's? Crooked or a straight dealer?"

"He seemed a decent sort. Only he loves to talk, and tell his story. And he will insist on reciting poetry. He was a forty-niner, and made a decent strike, enough to build a hotel. He'll direct you to Mr. Kanaway . . . but first, he'll talk your ear off."

"Now how can a preacher complain of a man talking your ear off?" Leon asked. "That's the pot calling the kettle black if ever I heard it."

Blevin took that dig with a smile. "My profession is given to prolonged loquacity, it's true."

"Just saying *prolonged loquacity* is prolonged loquacity," Leon said, pouring some coffee for himself.

Cleve cleared his throat. "Reverend, I take it Dave Kanaway suggested you could travel with us, when we head south?" Cleve was not keen on the idea. He preferred the company of men who were of practical use. Blevin didn't strike him that way.

"Yes sir! I will work my way there! I know you will be driving cattle. I did some sheepherding as a young man. I know how to do a man's share of work, sir. Not long ago, I took a job cleaning a stable. I will not ask anything but perhaps a plate of beans and the protection of your company. The trail there is said to be rough wilderness, aswarm with Indians and bad men."

Cleve said, "For now, you take your ease here and sober up, and then we'll talk. Leon, we'd best head to Winking Annie's."

The sign on the three-story wooden building said, *Winking Annie's Inn, AC McCutcheon, proprietor.* No Annie was seen within. At the front desk of the little hotel sat a scowling, balding man in spectacles and white shirtsleeves. Presumably McCutcheon. He looked to be in his forties, his long curly beard and side-whiskers neatly trimmed but his starched high collar yellowing. He was counting out greenbacks and silver coins as Cleve and Leon walked in—startled by their sudden arrival, he snatched a drawer open and drew out an old revolver.

Cleve put up his hands, smiling reassuringly, hoping he wouldn't die over a merchant's frayed nerves.

"Easy, mister," Leon said. "We're just here looking for a friend."

"Then why do you have two pistols stuck in your belt there?" asked the proprietor.

Cleve and Leon looked down at the offending belt.

"Hellfire," Cleve said. "I forgot about that. My friend here and I had a brush with one of the gangs in an alley, around the corner. A gentleman was being robbed and we interceded. Leon here took a gun away . . . and foolishly stowed it for all to see in his belt."

McCutcheon tilted his head to one side. "Put the guns on my desk, and step back then."

Leon hesitated till Cleve said, "My arms are getting tired, Leon."

Sighing, Leon carefully laid the guns on the desk.

McCutcheon lowered his gun and Cleve lowered his hands. "You'd be AC McCutcheon?"

"I am. I heard something about a shooting affray round the corner. You the men who wounded Jawbone Jefferson?"

"That the big fella's name?" Leon said. "He was robbing a preacher. The preacher had done well playing poker, do you see? Ol' Jawbone drew on us, but he was slow."

"I'm sorry you didn't shoot him dead. He is a thief and a killer."

Leon shrugged. "I missed. Cleve—he aimed to miss. Too softhearted, I'd say, if I didn't know he's filled many a grave in his time."

"What's your names, boys?" McCutcheon asked, sitting back to look them over.

"I'm Leon Studge. This here is Cleve Trewe."

McCutcheon's eyebrows bobbed. "Cleve Trewe of Denver and Axle Bust?"

Leon grinned. "The very man!"

"Well, well! I have read an account or two . . ."

"Newspapers like to embroider on the facts," Cleve said.

"And who are you looking for, Mr. Trewe?"

"Dave Kanaway," Cleve said.

"The colored fella? He was here, rented a room, but from what my Chinee nightman told me, Kanaway didn't come back last night."

"Mind if we check his room?"

"I guess I'll trust you with it, but leave the guns here till you go."

"Hell, you can keep that fella's pistol there, give you a backup, if you like, Mr. McCutcheon," said Leon. "When I get back, I'll take the other'n."

McCutcheon took a key from the wall behind him and tossed it to Cleve. "Number eleven, third floor."

Cleve and Leon climbed the flights to the top floor, knocked on number eleven, and got no response. Often it had seemed to Cleve you could tell when no one was in a room, when you knocked on the door, even before there was time for someone to answer. It was something he'd picked up as a lawman in Denver. The echo that came back from the knock spoke of an empty room.

But he called out, "Dave! You in there?"

No response. He unlocked the door and they found a small room with a bed, a cot, two bags, and a dresser, a tin water pitcher, a chamber pot, and nothing else. The window looked out on the lower roof of the neighboring building, where two gulls perched, looking back at him.

"His bag's here," Leon said. "And this one on the cot would be Reverend's."

"Seems like he'd have come back to sleep," Cleve said. "If he could. He's not a man to stay out all night carousing. These beds haven't been slept in."

"You're in the right of it," Leon said. "That's surely worrying."

They checked to see if Kanaway had left a note—he had not. They locked the room and returned to the front desk, where they found that McCutcheon had locked his money away somewhere, and was now scribbling with a pencil on a sheaf of paper.

"Ah, well met, gentlemen, I've just finished the first two verses of 'Cleve Trewe and his sidekick lay Jawbone Jeff low.'"

"His *sidekick?*" Leon said, bridling.

McCutcheon cleared his throat and began to read,

"Two worthies strode the Barbary Coast
*   a-seeking for a pard*
They came across a minister
Who liked to turn a card
The Minister was crying out
as Jawbone stole his money
And when Cleve said, 'You stop that now!'
Jawbone laughed, 'Why ain't you funny—'"

"Jawbone didn't say much but 'fook off,'" Leon muttered.

"Well, I'll finish 'er later," McCutcheon said, setting

the paper aside. "But perhaps you boys would like to hear my 'Rhyme of the Magnificent McCutcheon Mine?'" Not waiting for an answer, McCutcheon started in.

> *"The burning sun did not deter AC McCutcheon,*
> *for he's a man who seeks a shine on his*
> *escutcheon.*
> *And yet he was hard aweary when he stumbled*
> *in the hills*
> *where he beheld another shine, as he took a spill . . ."*

"A marvel of versification," Cleve interrupted. "I admire your rhyme of McCutcheon and escutcheon. But there's some urgency afoot, sir—Mr. Kanaway may be in a parlous state of affairs. We need to find him quick as we can."

Pouting with disappointment, McCutcheon said, "As to that— last I knew he was going to the Sunny States Music Hall, on Pacific Street . . ." He frowned and shook his head. "Come to think of it . . . maybe I shouldn't have recommended he go there."

"Why's that?" Cleve asked.

"Because the floor bull is a fella named Callum Sprague, come here from Alabama. He's a sesh—even now, almost ten years after the war. Was a slaver once himself. And he's bold enough to declare himself one of the Knights of the Golden Circle. And what with Kanaway being a colored man . . ."

* * *

"What's this Knights of the Golden Circle?" Leon asked, as they walked up to the Sunny States Music Hall.

"That's what my father called an 'SSSOB'—Secret Society of Sons of Bitches. They don't even do a good job of keeping the secret. Started a little over twenty years ago in Ohio, took root down in Dixie. Slaveholders saw abolitionists gaining influence, started the KGC figuring to establish their own country. They're still around, plotting for another secession; there's some here in San Francisco, so I heard. Saying the 'The South will rise again'—but they're in California, not Dixie."

"Hell, the South don't need to rise—it's already standing on its own two feet. Only a fool would want another Civil War."

"Amen to that."

The music hall was a one-story affair shaped like a boxcar, but longer. It might have started as a warehouse. It had one big door and a red-curtained window that wasn't rightly squared in its frame. A new sign in scarlet and gold paint had been added on top that didn't seem fitting for the weathered, slightly crooked building.

SUNNY STATES MUSIC HALL
~PRETTY GIRLS SERVING COLD BEER~

Cleve found the big front door locked, but he could hear someone moving about inside. He hammered on the door. "Open up!"

"We're closed!" came a gruff voice from inside. There was a slight Scottish burr to it. "Three hours on, come you back!"

"I got business with you!" Cleve shouted. "Open up!"

Heavy boot steps inside, and then a bolt scraped and the door swung back. In the doorway stood a man in a rumpled checked suit. In one hand he had an ax handle, without its blade. Cleve figured him for the floor bull, Callum Sprague.

Sprague had red eyebrows and a tussle of gray-red hair under a woolen tweed flat cap. His craggy face was gnarled around a permanent snarl. "I've nae business with you!" His breath reeked of cheap whiskey. "Don't know you from Adam nor Queen Victoria! Get you gone!"

Cleve spoke evenly, "I'm looking for a man who's working with me—David Kanaway. Black man, medium height. Not old or young. He was here last night."

"The devil he was!"

"Let me talk to the owner," Cleve said. "We'll clear this up."

"I own forty percent of this establishment and I say get you *gone!*" And with *"gone"* he jabbed the butt of the ax handle hard into Cleve's belly, to push him away from the door.

Cleve was braced for it, and kept his footing; grabbing the ax handle with both his hands, he jerked it from Sprague and, fast as an arrow to the bullseye, slammed its upper end into Sprague's jaw.

"Ach!" Sprague yelled, stumbling back and falling on his rump.

Cleve and Leon stepped inside. Leon clucked his tongue, and said, "I knew you was in trouble, Sprague, soon's I saw you poke the Major with that stick there." He shook his head. "You're going to have a piss-poor morning."

Sprague clutched at his swelling jaw. "You've cracked my gob bones!"

"If I busted your jaw, you wouldn't be able to squawk about it," Cleve said. He spun the ax handle thoughtfully in his fingers, glancing around the music hall. There was no one else there. The "music hall" was just a saloon; long and narrow, lit by a single gas jet. A short stage abutted a wall to the right; a banjo, a piano, and a bass drum sat waiting.

Behind Sprague was a mahogany bar that appeared to have come from some finer establishment. Cleve could see where the saloon's bar had been sawed in two, at the middle, so they could get it into the building. Beyond the bar were three ranks of bottles and above them a cracked mirror with a gilt frame. The place smelled like last night's spilled liquor and unemptied spittoons.

"Forty percent of not very damn much," Leon remarked, looking around.

"Even lacks the 'pretty girls,'" Cleve observed.

Clutching his jaw, Sprague said, "What do you want, damn you!"

"I told you. Kanaway. Black man. Medium height, neither old nor young."

"Probably wore his blue suit," said Leon. "Only finery he has."

"No such man was here!"

"You're lying," Cleve said. And he was sure of it.

"Go to Hell and give the devil your arse!" Sprague spat at them—blood in the spittle, some of which struck Leon's boot tip.

Leon shook his head again. "You see, you're foolin' with a puma thinking it's a barn cat! Now, Cleve . . ." Leon took out his pistol. "He spat on my fine Mexican-tooled horseman's boots. What do you say? Should I shoot him once . . . or twice?"

Sprague seemed to stop breathing and stared at the gun.

Cleve pretended to consider Leon's proposal. "Twice is tempting. But you might kill him. I need him to answer my question."

"You can see he's just going to lie anyway."

"You have a point. Maybe shoot him in the cojones." He pointed at Sprague's crotch.

"Now hold on, you!" Sprague shouted and winced with pain. "I'll tell you where he went."

Cleve watched Sprague's face carefully.

Sprague licked his lips. "He . . . he's gone off with a whore, a white whore with no teeth! Big blond wig she has! Her name is . . . is Sadie."

Cleve slowly and sorrowfully shook his head. "You're lying. That is not at all Kanaway's style. And anyhow, I can see the lie in you, as easily as seeing a snake crawl out of a hole. Go ahead, Leon. Avenge your boots."

Leon aimed—

"No!" Sprague said, holding his hands over his crotch. "He's with Turley! Sy Turley! They took him to the ship! *The Seattle Souther*—it's down to the dock! When a labor man jumps ship, they shanghai a new one—Turley and me, we have an arrangement. Go talk to him—he'll pay you to forget all about it! I expect Turley'd give you a hundred dollars for that black boy!"

Cleve stared at him. "You're Scottish. How'd you get mixed up with the Golden Circle?"

Sprague was taken aback. He looked back and forth between them. "How'd you know of that?"

Cleve shook his head. "Answer me."

"*Ach* . . . I had a ship . . . I delivered workers and women to New Orleans and the Yankees took my vessel . . . I . . . Who are you? Federal men?"

"No," Cleve said. "But I have a talk with Marshal Beaman over at city hall, now and then. I'll speak to him about you—so you'd best run, Sprague. Take what you can out of here and leave San Francisco. I'll give you five hours."

"Make it three," Leon suggested.

"Three it is," Cleve said, nodding.

Cleve took the ax handle in his left hand, drew his gun, and fired three times, shooting off the necks of three bottles behind the bar. Glass spattered and bottles crashed, spilling whiskey.

Cleve dropped the muzzle to Sprague.

"I'd like to burn this place down, Sprague. You don't leave town in three hours, I'll tie you to that bar there. That oak and mahogany, that'll burn slow and hard."

"I'll go! I swear an oath on it!"

Cleve pocketed his gun, raised the ax handle, and made ready to throw it.

Sprague gasped and hid his face behind his arms.

But Cleve threw the ax handle at the bar mirror. The ax handle spun through the air, struck hard, and sent shards of glass flying like startled birds.

"Gahh!" cried Sprague, as broken glass clinked and clattered around him.

Sprague scrambled to his feet, looked at the shattered mirror.

"You!" Cleve barked.

Sprague turned to face him.

"Three hours," Cleve said. "I'll be back to see."

Sprague nodded, his head bobbing frantically.

"You sure I can't shoot him?" Leon asked. "He helped the bastards shanghai Dave!"

Cleve shook his head regretfully. "We don't kill him unless he fails to leave San Francisco. We already shot Jawbone Jefferson today. That's shooting enough."

Sprague gulped. "You shot Jawbone?"

Leon got up a gob of spittle—and spat on Sprague's boots. Then he and Cleve went in search of *The Seattle Souther.*

This time they hired a coachman and paid him to drive the horse fast as it could go to the pier where *The*

Seattle Souther was moored. Arriving, they found that the big side-wheels were already churning seawater, thick black smoke was streaming from the chimneys, and the vessel was swinging out from the dock. A horn tootled, a bell rang . . .

Cleve jumped from the coach, shouting, "Pay the man, Leon!"

He ran past the lathered horse and seeing there was about five feet between the dock and the ship's stern, Cleve sprinted hard and leapt—and was almost sure he was going to have to swim back to the pier.

His flailing hands caught the ornamental deck trim under the railing, and he held on. A jolt pained his shoulders as his weight pulled him down, and his boots dragged in the waves. Gritting his teeth, he pulled himself up, grabbed a railing post, then another, then worked his way up the posts till he reached the railing. He pulled himself over it and was startled by a feminine scream.

On the deck, a round-faced lady in voluminous satin skirts, a buttoned-up jacket, and a pinned-on blue hat was gasping at the sight of him and backing away. Somewhere behind him, Leon was shouting angrily.

Cleve ignored them both and got his feet under him. He was glad he'd not quite lost his hat in his jump—and he tipped it to the lady. "Excuse me, ma'am. Left someone aboard."

He rushed past her, reaching into his coat for the Bulldog hideaway pistol, and ran down the sun deck toward the nearest door. Whatever he was going to do, it had better be fast: the ship was chugging away from the Embarcadero, cutting eagerly through the incoming waves. Up ahead the starboard-side paddlewheel was scooping up seawater and dumping it, so that a cloud of spume washed across the deck.

The hatch opened and a bearded man in a blue cap and dark blue peacoat stepped out, just as Cleve came skidding breathlessly up. The man had the look of a ship's officer. He gawped at Cleve and said, "Sir—are you—"

Then the words froze on his lips, as he saw Cleve draw his gun. "Mister, turn around and take me to where the coalmen work. Make it quick and quiet."

"But I—there's nothing of value there—"

"Oh, but there is! What's your name?"

"Me? I . . . it's Duckworth!"

"Well, then, Duckworth, keep your beezer shut and lead the way!"

"Ah . . . if we must . . . It's the stern ladder . . ." Shaking his head, the man turned and walked off down the passage.

Cleve could imagine Leon simmering on the dock. And it'd sure be mortifying if he'd read Sprague wrong—and Kanaway wasn't aboard at all.

They turned down a narrow passage toward the stern, then went down two steep, constricted flights of wooden stairs. The steam engine rumbled loudly down here; Cleve could smell coal smoke and felt the deck under his feet vibrate from the grinding turn of the side-wheels' axle.

Grumbling, Duckworth stretched out a key on a

chain from his belt and unlocked a narrow iron door. He
pulled it aside and they went through, Cleve struck by
the all-encompassing heat of the engine room's boiler.
Sweat immediately started out on his forehead. The
room roared with the flames under the big steel boiler
and vibrated from the rumble of the engine.

Most of the light in the low-ceilinged iron chamber
was from the open gate for the boiler so that everything
flickered with hellish light and shadow. To the right, a
massive iron chute dumped coal onto a steel floorplate.
Kanaway, shirtless, and a burly, squat Chinese worker,
also shirtless, were feeding the boiler with shovels. The
Chinese wore a queue, his hair shaved partway back, a
long braid hanging down his back.

To the left stood a hulking overseer, scowling puzzlement at Cleve. Head shaved, mustaches drooping with
sweat, the overseer wore suspenders over his shirtless
hairy chest and burly arms. On his belt was holstered an
enormous pistol—an Austro-Hungarian weapon, the
Gasser. In his right hand was a horsewhip. In his left
was an iron cudgel.

"He's got a gun!" shouted Duckworth, lurching to
the side.

The big overseer looked at Cleve's small hideaway
gun—and laughed. Cleve found himself missing his
Colt .45. But he aimed the Bulldog at the bearish engineer and shouted, "Drop your weapons!"

The overseer gave a gap-toothed grin, dropped the
whip, and tried to draw his pistol. But the Gasser had a
9-inch barrel—he didn't get it out of the holster before

Cleve shot him between the eyes. The overseer snarled and shook his head as if he had a gnat in his ear.

Impressed, Cleve fired twice more, into the man's forehead. The overseer sank to his knees and flopped forward.

Hooting, Dave Kanaway and the Chinaman both dropped their shovels.

"Take his gun, Dave!" Cleve shouted. He had to shout to be heard in the achingly loud engine room. "We're leaving! Your friend there, too, if he wants!"

Kanaway stepped over to the dead man, slid the big pistol from its holster, as Cleve turned to the terrified Duckworth.

"You—you murdered Abel!" Duckworth said, his eyes round, hands shaking.

Cleve shook his head and pointed at the passageway with his gun. "Your big Hessian there tried to kill me. Now get up—and walk slowly out the door!"

Duckworth sidled through the hatch, and Cleve followed, powerfully relieved to be shed of the hellish engine room. Kanaway and the Chinaman came along close behind.

"Take me to Captain Turley!" Cleve ordered. "The quietest way there is!"

Duckworth rounded on Cleve. "So you can kill him too? I won't do it! The captain's been good to me these five years."

"How about these men he ordered shanghaied? That makes him a slaver, not a decent man!"

"Why—they're but drunks, lowlifes!"

"That, mister, is a damned lie!" Kanaway declared.

Cleve raised his pistol and cocked it. "You take me to the captain or I'll find him alone."

Duckworth's face fell, and then he nodded and turned away. "Up the ladder."

They were soon up the narrow stairway, then up a ramp, goggled at by a black-bearded gent in a beaver-fur hat and coat. "Keep your mouth shut!" Cleve growled at him.

They followed a circular walkway to the back of the wheelhouse, and Duckworth raised his hands as if to let his captain know he was under duress. "Captain! There's a gunman here—he's killed Abel!"

Turley was a stout man with prodigious side-whiskers, a gold-buttoned blue coat, epaulets, and a braided cap. He glowered at Cleve as if he'd urinated on the deck. "What' do you mean by this, sir!"

"What I mean by this, Turley, is to offer you a choice—you can turn this boat around, take it to the dock you came from. Once we've gone ashore, I strongly urge you to head out to sea without delay. Duckworth here can feed the boiler. That's one choice. The other is, I can dump you overboard, right here, and take over the ship myself. Which do you prefer?"

Chapter 4

Cleve stretched his legs out, relaxing in the drawing room of their suite in the Montgomery Building. With him were Leon, Teresa, Dave Kanaway, and Alice. Kanaway had stopped over at the Winking Annie's to bathe and put on his work clothes. Now, sitting on a red plush parlor chair across from Cleve, he cradled the baby in a curled arm, tickling her tummy and making her chuckle. Kanaway was so happy to be away from *The Seattle Souther* that he didn't seem to mind what must be a painful lump on the side of his head. The late Abel had given him that.

"All things considered," Cleve said, as Berenice poured two fingers of Irish whiskey at the liquor cabinet, "I think we'd best light out for Sacramento on the next train, my Berenice. What do you say?"

"I say I think Alice and I are ready to travel," she said, handing him the drink. "Do you think Captain Turley will make trouble for you?"

"I doubt it."

"I never saw a man more scared than Turley, after you offered him his choices," said Kanaway wryly.

Berry brought a drink for Leon. Kanaway had refused liquor; he never drank anything but small beer.

"Turley wasn't any scareder than Duckworth," Leon said. "Once you let Duckworth go, he ran back to that ship like a rabbit from a wolf. And that ship went for the high seas with its side-wheels ablur! I doubt any of them will trouble us. Now, the Chinaman fairly danced down the street when we dropped him off in Chinatown. He'd never testify against Cleve, no, ma'am."

"Nevertheless, Leon, you shot a man," Teresa said, chiding him.

"Why, he's probably got the bullet out and a woman feedin' him shots of red-eye right now!"

"And Cleve had to kill that man in the boiler room. San Francisco is a more civilized place than Axle Bust—shootings are frowned upon."

"Is it indeed more civilized?" Cleve wondered. "Not in the Barbary Coast district. It's rougher than Dodge City, and that's saying something. Still, best be on our way. I'd figured to stay another week, maybe hire some men, talk to my banker, meet with a stock seller. But I've got a small herd waiting for me in Sacramento. They'll have to do. And from there we'll strike out for Sweet River Valley. We can breakfast with Drask and Mai before we take the train."

"What about getting Ulysses and Suzie to Sweet River?" Berry asked. "They didn't care much for the train trip here . . . Nor did Leon's horse, or Teresa's."

Kanaway nodded. "They did seem some het up, when I looked them over."

Cleve shook his head sadly. "Those horses will just have to put up with it."

"It's a risk to them, Cleve," Berry said, crossing her arms. "Teresa said a yearling had to be put down with a fractured leg when the engine stopped suddenly. And the foal is still quite small."

"Cleve," said Kanaway, looking up with a broad smile, "I'd be honored to trail that stock, yours and Leon's and Teresa's and my own. I'll bring them to you in Sweet River Valley."

Cleve held his whiskey glass up to the light as if scrying the future in its amber depths. He drank the liquor down, shuddered, and said, "Well, sure sounds good, Dave. That'd ease my mind—but it'll be a long ride, herding all those horses. There's the foal too."

"Suzie can be trusted to care for her foal. You know, Major, I was glad to work with you before this. But now . . . I was in full despair in that boiler room, I tell you true. And you come like an avenging angel and pulled me from the hands of devils! I'd drive those horses to Alaska and back for you."

Cleve was a little embarrassed. "I . . . well, you know, you're a valuable friend, Dave, and there's no need to feel, ah . . ."

Berry laughed softly. "Cleve does not take well to compliments or expressions of gratitude, Mr. Kanaway. But we shall be grateful to you if you can get our horses there safely. Can you do it alone?"

"Oh, I won't be alone, ma'am! The Reverend Blevin

will be coming along! He says he's worked with horses in his time."

"He worked with horse droppings, anyhow," Cleve said. "His last job, between pastor work, was cleaning stables."

Leon smirked at Cleve. "Thought you'd ducked ol' Blevin, didn't you, Cleve?"

"I don't mind the reverend," Cleve said.

But inwardly, he groaned. A minister along on the journey to Sweet River? And a troublesome one, too, prone to drinking and gambling. Who knew what other vices he might have hidden in his preacher's cassock?

The locomotive was wheezing up a steep grade, heading northeasterly toward the California state capital. The sunset reddening the westside windows tinted the plush railroad car a watered-down burgundy.

Caleb Drask and his beautiful Chinese wife, Mai, had come along to Sacramento with Cleve, Berenice, Leon, and Teresa, and that being the case, Cleve had spared no expense in renting a private Pullman car. As Leon put it, the car had "all the fancy a man can handle." The leather and brass booths had polished rosewood tables; there were dark blue velvet curtains framing the windows below curling brass hat hooks and ornamental green-glass lamps. But the grade was steep enough that they had to hold on to their coffee cups to keep them from sliding on the table. Berenice, Mai, and Teresa had taken the baby and gone to the observation car for a "postprandial posset." Berenice had startled some of the porters and passengers on the train with her insistence on carrying the baby on her back in a Paiute cradleboard. Fascinated with whatever she saw, little Alice didn't seem to mind at all. Berenice felt the cradleboard was the safer way of carrying a baby while walking through the jolting, jouncing railroad cars. One needed both hands sometimes to keep from falling.

"What's that 'postprandial' mean?" Leon asked. "I didn't want to let on I didn't know what she was saying."

"That's just Berenice's showy way of saying 'after supper,'" Cleve said, looking out the window at the rugged, boulder-strewn hillsides. He caught a glimpse of a mountain goat leaping from the top of an outcropping to a ledge. "I expect she wants to talk to Mai and Teresa about the Occidental Mission House. Which like as not means, Caleb, that Mai will be talking to you about donating some lawyer time for it."

Caleb nodded ruefully. "I've no doubt of it." He was a genial man in round-lensed spectacles, wearing a sulfur-yellow suit, and with a yellow bowler hat in his lap. He was weak-chinned but disguised it with a neatly cut beard, like something a pharaoh might have worn.

"I'm still obliged to you for clearing up the title to my uncle's mine," Cleve said. "I think I owe you some money."

"The accommodations you've provided for this trip are more than sufficient to cover it, Cleve," Caleb said, raising a hand from his coffee cup to wave away obligations, just as the train reached the top of the hill and started down the other side. He had to grab the cup as it slid toward him, and some of the coffee sloshed over toward his lap. Caleb looked mournfully at his hat. "You can buy me a new hat, too, however . . ."

Leon laughed. "I'll buy you a ten-gallon hat, Caleb!"

"I'll thank you not to do any such thing," Caleb said, dabbing at his hat with a linen napkin. "Cleve, you may as well tell me about the Occidental Mission House."

"The house is a sad necessity," Cleve said. "The anti-Chinese feeling being high, Congress passed laws making it harder for Chinese to come to the States, especially women. But thousands of these ladies were offered a free trip to America. They were told they would be well-paid servants in fine houses. When they got here, they were auctioned off on the docks of San Francisco. Sold into brothels. They are kept locked away, in cells with barred windows, and forced to surrender to any man who pays their pimp. All day long."

"Jesus, Mary, and Joseph!" Leon swore. "That's not any decent kind of bawdy house. Who'd tolerate such a thing?"

Caleb snorted bitterly. "Many here regard the Chinese as subhuman."

"Marshal Beaman tells me there's a power of police corruption too," Cleve said. "The police aren't well paid— except by the pimps. Beaman is putting pressure on the city hall, and Berenice has written letters condemning all this to the local papers. Me and Berenice and the marshal went to two of the brothels, and we, well, *persuaded* the guards to let the women go."

"You let Berry come along?" Leon asked, surprised. "Weren't you afraid for her?"

"You just try stopping Berenice when she's raring to help out a woman in need," Cleve said.

"But . . . where did you take the girls you rescued?" Caleb asked.

"The Occidental Mission House, founded by the wives of missionaries. But there are so many more. We need legal pressure, Caleb. You could bring suit for the women. With Beaman on your side—and the mayor, too, it happens—you can get more of them set free. And demand they get a new start."

Caleb flashed a smile. "When Mai comes back, she'll be fired up to do something, and I'll have no peace if I don't pitch in. Soon as my standing as a California attorney is officialized, I'll see what can be done."

"Cleve, you shoot any of those shit-heels who locked the women up?" Leon asked.

"That would involve Berenice in court proceedings. So I just cracked a few over the head."

Late the next afternoon, the party arrived in Sacramento, stepping off onto the redwood platform. Berry was carrying Alice on her back in a colorful Paiute cradleboard. Mai, wearing a jade-colored walking dress and bonnet, looked around happily. "State capital!"

"And we shall visit the capitol building before we go, dear," Caleb declared. "It's said to be a thing of splendor."

"Alice seems indifferent to Sacramento," Cleve said, seeing the baby girl was asleep in the cradleboard.

But Sacramento was noticing Alice. The colorfully

carved cradleboard worn by a white woman in a pretty blue walking dress garnered stares from the other travelers in the station.

There was muttering. "Is that a way to carry a baby? . . . She don't look like a redskin."

Cleve's mind was on the meeting he'd arranged in the hotel bar tonight. He'd telegraphed his purchase agent for word on the ranchland in Sweet River Valley.

They passed through the busy, high-ceilinged station. Outside, a horse-drawn tram rolled past; buggies and freight drays crowded the cobbled street. On the other side of the street were weathered buildings of brick and stone and wood, with occasional adobes. Higher buildings loomed beyond, including the marble dome of the state capitol.

"Quite a hubbub, ain't it?" Leon said, looking at the thronged street.

"Almost as frenzied as Boston," said Berenice.

Caleb frowned at his pocket watch. "Got to hurry, before the office closes." He waved a hansom cab over. "I'll see you at the hotel, dear!"

He kissed Mai goodbye, the two of them lingering over it so that Leon rolled his eyes and said, "You'll see her in the hotel later, you know. This same day!"

"*My* husband has little thought for romance," said Teresa, with a deadpan sigh.

Leon growled, "I'm just as romantic as *Cleve* is, anyhow."

"Cleve?" Berry shook her head and then mimicked Teresa's deadpan sigh.

Mai burst into laughter and pushed her husband away. "You go! I see you at hotel!"

Caleb hurried to his hired cabriolet; it required two hansom cabs to carry Cleve and the others to the hotel on the Sacramento River.

The broad green river was almost as busy as the streets, churning with steamships and sluggish with freight barges. "Such a big river!" Mai enthused, as they stood in the bay window of the hotel lobby.

"By God, Mai, it's not a patch on the Mississippi!" Leon declared. "Takes a week to sail from shore to shore of the Mississippi, and that's goin' full bore!"

"Oh, you are liar!" Mai said, laughing.

"No, ma'am! Mississippi used to be even bigger— belonged to Texas, in those days. But the damned Louisianans stole it from us."

"Leon lives in his own world," Teresa said, kissing him on the cheek.

"In *my* world, we'll get us some rooms," Cleve said, "and then I shall go to the hotel bar and order up a tall glass of beer . . ."

Cleve sat at a table alone, near an enormous stone fireplace. Leon was upstairs helping Teresa unpack, maybe trying to seem more romantic than usual, and Berenice was in the suite talking to Mai Ling about San Francisco.

Looking around at the dapper, pompous men in the bar, Cleve tried to relax in his well-padded chair. This was the most civilized and well-burnished saloon he'd been in since returning from Europe long years ago. The paintings were tasteful landscapes of Yosemite and the Pacific seaside; the bar was gracefully sculptured, all of brass and scarlet leather.

But Cleve felt out of place, as he looked around at the wealthy merchants in sharply tailored suits and barbered beards. They smoked fine imported cigars as they lounged in padded velvet booths, clearly styling themselves high on the totem pole. To Cleve, their kind always seemed shifty behind the gloss.

Two men strolled in, one of them as out of place as Cleve. The pair headed his way. Cleve had met the smaller man in the frock coat and black silk top hat before: Salvatore Newhouse, the purchase agent Cleve was waiting for. With his ascot, silvery vest, and pin-striped trousers, Newhouse seemed quite a contrast to his companion—who wore a six-gun holstered on his left hip. The stranger's long, horse-hide duster partly hid the pistol, but Cleve saw it as the coat flared back. His blue jeans were tucked into knee-high riding boots. The man's concession to the sophisticates of Sacramento was a white linen shirt and a black string tie. He wore no hat and his long black hair was pomaded back. His clean-shaven face was chiseled by gauntness, high cheekbones, and a strong chin. He'd have been handsome but for one peculiarity—his left eye was significantly higher than his right. The expression on that chiseled but cockeyed face wasn't friendly.

Cleve supposed Newhouse had brought a new rider for Sweet River Ranch. Many a good ranch hand could be some off-putting at first, proudly alert for any hint of mockery or insult.

"Afternoon, gentlemen," Cleve said standing. "Glad to see you, Newhouse. We've got a lot to talk about."

"We do," said Newhouse, but his glance seemed to carry a warning of some kind. "You might have to change some of your plans, Trewe."

"Oh, there's always some adjusting. A trail's blocked by a rockfall, you find a way around." Cleve decided he'd better make the acquaintance of the tall man. He stuck his hand out to the stranger. "Cleve Trewe."

The tall man smirked, and looked at Cleve's hand. Then he shrugged and they shook hands. It was a smooth hand, without the cowboy calluses. "Cullen Marske. I need a drink."

"Have a seat, boys, and I'll see to it."

They sat, and Cleve signaled the waiter. A smiling, well-groomed older Mexican in scarlet livery and apron hurried to them. "What can I get for you gentlemen?"

They ordered another beer for Cleve and two brandies. They each had a pull on their drinks, then Cleve turned to Marske. "You looking for work, Mr. Marske?"

Marske smirked again and shook his head. "Already got a job."

"That right?" Cleve asked, watching Marske closely now. So this man was no cowboy. "What job is that?"

Marske drank off some brandy, put his glass down, and said, "You don't need to know that. Newhouse—tell him what he does need to know."

Newhouse hesitated, licking his lips. "Well, now . . ."

Marske prodded Newhouse's shoulder, hard, with a stiffened thumb. "Tell him!"

"Trewe," Newhouse said, "I've got to tell you that it seems there's just no more room for ranching in Sweet River Valley."

Cleve sat up a little straighter. "You yourself found the man who wants to sell me his farm. Drake Samuels. I got a letter from him a fortnight ago!"

Newhouse cleared his throat. "A letter . . . a letter is not legally binding. There has been no signing-over of deeds. Nor can you, it appears, take possession of *any* land in Sweet River Valley. Now, I have an associate in Grass Valley who can find you a suitable place there. Splendid grazing land."

"Already looked at Grass Valley. Not much left there but small plots. I saw Sweet River Valley and, by God, I found a piece of Heaven!"

Newhouse cleared his throat. "No doubt. But it's a wild and primitive place, sir, most unsuitable for a man with a wife and baby along. The Indians are much prone to displaying their savagery, and . . . there are other considerations."

"What considerations are those?" Cleve asked.

"Mr. Asa Hawthorn. He owns Sweet River Valley."

Cleve shook his head. "No, he doesn't. I heard something about him. He throws his weight around down there. But the state hasn't granted him that whole valley."

"Oh, his ownership is underway," Newhouse said, in a voice that was a perfect merging of apology and insistence. "He shall have it, Mr. Trewe. There's simply no doubt."

Cleve didn't believe a word of this. He pondered his next move and kept tight rein on his rearing anger. "I will investigate the matter in person."

"Did I hear something about a pretty lady and a little baby child?" said Marske, his face mocking concern.

Cleve went very still. Only his eyes moved. He looked at Marske, who stiffened a little, maybe seeing something in those eyes.

"Careful, Mr. Marske," Cleve said softly.

"It's dangerous country, out south of here," Marske said, the smirk slipping from his face. "That's all I'm telling you." His left hand dropped below the level of the table.

"You don't seem stupid enough to fire on me in here," Cleve said mildly, easing a hand into his coat. "May as well put your hands up where I can see them."

Marske stared at him. Tensing.

"Marske!" Newhouse whispered hoarsely. "We are *talking*."

Marske took several breaths loud enough to hear. His shoulders relaxed, and he raised his hands as if surrendering and then linked them behind his head.

He leaned back and grinned. "I was just scratching an itch, Trewe. Don't you ever get an itch?"

Cleve just watched him. Waiting.

Marske put both hands flat on the table. "Sometimes folks got to learn to like what's on offer. You'll like it in Grass Valley. Mr. Hawthorn's willing to stake you to a nice little plot out there."

"Grass Valley?" Cleve changed tactics. "Maybe Sweet River's not worth all this growling and posturing, after all." He turned to the land agent. "I'll ponder it over the next couple days. Let you know."

Newhouse seemed to shudder with relief. "Good. Very good." He drank some brandy. "You know where to reach me."

Marske drank the rest of his liquor in one swallow and set down his empty glass with a *clack*. "I believe I'll go find myself a real drink in a real saloon. There's one over by the cattle pens. You—" He pointed a finger at Cleve in a way that had resulted in another man getting his jaws broken. "You take yourself one night . . . and *ponder.*"

Cleve envisioned throwing the table aside with his left hand and bringing a hard uppercut into Marske's chin with the other. But he had been a practical tactician in the war. And he knew a tactical retreat could bring on a chance to flank the enemy.

He gave Marske a faint smile, and he stood up and stretched. "I was two days on that train, gentlemen. I need some supper and a real bed. I'll be in touch."

He put on his hat, and walked briskly to the door,

thinking he was going to Sweet River Valley as quick as he could get the expedition organized.

Behind him, he heard Marske mockingly ask, "'Growling and posturing?' That what he said?" And Marske laughed.

Chapter 5

A light rain soothed the clamorous Sacramento train yard that early morning, as Cleve and Berenice stood near the cattle pen, contemplating their herd—just under four hundred head ploddingly prodded up a ramp and into stockcars by two husky men in overalls. He'd purchased a hundred-forty young steer, a hundred-sixty bulls, and ninety-four cows; for Cleve's aim was breeding stock, as much as fattening for sale.

The cattle bawled and stamped their hooves anxiously. Trains huffed on other tracks nearby and stock hands shouted at the beasts and the other workmen.

Cleve and Berry stood by the wooden fence, each thinking their own thoughts. He was wondering if he could keep his family safe in Sweet River Valley. His Colt Army .45 was holstered under his long, gray all-weather coat. He kept the six-gun close now, and he was conscious of its weight on his hip.

"There's a most peculiar pattern in my life right of late," Cleve said. "I seem to be right with the law—yet running from the law."

She looked curiously at him. "The matter of rescuing David Kanaway?"

He nodded. "I killed a man on that ship. Self-defense or not, they'd want it adjudged in court. I don't have the time for that—I've got to get the deed, and the land, and the cattle grazing and seen to, before winter sets in."

"There's no sign the police are searching for you. *The Seattle Souther*'s captain does not want his perfidy discussed in court."

"Still, the best thing would have been to see the thing through before a judge."

"You told Marshal Beaman about it. He didn't seem concerned."

"He's not San Francisco police. He can afford to let it go."

"Possibly he is still thinking of persuading you to work for the marshal's service."

Cleve nodded. "You are ever astute, my Berenice."

"And your pattern—first there was the shooting on the steamer, and then the encounter with this gunman at the hotel . . ."

"I held off on . . . on *clarifying* the matter with Marske. Because I don't want to get tangled up with the law in Sacramento. But backing off sticks in my craw."

"Yet it was the wisest course. If this man Hawthorn has powerful friends in Sacramento, you might have ended up in prison. I know you'd never cut a man down in cold blood, but they could frame the affair as they pleased."

You'd never cut a man down in cold blood. Cleve grimaced. He'd shot some men who were not even aware he was there, at Bull Run and in other battles. They were the enemy, and ambush was part of war. But it had gone against his grain. Some nights the memory gnawed at him.

He looked up at the sky, saw the clouds breaking up. "You're right. No telling how it would have gone. New-house was either bought, or scared into backing Hawthorn. Like as not he'd have lied in court."

Cleve looked at Berenice, and she gave him a sweet smile that seemed to say more than either of them could say aloud.

But he had to ask. He took her hands in his, looked into her eyes. "With Marske and Hawthorn making threats—is it too risky, too rough, bringing you and Alice out there?"

"Hawthorn is likely all bluff. But if we have to fight, you must know I'll stand beside you. We can both pro-tect Alice. No one's going to drive us from our new home."

"It's not just that. Even without the Marskes of the world, the ranching life . . . it's a lot to ask of you. You'll have some time to do your research, and write your papers, but . . . not always. A new ranch is hard work for everyone."

Berenice raised her eyebrows. "You think I can't carry my own weight?"

Cleve shook his head. "All the way from Axle Bust to Paradise, you never complained once. And it got hard. All the way to Gunmetal Mountain, in the snow, you did your part and more, every day and night. In the camp of the Bannock, you never turned a hair. On

Gunmetal, you showed more sand than any woman I've
ever known. You've got all it takes."

Berenice smiled sadly. "There are braver and stronger
women than me, by far. But men don't regard them
enough to know."

"It's just that, what we're going to do now . . . well,
it's a hard row to hoe and it'll go on for years." He
wrestled with how to say it. "I know you can *do* it . . .
but I don't know if it's right. You've got so damn much
to give folks. I feel like I'm going to hoard a treasure up
there in that lonely valley. A treasure that I shouldn't
keep for myself."

It cost him some to say that. But it was so. Berenice
was a woman of genius; a woman of vision. In Cleve's
mind, she was like Boadicea, or Cleopatra; like the sci-
entists Ada Lovelace, or Mary Anning; like Elizabeth I,
or Susan B. Anthony. And in Sweet River Valley, he'd
be keeping her cut off from most of the world.

He saw tears in her eyes, then, and he misread them.
"Berenice? I can sell these cattle off this very day."

"No, Cleve." Berry nestled against him, and he put
his arms around her, holding her close. For a moment
the lowing and bawling of the cattle, the noise of men
and trains, seemed to recede into the far distance. There
was just her breathing, her forehead pressed against his
neck.

Then she looked up at him and said, "Remember
when you came upon me at Axle Bust Falls?"

"Never will forget it."

"We spoke of my studies. Of natural philosophy—of
butterflies and bees. You *astonished* me by seeming

genuinely interested! I'd given up on men after I was widowed—but you lit a fire in me!"

He smiled. "That's not the usual way a man lights a fire in a woman. Talk of nature and bees!"

"Oh, it opened doors in me that had been long locked up, I assure you! And you are getting pretty good at lighting the other kind of fire too."

He laughed. "Getting pretty good? I'm getting downright expert! Why, last night you—"

She stopped his talk with a hand over his mouth. "I'm trying to say we are partners for life, Cleve. And I trust you. I trust you to allow me to be myself. In truth, I am convinced that we need each other. We simply belong together." She looked into his eyes. "We will go together to Sweet River Valley, Mr. Cleveland Terwilliger Trewe."

The train was to depart at five in the afternoon, headed for the sleepy town of Fresno, in the San Joaquin Valley. The engine was venting steam at the tracks, hissing as if impatient to be on the move, and black smoke writhed over the smokestack.

Cleve and Caleb Drask and Leon stood on the platform, speculating about the hired hands Cleve was to meet outside Fresno; Berenice and Teresa and Mai Ling Drask were talking excitedly of their visit to the state capitol building.

"They only finished it early this year," said Teresa. "Took them fourteen years to build."

"Oh, it was beautiful!" Mai said. "The columns—that is the word?"

"Yes," Berry said. "Corinthian columns. Apparently, there was some controversy about the pediment statue of Minerva. She being a Roman goddess—and Sacramento being named after the holy sacraments. Some people are overhasty in their interpretation of symbolism."

"Thank you, Berry, for enlightening us poor souls," said Teresa, a little snippy.

Listening in, Cleve thought that Teresa sometimes grew impatient with Berenice's scholarly manner. Berry could seem a mite self-important. But knowing her better, what Cleve heard was Berenice's quiet joy in ideas; in history and the arts and science.

"You've not met most of these men you're hiring, Cleve?" Caleb asked.

"Hm? Oh, they were signed on by the agent. Three fellas. I haven't looked them over. Well, there's a man named Milt Dumanis—I rode with him a time, last year. He's a capable cowboy. He might be waiting on me at Sweet River. If he's not in jail."

"All aboard, folks!" cried a porter.

Caleb and Mai bade them a warm goodbye and swore to pen a multitude of letters.

There were only two passenger cars on the train, the others given over to cattle and freight. In their sleeping compartment that night, Berenice was lying back in a nightgown, reading by lamplight. She held a weighty volume penned by Charles Darwin, *The Descent of Man, and Selection in Relation to Sex*. Baby Alice was asleep in her cradleboard, which had been snugged in on the carpeted floor, held in place by their luggage.

Lying beside Berry, Cleve read over her shoulder. "Now *that* I cotton to, as Leon would say."

"Which passage?"

Cleve read it aloud. "*As man advances in civilization, and small tribes are united into larger communities, the simplest reason would tell each individual that he ought to extend his social instincts and sympathies to all members of the same nation . . . This point being once reached, there is only an artificial barrier to prevent his sympathies extending to the men of all nations and races.* You know, Abe Lincoln reasoned the same." He sighed. "But people put aside their reason when they get greedy. Slavery fattened their purses, and that made them powerful unreasonable. So they fired on Fort Sumter and, in due course, more than six hundred thousand men died . . ."

He fell silent, and knowing how the Civil War lingered with him, Berry put a hand over his and nestled closer. The train click-click-clacked on and on, and its motion swayed them in their narrow bed. He thought of an army railroad trip he'd taken with a battery of mortars through Virginia cropland and seeing the destruction of several farmhouses bombarded by that same artillery. Mostly soldiers had died in the war—but not *only* soldiers . . .

Cleve thought he ought to derail thoughts of the Civil War. The means were at hand. "I read *The Origin of the Species* by Mr. Darwin—I can't remember the full title, which seemed most as long as the first chapter to me—and I began reading this book here, but kind of got stuck on the part about 'in relation to sex.'"

"You found it improbable?"

"No, I found it daunting. The idea is something like a young buffalo miss will choose her buffalo mister on the basis of his being strong and protective and maybe she likes his horns, and female birds will choose their mates because they are impressed by their singing, or their mating dances."

"Roughly, that's the general idea . . ."

"Now suppose Berenice Trewe met a man who was stronger, smarter, richer, better-looking, and more charming than me? And he sings and dances too! I know that man is out there somewhere."

"Is he indeed!" she said with a straight face. "Do you have his address?"

Cleve laughed and Berry kissed him.

"I would spurn that man, Cleve, because he is not my Cleveland Terwilliger Trewe. My husband and the father of my little girl."

"I'm not convinced that's enough to satisfy Mr. Darwin's thesis."

"As a scientist, I am always prepared for another experiment. Now come here . . ."

* * *

Two mornings later, Cleve woke up in a brand-new Conestoga wagon to a parade of odors, some of them pleasant. He could clearly smell manzanita, cattle, sheep—and coffee. The smell of brewing coffee surprised him. He was usually up before Berenice.

He wasn't surprised by the sheep. Sheepherding was widespread in the San Joaquin Valley. Making camp here outside Fresno, they'd met the Basque shepherds who kept three hundred head right on the other side of the fence.

Cleve put on his boots, sheepskin jacket, and his gray Stetson. His back twinged as he climbed out of the wagon into the brisk wind of early morning. He thought ruefully that he'd gone soft, sleeping in hotel beds. It would take a while to get used to sleeping on a thin mat laid over the wooden planks of a covered wagon.

He looked at the herd of sheep cropping at bunchgrass on the other side of the tree-branch fence. A lone Basque shepherd, looking quite relaxed, sat on a low sandstone boulder, his sheepskin-booted feet on the grass. He wore a red and yellow serape and a low-crowned, black straw Dilara hat. At the shepherd's feet, a shaggy yellow dog with a black snout alertly observed the sheep. Smoking a long, curved pipe, the Basque glanced at the cattle on Cleve's side of the wooden fence, then smiled and nodded to Cleve.

Cleve waved to him, feeling almost envious. It needed only a man afoot and a shepherd dog to watch a big flock of languid sheep. It took five riders to keep an eye on a moderate herd of roaming, restless beeves.

But in the long run, there was probably more money in beef cattle, and as Leon said, "A man don't have to shear a steer."

Closer, Cleve and Berenice's unyoked team of four mules cropped at shrubs and what little grass there was. Beyond the wagon were staked the three horses Cleve had purchased in Fresno; a gelding bay for Cleve, an Appaloosa for Berenice, and a black and gray mustang for Leon. Their usual mounts were on the way to Sweet River, in the capable hands of Dave Kanaway.

Cleve was here guarding his cattle, and Berenice insisted on being with him, so Alice was there too. Leon and Teresa were still in Fresno, staying at the hacienda of Don Josepe Diaz, the man who owned this property. Leon and Don Josepe were *compañeros* of long-standing, from a time in Texas when Leon worked for him, alongside a crew of vaqueros.

Berenice was sitting at the fire, cross-legged on a Shoshone blanket. He watched her use a stick of manzanita to stir up the fire under its iron grating. The baby lay beside her in the cradleboard, gazing adoringly at her mother's face. On the grate, a cast-iron pan held sizzling corn fritters and rashers, and beside it was the bubbling coffeepot. Cleve walked over to the fire and just stood there, contemplating his wife and child.

Berry smiled up at him, reaching to swipe a lock of her long, wavy chestnut hair out of the way.

His wife, his daughter, both lit rosily by the morning sun, were seated within a dozen paces of the herd they were to take up to Sweet River Valley. His future was prefigured in this moment, but his happiness was

already here. And as always happened when he felt
contentment, some part of his mind rebuked him with
the deaths of Union soldiers who'd fought under his
command. It didn't matter that he'd done nothing
wrong as an officer; that'd he'd always worked to keep
his men as safe as he could, and still do his duty.

He remembered lines from Walt Whitman, who had
served as a medic in the war:

> *Look down fair moon and bathe this scene,*
> *Pour softly down night's nimbus floods on faces*
> *   ghastly, swollen, purple,*
> *On the dead on their backs with arms toss'd*
> *   wide . . .*

And Cleve, during the aftermath of the battle of
Antietam. With far too few medics, hundreds of
wounded young men lay untreated. Cleve and other
volunteers tried to do what they could, but there were
always more wounded, and their cries became hoarser
and weaker, and at last silenced . . . and the moon shone
on their dead faces.

Cleve Trewe, though wounded more than once, had
been cared for immediately because he was an officer.
That knowledge left a perpetual shadow on his heart.
The feeling that he didn't truly deserve happiness.

But there was something in Berenice's eyes now,
that looked right at that shadow—and made it vanish
into the rising morning mist . . .

She turned away, poured coffee into a tin cup, and
handed it up to him, careful not to spill any on the baby.

"Good morning, Mr. Trewe," she said.

"Mornin' Mrs. Trewe. Up and making the coffee and breakfast?"

"I thought I ought to be of some use out here." She watched his face as he sipped the coffee. It was weak but it would do. "Not strong enough for you?"

Cleve smiled ruefully. A man couldn't hide anything at all from Berenice.

"It's just dandy, my Berenice. More frugal, like, this way. But . . . I guess I'm used to coffee that'll crawl out of the cup if you don't drink it."

"I'll make it stronger next time. Seems strong to me already."

"Just double the grounds and it'll put hair on your chest."

"And would you like me to have hair on my chest?"

Cleve laughed. "No, ma'am, I would not."

"Yet there's something to be said for a good pelt on a cold day. Winter's coming! Maybe I would do well to grow fur like a bear. Polar bears have fur that quickly sheds water, and the hairs are hollow, to trap warm air close in the cold water. It is a marvel of nature's ingenuity."

Cleve wondered how the conversation had made its way here. But it was not unusual, when talking to Berry, to follow peculiar trails. He supposed that if she could take a tonic that made her grow fur, she just might try it, as an experiment.

Berry had brought some dishes carefully packed in wood-wool, and now she used a fork to serve up their breakfast on the china. Tin plates might've been more practical but Berry had grown up in Boston . . .

As they ate, Cleve checked the sun, still doggedly rising, and nodded grimly to himself. That damned agent likely discouraged some of the men he'd tried to hire. *Ride with Cleve Trewe, you'll get yourself shot.* They should have been here by now. He'd said to get there by sunup.

How was he going to get this herd to Sweet River Valley, just him and Leon?

No use in fretting. Cleve soon set his plate aside and with the care of a man handling nitroglycerin, he picked up his daughter, cradling her in his arms. He grinned at her and she smiled shyly back. "She's just the most amiable child, Berry. When I've been around babies before, they've always been squalling. But by God, Alice is the calmest baby I ever saw."

"She's sweet-tempered indeed, and patient," Berry said. She bent over and kissed the baby's bare foot where it stuck out from the swaddling. Alice giggled. "Sometimes it worries me."

"How could her sweet temper worry you?" Cleve asked. He stroked Alice's cheek. "Why that's like being worried about a pretty spring morning, isn't it, Alice?"

Cleve heard hoofbeats and turned to see two riders coming, slowing to a trot as they neared the camp. One sat on a paint pony, the other on a larger mount, a bay quarter horse. They drew up and tipped their hats at Berenice.

The man on the bay was a stranger to Cleve—a clean-shaven man with a sardonic expression to go with his long glossy-black hair and flattish "deacon-style" blood-red hat. He wore a rust-red duster and red leather gloves and boots. His high cheekbones and the angles of his eyes spoke of Indian blood. But not their color. They were blue.

The man on the paint was a compact fellow, Luis Diaz, the son of Josepe Diaz. With his nut-brown skin and black eyes and thin smile, he looked much like his father. He had a sharp Van Dyke beard, curled mustaches, a black sombrero, and a short, rawhide-laced vaquero jacket; he wore rawhide chaps bossed in silver and black Mexican boots. His silver-plated pistol bore a mother-of-pearl grip.

Luis flashed a toothy smile at Cleve. "Hola, Cleve." He raised his hat to Berry. "*Señora.*"

"Good morning to you!" Berry said, nodding to them.

"Morning, Luis!" Cleve said, gently passing Alice to her mother. These were not the trailhands Cleve had been expecting. But he'd mentioned to Josepe Diaz that he feared his men would not turn up. "Your papa send you?"

"*Sí,* Cleve," Luis said genially, his hands resting on the horn of his Spanish saddle. "*Mi padre* says it's best if I find a job somewhere else, for a time. To learn what he does not have time to teach." He shrugged and pulled a face. "It appears I have made some trouble for myself in Fresno, and he wishes me to ask you for a job."

"You've got some experience riding herd, have you?"

"Most assuredly," said Luis, ducking his head in a slight bow. His English was fluent, his accent mild.

The other man snorted. "One herd from Phoenix to San Diego, Luis!"

"It is enough!" declared Luis. "Cleve, this vulgarian with me, he is Señor Smallwolf."

Smallwolf raised his hat to Berry and nodded to Cleve. "Lane Smallwolf."

Cleve had a notion he'd heard that name somewhere. He noticed that both riders had overfull saddlebags and bedrolls tied up behind their saddles. "Looking for a job, Smallwolf?"

"Yes sir, I am. The *jefe,* Luis's pa, he's gone full on to sheep herds, and I'm no hand with sheep. I rode with Chisum, and with McCall too. Had about every job but coosie."

A *coosie* being the cook. Teresa and Berry had volunteered to feed the outfit till they got to the town of Sweet River.

"You know the trail between here and Sweet River?" Cleve asked.

Smallwolf frowned and looked to the south. "I know a rider's trail. But a herd, you need a different trail. There is a way through Westcut Canyon."

Cleve liked that answer. It rang with experience and honesty. "You gents had your breakfast?" Both men nodded. "Well then, step down and have some coffee, and we'll talk about wages and such. You can decide if it suits you. And I'll tell you right now, I'd like to get started today, see what can be done before nightfall."

The riders dismounted, tied their horses to the wagons, and came to squat at the fire. Luis asked for sugar in his coffee. Smallwolf accepted his black coffee from Berenice shyly.

"Here is *la pequeña reina*," said Luis, taking his hat off ceremoniously to Alice.

"She is a little queen, for certain," said Cleve, with a nod.

The cowboys drank their coffee and admired the baby dandled on Berry's knee. Alice seemed inclined to chortle at them. They discussed the trail ahead, and the forage for cattle. Smallwolf said there was bunchgrass aplenty along most of the trail, especially Indian grass and switchgrass.

A creaking of wheels and the heavy steps of oxen announced Leon and Teresa bringing the chuckwagon. Leon tugged the reins and told the brace of oxen to stop and they did, but so close to the campfire that the nearer ox snuffled at the infant. She merely smiled at it and gummed a knuckle.

"She is a fearless child," said Smallwolf approvingly.

"As a queen should be," said Berry, pleased.

"Leon," Cleve said, "back that wagon up a little, and we'll get the camp packed up. Then we're driving the herd southeast."

"Right quick?"

Cleve nodded. "Soon's you had coffee." He wanted to set out before Hawthorn and Marske could try to stop him. "Appears the other hands aren't showing and it's going to be a long road. We've got to get rolling, and I'll be damned if I let anything get in our way . . ."

* * *

Eleven days on the trail.

There was a hint of autumn in the cold edge of the winds rushing down the long, flat Central Valley of California. But the days inched warmer as the men pushed the herd southerly.

Cleve riding the gelding and Leon on the mustang, they took turns riding point and scouting ahead. Smallwolf and Luis Diaz traded off riding in the drag and chousing the herd into line. Berenice and Teresa drove the wagons. After sundown, they took night-rider watches. It was a tough timetable, but with only two hired drovers, Cleve had to make do.

On the second day, Cleve took off after a few strays and quickly realized he'd lost some of his cattle-hand skills over the last nine years. Especially roping. Luis was adept with a lasso and couldn't help laughing at Cleve's efforts. Cleve took it with a grin. Long as the men followed his orders, he didn't mind them making fun of him now and then.

Evenings, if the herd was quiet, he called everyone together for dinner around the campfire. Cleve thought that people working together should get to know one another. Drinking coffee with a little brandy in it, Cleve drew Smallwolf and Luis out.

They learned that Smallwolf's father, Kuruk, was Mescalero Apache, who had worked for German immigrants. His mother was Annalise, the daughter of the German couple, and "she got her eyes full" of his father. As Smallwolf told it, she seduced Kuruk. She became pregnant, and the two had to flee the settlement. They took up with a Four Peaks Mountains tribe of Apache, and it was a hard life for Annalise. She died on a winter march when Smallwolf was ten. He stayed with the tribe for three more years, then tangled with the chief's son over a horse, and stabbed him—in self-defense, Smallwolf insisted.

His father gave him a horse and he escaped the camp, riding to a mission outside Phoenix. The *padres* were "not so bad" and they taught him English, how to read, and some figures. He left the mission at seventeen to cowboy for the local ranches. That's all he would say.

Cleve remembered having seen something in a Denver newspaper about Smallwolf's involvement in a range war and a shootout. He had been described as "deadly." Cleve chose not to bring it up.

Luis liked talking about himself so much, Cleve couldn't quite absorb it all. The young man had been sent to a college in Madrid, after a year and a half a letter from his father informed Luis his older brother had died—broke his neck in a fall, breaking a horse— and Luis must come home to take part in the *ranchero* south of Fresno. Sometimes he snuck away to the cantina in town to play cards and dice and to consort with "the friendly women." Fed up with these shenanigans, his father pushed him to marry the daughter of a caballero because her papa would give a fine gift of land for the wedding. Shaking his head, Luis described her in Spanish: "*Una chica gorda con bigote.*"

Berenice knew a good deal of Spanish. "'A fat girl with a mustache?' Really, Luis! She might be a wonderful person."

"I met her, Señora! She has foul breath and she sweats

very much and she scorned to talk to the servants. And she has no respect for learning! I tried to talk to her of Cervantes, but the only book she ever read was *Dios Habla Hoy.* And not so much of that!"

"Oh! She does sound rather awful."

"And so, I ran off to the cantina after that, and lived there upstairs for two days, and then a man insulted me, so I shot him. Not even dead! And yet, for this trifle"— He shrugged broadly—"my father sent me here."

The fifteenth day on the trail Cleve declared them within reach of Sweet River Valley. "Another thirty miles . . ."

There were more desert plants in the southern Joaquin Valley, including stands of prickly pear. Teresa had learned to eat prickly pear in an Arizona mining camp. Wearing leather gloves, she harvested the pears, skinned the husk, and cut slices to accompany breakfast. It tasted like watermelon and cucumber to Cleve. She and Berry boiled them down, added a little sugar, made them into a sauce ladled on biscuits and hotcakes. It was a welcome change from molasses.

After breakfast, the men rode out—except for Smallwolf, coming off night-riding. He bedded down for a few hours.

Gnawing on a knuckle, Alice watched cheerfully, propped on blankets in a Bannock-woven basket, as her mother and Teresa set to cleaning up after breakfast.

Cleaning pots with sand, lye, and rainwater—their barrel water was getting low—Berenice and Teresa were cheerful, if a mite caustic, when talk turned to the men.

"Who do you think snores loudest amongst that bunch, Berry?"

Berry thought it was Leon but didn't want to say so herself. "Cleve can get a good healthy snore working when he's had a long day."

"Don't you dodge the truth! It's Leon! I know you can hear him from your wagon. It don't matter if he's had a hard day or not."

"I'm more concerned with the metabolic response when we feed them beans."

Teresa laughed. They finished up, then saw to the oxen and mules, making sure they had forage and water. Water for the cattle was getting scarcer. Smallwolf said he knew of a spring on the trail, just before the turn into the canyon.

Now Berenice got one of her notebooks out of the wagon. She'd filled three others with her observations on kit foxes, kangaroo rats, gopher snakes, locust hawks, jumping spiders, and every manner of shrub. Teresa had marveled at Berry's ability to ferret out creatures no one else had spotted.

"Would you like to come along and see what we can find, Teresa?" Berry said, as she put the hideaway gun Cleve had given her in a pocket of her dress.

"Have we time? We've got to follow the herd."

"We shall follow them in just a few minutes. The Indian grass is blooming now. I want a quick sketch and a sample blossom."

"If we stay close to camp," said Teresa, pulling on her green bonnet.

"We shall." Berry picked up Alice's basket. "Cleve's an affable man but he grows fractious when he thinks I'm straying too far."

"Leon gets cantankerous too! Why can't they just trust us to use common sense?"

"And why can't they trust us to help with the cattle!" Berry said, as they started away from camp. "You and I are as good on horseback as any man here!"

"Excepting Smallwolf. That man could be a circus rider if he wanted. I'd take a turn herding if they asked, but it's probably rougher than you suppose, all those hours in the saddle. Eating dust behind the herd! And neither of us can rope."

"I could take the dusk watch, at least."

"Cleve's hat would spin on his head if you so much as suggested it."

"I'd have my rifle. I'm as good with a rifle as Cleve is." Her eyes scanning the bunchgrasses, with their high yellow blossoms sprouting from the bunchy grass, Berry added, "Women can do anything men can do." She gently put the baby's basket on the ground, and Alice looked around curiously.

"Berry, we can do something they can't—bear children. But I'm not built so's I can take a dogie down for branding. Still and all, I've seen women strong enough. Belle Starr could do anything on a ranch a man could do. She won every horserace she rode in." She laughed, looking at Alice. "Alice is looking at the plants just the same way you do."

"Have I the gaze of an infant?"

"Seems she's wondering about them just the same way. The apple don't fall far from the tree." Teresa reached down and tickled the baby's belly.

Notebook in one hand and pencil in the other, Berry peered at the sandy ground between two shrubs of Indian grass. Was that a snake track? Certainly. Which species? "As for strong women, Cleve knew a woman in the war who freighted supplies to the soldiers, and she was inordinately strong. Cathay Williams was her name. After the war, she disguised herself and became a Buffalo Soldier under a man's name—William Cathay!" She frowned and made a corrective mark on her drawing. "Cleve recognized Cathay when he stopped in at a Buffalo Soldier camp. She took him aside and begged him not to tell the others she was a woman. He never told, but he found out that 'William Cathay' was respected as a brave soldier, twice wounded in action."

"A good playactor she was, to fool all those men. What are you sketching, Berry?"

"The florets, the blossoms of *Sorghastrum nutans* . . . I'm tempted to follow that little animal trail. It may belong to a rattlesnake. I do like to observe them hunting."

"It's pure foolish to follow a rattler, Berry, for Heaven's sake—"

They were interrupted by the rapid clopping of hooves. It was Leon, riding hard and drawing up short. He'd finished breakfast early and ridden out to scout the trail through the hills. His face seemed even redder than usual now, and he was breathing hard, calling out, "Where's Cleve?"

"He's gone out to the herd," Teresa said.

Leon shook his head. "I figured he was here because the damn wagons are sitting where I left 'em. Why aren't you following the herd?"

"We were about to! What're you fussing on about, Leon Studge?"

"There's Indians!"

"Oh! Should we go for our rifles?"

"No, you don't see . . . they're mostly *dead!* The ones who aren't, why, they're hiding out there and they need help. Looks like these folks were ambushed. Go and wake up Luis, he's going to have to ride herd."

Then Leon turned his mount and rode hard toward the bawling cattle.

"Oh, Mother Mary and Joseph," Teresa burst out.

"Let us wake Luis and take account of our medical supplies," Berry told her. She picked up the basket, and they ran back to the wagons.

Chapter 6

Three vultures were disturbed in their feeding, flapping cumbersomely into the air as Cleve, Leon, and Smallwolf rode up at a canter. They drew up their mounts and stared at the scattered corpses, aghast. Cleve counted nine dead men, two dead women, and the fresh corpse of an infant boy. The child couldn't have been more than a year old. The dead wore beaded buckskin; some had capes of fur.

The bodies lay where they'd fallen, in a hollow between two hills furred with sage and craggy with crumbling granite. There were no arrows in the murdered Indians. Only bullet holes.

The vultures gone, flies returned and paced across staring eyes.

Cleve shuddered and took in the remains of a camp— half-burned wickiups still trailing a little smoke. A couple of abandoned travois. A single spear, with redtail hawk feathers attached to the blunt end, lay beside an elderly dead man fallen face down; his hand loosely upon it, as if he'd tried to defend the camp. He'd been shot through the head at close range. The back of his skull was a bloody crater.

Cleve saw no horses except a dead Indian pony with a fallen brave sprawled in a puddle of the horse's blood. He saw multiple horse tracks, heading off between low hills to the southeast, toward a distant gray-stone canyon cutting through a tableland. It was the Westcut Canyon, cited by Smallwolf.

The tracks to the southeast were marked by horseshoes. White men, most likely. But there—a smaller set of tracks—two unshod horses had run off due west, maybe spooked to hide in the boulders. The hoofprints going west weren't deep, as if they weren't carrying riders.

"Most here are Waashiw people," Smallwolf said, scowling about him. "You would say Washoe. Last time I was through Tahoe, I got to know them." He dismounted and went to look closer at the dead elder, a weathered old man with long white hair. "But this old man—he looks Paiute. The beadwork on his coat, and the headband—Paiute."

Cleve nodded. "Doesn't seem as if the Paiute was riding with the white men." Renegades sometimes rode with outlaws.

"No, you see"—Smallwolf pointed at the ground—"the old man's tracks come out of that wickiup."

"Paiutes traveling with the Washoe?"

Smallwolf shrugged. "This part of the country, it could be so. The settlers and the cavalry push people out of their home—some end up with other tribes."

Cleve looked at the dead child. Near cut in half with

a shotgun. He looked away, feeling as if the air around him had chilled like a January ice storm.

"They don't seem dead so long," said Smallwolf.

"You didn't see the gunmen, Leon?"

"Not to identify 'em." Leon rubbed his bristly jaw. "I heard shots, a fusillade, like. I rode to see what was going on. I come on this."

Cleve knew that Teresa would surely cuss Leon for doing so foolhardy a thing as riding toward gunfire, out on the range alone. But her husband was impetuous.

"When I got here, I saw white men, riding off," Leon went on. "Going like their tails were on fire. Too far away for me to catch up. Maybe five, six men."

"I figure those are their tracks," Cleve said, pointing. And surprised at how hoarse his own voice sounded.

"Yeah, that's just where they were headed. Long gone now."

"You said there was yet some of the Indians alive?"

Leon nodded toward a ridge of raw granite, about two hundred yards away, its boulder-strewn flanks extending down into the saddle between prominences. "They were up in them rocks. I spotted a peck of 'em before I went to find you boys."

"Hiding up there from the killers," Cleve said. He could see movement, between two boulders, partway up the ridge.

Smallwolf nodded. Climbing into his saddle, he said, "Hiding and waiting for a chance to come down here and . . ." He said something in Mescalero.

"And grieve," Cleve said.

"To pray for the spirits of the dead. Tell them, 'Go to Sky, do not stay here.'"

"They'll want to bury these folks," Leon said. "If that's what the Washoe do."

"They bury their dead, or burn them," said Small-wolf.

Cleve was thinking of following those tracks to the southeast. Settle if it was the white men who had done this. But he had Berenice and Alice to think of, and their well-being meant getting them safely to Sweet River. "Leon—you say there were six white men?"

"Maybe. There was a good deal of dust. But I saw a man lagging behind. He fell off his horse. One of the Washoe must've caught him with an arrow."

"Smallwolf," Cleve said. "How about you talk to the survivors, the best you can. Tell them we'll stand by them if those men come back. And tell 'em they can travel with us if they want . . ."

While Smallwolf was talking to the surviving Washoe, Cleve and Leon trailed the men who'd ridden southeast. He couldn't track them all the way, not yet, but he might get a notion of where they were going.

Cleve and Leon were grimly silent as they rode. About a quarter-mile on, they came upon the dead white man and paused for a quick look.

"You know him, Major?" Leon asked.

Cleve shook his head. "Nope."

"Me neither."

The dead man had thin black hair, fat mutton chops,

and the broken-veined nose of a drinker. There was an arrow jutting from his side. A Sharps rifle lay in the dust beside him.

"You figure them for outlaws?" Leon asked.

"Bandits won't waste time massacring Indians. No money in it." Did this man's partners know he had fallen? If so, they'd simply ridden on.

Cleve looked at their tracks. "Looks like they're headed through the hills. Up to that tableland that looks over Sweet River Valley." Cleve and his herd were going roughly the same way.

"Then there's a good chance we'll run across them, sooner or later."

"I was thinking the same thing. Like to have a word with those boys."

Leon gave a cold smile. "Yep."

"The time will come. Let's see how Smallwolf's faring." Cleve picked up the dead man's rifle. No use letting a good firearm go to waste.

As they trotted their mounts up to the Indian camp, Cleve and Leon found Smallwolf off to the side, digging graves with his small camp spade. The Washoe chanted their grief and their message to the dead. The Indians were in a circle, chanting and dancing, some moaning and falling to their knees. Two Paiutes, a man and a woman, were kneeling by the elderly dead man.

"I saw another dead white man, over by the rocks," Smallwolf said, as Cleve and Leon rode up. "Arrow through his neck."

Cleve nodded. "Seems that once the Washoe got into a good defensive position, and the riders had two men down, the sons of bitches decided they'd done their job, and hightailed it."

"You think they were hired?" Smallwolf asked, as Cleve dismounted and tied the bay to a manzanita bush.

"Someone sent them here, sure enough," Leon said. "That's how it looks."

"The old Paiute there . . ." Smallwolf pointed at the body. "He was once a chieftain. And he's the one who shot that arrow into the man's side—his son told me. That big shoulders fella in the fringed trousers." He nodded at a man kneeling by his father's body. The Paiute was chanting in his own lingo. "Wovoka is his name. He speaks some English. He says he and his father were Owens Valley Paiutes, from the other side of the mountains. The whites were making life too hard for them—demanding they work in the fields with almost no pay. The old man had a dream about Sweet River, and talked his son into heading there. They ran into the Washoe coming from Tahoe."

"Washoe are all from Tahoe, aren't they?" Cleve asked.

Smallwolf nodded. "The lake is all, to a Washoe. But the miners and settlers around Tahoe pushed them out. Most of them settled to the south, and east, along creeks feeding the lake. But this small band set out for Sweet River. And why?"

"A dream?" Leon asked.

"Yes. Ancestor Spirits came to them in a dream too! Now they say maybe they were evil spirits, because of what happened this day. But I say spirits do not know everything. Ghosts were once men. And men know little."

Cleve was interested to hear a metaphysical apologia from Smallwolf. The man had hidden depths.

"Kind of spooks me, all that spirit talk," said Leon, glancing out at the smoke rising ghostlike from the burned shelters.

"Hell, Leon," Cleve said, "you're spooked by black cats."

"For a damned good reason. I don't trust black cats, not a whit nor a whisker."

"Let's me and you fetch some rocks to cover the graves . . ."

That evening, the drive made camp at the foot of a high natural wall of sheer granite that stretched up to a tableland. Close by was the mouth of Westcut Canyon, which ran almost ten miles to Sweet River Valley. There were old wagon wheel ruts here, weed-grown but scantly marking a road. There was a spring, too, just as Smallwolf had said, at the foot of the butte. They re-filled their barrels and watered the stock at the pool below the spring.

A moonless night crept up on the camp, and Cleve decided he wanted full daylight to move the herd into the valley. They knew now that murderers rode these canyons, and he had no desire to expose the drive to a nighttime ambush.

The survivors of the massacre were camped with Cleve's drive, near the wagons pulled up close to the entrance to the pass. The tired cattle were bedded down on the other side of the camp, watched over by Leon. The horses were staked out, the weary oxen and mules were already asleep. Now six men of the band— a Paiute and five Washoe men—were at the campfire, finishing their meal, along with Cleve, Smallwolf, and Luis Diaz.

The rest of the Washoe, four children and four women, sat within the campfire's light but clustered nearer to the wagons. The hands of the Washoe women were abraded from carrying large, sharp-edged rocks to cover the graves, and Teresa had bandaged them. To Cleve's right, Smallwolf squatted as he ate.

Wovoka sat across the fire from Cleve, wiping the last of his gravy up with a hunk of bread. Beside Wovoka was Guama, son of the Washoe chief who was among those killed. Four other Washoe braves sat between Guama and Leon. Guama was a small, wiry man wearing buckskins and a beaded headband. He sat in scowling silence, his black eyes flicking from face to face.

Cleve sipped brandy in a tin cup and glanced over at the four surviving Washoe women. Mourning, they had cut their hair short with knives. They sat in the yellow glow of a lantern, with heads bowed over their plates.

Talk was flattened by grief and sorrow. Silence reigned over the camp, aside from the fire's crackling, the shuffling hooves of tired cattle, and the soft lowing of a calf.

Cleve tensed for a moment when a burning branch from a ghost gum tree popped in the fire, sending up a hissing admonishment of sparks.

He had been around a good many camps with native folk. They were normally talkative, discussing their day with one another; teasing and laughing. It had taken about an hour of persuasion at the burial site to get the little band to trust them this far. The Indians feared they were being taken into custody, maybe to some holding cell at a fort.

At last, Guama set his plate aside, and looked Cleve in the eyes. There was ever a deliberation, a sureness, in the young Washoe's motions. Though he could not have been older than twenty, he had stepped boldly into his father's position of leadership, and the others followed him. "You say, Cleve Trewe, that there is land given you. You say it can be shared with us."

Cleve nodded. "You can have six square acres to live on, with free access to the woods, to the water. The land is not quite mine yet. I made the deal by mail, and paid half of the price. I haven't got the deed in hand; not till I get there. But I'm confident I will. I guess you know what a deed is?"

"I do," said Guama. "No deed means no land. What you do with the cattle, if there is no deed—if there is no land?"

"Could be I'd lease some land for my cattle," Cleve said.

"But what will happen to us, if you must lease? We have no money."

The Paiute, Wovoka, spoke up then. "What choice, Guama? We will work for white men." He spat into the fire and it hissed. Wovoka was a stern, watchful man in a white man's Levi jacket and fringed buckskin trousers. He had a workman's mail-order boots, somewhat repaired with strips of leather. He shook his head slowly and grimly and his long black braids, hanging down the front of him, rippled with the motion. "For white farmers, we are dogs to be fed scraps. If we try to hunt—they hunt *us.*"

"We'll do what we can for you," Cleve said. "But today I can guarantee nothing."

Guama translated this for the others. Then Smallwolf said, "You didn't have any guarantee of what would happen when you got to the valley, Wovoka. You are men. You will find a way."

Silence fell again. Carrying a heaped-up plate of supper, Leon joined them at the fire. Luis got up to take Leon's place watching the herd.

"How do we find those who killed my father, and the Washoe?" Wovoka demanded suddenly, his eyes glinting with firelight.

"We'll find them," Cleve said. "I hope to get the U.S. Marshal after them."

Smallwolf shook his head, but said nothing.

"Cleve did give you a Winchester rifle, Guama," Leon said. "And Wovoka—he gave you a shotgun. And you've got your Sharps." When they found Wovoka's pony, the Sharps was still scabbarded on its saddle. "You just might have a chance to use them."

"There's something else you should know," Cleve went on. "There's an outfit belonging to a man named Hawthorn. They're trying to stop me from buying the land. He's trying to control the whole valley. Could be those killers work for him."

"Hawthorn?" Smallwolf looked at Cleve. "Asa Hawthorn!"

"You know him?"

"I had a . . ." He said a word in Mescalero. ". . . a run-in with him. In the town of Sweet River. I bought some rifle bullets in the store. Hawthorn was there—he did not like to see the Indian buying bullets. But it is not against the law. The merchant, Gunderson is his name, he took my side. Hawthorn warned me to go away, to leave town—and I did. But I heard talk from Gunderson and others there. It is not just Hawthorn. And it is not the land—but what runs through it."

"The river?"

Smallwolf nodded. "Asa Hawthorn is partner with a man named Payton. They want to own the river."

"Own it?" Leon said. "Water rights, is it?"

Cleve grunted. "You can own a water hole, maybe a small creek—but not a river. Least up until now. Maybe the Paytons figure to change that."

"I've heard of the Payton combine," Leon said. "Powerful folks. I've known range wars to start over water rights."

Cleve nodded. "Land's important, but a man's life depends on water." He took another pull at his coffee and brandy. He had been tolerably edgy, after the threats from Marske. Now he'd taken on an additional burden, offering protection to this band of Indians.

His plans were more than tangled. They were knotted in wet leather.

* * *

Early morning, Cullen Marske was standing watch, leaning on a lightning-blackened oak tree, rolling a smoke with his left hand, his right clasping the barrel of his Sharps repeater as if it was a walking stick.

As he stuck the Bull Durham quirly in his mouth, he saw three men ride into view, coming up through the notch on the south side of the bluff. He knew them by their silhouette: Asa Hawthorn wearing that tall-crowned white hat; Delbert Hawthorn, Asa's son, so gangly on his horse; and Harl Hawthorn, in his brown slouch hat, was Asa's jug-eared, big-bellied nephew.

They were a welcome sight. Marske was fair sick of waiting here with the complainers in this windy camp on the tableland. Nothing to do but watch for Indians, puff ever-scantier smokes, and play cards with men who were too stupid to see him dealing off the bottom of the deck. He'd started letting them win just to vary the play.

Marske thoughtfully ignited his quirly with a lucifer. Best let the others know the Hawthorns were here.

Grabbing the rifle up by the stock, Marske slipped down the hummock, calling out, "Hawthorns are coming!"

"Maybe now we can go into town," said Dipsey, scratching at his bushy head again. And then at his beard and crotch. Marske slept on a bedroll far from the others. He strongly suspected they were crawling with lice.

It flicked through Marske's mind how strange it was,

making a living this way. Keeping company with such men. Scurrilous, lousy back-shooters. Sure enough, it had been plain common sense to take the gun job with Twisty X for the Boone County range war, out in Missouri. No more punching cows, no longer eating dust all day, five times the pay to just keep your head down and shoot first. Kill some empty-headed Dutch squatters and a few rifle-toting sheep men. Bury the man to your right who didn't keep his head down during the shooting. Spend most nights at the My Darling's Delight Saloon. Hell, that was a job to kill for.

But gunning down the stunned, perplexed Washoe left him chewed at by the black dog. A fierce, dogged melancholy snapped at his heels. Marske caught himself thinking he was glad when Squeaky Jones took that arrow through the neck—it cut straight through his Adam's apple. Squeaky, who cut the toddler in two with the shotgun.

Hawthorn had said, *Make sure they can't get into the valley. Not by any route.* There was only one way to make certain of that. But shooting a little boy and his ma wasn't called for. Maybe it bothered Marske because he was himself a quarter Comanche. After the kid was shot down, Marske figured they'd made their point, time to ride out.

After the Boone County War, Marske drifted west to California, where he'd run into Asa Hawthorn, once Marske's captain under John C. Fremont in the Union Army. Marske had made sergeant and he had done his part in fighting rebs. Hawthorn remembered him, and recruited him as a gunhand for Hawthorn Enterprises. Marske never much liked Hawthorn, but the man had a growing cattle ranch. He was planning irrigation canals, and going to lease water rights. Here was a powerful, money-dripping man. So Marske put his dislike of Hawthorn aside.

Now he looked away from the men around the breakfast campfire as the Hawthorns rode up. As they reined in, the gunmen stood up, to show some respect for the man paying their wages.

Asa Hawthorn had a long face, and one of those mouths with a lot of room between the lips and the nose. Most men would cover that expanse with a mustache, but Asa shaved it clean, leaving only a fringe of jaw beard. He wore a tailor-made black riding jacket with leather lapels, khaki trousers, and high black boots. Del got his skinniness from his pa, but the elder Hawthorn was wiry, and his hands were rough from work. He could handle a rope or a rifle good as any man in his outfit.

A pale young man with a sparse mustache, Del wore a pea jacket and a tweed cap he'd gotten in Boston when he'd gone to school out there. He pushed his spectacles back with a finger and stared at Marske, as he always did.

Harl Hawthorn sniffed and rubbed his nose and squinted at Marske. Probably needed spectacles himself.

"Marske," said Asa, pointing a finger. "You get the job done?"

Marske nodded and plucked the quirly from his lips.

"Half of the Indians are dead and buried, Mr. Hawthorn. And we lost two men."

"You *buried* them red bandits?" Harl blurted, gawping in disbelief.

Marske shook his head. "Nope, I rode over at first light this morning, to see if the rest of the Indians had lit out. I found the graves. The ones who hid in the rocks— they'd moved out. Tracks say they went back north."

"Why didn't you kill them *all?* " Asa demanded.

"We killed enough—the rest gave up and went home."

"You don't know they went home," said Asa. "You want to get paid, you'll find out! If they're coming at the valley from any direction at all, you're to do what has to be done."

"How did the fight start?" asked Del suddenly. He licked his lips, glancing nervously at his father. "I mean—did they force your hand?" It appeared that Hawthorn hadn't told his boy much about the raid on the Indians.

More like we forced their hand, Marske thought. They'd shown no fight until Hawthorn's men opened up on them.

"I told him to make sure," Asa said. "I'm just sorry the job wasn't finished."

"We did lose Hungry Griff and Squeaky," Dipsey piped up. "We figured—"

"Shut up, Dipsey," Marske snapped. "No one gives a damn what you figured." He nodded to Hawthorn. "We'll finish the job, Asa."

"You do it and you'll get the other half of your pay

and a bonus!" Hawthorn turned to Del. "What did you say, Delbert—you questioning my decisions?"

"I . . . I think it unfair to interpret what I said that way, Father."

A couple of the men sniggered at that.

"You want to step down and have some coffee, Mr. Hawthorn?" Marske asked.

Hawthorn glared at him. "You men haven't got time for coffee. Get your bunch to the north side of this bluff and see what the heathens are doing! You get a chance to take care of them—do it!"

"Yes, sir."

Asa turned to his nephew. "Harl—they'll be coming up the Westcut, once they figure Marske and his boys are gone. You get over there, take a post on yonder southwest cliff, and you keep watch. Stay till nightfall, if you have to. Have your rifle out and ready—you might need it. You see any Indians come south on that canyon, open fire. Once it gets dark, you come and report to me."

Harl hesitated, not seeming happy about spending hours lying out on the edge of a cliff. But let out a whoosh of breath and said, "Sure, Asa. You bet."

Del cleared his throat. "I cannot but observe that state and federal laws—"

Hawthorn flashed that pointing finger at Del, silencing him. "And you, boy—I'll talk to you at home. Just keep your peace and come along."

He backed his horse, turned it, and rode back toward the notch. Harl headed his quarter horse toward the southwestern lip of the cliff.

Del closed his eyes for a long moment, then looked at Marske. "I'll . . . be seeing you." He turned his horse and cantered off after his father.

"Well, boys, saddle up," said Marske dryly, turning toward the horses. He flicked his still-smoking stub away and strode to his horse. "Captain Hawthorn has given us our orders."

The sky was almost cloudless but the air was nippy as Cleve and Leon rode down into the Westcut Canyon, ahead of the herd. Cleve wanted to scout ahead. Whoever sent the killers after the Washoe band might be set up for ambush.

"You sure got yourself into another pickle, Cleve," said Leon. "What with this Payton combine now. Money like that can hire all the guns it needs."

"I know, Leon." He slowed the bay to a trot. Didn't want to canter into someone's gunfire.

"You know what this reminds me of?" said Leon, his eyes scanning the top of the tableland. "Like you're that David from the Bible story, but this time he ain't just fighting that Goliath—he's fightin' Goliath's giant big brother and his uncles too!"

Cleve grunted. "Why is it you sound pleased about it?"

"I sure as hell ain't pleased!"

"Amused, then." He guessed that Leon was still feeling cold and heavy after finding the massacre site. A child killed with a shotgun. Cleve felt the same way.

And this flippancy was Leon's way of keeping his mind off it. Whistling past the graveyard.

"Maybe I am a little amused," Leon went on. "Kinda funny how Major Cleveland Trewe can take the quickest road to the quicksand. Axle Bust? Caught between outlaws and a mining boss! San Francisco? Gunfights in Barbary Coast, jumping off a dock onto a boat, up to your neck in coal and steam while that big man—"

"I *remember,* Leon," Cleve interrupted, feeling provoked. He hadn't slept well and he was on edge. "I'll buy you out of this herd if you want."

"I didn't put any money in yet."

"You're working as foreman for your share. If Goliath and his uncles worry you, I'll buy you out and you can take Teresa and go on back to Sacramento and—"

"Dammit, Cleve," said Leon, visibly gritting his teeth, "once more you are insulting me. Saying I got the white feather in my hat!"

"Don't get started on that again! I couldn't ask for a better man at my side. I guess that . . ." He shrugged. "Maybe you're ragging on me because you're worried about Teresa."

Leon opened his mouth to retort—and then closed it. "Mebbe so."

They were silent then, another mood taking them both. Quiet, unspoken dread for those they loved.

They clopped slowly on, seeing little but scree under the cliffs, scrub brush and Indian grass. The herd was about a quarter-mile behind them.

"I do have a worry," said Cleve after a time, "that I might be dragging Berry into a cross fire."

Leon nodded. "I told Teresa, maybe you should stay in Sacramento for a time, and I'll send for you when everything's safe. She nearly bit my ear off! Says she can take twice the hell I can and she can do it before breakfast. Told me some stories about her alone in the mining camp. You know, she shot a drunken miner in the gizzard, down in Coloma, for trying to violate her. He lived, though. And who do ye suppose tended to him while he mended?"

"Teresa?"

"She did! He wept when he came to and saw who it was. Then Teresa told him she'd shoot him dead if he tried to manhandle her another time."

Cleve smiled. "No wonder she and Berenice are such good friends. Berry, she won't follow a man, but she'll walk beside him—if he earns that privilege."

"Did she say that? If he *earns* it? Ho-*ho!* I'm right curious to know when she'll get smart about you and give you the air!"

"Now don't start in—"

"Cleve—hold up." They reined in the horses. "You see something flash on that bluff there?" Leon pointed at the top of the tableland on the south side of the cut, and closer to the Sweet River Valley.

Cleve looked, saw a winking of silvery-blue light from the edge of the caprock. "If that's not gunmetal, I don't know what the hell else it could be."

"I knew a fella had a silver front tooth. Could be him grinnin' at us."

"You are a fount of merriment today. I'm wondering how we're going to get the bulge on whoever that is up there."

"Let us move out of range and mebbe we can flank the bastard."

"We're probably out of effective range. But come along this way." He started toward the eastern cliff and Leon followed. "I've got a notion forming up in me . . ."

Cleve rode quickly over to the eastern cliff. They were sheltered here from the rifleman by a big outcropping where the canyon wall bulged out.

Hugging the cliff wall, they rode back north till they found Smallwolf alongside the herd, trying to keep the cattle from straying after bunchgrass. The steers complained, bawling when he chivvied them with his spinning rope ends.

"Smallwolf!" Cleve called, as they rode up. "Let the herd slack out right here. Where's Wovoka and Guama?"

"Taking up the drag, boss. Here is Luis."

"Señor Trewe!" said Luis Diaz, riding up. *"Qué pasa?"*

"We're going to check the backtrail. We need you to ride up to the point and keep the herd back. There's a man with a rifle down that way. I don't want the herd going down there yet, nor you boys either."

"But—where are you going?"

"Got no time to talk, Luis. Just get it done."

He rode away, leading Leon and Smallwolf at a canter to the rear of the herd, where Wovoka and Guama were on their ponies—Wovoka on the black and white pinto, Guama on the brown and white. Wovoka's pony had a circled Paiute hand mark on its flank.

"Ho-ah!" Cleve shouted and coughed in the dust pluming back from clumping cattle hooves.

The two Indians rode over to him, drew down the bandannas Cleve had given them against the dust. Wovoka said, "You call?"

"Hold on a moment." Cleve reached for his canteen, took a drink to wash away the dust, and said, "We might have a chance at the cowards who shot your folks . . ."

Chapter 7

Five men rode side by side. Cleve, Smallwolf, Leon, Wovoka, and Guama.

They cantered northeast, through the thin growth of scrub, and on past the wagons. Berenice was driving the Conestoga, the baby in a sling on her chest. Some of the Washoe women were riding in the wagon. Cleve waved at her and Teresa, bringing up the chuckwagon. He knew they'd want to know why the men were cantering away from the herd—but there just plain wasn't time to explain.

"Leon!" Teresa called, as the men rode past.

"Don't you worry, darlin'!" he called to her, spurring his horse to more speed.

They passed the rest of the Indians walking behind the wagons. The Washoe frowned at the passing riders but said nothing.

Cleve knew what he was figuring on might be flat wrong. But they rode onward for fifteen minutes, till they came to a place of tiered rock ranging down this side of the tableland. Cleve signaled a stop. The riders reined in and Leon turned to Cleve.

"I'd sure like to know where in hell we're going!" Leon said, wiping dust from his eyes.

"You see that trail coming down off the bluff there? Behind the big red rocks."

"I make out some of it."

"That rifleman was watching the Westcut for a reason. If that murderin' bunch is on the caprock up there, could be they're coming down this way to finish the job. This is the only way down on this side. Like as not, they spotted the Indians following the herd. They could ride up behind and cut them down."

"If you're wrong . . ."

"Then we lose nothing but a little time."

"I'll lose a heap of time explaining to Teresa."

"Let's leave the horses here," Cleve said. The five men dismounted and tied the horses to tall, sturdy manzanitas in the shadow of the rimrock. Cleve took his Winchester from its saddle scabbard and carried it in his left hand, his right resting on the butt of his Colt Army .45.

"Riders coming," Wovoka said softly, hefting the rifle in his hands.

The men kept quiet, listening. Cleve could hear it now, horseshoes on rock, somewhere above.

He chambered a round in his Winchester and whispered, "Move into the rocks across the trail. We'll get a better shooting angle. Catch them from cover."

"Suppose it's not them?" said Leon softly, as he followed Cleve to the trail between the boulders. "Could be just some drovers out looking for their beeves."

Cleve turned to Wovoka and Guama. "Would you know their faces?"

Both men nodded.

"Tell us if it's them—and don't shoot if it isn't. We agreed?"

Wovoka said, "Yes, Cleve Trewe." Guama nodded.

"There's another thing. If we can get the drop on them—maybe I can get them to surrender. You might get to watch them hang."

Wovoka shook his head. "Just kill them."

"I'd feel the same if I were in your place. But if you want me there—we kill them only if we have to." The Indians looked at one another with uncertainty. Cleve reflected that sometimes he forgot he was not leading a cadre of military men. "I'll say it plain—if they open fire, then we have no choice but to fire back."

Smallwolf said, "I will go where Cleve leads."

"Me too," said Leon.

Wovoka growled in his throat. Then he nodded.

Cleve clapped him on the shoulder. "Come on, then."

That pause might have cost them some. They stepped out on the trail—when thirty yards up the hillside, five riders rode hard around a bend and down toward them.

There was not a second to get to cover—the riders were galloping down at them, pistols raised. Two of the riders opened fire and bullets cracked by.

"It is them!" Wovoka shouted, raising his rifle.

And Cleve knew there was no capturing these men, not now.

"We got 'em boys!" shouted a yellow-haired rider

with wild eyes and a blazing grin, as he rode hard at Cleve. "Cut 'em down!"

It was his last grin and his last call to arms. Cleve drew the Colt, letting experience and instinct aim for him as he fired from the hip. He fired twice, his first bullet smashing through that grin, knocking the gunman back, the second taking him under the chin. The yellow-haired rider fell and his horse dragged him on down the hill, one boot stuck in the stirrup, as Cleve swung for another target—a big man with a bushy black beard riding down on the three Indians.

But the Washoe and the Paiute fired at once, from five yards away, both shots catching the bushy-maned gunman in the chest. He fell heavily back into the dust left by his spooked horse as Leon and Smallwolf shot a lean-faced man with a black eye patch, Smallwolf's round taking out the other eye.

Cleve sidestepped an onrushing horse, barely evading the slashing saber wielded by an ex-Confederate, judging by the gunman's torn gray coat and crumpled gray hat. The saber came close enough that its tip scratched Cleve's jaw. Cleve pivoted, firing at the same time as the gunman turned in his saddle to fire back at Cleve. The bullet cut close by Cleve's right ear, humming like an angry bee as Cleve fired twice, his rounds smashing through the Confederate's rib cage. He turned away before he could see the gray-clad gunman fall, for a fifth rider up the slope had held back, his horse rearing in the rising dust. He was a dust-draped blur, but his long black boots and his horse-hide duster were familiar.

Was it Cullen Marske?

Cleve couldn't make out the gunman's face, but saw the muzzle flash of his pistol. Bullets cracked into the rock on Cleve's right, stone breaking up like cannonball fragments. Cleve felt a vicious sting at the corner of his jaw.

Leon and Smallwolf fired up at the last rider—and Cleve let go a shot without a chance to aim—and knew the bullet went wild. The rider returned fire at Leon and Smallwolf, who ducked behind an outcropping as bullets kicked up dust at their feet.

Cleve holstered the Colt, brought the Winchester to the right shoulder, and fired as the rider turned and rode back up the hill, overwhelmed by the gunfire. Cleve missed again, maybe, but it was close.

Irritated with himself, Cleve turned and ducked between the boulders, ran into the manzanita clump to look up at the rimrock, hoping for a shot.

He caught a glimpse of the gunman between two boulders, riding hell-bent for leather up onto the tableland, hatless head ducked low, long black hair streaming back. Cleve brought the rifle up and fired. He thought he saw sparks from a boulder near the rider's head.

"Dammit . . ."

Then the gunman was gone, hidden behind the rimrock.

Gun in hand, Leon huffed up to him. "You get him?"

"Couldn't get a good shot."

"Sure rabbited out of here, didn't he?" Leon said, squinting up at the rimrock.

"He saw his men cut down. He figured the odds. Don't make him a coward. Just not a fool."

"You think he was their boss?"

"Boss of this bunch here, anyway. Might've been Cullen Marske."

"You sure enough to swear to it in court?"

"Nope."

"We going to bury these owlhoots?" Leon said, as they turned toward their horses.

"Think we should?" Cleve asked.

"I looked close at a couple of those bodies. They got lice. I don't want nowhere near 'em. I had to talk Wovoka out of taking a scalp. They don't deserve burying anyway."

"Let's go after the bastard who got away . . ."

"We followed him up onto the butte," Cleve said, as he watched Berenice washing the baby in a ceramic tub. The tub was set up on a barrel top outside the Conestoga. Alice splashed at the water, sending some up onto her mama's chin. "Found some blood up on the trail. Not much—but it seems one of us hit him after all. Tracked him to the far side, and down the trail a piece . . . just couldn't follow him farther. Not with you and Alice waiting back here." His account was something of an apology for being gone so long. Knowing the women had heard the gunshots and were wondering if their men would be coming back.

Cleve, Smallwolf, and Leon had spent hours looking for Marske, if that's who he was. The tracks led past a faintly smoking campfire near a blasted oak, then to the cliff edge close to the southern side of the butte, and they could see the crushed grass where the rifleman had lain, watching the canyon.

Two sets of horse tracks ran from the cliff across a corner of the butte and down through a notch, then along a trail slanting against the tumble of rock at the foot of the rimrock, and into Sweet River Valley.

Fringing that side of the valley was a thick motte of cedar and juniper. The gunmen could be in there somewhere, watching their back trail. They'd have a clear shot at Cleve and his companions from down there. The trackers reluctantly turned back.

"Your blood was up," Berry said, as she diapered the baby with gingham. "But you shouldn't have pursued them, Cleve. We didn't know what to do here, till you got back. We heard some of it from the Indians."

Cleve nodded. "You're right, as usual." He bent over and kissed the back of her neck.

"That's not going to get you on the right side of me," she said. But even without seeing her face, he knew from the tone of her voice that he was forgiven.

She closed up the diaper, took the cooing baby in her arms, and turned to face Cleve. Alice reached out toward Cleve's nose.

"You want it, Alice, you got it," he said, leaning close so she could grasp his nose. She took a firm grip on it. "I didn't say you could take it with you!" He took her hand from his nose and kissed her small chubby fingers. The baby pulled her hand away and gnawed at a knuckle, gazing at him in a way that he told himself was fondness but might be more like scientific interest.

When he straightened up, what he saw in Berry's eyes was a kind of fatalistic sorrow. "You and Leon can't do this alone. Hired cowboys aren't an army, Cleve."

"What do you want me to do, my Berenice? You know, these are the men who massacred the Washoe—and we were hunting another who got away."

"I know. You did the right thing. Tell me this, are you going to walk away from this shooting too? There are four men lying dead out there."

"I didn't kill them all."

"I know that. Still and all . . ."

"I'm going to send a telegraph, first chance I get, to Marshal Beaman. And I'll write him a letter to give him full details. He used to be an Indian agent, on a reservation for the Eastern Paiute—far as I heard, one of the few agents the tribes liked. He set up a tribal police and a tribal court on the reservation, so they could run their own affairs. He has no love for folk who treat the Indians as if they have no rights in this country."

"So he'll be sympathetic to the Washoe in this? And to Wovoka and his wife and their boy?"

"Beaman will be *fair*. He won't dismiss their story just because they're Indians. I'd bet a thousand in silver he'll make the trip out here himself."

"Alice, your papa has taken a weight off my shoulders. Let us reward him." She stepped in close to Cleve, and they gently snuggled the baby between the two of them. Alice wriggled and chirped at them, and for a time Cleve didn't have to think about the four dead men lying out on the bloody trail.

It was dusk as Cleve stepped down from the rear of the wagon. He stood there gazing at Sweet River Valley.

The woods off to the north were taking on a grayness, as the sun began to set, and the Sierra Mountains rising sixty miles to the east were caped in velvet-red. Stretching out from the foothills of the Sierras, unrolling toward the camp in breeze-rippled green and ripple-glinting silver, was Sweet River Valley. Running down the middle of the basin, a little south of dead center, was Sweet River itself. Clear and cold, fed by springs and snowmelt and seasonal rains, jumping with rainbow trout, Sweet River ran on far to the west, eventually joining the San Joaquin River.

Looking at it, Cleve smiled.

The cattle grunted, as two restless bulls clashed their horns together. The older one backed away and shuffled off. The rest of the herd was quietly bunched, beginning to bed down after gorging on the deep green grass.

Leon and Teresa were at the back of the chuckwagon, talking about the evening meal, she proposing yet another stew. But the Washoe were already out fishing with handmade nets of hemp, and soon they could catch trout for supper. The Washoe were a fishing people, as were the Owens Valley Paiute, and the sight of the river cheered them up.

The Indian women had made their own fire a little

distance off and were ranged around it talking. The Washoe had danced with joy and song when the men returned to report four of the murderers dead. But Wovoka and Guama nearly mutinied when Cleve told him they wouldn't be trying to catch all the dead men's horses. He didn't want anybody saying they'd killed those men to rob them. Still, he allowed them to take one horse, for the band's use—the unbranded chestnut mare that was slowed by dragging its dead rider. They cut the dead man free and the mare was now in the Indians' camp. The other horses they unsaddled and set loose, Wovoka and Guama shaking their heads with disgust at this loss of good saddle horses. But Cleve had given them the guns and ammunition from the dead men.

He looked back toward the tableland. Four dead men lay at the foot of that butte, probably feeding vultures and coyotes now. He had hoped to catch them unawares, demand their surrender. Find a hooscgow to stow them in till they could be turned over to the U.S. Marshal. But they had come on firing. Well, the world was a little cleaner without them.

Luis Diaz was scowling as he squatted by the cooking fire, adding a few sticks of cedar. He looked up at Cleve without moving his head, just those eyes glaring up at him.

Leon walked over, grinning, nodding toward the valley and the mountains beyond. "Lord, Major, she's a beauty, ain't she?"

"She is at that. Tomorrow you and me'll ride on up

to Drake Samuels's place, pay him off, and claim the deed."

"You don't think it's likely Hawthorn has gotten to him? Maybe offered him more?"

"Samuels does not seem a man to squirm out of a deal. And I paid him well." But in fact, Cleve was far from certain. He glanced over at Luis, who was staring into the fire, moodily smoking a thin cheroot. "Leon, has Luis got his back up about something?"

"Oh, only that you made him stay behind and took all the other men to a fight is all! What young feller wouldn't kick at that? There was some excitement about the fight when we come back and he got a look of thunder to him. You could've got one of the braves to watch the herd."

"His father fed us and put us up, then let us pasture the herd on his land. Wouldn't take a *centavo* for it. He's a good man. I didn't want to have to write him a letter saying his son was shot dead."

"There's something to that. It's a miracle none of us was shot bad. I got a graze on my hip, didn't amount to anything, and Wovoka caught a round in his left arm."

"I thought I saw some blood on him but I thought it belonged to them we killed. He didn't make a peep about that wound."

"He got Marigold to dress it. The bullet missed the bone, it's not bad. Must smart some."

"Who's Marigold?"

"She's his woman—how is it you don't know that? That's her, sitting over there with the Washoe—the one in that ribbon dress. She's Paiute like Wovoka."

"Has anyone spotted riders? Maybe around in those woods, or along the river?"

"Not so much as scared-up birds. Right peaceful. Saw some tule elk over there by the trees. The Washoe wanted to hunt them but I said let's wait, stay together tonight. Plenty of time for hunting when we know it's safe."

"Makes good sense." Cleve decided he'd take first watch himself. He wasn't going to let Marske get the bulge on him. But with four men dead, there was a good chance Hawthorn was undersupplied with gun hires. "Leon, if you're going with me tomorrow, be ready to rise before dawn . . ."

"Well, of course, I'm coming! I'm ready to rise just as early as you want, Major!"

"Dammit, why'd you wake me up, Cleve?" Leon mumbled. "I was having me a dream I was winning a horse race in Austin . . ."

"Hush up, or you'll wake Teresa," whispered Cleve. He hunkered just outside their bedding, which was laid out under the chuckwagon.

"I'm already awake," Teresa said, without opening her eyes. "And damn you, both. You just get him back here in one piece, Cleve Trewe."

"Yes, ma'am, I will. Come on, Leon."

As they saddled their horses, Leon asked, "What was you doing up so late last night? I know it wasn't canoodlin'. I seen your shadow on the canvas, sitting on a chest or somethin'."

"Cleaning my guns. Oiling my guns. Checking the cartridges for my guns. Loading my guns up. Even the shotgun and my hideaway."

"You're loaded for bear, Cleve. Maybe three bears." He glanced off toward the southeast. "You got one of those—*feelin's?*" They were both veterans of the Civil War. They knew about 'those feelings.' The premonition of danger afoot.

Cleve tightened the cinch on his saddle and climbed aboard. "Finding a crowd of men and women shot dead will do that. Then there was the fight with Marske's boys. We don't know where he is now. I'd guess his boss is hiring more men."

Leon mounted up. "Teresa doesn't like it if I keep the light on when she's ready to sleep. You don't get that naggin' from Berry?"

They turned their mounts toward the valley in a trot. "Nope. Half the time she's the one up late, working on those notes of hers. Scribbling and yawning. Yawning and scribbling. But when she's ready to sleep, a light won't keep her up. Teresa and Berry work as hard as any man in camp. Driving the wagons, cooking, cleaning up, taking care of Alice, washing clothes, a multitude of other chores." After a moment he added, "Soothing their men with flattery and affection—that's hard work too, I suspect."

"Why, I don't need flattery."

"You need it double."

Leon snorted. "Don't get much of that from Teresa no-how."

Half an hour later, they were heading east up the

valley, riding alongside the river as the sun rose between
two peaks of the Sierra. The last flowers of the season
were blossoming. California poppy dappled swells and
hummocks; wild sweet pea flowered along the river.
Pansies and Shasta daisies interspersed the grasses.

"Why, it's most like a garden!" Leon marveled.

Cleve nodded. Hummingbirds shimmered over from
purple aster; towhees and goldfinches squabbled over
beautyberry along the river. Trout in the river jumped at
the first damselfly of the morning. Off to the north,
Cleve saw five elk roaming the grasslands. A buck
raised its grandly antlered head and contemplated the
horsemen, perhaps meditating a warning rush at them.

Leon pointed at the craggy horizon. "What's that big
mountain there, Cleve, the one with the snow?"

"Mount Whitney. Paiutes call it *Tumanguya*. Means
'the old man.' Some of this river water comes off
Whitney's slopes as melt. That mountain over there—"
He pointed. "That's Mount Emerson. Named by John
Muir. Hope to meet Muir someday."

"Muir? Why?"

"Because he's a man who looks at the world with
his soul."

"I'll take your word for that. What county is this
anyhow?"

"Inyo County. This valley is one of the greenest
spots in it. Some of Inyo is desert—specially up in the
foothills. Death Valley's over yonder, southeast. Couldn't
get dryer than that."

"It's a forever drouth, I heard. They say Death Valley
was named by prospectors—seeing as a power of miners

died there. Kinda surprised Sweet River Valley's not all settled."

"Southern Miwok occupied it and that tribe's pretty tough. That slowed settlement some. But they moved on, and settlers started coming in, like ol' Samuels. Not such a big valley—twenty-four miles wide at its widest, maybe seventy long. It'll get crowded soon enough."

"If that syndicate allows it." Leon sniffed the air. "Surely smells sweet in the morning here. Lord, but you could fatten a herd on that grass."

"And Hawthorn thinks he can claim all that and most of the river for himself."

"How you going to get your deed registered?"

"I can send a claim by wire to Sacramento, once it's signed and witnessed—nearest telegraph and court-house is in Independence, up northeast. That's the county seat."

"Where's Hawthorn's outfit?"

"His ranch house is on the south side of the river. We'll see it as we pass. Best not linger thereabouts."

"We're lingering, right here. Let's pick up the damn pace, Cleve."

"I'll race you to that river bend!" They galloped up along the river for a time, just to get the horses stretched out, then slowed to a hard trot. Cleve was impatient to get to Samuels's ranch.

Hawthorn would keep on trying to block him from buying that land. If Marske was any indication, Haw-thorn would use guns if he had to.

Cleve gazed again at the green and silver splendor of the valley and knew it was worth fighting for.

* * *

Delbert Hawthorn was awaiting the moment to speak his piece. Awaiting it, and dreading it. He feared his father's response.

"It's a simple matter, boy," said Asa Hawthorn, tapping the map on his desk. "'If a man is bold, he grabs a hold.'" He was prone to quoting his Uncle Rastas, who'd raised Asa Hawthorn. Rastas was a fount of rhyming epigrams. "You have the simplicity for a simple matter, Delbert, but you don't have the boldness."

Del shivered, maybe at this casual double insult from his father, or maybe because the room was cold. The fire had gone out hours ago. But the insult stung. He shrugged, knowing himself to be like the man who kept bees and was used to stings.

They were standing together at the desk at one end of Hawthorn's big bedroom. The long room contained a river stone fireplace and a four-poster bed, made up every day by the colored housekeeper, Millie. There was a settee covered by a grizzly fur and a sprawling mahogany desk. At either end of the room broad windows of clear glass, imported all the way from San Francisco, looked out on a meadow where a small herd of horses grazed near a motte of live oak.

"We had a setback," Hawthorn went on. "We lost some men. Don't think I won't get Judge Payton to go after this man Trewe for gunning those men down."

Delbert cleared his throat. "I heard Marske tell it. He and his men went in shooting."

"He'll tell it the way I want him to if it goes to court! And so will you!"

Del nodded. It was a reflex. "Still—there's a U.S. Marshal. He said in the *Sacramento Bee* that just shooting Indians down will no longer be overlooked in this state—"

"Boy!" Hawthorn barked. "Hush!"

Staring into the cold fireplace, Del licked his lips and waited.

"Delbert—you hear me and hear me well! Those Indians killed *white prisoners!*"

Del blinked in confusion. This he had not heard. "When did that happen?"

"When I decided it did. We're going to say the whites are buried out in the rocks. And the Indians fired on my men!"

"That's . . ." He wanted to say, *That's quite a high stack of mendacities. It might just fall over of its own weight.* But he dared not. "I see."

"I am saying a Hawthorn does not accept a setback. We set out, to make out! We're going to own every square rod and acre of land out to a mile on both sides of Sweet River!"

Del kept his expression bland, his voice all puzzled innocence, as he asked, "Will we own it—or will the combine?"

"Why, it's a joint ownership, the Paytons and us!" His face clouded. "Are you needling me, boy?"

"No, sir, I just want to get it all sharp and square in my mind. How . . ."

"How what? Spit it out!"

"How, ah . . ."

Del knew what he should say to please his father. And it was the last thing he wanted to say. What he really wanted to ask was if he could go to the state university in San Jose. But he needed to think of some way his going to that school could help his father. Maybe he could study law. Though he'd prefer to study geology. San José State University was not close to Sweet River but it was closer than Boston. Maybe he could persuade his father that geology could lead to finding precious metals or at least coal on the Hawthorn ranch. "I wanted to get clear, father, just how . . . how I can help you with the, ah, the water rights and . . . and the matter of, ah . . ."

"How can you help? You will show me you have a scrap of manhood! 'First things first or things get worse!'"

"I was just thinking I could study up on—"

"Now, Marske is wounded," Hawthorn interrupted. "It'll be a month maybe before he's back in the saddle. He has recommended some men who can be of use to us. They're in jail in Independence, but your Uncle Sully can aid us with that. He won't like it. But I got him elected sheriff and he owes me powerful. He'll turn those men over to me, so's we can deal with these Trewe squatters—Sully Morse will do it or I'll make him sorry."

Chapter 8

A windy late afternoon, in the riverbank settlement of Sweet River, California. Cottonwoods by the river bent in the damp breeze and let go a scattering of leaves that blew across the rutted dirt road as Cleve and Leon rode in. The town resounded with work being done: a hammer clanging rhythmically on iron; a circular saw buzzing. A hostler calling after horses.

"Not a whole lot to this town," Leon remarked. "About enough to fill a gopher hole."

"Nonsense," Cleve said, smiling. "When I was here early this year there were eleven buildings. Now there are twelve! It's growing by leaps and bounds."

"Looks like that new one's a saloon."

"Last time I was here, the only place to share a drink was Gunderson's Trading Post. He uses a couple old barrels for a bar."

The town of Sweet River was crowded around a bridge of pine logs and clay mortar built over a narrows. There were a few cabins and a tent on the other side of the river, near the river. Most of the shops were on the riverside; two frame houses and two cabins took up the other side of the road. A freight wagon pulled by four draft horses rumbled away across the bridge, carrying goods from Gunderson's to some spread on the other side of the river—like as not, Asa Hawthorn's, a quarter-mile west.

As they rode at a walk into town, past pine stumps and a few birches swaying sinuously in the wind, Cleve looked closely at the few people outside. At the farther side of town, a man in a droopy hat was slumped on a bench in front of the saloon, nodding with drunkenness. At this end, a young man, not out of his teens, was getting off his horse at a small sawmill, where waterwheels provided power to the circular saws. Close by was an open-air blacksmith's workshop. The broad-shouldered, clean-shaven smithy—in a leather apron, trousers, and boots and nothing else—was hammering a red-hot horseshoe at the anvil. He was scowling over his work, but the scowl vanished into a flashing smile as Leon waved to him. Cleve saw nothing of Marske, or men with the look of gunhands.

"You think Samuels will be here?" Leon asked, as they passed a few cabins.

They rode past a meat shop offering venison, beef, grouse, rabbit, and whatever a "river coney" might be. As they clopped up to Gunderson's Trading Post, Cleve grinned, seeing an old friend trotting up to a corral fence in the lot beside the store. "There's Ulysses, by God! There's Suzie too—and there's your Danny! Kanaway's got here ahead of us!"

Leon slapped his thigh and hooted, seeing their own horses waiting for them in the corral. "They've seen us!"

Ulysses was rearing up, Suzie was running back and forth, tossing her head, Danny was neighing and trying to climb the fence. Leon laughed. "Now, where's Kanaway got to?"

"Hold on—there's Samuels!"

A big, broad-shouldered man, middle-aged and sunburned, was stepping out of the Trading Post. He had a rust-colored, gray-speckled beard, and thick eyebrows. He was leaning on a staff; his left leg was bandaged up and splinted. He wore overalls held up by suspenders, and a floppy brown hat with a brim that near drooped over his eyes.

"Drake Samuels!" Cleve said, relieved to see him. He dismounted and shook hands with the widowed farmer.

"There now, Trewe, you've got yourself here," said Samuels.

"Been on the way here for a goodly time. Your leg giving you trouble?"

"Hawthorn give me the trouble and the crippling too! He wanted me to sell out to him. I'll tell you true—I've been thinking on it." He stopped suddenly to lean against the doorframe and take a corncob pipe from a pocket of his overalls, occasioning impatience in Cleve, who was unsettled by Samuels's willingness to consider Hawthorn's offer.

Slowly, Samuels took a little baccy bag from another pocket, frowned over the pipe as he tapped a little tobacco in. He then took his time putting the pouch away and searched in another pocket for a match.

Growling in his throat, Leon took out a lucifer, lit it with a thumbnail, and held it out.

"Allow me, Mr. Samuels."

"Why, thankee." He squinted through the pipe smoke at Leon. "Who'd you be?"

"This is Leon Studge, my business partner," Cleve said. "You were saying about Hawthorn . . ."

"Yup. He was offering more money than you." Samuels pointed the pipestem at him. "I could pay your down payment back to you, and still come out ahead. But I don't take to him or his ways! I won't be rushed and I liked the way you talked to me better. Then he sends this Marske around and the son of a goat shot me in the leg! He said he was real smart careful to miss the bone this time. Said next time he'll shoot me in the knee if I don't do the deal. Can't say he didn't scare me. I'd rather be dead than crippled."

"Maybe go to the county sheriff in Independence," Cleve said.

"County sheriff is Hawthorn's half-brother," Samuels said, clearly feeling no further explanation was needed.

"I see."

"Cleve paid you half the money for the land already," said Leon. "Now you can pay him back but once you take that payment, there's sure enough an obligation, seems to me."

Samuels squinted darkly at Leon as if he didn't like the implication.

"Let the man finish what he was saying, Leon," Cleve said softly.

"Got another think on it too," said Samuels. "Still got crops to bring in. Don't want to be hurried. I must hie myself to Independence to peddle them taters and turnips and corn and all that grain, and it's a goodly trip. And it's late in the season—bad luck is why. I didn't plant in the dark of the moon so the crops were slow to come up." He sighed. "Why didn't I plant when I should've?"

Leon scratched his head. "The dark of the moon?"

"Why sure—any roots must be planted when the moon's hiding! Now corn, you got to plant that on the *waxing* of the moon. That's just farm sense. Just like you butcher hogs when the moon's increasin', otherwise the meat'll go bad!"

Leon opened his mouth, seeming about to contest this wisdom, and Cleve quickly put in, "Did Hawthorn offer to help you with the harvesting of your crops?"

Samuels raised his bushy eyebrows. "Why, no!"

"You got a crew doing it?"

"Not no more! Hawthorn scared them off! Shot himself in the foot on that one. Made me dig in and wait for you when he done that!"

"Drake, if you'll take the rest of your payment, and sign over the deed, I'll help you finish your harvest," Cleve said. "And I think I can get you some more hands. You'll have to pay them—but you won't have to pay me. I'll get you to Independence with your goods too."

Leon looked at Cleve in surprise, but said nothing.

Samuels frowned at his pipe. "Where d'ye get these workers at?"

"I know some good Washoe men can do the work. I think they'll do it for a fair wage, and maybe a few bushels of produce. It'll be a start for them hereabouts, and a quick way for you to finish your business—if you're still planning on leaving the valley."

"I am! I'm going to take care of my sisters and their farm over in Visalia. Hazel's a spinster and Flora's a widow."

"And—we can protect you from Hawthorn's men, as we get the harvest finished."

Leon nodded and patted his holster. "Cleve and I were both lawmen. We'll keep a close eye over you."

Samuels puffed his pipe thoughtfully for a moment, staring critically at the sky over Cleve's head like any farmer worried about the weather. Then he looked sharply at Cleve and asked, "You bring the rest of the money?"

"It's in my saddlebag, right here."

Samuels stuck out his hand. "Well, if you'll help me with the crops, just how you said—"

"I give my oath on it!"

Samuels stuck out his hand. "Then you have yourself a deal, Cleve Trewe."

Marske forced himself to get up out of the cot and shuffle toward the wash bin on the cedar dresser. As he went, he cussed out the pain in his lower back. Just standing up hurt like a wolf was chewing on his lower back. But he was lucky, he knew that. The bullet had just missed his spine. It had cut in crosswise, burrowing atop a hip, passing through muscle, coming to a stop up against his spine just above the tailbone. "You were damned lucky," Purling had told him.

Old Beal Purling had been an ambulance man during the war, slinging the wounded into the wagon, driving the horses, sometimes assisting the surgeon when it was nip and tuck. Now he was a bullwhacker and the closest the Hawthorn outfit had to a medical man. Purling declined to use anesthesia, claiming, "Ether is costly, and so is laudanum, and this here operation wouldn't make a baby whimper." But it hurt so much, Beal Purling was just lucky Marske couldn't reach his gun. He struggled to hold still the whole time, knowing that Purling's was probing with rusty forceps close to his spine. In the war, he'd seen what happened if a man's spine was parted. Most of those men ended up blowing their brains out.

After pulling the rifle bullet, Purling disinfected the wound with an excruciating wash of grain alcohol.

Now Marske splashed water on his face at the basin and looked into the oval, polished-silver mirror above the basin—the man he saw there was haggard, unshaven. Time to ask Millie for some hot water, so he could shave.

Looking into the reflection of his own eyes, Marske saw a troubling uncertainty. A man should know his way in the world with firmness and certainty.

He needed something to get his mind set again. He figured that was Cleve Trewe. Marske hadn't expected him and his men waiting at the bottom of that trail off the tableland. But seeing Trewe down that hillside had startled him. He'd figured Trewe might show up out here, despite what he said in Sacramento. But Marske hadn't counted on him being ready and waiting, with a gun in each hand . . .

Cleve Trewe. The name had nagged at Marske. Somewhere, way back, he'd heard the name. The land agent had mentioned that Cleve Trewe had a gun reputation. Marske made inquiries at the *Sacramento Bee*. After he'd passed out a gold eagle, the clerk found him an old edition repeating stories about Trewe in Nevada and Colorado. It said Trewe had been a decorated major in the Union Army. Reading that brought back the memory: In 1863, after Vicksburg surrendered, John Fremont had mentioned a captain who'd distinguished himself in the battle that led to the Siege of Vicksburg. The man was awarded a battlefield commission of major—awarded by Ulysses S. Grant himself.

Major Cleveland Trewe.

Marske remembered being envious when he heard the story.

And now he had retreated before that man. Still and all, Marske had his pride.

Marske had seen five armed men down below, including two Indians he recognized from the raid on the Washoe camp. Indians armed with firearms, not bows and arrows.

So he drove his men down ahead of him, shouting, "Charge 'em boys!" And the gunmen galloped down the hill, missing their shots because they were no marksmen on horseback. He'd known Hawthorn's gunnies would die before it was over. Probably Trewe would take down two or three. But Marske calculated that those Indians, maybe that cowboy with Trewe, would go down before the charge. Improve the odds.

Nope. Not a one. It was Marske's riders who went down. All of them.

He didn't feel any regret about that. Hell, Hawthorn and Fremont had done it. More than once in the war, they'd picked out men who were basically useless, put them out front to take the first volleys; the first cannon blasts. Cannon fodder.

That didn't bother Marske. That was the most use those four yacks had ever been, most like.

What bothered him was retreating from a man like Cleve Trewe. It was a sour memory. But he was outgunned and a fusillade filled the air with leaden hail.

He'd spurred his horse back up the trail, under cover of the boulders. A bullet fired between the rocks snagged him and now he had a spearing pain in his back.

Just where you deserve to get it, he thought.

Marske opened the dresser and took out a bottle of Overholt. He poured himself a shot, and then one more, easing the pain. And steeling his determination.

Cleve Trewe was a man worthy of respect, even if he'd seemed to back down at the hotel bar. Hadn't Trewe hinted he'd forfeit Sweet River for Grass Valley?

But Marske shook his head. Trewe had simply shaken off the fight, like a man shrugging off a mosquito. And the look in Cleve Trewe's face and eyes never changed. He never dropped his gaze.

Marske calculated to mend up, and then he was going to call Cleve Trewe out. Man to man, the two of them.

It was something Cullen Marske just had to do. His father had failed at everything he'd turned his hand to. Young Cullen had sworn he wouldn't fail. He had a government payout after the war, and bought some land, started up a ranch of his own. But the land was plagued by drought. Six years, doing poorly. *Comancheros* had stolen most of his cattle and he'd had to sell out.

He'd gone from landowner to hired cowboy. Drifting north to Missouri, Marske found himself another war— a range war. War was something he was good at. Until he'd ridden away from Cleve Trewe, at Westcut Butte. He'd had to move fast, in vicious pain, to get away . . .

"You turned tail," he said, to his sickly mirror image. "But no more."

He corked the bottle and put it back in the drawer, thinking that now he had another war. Because this man he admired, this man with a reputation that smoked like a hot gun, was exactly who he needed to kill. Cleve Trewe was the enemy.

"That steel-dust stallion there is Kanaway's," Leon said, as he and Cleve led the mustang and the bay up to the corral. "Say now, where's the filly?"

"I don't know!" Be a sorrow if they lost her. Suzie would grieve—and so would Berenice. He looked around for the little horse. To the left, built so it connected the corral fences, was an open-air horse shed, with seven stalls. Four saddle horses shifted pensively in the stalls. Out of the shed stepped Dave Kanaway, leading Suzie's filly by a small rope bridle. Kanaway smiled at them and gave a small salute. Cleve saluted back, relieved to see the foal. When Kanaway removed the bridle, the little mare leapt about as if celebrating and then ran whinnying to Suzie for an afternoon nursing.

Kanaway came over and shook hands. "Good to see you gents!"

"Dave, you got the stock here in fine shape," Cleve observed. "But your horse looks to have some bite marks around his muzzle."

Kanaway chuckled. "Yep, Dusty was arguing with your Ulysses over Suzie. I've been trying to keep them separated."

"I'm going to put up this bay and take Ulysses with me anyhow."

"All that stock in the shed there—they're all yours, Major. I got a good price for them in Independence. They're all cow ponies! You can buy them at my cost for the remuda."

"That's fine, Dave!" Cleve reached into his coat pocket. His roll of bills was smaller now, after completing the deal with Samuels. "I've got your pay for bringing the horses out right here, and the money for the new stock too . . ."

Kanaway stepped back, smiling and raising his hands. "No, sir, I will not take pay for bringing the horses out." He put his hands in his pockets and looked at the filly nursing on her mam. "I do believe I'd have died on that steamboat if not for you. I still have money left from selling my outfit in Axle. But Major, if you want to hire me as your sutler and horse jangler, why, I'll earn my wages."

"Now, let me see," said Cleve. He turned to Leon. "I have a chance to hire a man to work for me who's master at his trade, is dependable and trustworthy, and he can play the fiddle too . . . do you think I should do it?"

"If you don't, I will! But I couldn't pay you as much as Cleve here, Dave."

They laughed and talked wages. And then Cleve said, "Let me get Ulysses and we'll celebrate over a glass of beer at that new saloon."

Leon nodded. "Now you're talkin' turkey. I'll just switch out this here mustang with Danny, before he gets any ideas about Suzie. I don't want him all kicked and bit like Dave's horse."

Tucking Alice into the cradleboard for a nap, Berenice was thinking the growing baby would soon no longer fit into it. Perhaps she could trade something to Marigold to have a larger cradleboard made. The baby yawned and went immediately to sleep and then Teresa rushed up to the back of the wagon.

"Berry! There's some men approaching the camp!"

"How many and from what direction?" Berenice asked. She felt a chill. The massacre, the gunfight at the tableland, now strange men riding into camp. But her mind instantly went to defensive tactics. She was calm when trouble arose, but she had also been schooled in tactics by a husband who'd served as an officer in the army.

"Four men, riding from the southwest," Teresa said, coming into the wagon. She scooped up a shotgun lying atop a crate of salt and spices and climbed out of the wagon.

"Teresa, kindly do not get jumpy with that weapon!" Berry called. "Flank them and hold it on them!"

Berry caught up her Winchester and with a final glance to see Alice was asleep, she stepped down from the wagon and walked composedly toward the riders. They were coming at the camp in a skirmish line, riding roughly abreast.

The older man in the middle, a gaunt man with a tall-crowned white hat, raised a hand and drew up, the other three reining in beside him. Yellow dust rose about them. The clean-shaven face of the man in the white hat was a glowering mask of authority. The man on his left, young and wearing a cap and a pea jacket, made Berry think of Ichabod Crane, so thin and unsure of himself he seemed; he lacked all the certainty the older man emanated. He gave Berry a tremulous smile and touched his hat respectfully. On his right was a heavyset, bearded man, wearing suspenders over a dirty white shirt, and a slouch hat. On the older man's right was a young rider, his hair a thatch of straw. He had an impish smirk on his face. He wore a jean jacket, and cowboy boots—and a six-shooter set up for cross draw.

He nodded to her, recognition in his eyes—and then she remembered him. Crofton. She and Cleve had a run-in with him in the foothills of Gunmetal Mountain. He'd almost forced Cleve to shoot him.

"Missy," said the man with the long white hat that seemed to mock his long white face, "did your man leave you here all alone?"

At that, the heavyset bearded man leaned on his saddle horn and gave Berry a candid look of appraisal that made her want to close the top button of her blouse.

"She ain't here alone!" called Teresa, stepping out from behind a wagon to point her shotgun at the men. "This is a double barrel shotgun, with two triggers, and you men are fully in range!"

The young blond man gave a brash imitation of laughing at this—but it was a nervous laugh.

The older man raised his bushy eyebrows at Teresa. "Do refrain from pulling the trigger, young lady," he said. "We're here for a talk, not a fight!"

"Would you be Asa Hawthorn?" Berry demanded.

"Good guessin', missy! May I introduce Mr. James Crofton." He hooked a thumb at the young blond man. "Over on this side, wearing that goddamned Boston cap is"—he looked at the young man and sighed—"my son, Delbert." He nodded toward the heavyset man. "The man that looks like he can't leave the pie alone is my nephew Harl. Now—who would you be?"

"I am Berenice Trewe."

"Ah. Mrs. Trewe. And those cattle"—he tilted his head at the herd, grazing about fifty yards off— "are they headed up east?"

"They are."

"Well now—" He broke off, staring, seeing Wovoka

and Smallwolf galloping up, both with six-shooters in hand.

"Hold your fire!" Berenice called to them. The cowboys reined in and she said, "Wovoka! Were any of these men at the massacre?"

And as she said it, she raised her rifle to her shoulder, pointing at Hawthorn.

Wovoka shook his head. "Not these."

"That's four guns pointed at us now, Asa," said Harl, swallowing.

"What's this about a massacre?" Hawthorn asked.

Berry noticed that Delbert looked at his father then, as if he wanted to say something. Then he licked his lips and dropped his eyes.

"More than half a band of Washoe were killed, and two Paiute traveling with them," Berry said. She lowered the rifle. "We don't know why they were killed. But a man named Marske who works for you was seen with the killers. At least—they're fairly sure it was Marske. And he tried to shoot my husband down."

"And was it your husband who shot at him and four of my men?"

Berry hesitated. Then decided she must tell the truth. "They fired on him, and his companions—they all returned fire."

"That's his story! Say, I've been in the saddle awhile. How about I step down and we can talk this over."

She shook her head slowly and firmly. "You are not visitors seeking coffee at the camp. I suspect you had a part in the massacre of the Washoe and the Paiute."

He flicked a hand contemptuously. "The incident

was no massacre! Those Indians opened fire on my men. My boys were looking for some whites held prisoner by a band of Indians. They came to ask about it and fired back to defend themselves."

"There were no white prisoners," Berenice said firmly.

"And they shot a two-year-old boy to defend themselves?" Teresa shouted.

Berry glanced over, saw Teresa's knuckles were white on the shotgun. "Teresa, please lower the gun, until it's needed. *Please.*"

Reluctantly, Teresa pointed the gun at the ground.

Delbert looked at his father. "They shot a child?"

"And a defenseless old man and two women!" Teresa said. "And men who had no chance to defend themselves!"

"I know nothing of that," Hawthorn said, shaking his head. "I heard nothing about a child. Marske is healing up from a bullet wound. I'll ask him about it. Can you produce the bodies of these women and children?"

"They are buried, of course," said Berry.

Wovoka walked his mount toward the four riders. He was staring at Hawthorn. *"You!* You sent those men!"

Hawthorn said, "I sent them to inspect my land. Nothing more. And to watch for any whites held prisoner."

"It's not your land," said Smallwolf flatly.

Hawthorn looked disdainfully at Smallwolf, then noticed that Crofton's hand had gone to the butt of his Remington. "Crofton! Hold! We are flanked and outgunned. Look there!"

He nodded toward Guama riding up, with a Sharps rifle propped on his hip. And two more Indians were coming out from behind the wagons, carrying pistols cadged from the four dead gunhands.

Crofton dropped his hand from the pistol.

Wovoka pressed his lips into a tight line, and Berry had a terrible certainty that he was going to shoot Hawthorn down if she didn't stop him. "Wovoka!" she called sharply, walking over to stand in his way. "The U.S. Marshal from San Francisco is coming. He will investigate this!"

Wovoka's eyes were wild. His nostrils flared. Then he holstered the six-shooter, turned his horse, and rode hard, his heels angrily spurring his mount into a gallop, back toward the herd.

"There's another drover coming from the herd," Teresa said, tilting her head toward Luis Diaz, riding up. "And we have more armed Washoe with us! You men need to get out of our camp!"

"We're going," Hawthorn said. His voice was mild but his eyes glittered with fury. "When does Trewe come back, missy?"

"Soon," she said. She added calmly, "If you make him mad enough, he'll kill all four of you."

Harl snorted at that. "All on his own?"

Crofton cleared his throat. "If any man could do it, he could."

Hawthorn frowned at him. "You know Cleve Trewe?"

"I ran into him a couple times. I saw him do some shooting in Pisswaller. I know his reputation. And I heard what happened on Gunmetal Mountain. So I guess I'd say if you make him mad, you better be sure you've got two or three guns trained on him first."

Hawthorn grunted. "I'll keep that in mind."

"You, Crofton!" Teresa said sharply. "Were you there, at the shooting in the Westcut?

He looked her in the eye and shook his head. "I was not, ma'am. I never met those gents—I just signed on a day ago."

"Where's your husband, Mrs. Trewe?" Hawthorn demanded.

"He went to town, on business. He'll be on his way back."

Hawthorn looked east, and began to turn his horse that way.

Berenice raised her rifle again. "Just you put that thought out of your mind, Mr. Hawthorn. You are not going east and shoot him from cover. You will ride out of here back the way you came. Cross the river at the ford to the southwest—you doubtless came that way, so you know right where it is."

Hawthorn stared at her, amazed. "You are the very soul of impertinence! But as you are a lady—I will allow it this time."

"She does not give you a choice," Smallwolf corrected him. "You're lucky she don't shoot you out of your saddle."

"Now you are riling me," said Hawthorn, glaring at Smallwolf.

"Do you feel insulted?" Berry asked. "I could do better: Men who kill women and children are cowards—"

"I killed no women and children!"

"And the men who sent them are worse than cowards! But we will not underestimate you, Mr. Hawthorn. We will keep sharp watch for you and your men. And remember that Marshal Beaman is coming."

"The U.S. Marshal will find it was just as I said," Hawthorn growled.

"I truly doubt that," said Berry, smiling.

Hawthorn's scowl deepened. "Let's ride out, boys. We're not going to shoot any ladies." He turned his horse and rode off toward the west. The others turned silently to trail after him with all the dignity they could muster.

Berry guessed he would head west along the river, take the ford to the south. Would he then ride up east, on the far side of the river—and look for a place to ambush Cleve from there?

Only then did she realize how fast her heart was beating; how cold her hands were, how dry her mouth.

Letting out a long sighing breath she lowered the rifle and looked past the herd, to the foothills of the Sierras. That way lay the town of Sweet River.

She hoped to high Heaven that Cleve would be back soon.

Chapter 9

Cleve and Leon galloped Ulysses and Danny around the big field to the north of the town, a quarter-mile square it was. They raced 'round it four times, just to give the horses a stretch and calm them down. They raced along so fast the headwind stung Cleve's eyes.

At last, the horses sweating and breathing hard, Cleve and Leon reined in at the saloon. They dismounted next to a plow horse yoked to a buckboard. They let the mounts drink from the water trough, then tied them to the rail. The man with the floppy hat over his face was snoring, a half-empty bottle beside him on the bench.

It was just a short walk from the corral and now Kanaway sauntered up. "You gave them a fair run. Kind of sudden for them. I might've worked them into it slower."

"They going to be all right?" Cleve asked, looking at Ulysses. "They're not foundered or winded?"

Kanaway contemplated the two horses and smiled.

"No, they're not favoring a foot or gasping, nor coughing neither. They're damned good horses, is why."

"You could've come up and waited for us inside, Dave," Leon said.

"Haven't been in this benzinery yet. Not sure how they take to colored men. Differs one to the next."

"Well, they'll serve you in this one," Cleve said.

Leon did a couple of quick squats, grimacing. "Might be I'm the one winded. Anyhow I think I foundered my rump."

Inside, the new saloon smelled almost as much like freshly cut pine timbers as spilled beer and spat tobacco. Out of habit, Cleve paused and glanced around for trouble. Leon and Kanaway stopped beside him, figuring he must have his reason for not going over to the bar yet. Cleve saw two bearded men in overalls at a table in a corner, playing checkers and sipping from the same bottle of unlabeled liquor. Farmers, Cleve figured.

In the opposite corner, a darksome fiddle player sat in a chair tuning his instrument. He sported a blue round-top bowler, matching blue frock coat, and a small, sharply trimmed forked beard. The fiddler smiled up at Cleve, showing buck teeth.

Near the bar stood an Indian woman in a ribbon dress, buckskin boots, and shawl; she seemed to be waiting for a cowboy who was having words with the bartender. Cleve recognized her. *Pamahas.*

"Ain't nobody going to give a damn if I bring my bride in here, whoever she's related to, dammit!" the cowboy declared.

"They just might give a damn and they might give

you hell too!" the bartender retorted. He was a stocky man with long lanky hair, and a red undershirt to go with his red-rimmed eyes. His hands were dark with grime. Cleve disliked seeing a barman with befouled fingers.

On a single shelf behind him was a row of bottles, all of them without labels. Some looked to be a purplish wine, the others contained a clear liquor likely straight from a still.

In the bartender's hands was a large jug that might contain beer. "Now," the bartender said, "you just send her outside and I'll pour your beer."

"I'll toss *you* outside first!" the cowboy declared.

"Milt Dumanis!" Cleve called. For he knew that cowboy's voice.

Milt spun to face him. "Now who the—" Then he grinned. "Cleve Trewe!"

Milt had cleaned himself up since last Cleve saw him. His dark brown hair was neatly barbered, and he wore a new Levi jacket to go with his trousers. On his hip was a Smith & Wesson six-shooter.

"You in trouble already, Milt?" Cleve asked dryly, approaching the bar. They shook hands.

"By God, Cleve, it's good to see you! I was afraid I'd come out here for that job, and you had maybe decided to go to Colorado or Alaska instead!"

"The Major is not easily hindered, when he decides to go somewheres," said Leon.

Cleve introduced Kanaway and Leon to Milt. Hands were shaken all around. Cleve was glad to see no un-friendliness toward Dave Kanaway on Milt's part.

"Dave here has accepted work as remuda hostler, horse breeder, and everything requiring equine expertise."

"*Ee*-quine?" Milt asked, blinking.

"Horses," said Kanaway.

"Oh!"

"That . . . that colored fella," called the bartender, "I can't let him in here neither! I've got appearances to keep up and such."

"Now, look here," Leon began. "Dave Kanaway here is a personal friend of mine and he can outwork, out-ride, and outshoot any man in town!"

"I prefer not to put that last one to the test," Kanaway murmured.

The bartender's whole face pouted. "We don't have affry-kins or abergoins in here—I don't want the trouble of it!"

"Abergoins!" Cleve said, laughing. "Haven't heard that in some years." The term, like aborginny, was a corruption of aborigine.

Leon put a hand on his gun. "I am full fed up with this yack!"

"Leon . . ." Cleve put a hand on Leon's gunhand. "Let me talk to this . . . gentleman."

Cleve stepped to the bar. He took off his hat to the Indian woman, the very woman Milt had been smitten with in the Bannock camp, not far from Gunmetal Mountain.

She smiled shyly at him. "Mr. Cleve."

"Pamahas, it's good to see you."

"Pammy's my *wife* now, Cleve," Milt said. There was something in his voice that warned people not to speak of her in any other way. He wasn't going to stand for "squaw."

"If she's been kind enough to marry you, Milt—you're a fortunate man."

Pamahas put a hand over her mouth to cover laughter.

Cleve turned to the bartender, who looked him up and down, and swallowed. He saw something in Cleve's face that made him nervous.

The bartender cleared his throat and said, "You got to understand, mister. This here saloon opened on second of August and I ain't making out, hardly at all. I'm going broke here."

"It's because you got bad beer and bad whiskey!" shouted one of the men playing checkers.

"You shaddup or you ain't getting no more of my 'bad' beer and whiskey!" the bartender shouted.

"You make your own supplies?" Cleve asked, nodding toward the liquor bottle.

The bartender nodded. "Takes a long time to import fancy brave-maker out here, and it's costly! Gunderson won't sell it to me! I bought some elderberry wine from Mrs. Rinaldi, howsomever. Now, these people here, whatever ye care to call them." He gestured toward Kanaway and Pamahas. "They got to wait out back."

Cleve had an impulse to cold-cock the bartender with a right hook and serve the beer himself. But he could imagine townsfolk saying, "*He got all high and mighty with that bartender and rapped him in the mouth! Laid him out and took over his saloon!*"

Wouldn't make a good first impression on the town.

"What's your name, friend?" Cleve asked.

The bartender seemed startled by Cleve's mildness. "Me? It's . . . I . . ."

"He cain't remember 'cause he's been a-drinkin' his own whiskey!" yelled the man at the checkers table. The other man laughed and so did the fiddle player.

"It's Jack Noble," said the bartender, glaring at the fiddler.

"Noble!" Leon said. "Well, ain't that ironical."

Cleve said, "Mr. Noble—you say you're losing money on this place?"

"I am! I'll tell you, people are awful damn choosy out here in this little hidey-hole on the edge of nowhere special!"

"How much you did you pay for the land, and building the saloon?"

"A hundred seventy dollars for two acres of land. I bought it from Mr. Gunderson. And I paid some hammer-hands near two hundred dollars to get 'er built."

"Couldn't spring for a lick of paint?" Leon asked.

"How about we do a deal," Cleve said. "I'll give you four hundred dollars right now for the land and the saloon."

Noble blinked. "But—this here's my home. I live in the back room. That's the onliest place I got to live. And there's the shed out back—I paid to build that too."

"That shed where you brew the chock and distill the corn?" Cleve asked.

"I don't like to say."

"Whole town can smell it!" shouted the man at the table.

"You can take your loud mouth out of here, Tweedy!" Noble snapped. Then he turned a sidelong glance at Cleve and shook his head. "What you offer ain't enough!"

"How about five hundred?" Cleve asked.

"Make it a thousand and it's a deal!"

Cleve shook his head. It just seemed too much for this ramshackle saloon and two scrubby acres.

"Wait a minute now," Leon said. "I always wanted to own a saloon."

"Seems like the last thing you should own," Cleve said.

"How about I put in with you and make it seven hundred and fifty between us!"

Noble said, "Nine hundred and eighty!"

Cleve chuckled and made a counteroffer.

Noble finally settled for eight hundred and thirty dollars, Cleve and Leon each going in four hundred and fifteen.

"I'll just clear out right now, by damn!" Noble said, putting the jug down on the bar.

"I was going to suggest the same," Leon said.

Cleve and Leon paid the money over, and Noble went into the backroom to pack up.

"What we going to call this place, Cleve?" Milt asked.

"We should call it the *Why the Hell Saloon,* because our wives will ask why the hell we bought it."

There was general laughter. "The Why the Hell it is!" Leon declared.

Cleve went behind the bar and poured beer into five wooden cups. He took a sip. It was flat, warm, and just drinkable. "One free beer on the house!" he called out.

He offered a cup to Pamahas who shook her head and pushed the cup away, but the men all drank some. Kanaway made a face as he tasted it.

Milt took a cup of beer and cleared his throat. "You still offering me that job, Cleve? It's been near a year . . ."

"Leon is foreman," Cleve said. "If he has no objection, you begin today!"

Leon drank some beer. "If Cleve vouches for you, the job is yours. I won't pretend we don't need more men."

"My wife can cook, and not just Injun fare. I'd like to bring her along with us."

Cleve nodded. "Our wives are cooking for the outfit right now, and they've had just about enough of it. We'll pay her a cook's wage—but we got to taste the food first."

Pamahas's eyes lit up and she said something in Bannock, adding, "You will see! I worked five moons cooking for lumbermen! I learn many more cooking!"

"I taught her how to cook *barbacoa!*" Milt said proudly.

Cleve turned to the other three men in the bar. "Join us, gents? It's on me today!"

They came grinning to the bar. "I'll be glad for

some wine," the fiddler said. He had a slight Eastern European accent.

Cleve found another cup, poured the wine for the fiddler, and then drank a little out of the bottle. "This is good!" He dumped his beer into a bucket and poured wine into his cup. "We're going to have a talk with Mrs. Rinaldi. I hope she's got a lot of elderberries."

The grinning farmers came up and introduced themselves. They were cousins, Harry and Shamus Tweedy.

"Cleve, who's going to run the Why the Hell?" Leon asked.

"I only know it won't be you, Leon."

"As to that, sirs . . . and ma'am . . ." said the fiddler, tipping his hat to Pamahas. "I am Mikhail Chocholak. I am quite capable and so very honest. I have tended bar before!

"And"—raising a finger to emphasize the *And*—"I can provide music, when the customers ask, for a small consideration."

"Well, that's fine, Mikkel!" Leon said.

"Mikkel? Perhaps, call me Mickal."

"Mickal it is."

Cleve looked gravely at Mickal. "If you wish to work for us, you must pledge that anyone is to be admitted, regardless of their race, so long as they are here peaceably."

"I give my oath upon it!" Mickal said, taking off his hat.

Leon looked at the clear liquor bottles. "Cleve, how about I try some of that corn liquor?"

"That's a good idea," Cleve said. "Then I can wait to see if it leaves you blinded before I try some myself."

Leon looked at him askance. "Blinded?"

Kanaway nodded gravely. "When men make their own liquor, if they don't do it right, folks get sick. Blindness sometimes."

"Never mind then. But what you going to do with it?"

Cleve shrugged. "Keep it in case I need paint thinner."

"Mind if I have a touch on your fiddle, Mickal?" Kanaway asked.

"Not at all, sir!"

He passed it to Kanaway, who tucked it under his chin and bowed up a quick lick on it. He tightened a peg and tried another tune.

Cleve poured a round of wine. "We've got to head out soon, Leon, so drink up. Long ride back to camp."

"You bring a herd up here, Cleve?" Milt asked.

"We did. Leon and I and a few other fellas. Not quite four hundred head. Middlin' long drive."

"Long drive with few drovers."

"Pish, that ain't nothing," Leon said. "I was a cow waddie and a brush hand in near the Pecos for four months. This herd of Cleve's is tame as house pets. We went after wild cattle, and we did it in the thorny brush, eating dust from dawn to sundown and sometimes after. Now, Dave, that's where you get your real cow ponies."

Kanaway nodded. "I've seen them in action. Best cow ponies are the ones who can chase down the wild cattle."

"They don't always live through it, nor the cow hands neither," Leon said grimly. "Weaving at a gallop in the brake and cactus, miracle more men aren't killed—many a cowboy crushed, their horse falling on 'em. And Indians! Meaning no offense, Pamahas, but them down there, they hated our guts, and we had to keep constant watch. Always raiding our herd. Lost a good friend to arrows, another was scalped and crippled. They never let up for long."

Cleve said, "For once, Leon's not exaggerating."

"I never exaggerate!" Leon protested.

Cleve ignored that prime falsehood and went on, "I tried that work for exactly three weeks. I got a cracked jaw, knocked off my horse when I ran into a branch chasing wild bulls full bore out there. Arrows flying, horses and men getting gored." He shook his head. "Easy work coming here, compared to such—but we ran into some trouble all right." He told Milt and Pamahas and Kanaway about the massacre, and the consequent gunfight. "If you want to work for us, Milt—the honest truth is, I'm not sure you won't have to use that sixer of yours on more than snakes."

"I'll do what needs doing," said Milt simply, reaching for his wine.

"Then you'll do," said Leon. "Say, Dave—where's that preacher of yours gone to?"

"Reverend Blevin?" Kanaway lowered the fiddle, looking puzzled. "You walked right by him! He's sitting out front, snoring away! I thought it best to let him sleep."

Cleve huffed out a long breath, shook his head, and swigged his elderberry wine as Dave Kanaway once more took up the fiddle, sawing away on, "Hard Times Come Again No More."

Wearing a rain slicker, Cleve rode due east, scouting ahead of the herd.

They'd taken three rainy autumn days, taking the herd to the basin at the foot of the Sierras. The ground was softening, hooves churning good grassland into mud. The drovers did what they could to chouse the cattle to higher, dryer ground. The weather wasn't bitter, but it brought its own miseries.

Still and all, they were nearly to the town of Sweet River. But for Cleve, this last leg of the drive was nerve-racking. Hearing about Hawthorn's visit to the camp—a visit that almost turned into a shooting affray—his feelings churned like the red soil under the herd. A deep pride in his wife, for handling things better than most men would have; fear for her, and for Alice.

Seemed that "Lightnin'" Crofton was filling in for Marske. Cleve smiled at the thought. For reasons no real grown-up man could appreciate, Crofton wanted to be a gunfighter. The next Wild Bill. He was little more than a kid who practiced draws in front of a mirror.

But a man who wants to prove himself could be a wild card. And a wild card is dangerous.

Blevin had been deeply penitent at becoming sodden drunk at the Why the Hell Saloon, and he was sober these last few days, but Cleve still found him to be a saddle burr.

Blevin had found a few of the Washoe who had some learning of the Christian doctrine from a Catholic missionary. There was Marigold, a Washoe wise woman, who was married to Wovoka the Paiute, and her fidgety twelve-year-old son, Raincatcher, who liked to call himself Cliffy though his mother insisted it was not his name. They both liked to listen to Blevin's preachments, though it was hard to tell if their interest was theological or just a desire for entertainment. Cleve thought the preaching tiresome, after a long day in the saddle, though Blevin wasn't a bad speaker.

Then on the second day of the drive up the valley, Reverend Blevin became very serious. He declared the Lord had chastised him, in his heart. He must take up his mission to Kerosene Corners. He'd taken his pay for helping bring the horses to Sweet River, had purchased a mule, and trotted off toward the mining camp in search of his friend Moss. Cleve was glad to be shed of him.

Despite the weather, the men were cheerful, singing drover songs around the evening campfire, and trading windies. Milt made a show of pretending to believe Leon's *If'n you think this weather is bad* stories. "So you pried icicles out of your nose and mouth so's to breathe, Leon? Well, I'll be damned." When the rain abated of an evening, Dave Kanaway brought out his own fiddle and played a tune. The Washoe came from their own fire to listen, some doing a shuffling dance to a Kentucky ballad they'd never heard before.

Cleve remembered one night, lying in the Conestoga, Berry dozing beside him, when he heard Leon begin a story "about Cleve Trewe in Axle Bust." Cleve frowned, hearing that—he did not want Leon spreading more exaggerations. He considered getting up and telling the men they needed to turn in. But he listened for a while, and as the story was a true one, and he didn't want to disturb the baby lying close beside him, Cleve decided to stay where he was . . .

"Now toward the end of his time in Axle Bust," Leon said, "Cleve was saddled with a reputation, what with the gunfight with Buckskin Jacques, and the shootout with the Bosewell gang. Cleve was the law then, and hearing a gunshot he went on into the Tom Cat Saloon to see what the ruckus was. I was at the bar that night and I saw it all. A young drifter playing poker there was called Kid Claiborne. He was a gambler, maybe a horse rustler, from Texas, come up to prospect, and he was trying to gamble with a nugget of gold. He'd run through his cash but he declared the nugget worth two hundred dollars. 'No,' said Brixton, for he was the dealer. 'That looks most like quartz. Might have ten dollars of gold in it.' Claiborne stood up and cursed him and fired a shot down through the table, right through the cards, and said the next one is for you.

"Now, Cleve come in and he seen the smoking gun, and he pointed his Colt and told Claiborne, 'Hand that gun to the bartender, and I'll stand you a drink. But you're done shooting tonight.'

"Now I spoke up and said, 'This is Cleve Trewe, and you don't want to fight him, Claiborne.' The Kid saw that Cleve had the drop on him so he holstered his gun. 'There,' he said, 'That's holstered, but I ain't going to turn it over. I heard about you and I don't care who you are. You put that Colt in its holster and we'll finish this in the street.'

"Cleve surprised me then, boys—he said, 'That'll be fine, but I just need you to write something out for me first. If you can't write, we'll have it writ.'

"'What's that?' asked Claiborne.

"'Just the address where your folks live, so I can send a letter there, saying how you died and where you were buried. And I can send your things and any money you have. I'll sell your horse and saddle, send them the money for that. But I need you to write it out. It's a sad thing, not having a way to tell folks how their boy was killed.'

"Claiborne says, 'You think you're funny!'

"Well, I knew what Cleve was up to and I said, 'He ain't joking, boy! You see anyone laughing in here? You will die tonight and he'll want to know where to send your things. It's the right thing to do. It's sad when we got to bury someone and can't tell their family.'

"Right then, Cleve holstered his sixer and he goes to the bar to get the paper and pencil and he asks, 'What's your name, son?'

"'Why, it's William Claiborne, said the Kid'—he's getting kind of pale.

"Cleve writes it down and says, 'I'll write down where your folks live. Where'd that be?'

"Cleve seemed so serious, the boy told him where his folks lived in Texas. Then Cleve asked him, 'Are you a Catholic? That's for the choice of cemetery.'

"The boy was kind of swallowing hard, then he says 'Yes. I'm Catholic.'

"Cleve nods and writes it down and says, 'We'll send the body to Virginia City then.' Then Cleve asks, kind of quiet, 'Any message to your family?'

"Now, all this time the boy's studying on this paperwork and what's been said and he's pretty cooled off. Then he says: 'This here is too much paperwork. I never heard the like. I believe I'll take my nugget and go.' And then he did, and rode out of town fast as he could!"

"Was that a true story, Cleve?" Berry asked sleepily.

"Yes. You were in Virginia City at the time."

"You really are a softhearted man inside. Give me a kiss . . ."

Cleve smiled at the memory.

Now, the rain eased to a faint drizzle. He saw no danger ahead, nothing but seething gray clouds and the silvering of the grass as the wind swept over it. A formation of geese made its honking way south over the foothills rising some miles ahead. "Ulysses, let us go back to the herd, you need to get a little more used to working around cattle. I know you didn't sign up to be a cow pony . . ."

Cleve turned back and rode two miles back west. The wet grass was four feet high, hissing as they passed through it. His pant legs were soaked. He figured on riding to the wagons, checking on the women and the Washoe bringing up the rear; some of the Indians on horseback, trotting along, some marching.

He soon spotted Milt Dumanis galloping on a remuda pony, chasing a young steer in search of greener pastures to the south. Cleve knew Milt would bring the steer back quick as he could, and ride onto the next thing to be done to keep the herd moving.

Every day and night, Milt Dumanis showed Cleve he was an experienced, hardworking drover. Leon liked and trusted him. Cleve hadn't told anyone but Berry that he'd come close to killing Milt when he first ran into him. He'd taken the wayward cowboy into custody for attempted horse theft. But Milt had been desperate, and Cleve saw in him a good man tangled up with bad company.

Leon rode up to meet Cleve at the south side of the herd. "They don't like that muddy hill," Leon said, raising his voice to be heard over the bawling and stomping of the cattle.

The valley sloped up some here, eventually rising to the lip around the basin sheltering the Samuels farm. The cattle had to labor hard to make the hill here. Small-wolf threw a small-loop over a bull that was about to trample a calf in his confusion. Other cattle tried to split off from the bunch.

Cleve grunted. "We should've waited till the ground dried, Leon."

But then he noticed Smallwolf cantering up. Darting his pinto into the herd, the Paiute rode up to the biggest bull, the "boss cow" the others were prone to following. The bull was torquing off to the right, panicking as its hooves slipped in the slick mud. Smallwolf bent down and spoke to the bull, and tugged at its left ear . . .

The bull dug in its front hooves and turned back to the herd, made a rush up the hill, slipping once or twice, and was quickly gone over the crest. The other cattle followed.

"Never seen a man turn a bull like that," Leon said.

"I knew some Paiute to have close ways with animals," Cleve said, thinking back to the season he'd spent with the tribe out on the plains. "Like they're talking to its spirit."

"We almost in sight of the ranch?"

Cleve watched the herd flowing over the lip of the basin. "Just about four miles . . ."

It was trembling on the edge of dark out when the Conestoga arrived at the western edge of the Samuels acreage. Berenice sat beside Cleve, Alice sleeping in her arms. Leon and Teresa, in the chuckwagon, were not far behind them.

Cleve pulled up at the western gate of the acreage, jumped down, and opened the leather-hinged gate in the half-fallen wooden fence. He returned to the wagon, drove through the gateway, stopped when there was enough room for the chuckwagon, and climbed down again. Leon drove through the gate, saying, "You're pretty spry, boy, I may have to keep you on here."

Cleve declined to laugh. He closed the gate, jogged up to the Conestoga, climbed up beside Berenice, and on they went.

The wagon bumped along the rutted, mud-puddled road for several miles, sometimes slowing as the mules struggled to pull it through muddy spots. Cleve urged the mule team between fields of corn and root crops.

"We seem to be coming upon a rather steep hill," Berenice said.

"We won't have to climb it. At the foot of that hill is our new residence."

There were hills backing Samuels's farm—which was about to become the Trewe Ranch. And within the side of the modest hill just ahead, was a soddy dugout.

Cleve could see the lantern hanging outside it, illuminating the front of the wood-framed hole in the hillside. He called "Whoa!" just twenty paces from the soddy's door.

Alice cooed as she looked at the sunset-lit prospect of their new home. Berenice stared at it.

"Is that . . . some sort of earthen barn?" Berenice asked.

"No, my Berenice," Cleve said, wincing. "That's where we're going to live—just for a time. It's a soddy."

Berenice was staring open-mouthed at the dugout.

"You've seen them before, surely," Cleve said.

"I have seen them used for cattle and goats!"

"This kind is for people. It's got a stove and a bed. It is a house built into a hillside."

"A house? Would you characterize it that way? Does it have a dirt floor?"

"I haven't been inside this one." But the floor might be packed dirt. "With a little straw on the floor, it will be, ah . . . habitable. For a time."

Cleve reflected that he had, in a sense, plucked Berenice out of a fine house, with chandeliers and parlors and staircases and servants, back in Axle Bust. And now he was proposing to install her in a dugout soddy. She'd camped rough, after leaving Axle Bust. For the first leg of their journey, they'd slept under the stars, or in a wagon—and sometimes under it. And Berry had never complained.

But this was to be her own *home*.

"Does it have *windows?*" she asked.

"I . . . well . . . I think I see one. If that's what it is."

There was a silence that was chillier than the misty evening air. The chuckwagon, driven by Leon now, drew up beside them.

"It's a . . . a fine *site* for a house!" Teresa said, encouragingly, as she climbed down to the turf. "Maybe on top of the hill. Come the summer . . ."

Drake Samuels came out of the soddy, smiling broadly, one hand holding onto a suspender, the other his cane. "By gum, you have come at last! We can make plans for the harvest and the trip to Independence!" It seemed Samuels wanted to be clear he expected that part of the bargain to be fulfilled.

"That's just what we'll do, Drake!" Cleve said, jumping down.

"I expect the lady will want to get a gander at her new home!"

"Certainly, the lady would," Berry muttered, climbing down. "It is best to see calamity coming, so one can be prepared . . ."

Chapter 10

Berenice hitched up her skirts a few inches to keep them clear of the floor. The floor did involve some wood—that is, there were planks, with sawdust dumped over them to absorb the moisture. But the sawdust was quite overwhelmed by rising water and, in some places, brown water seeped up between the planks to form puddles, which gushed and spread when Samuels walked over them.

"Been meaning to get a good floor put in," Samuels said, seeing the look on Berry's face as she took in the smoky little room. "But I kept thinking I was going to build a frame house. Didn't quite get there."

The single room was about thirty feet by twenty-five. A rusty Franklin stove stood in one corner, glowing with a dying fire. Its iron chimney passed up through the roof, in a place where the ceiling logs had been cut away. The door had a timber frame, and timbers in the corners of the dug-out rectangle were held up by raw timbers. Chinked logs, just a foot over Cleve's head, constituted the ceiling. Atop the logs were sod blocks, thickly grown with grass. In two places, a little water dripped down between the logs. Wooden buckets were set up to catch it.

The walls were dirt, scrappily covered by burlap, filthy cotton fabric, and crumbling newspapers. Several chests and wooden boxes were against the dirt walls, close by a wooden barrel. A ceramic chamber pot stood by the cot. Almost crowded against the cot was a small wooden table and a single chair.

Looking at the sagging, discolored cot, Cleve's only thought was, *That must be replaced, and with all speed.*

There was sort of small window near the door, a foot-square horizontal cut in the dirt to the outdoors. The canvas flap on this side was pinned up and a little light and breeze came through. The stove smoked, the pine smell mitigating the rankness of unwashed male and dirty clothes.

"It's . . . cozy," said Teresa, looking through the door.

"A soddy stays warm in the winter and cool in the summer," Cleve pointed out.

Berenice said nothing.

"Now, up here by the river, and up in these hills," Samuels said, taking out his pipe, "why, it can be a might parky. Howsomever . . ." He didn't finish the statement, as he was frowning carefully over the pipe, fiercely concerned not to drop any of the precious tobacco on the ground.

Berenice watched him work at it. She waited.

At last, he puffed the tobacco alight, and went on, "Up here, we're not so much north but we ain't so much south either. And close to the river and the hills, like I said, well, it can get frosty in the winter. We get a little snow, now and then, but it don't stay long. There's a wind comes out of the pass up east, and it'll shiver your bones! So's you need this here"—he patted the wall. A bit of dirt came trickling down to the floor at this—"this good thick soil here, to keep you warm."

"It is not yet terribly cold out," Berenice said. She glanced at the door as if she wanted to make a break for it. "The wagon will suffice us for a time."

"Anyway," said Cleve, "Drake will be here for a few days more. Then me and Leon will help him take his harvest to Independence. And . . . some chests and such . . ."

"I'd best go and see how our Indian friends are faring," Berenice said suddenly. "We'll need a camp-fire."

Skirts rustling, she hurried out the open door.

In the morning, Berenice found enchantment on the banks of the Sweet River.

It was a mild day, cool but partly sunny. Clouds skated east to west, but few enough that the sun flashed through.

Marigold was watching the baby at the wagon, and Berry and Teresa were riding the property line with Smallwolf. Berry and Teresa were wearing split-skirts for riding, jackets, and boots; Berry wore a straw boater, tied under her chin with a ribbon; Teresa wore a bonnet.

Cleve had insisted Smallwolf come along to keep watch over the ladies.

They'd passed the croplands, where Cleve and Leon and the Washoe and Paiute were harvesting the remainder of Samuels's crops; they'd seen the woods on the northern edge of the property and the posts of rock Samuels had set up, marking the eastern border. They'd looked into his barn—just a wider dugout with a couple of mules and a cow in it—and they'd seen a wooden shack, covered with tarpaper, for his plow and harrow and tools.

Now they reined in beside the river. Sweet River sang and tumbled so close Berry could smell the green life of it. Crystalline-clear near the bank, it was silky green in the deeper pools. Dragonflies darted and a white crane waded, bending its neck to aim its long sharp beak at some unseen prey on the riverbed.

Smallwolf and Teresa sat their horses with Berenice, gazing at the river and the land beyond it. And Berry was enchanted.

"I have come to *live* here," she said, mostly to herself. "It's a wonder, isn't it?" She leaned over and spoke into Suzie's ear, hugging her neck. "Is it not a marvel, Suzie? Cleve and I and Alice and you and Hippolyta; Ulysses and Teresa and Leon—all of us here?"

"I see we're down the list from the horses," Teresa said.

Smallwolf let a smile flicker at that. "Who is Hippolyta?" he asked.

"Why, our filly!" Berenice said. "Though Cleve calls her Polly."

Berry sat up straight in the saddle, sweeping an arm

to encompass everything around them. "I do feel like this is the home I didn't know I was waiting for. I understand Cleve better now. Why he was set on coming here. And why this is a place to be defended."

"The water's so clean you can see every scale on that fish," Teresa said, pointing at a long, thick fish swimming upriver. "A powerful big fish too."

"That's a white sturgeon," Berenice said. The long, powerful-looking sturgeon seemed to be slowly working its way upstream. The sun coming through the water made its thick scales look like polished steel. "I regret I don't have my sketchbook. Such fish have a primeval look."

"Maybe I can get him," said Smallwolf. "Slap him to shore."

"Oh, there are so many trout to be had—and this sturgeon is so magnificent—I hope you'll let him be today, Smallwolf. Perhaps, someday, if we're short on rations . . ."

"'Short on rations,'" Teresa said, with a smirk. "So speaks the wife of a military man! I recall downriver, when you went out to face off with Hawthorn, you said to 'flank em!'"

"And you did flank 'em!"

"Berry—" Teresa lowered her voice. "Was you scared, then? Maybe I didn't sound it, but I sure was."

"I was terrified—but I didn't know it till after."

Smallwolf surprised Berry by saying, "That I know. The fear that comes after."

Across the river was some of Cleve's land too—a strip

bordering the southern riverside, a mile long and five hundred yards wide. It was tree-studded there, and rocky, with granite outcroppings to the west seeming connected to the rugged gray ridge slanting down from the foothills.

"Too many big rocks for farming, on that side," Smallwolf said. "That stone is the knuckles of the mountain. All one, under the ground."

"But there's forage there," Berry said. "All the fine grass growing between. There's lumber in those pines. If there was to be a bridge, cattle could be moved across when we need more room."

Teresa shook her head ruefully. "Berry, it's strange to be part of a cattle range. Leon, a partner in it. I never thought I'd see the day."

"You're just as much a partner, Teresa. Not only Leon."

"Berry—are you going to sleep in that dugout when Samuels is gone?" Teresa asked.

"Perhaps. Cleve asked Milt and Pamahas to go into town, buy us a new cot. Kanaway says Gunderson sells them. Give them a chance to shop for coffee and rations too—ah, vittles, I mean. But before I move into the soddy, I shall wait till the weather turns bad. *Very* bad. Majestically bad! Then—I suppose we shall creep into the burrow, like three badgers. Cleve and I once slept in the dust under a sandstone overhang, deep in the Badlands, northwest of Axle. That seemed cleaner than the soddy."

"If it's bitter cold out, Alice will benefit from that dirty little hole in the ground."

Smallwolf pointed across the river. "Riders coming."

Berry saw two familiar figures riding up to the farther bank, and she named them. "James Crofton and Harl Hawthorn." Harl's rifle was in his right hand, propped on his hip. They drew up under a gnarled pine tree. Harl shouted something at them. It was lost in the hiss and tumble of the river.

"Did he say move on?" Teresa asked.

Smallwolf nodded. "They're trying to scare us, again. They have a clear shot from there."

Teresa took a deep breath, cupped her mouth, and shouted, *"Go to hell!"*

Smallwolf smiled.

"Draw back with me, you two, if you please," said Berry.

She backed Suzie up; the others backed their horses beside hers, some forty feet, to an outcropping of granite. "Far enough, I hope. Smallwolf, will you be so good as to hold my horse?"

She passed him the reins, then unscabbarded her saddle rifle, and slipped off the horse.

"Berry!" Teresa hissed. "What in Heaven's name are you up to?"

Berry kept the rifle tucked against her side and trained on the ground as she walked to the outcropping, which was a little over five feet high. She pointed at the outstretched branch of the pine tree over the Hawthorn riders. They looked at one another in puzzlement.

Berry laid the rifle over the rock, steadied it on the sun-warmed stone, and took careful aim. She'd been a good shot since her first lessons at the age of fourteen, but Cleve had continued her instruction.

Harl was shouting something unintelligible at her.

Berry picked her targets and fired.

A pine cone exploded over the Hawthorn riders. Their horses shied, and the men struggled to control them, as Berry chambered another round and picked out a second target. She fired. The next pine cone up the branch exploded.

Then she chambered a third round and fired at the branch itself, where it was narrowest. It split, not quite parting but slapping down at Harl.

He yelled something she couldn't make out, as he drew his horse back, but she could tell he was cursing. Smallwolf was laughing aloud now.

Harl steadied his horse and raised his rifle, Crofton reaching over to grab his wrist, shaking his head at him.

Harl shook off Crofton's hand but lowered the gun.

Crofton pointed at the pine branch and took off his hat in a salute. Then he said something inaudible to Harl and the two men rode off to the west, along the river.

"I guess they got the message," Teresa said, as she and Smallwolf rode up to Berry. "But if I was you, I wouldn't tell Cleve what you did."

Berenice gave a quick nod. "Most sensible. Let us return to camp. I'm pining for Alice."

"Cleve . . ." Leon began. "Is this . . . I mean, how much more . . ."

"You're going to complain, aren't you, Leon?" Cleve

said matter-of-factly as they made their way across the field to the wagons.

Clouds were gathering on the cusp of evening. Cleve and Leon were carrying sacks of potatoes, one large sack on each shoulder. It had been a long day of completing Samuels's harvesting, and they both had aching arms and shoulders. "I was hired to be a *foreman*," said Leon. "Not a dirt farmer."

"This property is going to be as much farm as ranch," Cleve said. "This land is pleading to be farmed. Anyway, the Washoe did most of the work today. And Dave got a lot done with the draft horses."

"I did a smart lick of this donkey work today m'self, by God."

They tramped to the back of the freight wagon, loaded in their burdens, Leon groaning with relief. "Lord, my back . . ."

There were three wagons for the trip to Independence. They were lined up on the dirt road at the western edge of Cleve's new property.

Cleve glanced up to Drake Samuels, who was at the front of the line, where four riders were approaching. At least one of them, even from here, had the look of a gunfighter.

Cleve tensed, seeing three of the men get off their horses and walk toward Samuels. "Look at that, Leon."

"What in blazes is this now!" Leon said, slapping his hip for a gun that wasn't there. "I don't have a gun on me, Cleve!"

"Hellfire," Cleve muttered. He was in the same fix. His Colt was in the Conestoga.

He strode up to the front of the wagon, reached up to the seat, grabbed his Winchester rifle, and walked fast as he could without running, up toward the head of the line.

"Cleve!" Leon called. "Dammit!"

Leon ran to catch up, clutching a horsewhip.

"Dive under a wagon if they start shooting," Cleve said.

"You think I'd do that, do you?"

"You haven't a gun."

"Now look here, Major—"

"Suit yourself, Leon," Cleve interrupted. "Berenice, what are you doing!" he blurted, seeing her riding up to the four men.

He rushed up the line of wagons, breathing hard, seeing Berry dismounting from Suzie, her Winchester in hand. Where was Alice? Maybe Teresa had her. Still and all . . .

Asa Hawthorn, James Crofton, and Harl Hawthorn were standing side by side in the field by the dirt road, even Old Man Hawthorn with a gun on his hip. Cleve knew them from Berry's description. The fourth one, who looked some out of place, sat on his horse. He was a thin young man in spectacles, wearing a wrinkled suit and a cap. Berenice had mentioned a Delbert.

Luis Diaz rode up then, one hand drawing a six-gun. Seeing that gun come out of its holster, Drake Samuels scurried behind a wagon with a quickness that defied his limp.

Cleve strode up to Berenice, in time to hear her say, "You are once more outnumbered, Mr. Hawthorn."

The gaunt older man answered, "And we're not here for a fight, Mrs. Trewe." He glanced at Diaz and back at Berry. "I understand you did a shooting exhibition, put my nephew here to flight."

"I wasn't flighting nowhere," Harl growled.

Cleve lowered his rifle. "A shooting exhibition?"

"She just showed how she could bust some pine cones from a branch and the branch, too, from a fair piece off," Crofton said, chuckling. "She convinced me! But we weren't looking for a fight either."

"What do you want here?" Luis Diaz demanded, cocking his pistol.

Cleve figured Diaz could start a gunfight where none was needed. "Luis!" Cleve said sharply. "Holster that iron!"

Diaz glared at Cleve, looking like he would refuse. Then he snorted, eased the gun off cock, and holstered it.

"You would be Cleve Trewe," said Asa Hawthorn, looking him up and down.

Cleve nodded. "I am," said Cleve. "This is Mr. Leon Studge. In my absence, Hawthorn, you threatened my wife, Leon's wife, my men, and my herd. And in Sacramento, you sent your man to threaten me. Here I am in the flesh. Now have your say and ride out."

"You make it out worse than it was," said Hawthorn. "I was just . . . testing the water. A man needs to know where the borderline is. Don't you find that's so?"

"You stepped over it twice," Cleve said, thinking of this man threatening Berenice. "I should kill you now." The last five words came out of him as if someone else had said them. Someone deep inside him.

Crofton put his hand on his gun. "You can't get us all, Cleve Trewe," he said.

Cleve looked at him—and snorted. "Lightnin' Crofton. Your folks know you're away from home?"

Crofton tensed. His eyes narrowed. And then he relaxed, laughing shortly and softly, and Cleve saw him let it go.

Berry spoke up. "If you're not here for a fight, Hawthorn, why are you here?" There was just the faintest tremble in her voice.

"To make an offer to your husband, ma'am."

"The answer is no," Cleve said.

"You haven't heard me yet. I'll give you twice what you paid. I'll give you some land on the other side of the valley, away from the river. There's a spring there. But you can't have this piece of land."

"Grenville Payton decide that, or you?" Cleve asked.

Hawthorn frowned and shook his head. "Who give you that idea?"

"It's as clear as Mount Whitney over there," said Cleve. "Nothing new about that game. They want to control the river, sell access to the water, keep most of it for their own cattle combine. When I was in New York, I saw a man with a monkey on a leash. He made it dance so people would throw him silver. I figure that's you—you're a dancing monkey for the Paytons."

Hawthorn caught his breath. His eyes flared with rising fury.

"You think to push the man into a fight with insults?"

Crofton said quickly. "Mr. Hawthorn is smarter than that." He gave Cleve a significant look—and it occurred to Cleve that Jim Crofton was maybe more interested in stopping a fight than starting one.

"Three times what you paid, and that's the last offer," Hawthorn growled.

"You're behind the killings of the Washoe and Paiute, out at Westcut Canyon."

"Now hold on—"

"You hear me clear, Hawthorn!" Cleve interrupted. "You could offer me the Bank of San Francisco and everything in it and I'd tell you to go to hell." Feeling his anger rise, Cleve pointed the Winchester at Hawthorn, aiming it from the hip. *Now get off my land!"*

"It's not your land," Hawthorn said. "But we're leaving for now. It's a long trip to Independence with those wagons, Mr. Trewe."

Then Asa Hawthorn turned and went back to his horse.

Crofton and Harl glanced at each other, shrugged, and went to their mounts too. They mounted, and the four men turned away, and rode toward the west.

Except . . .

In under a minute, the young man in the cap and spectacles turned back toward the wagons. He rode with one hand up, palm outward in a sign of peace, right to Berenice. Then he gulped, and took a deep breath, and said, "Ma'am . . . Mrs. Trewe . . . I am Delbert Hawthorn. Are you indeed the Berenice Trewe who wrote the monograph 'On the Modernization of Hydraulics in Hard-Rock Mining?'"

Berenice's mouth dropped open in surprise. "I am! Where did you see it?"

"In the *American Geology Review,* the August issue of that journal."

"So they did publish it! I have not seen a copy!"

"Oh, it will catch up with you, I'm sure, ma'am. I just wanted to say—it is my dream to work in geological hydrology. I admired your workings on it, Mrs. Trewe, it was like a great dawning for me, I assure you! If only we could talk of it sometime. I have some diagrams I'd like to show you. I know this is awkward, my father is troublesome but . . ."

Cleve laughed bitterly. "Awkward! I nearly had to shoot your father, boy!"

"I do understand, sir," said Del, undisturbed at the remark in a way that made Cleve wonder if he wouldn't have minded so much if his father had been shot.

"Cleve," Berenice said, turning to him. "This man is clearly a scientist, and he deserves your respect."

"You have anything to do with the massacre at Westcut?" Cleve asked him.

"No, sir," Delbert said. "I was not there."

Cleve scratched his head. "I . . . very well then."

This was a strange position to be in. Leon was chuckling at it.

Berry turned back to Del. "I would be pleased to discuss hydrology with you, at a suitable time. And *my husband* will surely recall that he nearly died in a hydrological mining disaster!"

Leon chuckled. "She's got you there, Cleve!"

Del slapped the saddle horn in delight. "Your discussion of that disaster and your solution to it—why it moved me, ma'am! Simplicity, precision, timing—a great moment for the science of mining!"

"You are very kind, Mr. Hawthorn," she said. Cleve could tell she was inordinately pleased. It welled up in her voice.

A gunshot sounded and they looked to see the other three, reined in a distance away and looking back at them, Hawthorn with his gun pointed at the sky.

"I believe your pa is calling you, Delbert," Leon said.

Del Hawthorn looked back at his father who was gesturing angrily.

Del sighed and raised his hand to Berenice. He gazed at her reverentially, and said, "It has been the great honor of my life to meet you, ma'am."

Then he turned and rode hard to rejoin his father.

Leon said, "Major, it looks like you've got to work right smart to keep that young fellow from stealing your wife away."

Berenice laughed. Then she poked Leon in the chest with her forefinger. "You can just . . . just *shut your bazoo,* Mr. Studge."

Cleve grinned. But he was still hearing Asa Hawthorn's parting words in his mind.

"It's a long trip to Independence with those wagons, Mister Trewe . . ."

Chapter 11

Leon was driving the lead wagon, Cleve was riding alongside, at the head of the caravan of three big wagons trotting their slow way to Independence. Samuels was driving the second wagon, Smallwolf the third, his cayuse tied behind, alongside Leon's Danny. The temperature had dropped some overnight, and it was a crisp morning, their hands cold on the reins. Cleve was keeping close watch on the distant hills and ridges, on mottes and underbrush along the way, any place a man could conceal himself.

Leon noticed. "Watching for Hawthorn's men?" he asked.

"I am," Cleve said.

"Asa Hawthorn seems better at threatening than doing."

"He had half a band of Washoe murdered," Cleve reminded him. "And the Paiutes with them."

Leon grunted, his face glum. "They're still mourning at the Washoe camp. Them and Wovoka and Marigold."

Cleve nodded. His mind was troubled by those he'd

left to fend for themselves, while he made this jaunt to Independence. Hawthorn might choose to strike at the Trewe Ranch, or he might have a run at the Indians while Cleve was away.

Yet to Independence he must go, to get the deed settled, and fulfill his vow to Drake Samuels. Milt and Wovoka and Luis, well-armed, were watching over the herd and the wagons. Guama and two braves, Broken-wing and Datsa, were now "captains," as the Washoe liked to say, of the Indian camp. They kept their weapons close. One of the Washoe children had come down sick, but apart from that, the band seemed to be stolidly settled.

Cleve had sent Milt with three hand-written notices to post in Sweet River, one of them at the Why the Hell Saloon, to let townsfolk know these Indians were per-mitted on his land, and under his protection. Suppose one of the braves ran afoul of a settler? The Indians were uneasy and mistrustful after the massacre. They spoke little English. A misunderstanding could lead to a skirmish—even a battle.

Still, Berenice had become friends with Marigold and was learning from her to weave baskets. She was studying the Washoe and Paiute languages; their medi-cine and mythology. Berry was a persuasive woman. She would surely intervene if there was trouble between the Indians and the settlers.

But was that supposed to comfort him? Berry could get herself shot if some local Indian hater took offense. There was Alice to think of too. Teresa Studge was a force of nature her own self, and a second mother to Alice, and he had no doubt that the cowboys, who doted on Alice, would give their lives to defend her. Still, there was no telling what Hawthorn would try next. Would he try to burn them out?

Cleve growled to himself. He had to get to Independence, file that deed, and get back, quick as ever he could. But he had to meet with Marshal Beaman in Independence, too, if he was still at the Whitney Hotel. And he had to get cash to pay the men, which meant sending a telegram to his bank, having them wire the money to Independence. That could take time . . .

He shook his head. Just have to have faith in Milt and the others.

For there was no quick way to escort a string of brimming harvest wagons, drawn by oxen and draft horses. It would take two days. The stock couldn't pull the wagons all night, so Cleve would have to call for a camp, partway there. That would take them close to the woods along the base of the hills to the north.

And that darkly shadowed strip of forest would be a good place for an enemy to hide, until ready to attack . . .

"Oh, dear," Teresa said. "I do believe your fingers are bleeding, Berenice."

Berenice drew her hands back from the half-finished basket. "Has it come to that? So it has."

Berry and Marigold were sitting on logs beside the small fire, basket-makings in their hands. Berry wore blue jeans and her riding coat and a woolen scarf over her head against the occasional showers. Teresa sat cross-legged on the ground nearby, Alice in her lap. She wore a long brown cotton dress and matching bonnet. Alice, in a little dress and coat Teresa had made for her, was gazing fixedly at Marigold's basket, seeming to absorb every movement of those expert fingers. Marigold's weave included interwoven black bark formed into the outlines of fir trees.

"You soak your fingers in vinegar, and let them dry wet," said Marigold, looking up from her own basket. "Rub your fingers on soapstones, later, to make them hard."

"I thought they were rather calloused already," Berry said, looking at her frayed fingertips. "Yet I'm getting blood on the straw. I am agog at the toughness of your hands!"

"Agog?" Marigold grinned. She was missing two teeth, one above and one below, but that did not make her dark, amiable face less pleasing. "Yes, you clean off this blood, Lady Berry, then you try the vinegar and soapstone, and rest your fingers."

Marigold had taken to calling her Lady Berry. A term of affection, Berenice decided.

Berry fetched a rag from the laundry pile, wet it, and cleaned the blood drops from her basket as well as she could, as she asked, "How are the children, Marigold? The ones who ail."

Marigold shook her head, her fingers continuing weaving as she said, "The younger one, So-an-ah, maybe the next world wants her. She is . . ." Marigold touched her neck. "So big here."

"Swollen?"

"Yes. The fever is very bad. On her arms, sores. She sleeps now."

"Sounds like diphtheria," said Teresa. "They did have the good sense to isolate the children. Each one to their own lean-to. Raincatcher was sick."

"Cliffy?" Raincatcher, also called Cliffy. "He is recovered?"

"Yes."

Berry stopped what she was doing and looked at Alice. "Did you go near the ailing children, Teresa?"

"I did not. I have too much contact with Alice."

Berenice relaxed a little. Yet Alice might still catch the disease. Four days ago, she and Alice had visited the wickiup of the woman with the sick baby—the child had not been noticeably sick at the time.

Berry knelt in the grass and she stroked the baby's plump, soft cheek, and felt no fever. "Doctor Fourgeaud believed diphtheria is carried through the air through small droplets, projections of sneezing and coughing. If you go near the children, you must wear a scarf over your mouth and gloves, and both must be boiled afterward."

"You would boil the children?" Marigold said, gaping in horror.

"No, no, my dear, I meant the scarf and gloves."

Marigold laughed. "Even that—why?"

Berry did her best to explain germ theory to Marigold,

who cocked her head in skepticism. "Much-very-little animals on the body?"

"Of a sort. You have seen telescopes?" She mimed using a field glass.

"I have seen."

"They use glass lenses to make things seem nearer. To see these . . . these tiny animals . . . one needs another kind of glass lens, that makes small things visible . . . seeable . . ."

Teresa kissed the top of Alice's head. "Diphtheria affects the lungs. My granny made a tonic against breathing ailments."

"Oh, I've little patience with 'granny cures,'" Berry declared. "Folk medicine speaks of balancing the humors, as if it were two hundred years ago."

"But we both use some old-time remedies, willow bark and mint and such. And the Indians have a tea for nigh anything."

"The natives—the wilderness is their apothecary. Their *materia medica* is the speech of their grandparents, and their memory. Their laboratory is history. Experience yields treasures. Some of these traditions, however . . ." She shrugs. "If Marigold will forgive me, I feel that the burning of sage and pine needles to drive away the spirits of sickness is not efficacious and certainly not conducive to the vitality of one's respiratory functions . . ."

"What language is she speaking?" Marigold asked, looking at Teresa.

"It's her grand ol' version of English, hon," Teresa said. "Berenice, you'll anger our Washoe friends with this kind of talk about their smudging and such. Those doings are part of their lives."

"I suppose you're right. Ritual can be a comfort. After all, attitude seems to affect healing. René Descartes tried to cut the cord between mind and body, and I suspect he went too far. And I go too far too . . . I am a bit distracted, with this talk of diphtheria. Does . . . does Alice look a little pale to you?"

Alice chose to cough at that moment. It was only a small cough, but Berenice felt an icy hand clutch her heart.

The sun was smothered in the clouds at the western horizon. With the light gone gray, and the trees losing their leaves, everything seemed elderly and tired. The stock was tethered near the camp; some grazing, some already sleeping.

"There are wolves, 'round this way," said Smallwolf, looking up from stoking the campfire. "We better post a watch, boss."

That's the least of it, Cleve thought. "We'll do it. You stand first watch. Wake me before midnight, I'll watch till dawn."

"You wake me, Cleve," said Leon, spreading his bedroll. "I'll take a turn. You don't need to miss all your damn sleep."

Cleve looked toward the shadow-wreathed woods thinking they should've camped farther east of the forest, at least a mile. It was out of their way, but it'd make it harder for a sortie to catch them unawares. It was Drake Samuels who'd insisted on stopping right here. He was old and had an injured leg, aching after a long day on the juddering wagon, so Cleve couldn't blame him. Samuels was sitting on the ground, his splinted leg stretched out, cutting up vegetables and meat into a pot for supper.

The sun sank and the dark woods seemed to thicken, as if the shadows gave the phalanx of white pine and juniper and oak a new massiveness.

Cleve noticed one opening in the thick undergrowth of the woods. There, a little to the north end, at the foot of a hill.

He picked up his rifle and said, "I'll be back. You boys go ahead and eat when there's food."

He turned, stalked toward the woods.

"Now where you going?" asked Samuels with a snort.

Leon chuckled. "Call of nature, I expect."

Drake Samuels slapped at a mosquito, muttering about "triple-damned gallinippers."

Cleve headed into the deepest shadow near the camp, walking fast, keeping an eye out for so much as a twitch or a flicker in the dark brush of the forest edge. There— a flash of movement, a harsh cry. But it was just a blue jay, flitting through the trees, looking for a little something more to eat before it bedded down.

Cleve felt badly exposed here, walking across the meadow into the woods, and he knew he was taking a chance. But it would be hard to rest without scouting the thickets.

He reached the woods, strolled down to the opening in the thicket, and stepped into a deeper darkness. He was amongst the trees: the piney smell, and a strong animal musk that might be brown bear; the spice of fallen, decaying leaves, all of it stirred into the deep, damp coolness of the woods. An owl overhead screeched from one tree to another.

Cleve waited till his eyes adjusted and moved onward, keeping his head low and slowly searching this end of the woods. He tried to keep to the mossy ground; easing between shrubs to make as little noise as he could. His senses were taut as a bowstring. He heard mice rustling in fallen leaves, felt the ghostly touch of the evening breeze probing about the tree boles.

He stopped dead, peering at a silhouette. Was that a man, against that yellow brush?

No. Just a snag of a dead tree.

Hunkering down, Cleve went still, watching and listening. Seeing little, hearing nothing but the familiar rustling of small night creatures.

At last, he stood up and headed back. At the edge of the woods, he looked out toward the camp, seeing the circle of firelight, the dim forms of stock, and a man he took to be Smallwolf, looking his way.

Cleve hurried across the meadow, strolling up to the campfire as if nothing worried him. How's that stew coming?"

* * *

He slept lightly, uneasily, waking up half a dozen times. At last, Smallwolf padded up, touched his shoulder. "You want to take a watch?"

For answer, Cleve sat up and pulled on his boots. He put on his hat, his gunbelt, and picked up his rifle. He could hear Leon and Samuels snoring from their blankets near the red coals of the fire. "Anything move out there, Smallwolf?" he asked in a whisper.

"A couple elk and many bats."

"Get some rest." Cleve found cold Arbuckle's by the fire, drank some right from the coffeepot.

Then he went to sit with his back to a wagon wheel, holding the Winchester '73 across his lap, watching the woods.

Thinking, *I'll feel like a damned fool if they come from somewhere else.*

He watched that gap in the thicket, where they'd most likely be coming out, if they were coming at all.

It was cold here, and the night seemed to press against him. The darkness was too intimate, too open to anything happening, anything at all.

He kept his eyes on the woods, but his mind turned to thoughts of Berenice. He smiled, thinking of how she'd bitten her lip to keep from utterly condemning "the mudhouse," the old soddy he'd offered her on buying Samuels's place.

He envisioned the house he would build for her and Alice. There was a small hill overlooking the river, high enough to be clear of spring floods. Its crown offered just enough room for a large house. He'd start small, a structure of wood frame and stone, with a slate roof, a bedroom, a main room—both parlor and nursery—a shed off the back containing a stove, and a pantry. A root cellar. A covered walk to a large privy out back, its pit lined and directed to turn the contents away from the river.

The main house would be constructed to make it easy to add upon. As his fortunes grew, so would the house. A second story, then an extension to the side for Alice, her own room as she got older. More rooms for more children, if Berenice was agreeable. A smokehouse too . . .

The river contained a great many large, round stones. He would use them to build the fireplace. His father had taught him some masonry. He'd get the finest curtains he could find for Berenice. Perhaps a piano.

There would be a barn, of course—a substantial barn with a loft. The soddy could be used for cowhands and farmworkers till bunkhouses were built.

But he'd forgotten Berenice's study, for her natural history writings. A cubby, at least, with a desk and bookshelves. That would please her inordinately. Someday they'd have gas lighting . . . Yes, and a porch, a big porch, where they would all sit of an evening and look at the sky, and Berenice would name the stars for the children . . . the several children . . .

He was building the house, had the first story almost completed, when the raiders came in, their faces covered with flour sacks, guns blazing, torches thrown on his works, the fire licking at the sky, Alice crying . . .

Cleve's eyes snapped open.

He damned himself for dozing. How much time had

passed? There was dew on his clothing. His hands were cramped with cold.

Flexing his fingers, he scanned the dark meadow. A little moonlight had broken through the clouds, and he could see swells in the ground, a few shrubs, and the edge of the woods. And that dark, natural gateway thick with shadow . . .

Where he glimpsed something moving.

There was a glint of moonlight on metal. A rifle.

Careful to make no sudden movement, Cleve eased himself to the ground, wriggled to lay flat on his belly, one elbow planted. He levered a round into the chamber of his Winchester, and aimed at shapes emerging from the wood.

A man for a certainty, and skulking too. The skulker was half crouched, head low.

Could he open fire on the man, here and now?

But it could be a hunter who'd gotten himself lost. Or some Indian, maybe western Paiute, cautious about the camp, but not necessarily an enemy. It was even possible one of his own Washoe friends had wandered up this far north.

Hold your fire, he told himself. *Wait. Let them fire the first shot.*

It was risky, doing it that way. But he hadn't yet confirmed this was an enemy, and the risk was better than having to live with murder.

A second figure emerged from the woods, hunched low as they started across the meadow. Just human shapes, a little darker than the prevailing darkness. Now and then a glimpse of metal in their hands. They moved like hunters—hunters of men.

Cleve thought about rousing the camp. But these gunmen, whoever they were, didn't know he was aware of them. He had an edge so long as he kept quiet. And lying in their bedrolls, Leon, Smallwolf, and Samuels were less likely to catch a bullet.

A third man came skulking from the woods, coming up close behind the first two. They spread out, and Cleve knew a skirmish line when he saw one. But still, he waited. And still, they came toward the camp.

One of them, a little in front, turned and signaled to the other two. They stopped. They raised their rifles to their shoulders.

"The hell with it," Cleve muttered. He took a bead on the man in front. And he shouted, *"Drop your weapons and put your hands up!"*

They answered with gunfire.

Gun muzzles flashed. Bullets cracked by. Lead thwacked into the freight wagon behind him.

Cleve opened fire on the nearest raider, instantly levered another round in, cocking and firing again—all in under a second. The man went down with two bullets in his chest. Cleve levered another round into the chamber, cocked the rifle—and saw a muzzle flash, an instant before the bullet sizzled past his right ear. It ricocheted off the metal of the wheel rim. There were shouts of alarm from the camp.

One of the intruders had gone down in a shallow dip in the meadow, kneeling to fire from behind a swell. His gun cracked and one of the stock animals screamed.

Another raider ducked behind a shrub off to the north. Cleve fired through it, but he didn't figure he hit anything.

Two muzzle flashes, gunshots from the depression in the meadow. Cleve heard wood splintering, and a returning shot from somewhere in the camp.

Cleve fired three quick rifle shots at the gunman in the slough, then got to his feet and tossed the Winchester aside. He sprinted slantwise south and west, drawing and cocking his Colt Army. A bullet grazed his belly—he could feel it dig out some skin. He dodged right, then slanted back west toward the low place where he could just make out the gunman, turning his way. Cleve turned sideways to the man and fired the Colt three times, each round giving him a split second to more accurately direct his aim. The gunman shouted in pain and fell back, dropping his rifle and writhing. Cleve approached—and the gunman sat up, pistol in hand, and fired. The bullet cut close by, but Cleve's return fire found its target. The man's head jerked and he fell limply back.

A shotgun boomed from close behind—Cleve turned to see Leon, shotgun in hand, and a man to the north stumbling back and falling. Cut down by the scattergun.

Cleve realized that was the man who'd ducked behind the shrub. He must have circled to flank him. He'd have shot Cleve down if not for Leon.

"Look at that, Cleve!" Leon said, shaking his head. "You're a damn fool, letting that man creep up behind you! You should've woke me!"

Cleve grinned and said, "Leon, I'm just glad you were there!"

"Best get behind the wagons, boss!" Smallwolf called. "There could be more!"

Cleve nodded. He and Leon hurried back under cover of the wagons.

"Somebody better heat up the coffee," Leon said.

Chapter 12

"Three is all there were?" Samuel asked, as they examined the three bodies.

"So it appears," Cleve said.

Cleve had decided to turn the dead over to the law in Independence. They now lay on their backs at the edge of camp, laid side by side in the dawn light.

"Them two seem Injuns," said Samuels, leaning against a wagon wheel. He was in a foul mood, Cleve could see, scowling first at the dead men, then at his dead draft horse, lying past the wagons. It had caught a bullet in the neck and had bled out quickly.

"These two are not unknown to me," said Smallwolf. "That one, missing the tip of his nose, that's Wild Dog. Half Comanche. He kills for gold. The man shot in the head, I think that's his nephew Rio. Both of 'em are half Mex. The fellow in the buckskins, with the long hair—he looks like a white drifter."

"Not no more he ain't," said Leon. "Cleve put two right where they did the most good."

"Wild Dog was crafty," Smallwolf said. "He don't

want a gunfight. Sneak up and cut throats, that was his way."

"Didn't count on Cleve," Leon said. "Now I'm wondering was it Hawthorn sent them or were they just some trail trash looking for someone to kill and rob?"

"I'm satisfied it was Hawthorn," was all Cleve said.

Leon nodded. "What about their horses? They didn't walk all the way out here."

"Their horses are in those woods, maybe on the south side, be my guess," Cleve said, squinting in that direction. "Let's backtrack them. Put two of their horses to pull the grain wagon, to replace the one we lost, if we can gear it up that way. Put one of the dead men on the third horse. The other two we can chuck across the oxen . . ."

The sun was right overhead, good and hot, and Cleve could smell the ripening corpses strapped to the stock behind them.

"The way these mountains are hoisted up all around us, it spooks me some," said Leon, as he and Cleve rode ahead of the train of freight wagons. He looked right and left at the craggy, deeply etched snow-topped mountains rearing over Owens Valley. "Feels like they're like to fall on us."

"Maybe because this is the deepest valley in the west. Some think it's the deepest in the whole country."

"Anyway, I heard these mountains do get to falling. Smallwolf said there was a town called Kearsarge, close under these mountains, was going to be the county seat, till the biggest avalanche anybody seen around here done fell right on top of it." Leon shook his head. "A man just never knows for sure what's coming."

The Owens River Valley was considerably bigger than Sweet River Valley, but much of it was cracked alkali flat. Around the Owens River, running southwest, was a green belt, and even the alkali flat was set out in lines of pink checkerbloom, the flowers' tattered petals sent spinning away by the autumn wind.

On they rode, talking little—unusual for Leon. Perhaps it was the presence of the dead men. Leon glanced back at them from time to time, frowning.

Cleve kept watch on the mountain passes, and the copses of oak and pine, just in case Hawthorn had some more surprise greeters awaiting them. But they saw no trace of people, except the rutted road and gray, wind-blown smoke from a couple of cabins far off on the lower slopes of the mountains. They were greeted only by southing flocks of honking geese, arrowing toward Owens Lake.

The caravan made two brief stops to let the stock rest while the men gnawed on jerked meat, drank some water, and listened to Drake Samuels prose away about his plans for his sister's farm. How he was going to use a dowsing rod to find a new well, for theirs was running dry. He also made a vow never to plant on a Friday, for that was bad luck . . .

"Drake," Leon said, "I don't care for talk of bad luck." He looked over at the dead body of Wild Dog. "You'll have me worrying about Indian curses. I don't look for them, but I don't doubt 'em either."

"I believe we shot him, before he could put a curse on us," Cleve said, smiling.

"A man's spirit can put a curse on you, so I hear," Leon said.

"Wild Dog's kept too busy in Hell to have time for cursing us," said Cleve.

Smallwolf grunted and nodded. "That's so."

It was twilight when they got to Independence, a middling town with a courthouse at the end of a cobbled main street crowded with neatly painted shops. The county seat was built around mining, and a wagonload of ore passed them by, headed for a foundry.

All four men were glad to see the town unfold about the road. Glad the wagons could be delivered, and the dead men too. None of them enjoyed the company of the bloated bodies.

People along the wooden walks stared at the corpses strapped to the oxen and horses. Cleve kept his eyes peeled for a sheriff's office.

On the east side of the street was a three-story, passably ornate manse that had become The Owens River Hotel. In front of it, Cleve spotted someone he knew.

Shouting at the others to hold up, Cleve reined Ulysses in, dismounted, and hurried over to the horse that bore Wild Dog. Tugging his knife from its sheath, he cut the body loose, let it fall, and dragged it by the collar, his nose full of the reek, over to Asa Hawthorn, who was standing out front of the hotel. With Hawthorn was James Crofton and a thickset man with drooping mustaches, a shield-shaped badge on his shiny blue vest.

"Hawthorn!" Cleve called. "I have something belongs to you!"

The three men gawped as Cleve dumped the body at Hawthorn's feet.

Asa Hawthorn stepped quickly back. "What in God's name do you mean by this!"

"You sent this man and his two friends there to kill me, Hawthorn. To kill me and these three riding with me."

"That's a damned lie!"

The man with the sheriff's badge was sizing Cleve up. He was a big man with a square jaw; wore a modestly sized black sombrero and silver spurs on his black Mexican boots. On his badge was impressed the name *H. Morse.* "Who's this man telling the damned lie, Asa?"

"He is Cleveland Trewe," Hawthorn said, snorting. "A notorious gunfighter. He's killed many a man."

Sheriff Morse seemed unruffled. "I've heard. Well, Trewe—how come this here man to be dead?"

"He came at us guns blazing, and I killed him," Cleve said, his voice flat. He was trying to keep his temper. He kicked the body lightly with his boot. "This body is identified, to my satisfaction, as the bandit Wild Dog. He and his men tried to kill me and Drake Samuels—and these other men here. Leon Studge and Lane Smallwolf."

"Wild Dog!" exclaimed Morse, hunkering down for a closer look. "Well, he's some puffed up but that sure looks like his picture. Bullet holes in the front of him too. That's good."

Leon strode over and said, "It's like he says, Sheriff. I'll swear to it. I'm Studge—I was town marshal in

Axle Bust. These men came at our camp, set up a hail of fire. Killed one of the horses and near got me in the bargain."

"That Drake Samuels, is it?" the sheriff asked, looking at the farmer on his wagon. "Him I know. He's a solid sort."

"Very well, they were attacked by bandits," Hawthorn allowed. "But this man defames me!"

"Trewe, what makes you think these men were working for Hawthorn?" Morse asked.

Cleve noted the sheriff didn't seem surprised by the allegation. The notion that Asa Hawthorn would hire killers did not seem foreign to his thinking.

"Hawthorn threatened me, and my wife, and Samuels there. Samuels will tell you what he went through. He was wounded by one of Hawthorn's men . . ."

"You want to allege that in court, you'll need witnesses," said Morse simply. He stood up and turned to Hawthorn. "Asa, I'll need you to make a statement. Go ahead to my office, you and Crofton, and do me the kindness of telling the undertaker to come and get these cadavers. He's right next door to my office. Pflug's his name. He'll be happy to see you."

Hawthorn nodded, scowled at Cleve, and hurried quickly away, giving the dead man a wide berth. Crofton grinned at Cleve and tailed after his boss.

"Trewe," Morse went on, "I'll get a statement from you and these other men a little later. Just drop by the office, say in an hour or so. Asa won't be there. I've got some good whiskey in a drawer, I'll pour us all a drink—and you can tell me about the fight." He winked. "I'm fair breathless to hear it! Now—let's get these other bodies off the stock, get someone to take them to ol' Pflug."

Cleve found Marshal Beaman in the same hotel Asa Hawthorn was staying in. The U.S. Marshal was seated in the lobby, reading the *Sacramento Bee*.

"Marshal," Cleve said, a little breathless from hurrying here after half a dozen errands. He'd had to hire men to unload the wagons, send telegrams, close out his deal with Samuels, and make his statement for Sheriff Morse.

"There you are, Trewe!" Beaman said, taking off his half-glasses to look Cleve over. "You look like a man who's had a weary time of it!"

"That I did, sir."

Beaman tossed the newspaper onto a lamp table, stood up, and stretched. He was a tall man, but going stooped in late middle age. He wore a black, neatly tailored suit, a red silk tie, and a bowler hat. His lined face was edged with a short graying black beard. His dark eyes were hooded but piercing. "You had your supper?"

"Was just wishing for some."

Beaman smiled. "You'll be feted by the U.S. government tonight. Dining room's right over here. But you might want to check your gun at the front desk. The hotel tries to be high-toned."

The hotel's dining room was poorly lit by oil lamps;

the effect was eased by the lithographed wallpaper showing blue mountains topped with snow. The view of the Inyo Mountains was the pride of Independence. Cleve and Beaman drank coffee in china cups as they waited for steaks at a shinily lacquered live oak table on an imported braided rug.

Not wanting to rush the U.S. Marshal into their business, Cleve said, "I got used to gaslights in San Francisco. Seems darker indoors out here without it."

"Oh, it'll be along. Civilization's picking up steam like a runaway locomotive. Going to need more vigorous law enforcement. I hear you had an eventful trip here."

Cleve told him about the fight with the Wild Dog bunch.

"I see. Delivering that body directly to Asa Hawthorn must've been satisfying. But it couldn't be called prudent."

"You're right," Cleve admitted. "I let my anger get the best of me. Hawthorn threatened my wife, Marshal."

Beaman rumbled in his throat and gave his beard a thoughtful tug. "I see. And I understand. But it doesn't sound to me that you have direct evidence Hawthorn sent those men after you."

"Yet I am certain of it. Consider what he did to the Washoe band—Washoe and Paiute, I should say."

"I received your letter on that affray. You've no clear proof that it wasn't as he said—a search for missing folk and a fight with renegades. I'll grant you that Marske may well be Hawthorn's man. That's what I'm hearing in other places too. But I spoke to Hawthorn, and he says the men you and your men killed at Westcut Canyon were going to demand you leave the area. And you opened fire."

"He's a liar. They opened fire and we returned fire. Nothing was said about trespass—and we weren't trespassing anyhow. Hawthorn claims ownership of more land than he actually owns."

"I'm inclined to accept your version of events. I visited that hillside, Cleve. I saw more to support your claim than Hawthorn's. But not enough to be sure either way. A judge will decide, not me. But I'll testify for you. I looked through the pockets of the dead men—and found papers on two of them. They were wanted men. I also found the gravesites of the massacred Indians." His face darkened with anger and Cleve remembered that Beaman had been an Indian agent, overseeing a reservation, and had shown a high regard for native people. The marshal went on, "It does look to me like an unexpected attack on the Indians, not some case of white men defending themselves. But establishing that Hawthorn is behind it is going to be fearsome delicate."

"The Washoe band and two Paiute survivors are ready to testify."

"Yes. But they did not see Asa Hawthorn there." He sighed, and drank a little coffee.

Cleve had an inclination to order a whiskey to sweeten his Arbuckle's, but decided against it. He knew Beaman to be a teetotaler.

Beaman put his cup down and shook his head. "It makes me bitter angry, Cleve. Quite furious." He lowered his voice and leaned forward. "Do you know how many Indians have been killed with impunity in the state of California? We believe it to be at least ten thousand—some systematically cut down—as when Charles Fremont led an expedition that slaughtered whole villages. Others were killed for bounties. Can you imagine? Bounties for women and children—just because they were Indians!"

Cleve nodded. He had heard of it. "That history— that's how Hawthorn figures he can get away with it."

"Yes. Politics prevented anyone from being prosecuted for these depredations. The state of California, the local U.S. Cavalry, even my own service—they all looked away. Monstrous, sir! But, times are changing. The state administration has changed, the federal policy, too, and we will not allow these massacres to resume. The word has gone out it is no longer to be tolerated."

"That's what my father would call too little, too late."

"It is that—but it's all I have to offer. If there is any means to tie Hawthorn to these murders, something we can take to court, I will see him arrested. Do you know, by the by, who Hawthorn served under, in the war?"

"I do not. I never encountered him, that I know."

"He served under Fremont!"

Cleve grunted. "I heard tales of Fremont, from a sergeant who'd served under him. He was known as a cold man who would do anything to further his ambition. Even if it meant throwing away the lives of good soldiers."

Beaman nodded. "And a senior military officer will

choose his own kind to follow him, when he can.
Hawthorn was Fremont's bootlick! But listen now,
Cleveland Trewe—if you're to take Hawthorn on, and
indeed, the Paytons, you must do it in two ways. First,
you must do it impartially, despite your hard feelings.
Second—you'd best have some force of law behind
you. Now I know you well enough, I don't believe you
will drag this down to a personal fight."

Cleve was puzzled. "Force of law, Marshal?"

"I have made some inquiries on your behalf. I have
some paperwork here for you to sign, if you are willing.
You turned me down once—but this time you may be
in another frame of mind. If you are agreeable . . . I have
this for you."

He took a U.S. Deputy Marshal's badge from his
coat pocket, and placed it on the table, beside Cleve's
coffee cup . . .

Chapter 13

Cleve was sitting up in bed, his every slight movement eliciting a squeak of protest from the rusting bedsprings. On his lap was a thick book, given to him by Beaman, a blue tome of marshal service regulations, and all laws pertaining. He had it open to common law property rights, and so far as he could see, Hawthorn had not established common law property over the whole of Sweet River Valley.

Cleve was spending an uneasy night at the Silver Miner's Inn, a ramshackle two-story affair located near the mining cart track near the end of the Independence's main street. He had to wait in town till tomorrow for he'd come in too late to establish his deed of property at the courthouse. But he would certify ownership of the Trewe Ranch first thing tomorrow. It was the silver badge lying on the table by the creaking bed, catching the glow of the lantern, that kept him from sleep.

The ore carts clacked by, coming and going, and his mind went round and round the burdensome responsibility of being a U.S. Deputy Marshal, ever returning to the opportunity the appointment presented to help civilize Sweet Valley.

Cleve could give the badge back—or he could sign the Deputy United States Marshal appointment papers. If he accepted the appointment, Beaman would swear him in on the spot.

There was still time to say no. Of course, Cleve could resign from the position most any time, but he wasn't a man to agree to a thing, to be sworn in, and not do the job, at least long enough to see his obligation settled. If a man's word was no good—how good a man could he be?

He knew what Leon would say, and likely Caleb too. They would assure him it would be folly for a man to undertake the appointment when he was starting out with his own ranch—a considerable ranch calling for considerable work. Especially when this man had an infant child, a wife, a crew of cowhands, and even an adopted band of Indians under his care.

Folly.

And what would Berenice want?

She knew he was a man who liked to set things right. *There are two kinds of peacemakers, Cleve,* she'd said to him once. *One is the easier sort. The one who we go to for diplomacy. The other is the hard kind of peacemaker. We wish for the first one. But sometimes we need that second peacemaker. Like that ironic name they give to the Colt six-shooter. You have kindness, and gentleness in abundance, my love. You do not settle every conflict with a gun. But when it comes to it—you are the hard kind of peacemaker.*

She said it in a tone of resignation.

Berenice would accept his decision. But in her heart, what would she truly want?

She would want him to stay close to her, and Alice, and the ranch. That's what would make her happiest. A U.S. Deputy Marshal might be called away from home at any time.

Still . . .

Cleve kept returning to something Beaman said, after dinner. He had pressed the badge into Cleve's hand, and said, "Take it with you tonight, while you think it over. Consider what it represents. I know your war record, Cleveland Trewe. I am not thinking only of your medals—your decorations. I am thinking of your devotion to *the Republic*. I know too that you beheld horrors in the war, and you had your doubts. But you knew what the real meaning of that war was—*justice!* Do you suppose men like Hawthorn will cease to murder the likes of the Washoe and the Paiute? Some Indians have been enslaved—in California, and in Arizona, and other states, Indians are yet held in slavery, long after the negro was freed by the Emancipation Proclamation. Then there are men like Drake Samuels—forced to flee his land by bullies breaking the federal law! Oh, some of it I cannot yet prove, but I know it's so. I ask you to take up this badge, this silver banner, in the same cause that sustained you in so many battles for the Republic. And for a higher cause!"

Cleve smiled wryly, remembering Beaman had gone so far as to quote *The Battle Hymn of the Republic*.

"You know the song, Cleve. *He has sounded forth the trumpet that shall never call retreat!*"

The U.S. Marshal had seen into Cleve's heart; had struck it like ringing a bell with a hammer.

Cleve reached out, picked up the badge, and held it in his palm, tilted to catch the lantern light. It was fancier than some he'd seen, cast all of sterling silver, a five-pointed star within a circle, and in the center of the star was carved the eagle—wings spread, talons lifted—of the United States of America.

His holstered six-gun was in its gunbelt holster on one of the bed's brass posts, close to hand, and the Colt's glinting cylinder shared the lantern light with the badge.

Cleve smiled sadly, and nodded to himself. He turned to his holster, and attached the badge firmly to the black leather, close to the blue steel of his Colt . . .

"You done gone completely out of your poor ol' mind this time, Cleve," Leon said, as they drew up at Chumash Creek, where it poured itself into the Owens River. It was late afternoon on a windy day, and the sun was edging low. Cleve, Leon, and Smallwolf had a long ride and there were still many hours of hard riding ahead to Trewe Ranch.

The three men dismounted, and let their horses water. Leon shook his head, watching Danny drink from the creek, and added, "What do you think Berry's going to say? She'll say you take that badge right back to Beaman!"

"What worries me is what she *won't* say," said Cleve, patting Ulysses on his neck. "She'll *say* I must go with my heart and conscience. But she'll be thinking I should stay at home and protect the family and build up the ranch."

"Damned straight you should!"

"Once I take care of this first arrest, I'll have time for everything else."

Leon looked at him. "The marshal give you papers to serve, did he?"

"This morning. Man named Carter Tucky. Known for running a horse-thieving gang. Killed a sheriff and his deputy down in the Sierra Madre. There's a report says Tucky figures to set up another outfit out here, where the grazing's so good."

"Where's he at now?"

"Last word was, Tucky and three others have a camp over in the North Valley woods, just about two miles north of where we brought the herd through the hills."

"Don't want anyone stealing our horses," Leon observed. "Can you deputize me?"

"The marshal service doesn't pay much. Fifty cents a mile for trailing, and twenty dollars. I'm not getting paid much better myself."

"The skinflints! When do you figure on going?"

"Tomorrow, I hope. Get it over and done with."

"I'll come too," Smallwolf said.

Cleve shook his head regretfully. "I'll need you to get back on the herd, Lane. And keep an eye on the ranch. And as for Leon . . . well . . ." Cleve gave a droll little smile. "Depends on if Teresa lets him go."

"Teresa!" Leon said, snorting. "Why she'll just have to tend to her pots and pans! I'm not going to let you go after those owlhoots alone!"

"I'll bet you five dollars Teresa won't let you go with me," Cleve said.

"I'll take that bet! But I'll bet you ten Berry'll give you a tongue-whipping about the whole damn thing!"

Smallwolf grinned. "White men! Frightened of their women!"

"Indian women never give their men trouble?" Cleve chuckled. "I remember, when I was camping with the Paiutes, a war chief's woman tried to cut his throat when he slept! He lived because all she had was that old flint knife."

"Sometimes, if you make them angry enough . . ." Smallwolf allowed.

"We'd best move on. It's getting late. Not sure if we'll get therc tonight."

"There is a storm coming," Smallwolf said, pointing at the black clouds banked against the Sierras. "Maybe rain, maybe snow."

Leon looked at the clouds skeptically. "You can tell that from them clouds? They're a long way off."

"You will see."

They saw it and they felt it, a blast of cold, a mix of soppy snow and rain, pressing furiously at them from the northeast. The storm was coming face-on and the horses, already exhausted, were shivering, stumbling in the windchill. Somewhere close to midnight, Cleve decided they wouldn't make it to the ranch tonight. He called a halt in copse of oaks and birch, on a knoll along the road. They made camp on the lee side of the hill in a small clearing, building a fire amongst the remains of a dried-out old stump. They drew the horses close to the fire, and rubbed them down, giving them grain with sorghum to give them extra strength.

The men spread their own blankets over the horses and made them lie down. Within a rough triangle of three reclining horses, Cleve, Leon, and Smallwolf were passably snug, even as the treetops lashed about and shrieked in the wind, their branches whipping icy drops of water on the camp. Huddled in their coats, hats pulled down, the three men gave way to exhaustion, and slept . . .

Delbert Hawthorn felt strange walking into a jailhouse with his father. Especially at past midnight. Asa Hawthorn had woken Del personally, compelling this descent into the rank darkness. Asa had refused to explain.

The twelve jail cells opened on both sides. Down the passage, five ceiling lanterns offered pools of frail illumination. Some of the cells were occupied by foulsmelling drunks, sleeping off their spiritous confoundment. Other prisoners cursed the Hawthorns and Jim Crofton as they followed Sheriff Morse toward the last of the cells.

Father carried a pair of wrist gyves, the chains clanking as he walked, Crofton carried another. The sheriff had a lantern in one hand and a ring of keys in another. They passed a cell where a woman in a torn, muddy gown, her hair straggling astray, stared desperately. "When you gone let me out, Sheriff?" she asked hoarsely.

"Maybe come morning if the circuit judge gets here, Maude," he said, not slowing his stride. "You shouldn't try to knife my deputy."

They reached the end of the hallway, and Del was startled by the two faces, on the other side of the bars, caught in the yellow light of the sheriff's lantern.

"This is them," said Morse. "The Denk brothers."

The two men blinking in the light made Del think of startled possums. Seated on the same bunk, the brothers had deep-set, strangely small black eyes, hatchet faces, weak chins, unusually thin lips. They wore ranch hand attire, with tattered jeans, buttonless vests, down-at-heels boots. Their long, lank jet-black hair was ungraced by hats. "Gentlemen," said Morse, in a dry tone, "Here you behold Monty Denk, he's the shorter one missing his front teeth, and Chadley there, the taller one missing his right ear. Seems he was born without it."

Del half expected the men to hiss like possums, but Chadley spoke up clear enough. "Sheriff, what's all this here 'bout?"

"It's a lynching, Chadley," said Monty, his voice creaking with fear. "Why else they come in the dead of night?"

"I could wish it were," said Morse. "But sadly, I must release you into the custody of these gentlemen. They've got papers from Judge Payton. Seems it's got to be. Marshal Beaman tried to stop it. He wanted to send you to Kansas on federal charges. Judge Parker has a couple of fine new ropes for you boys. But it seems . . ." He muttered an invective and unlocked the jail cell. "Come on out, you Denks!"

The Denk brothers shrugged at one another and emerged from the cell. "Turn around, men," Del's father growled. They turned around, put their hands behind their backs.

"Well, they know how to do that much, anyhow," said Crofton, chuckling, as the elder Hawthorn clicked the gyves around Monty's wrist. Crofton did the honors on Chadley.

Morse locked the door of the cell, hung the keys on his belt, and took a folded paper from his shirt pocket. "This here," he said, waving the paper under Chadley's nose, "is the orders to turn you two willow rats over to Mr. Hawthorn. Don't you give him no trouble now. He's"—Morse glanced at Asa Hawthorn—". . . *supposed* to take you to Sacramento."

Handing the paper to Del, Morse started off down the hallway, and they all followed him out.

"You can have a nice poke with me right here if you'll let me out after!" Maude said, as the sheriff passed her.

A drunk called out, "Me too, Sheriff! I'll give you a nice poke your own self!"

There was laughter up and down the hallway at that. Morse ignored that too.

But Del shivered, and buttoned up his coat, suddenly cold.

Outside, in the cold rain and meager light, Morse turned to Hawthorn and said, "I suppose you could chain them up in the stables till the morning."

"No, we're leaving soon's we can get saddled. Why'd you think I got you out here at this hour?"

"To ride out ahead of Marshal Beaman, I expect."

Hawthorn scowled. "You're getting above your station, Sheriff."

"You showed the papers, and this is on your head, Asa," said Morse. "I wish you luck."

He turned and stalked off toward the Kindly Ladies Saloon.

"We really riding out this minute?" Crofton asked.

"Soon's as we get our goods strapped to those horses," Hawthorn said. "Beaman woke up the telegrapher, a couple hours ago. I don't want us to be here when the answer comes to whatever he sent."

"You taking us to Sacramento?" Chadley asked.

"Nope. We're taking you to my place on Sweet River. It seems you are destined to escape along the way."

Crofton chuckled again. "I swear, you got it all figured, boss."

"You hear that, Chadley?" asked Monty. "He's gonna shoot us out there and say we tried to run!"

"Nope," said Hawthorn. "We'll let you out of the chains in half an hour or so. And we have horses for you. But if you try to ride off, Lightnin' here will shoot you down."

"And I'll be pleased to do it," Crofton said.

"You men are going to work for me," Hawthorn went on. "If you want to live—and prosper. Now come along. We need to ride hard for a time."

* * *

The wind subsided around dawn, followed by a lazy fall of snow, drifting down aslant. Despite the miserable cold wetness of the morning, through some miracle of Mescalero campcraft, Smallwolf got a fire going inside a hollow stump and they managed to brew coffee.

Leon had brought eggs along in his saddlebag, but every last one of them was broken. He ladled them out with his hand, dumped the runny egg stuff on a pan, and got it something like cooked, and stubbornly ate it all, bits of shell and cloth lint included.

Then they grained and saddled the horses, and mounted up. Cleve was worried the snow might not let up. They could lose sight of the road, wander off into the wilderness.

But the flurries ended after half an hour on the trail. The ruts were hidden by five inches of snowfall, but they showed as white humps. To avoid the risk of a horse breaking an ankle, the three riders kept to the roadside, in the grass.

The snowy plain seemed to stretch on forever, gleaming like metal in the dull light of the half-veiled sun. Their clothes were wet, their breath came steaming out in gasps, but half past noon, they saw the covered wagons. They rode faster, cantering up to the snow-wreathed Trewe Ranch. Cleve was relieved to see Berry and Teresa emerge from the soddy. The women were dressed in men's clothes, apart from Teresa's bonnet, and much bundled up.

Berry smiled wanly. Teresa was frowning. "You boys better get in the wagons, get some dry clothes," she said.

"I go to look at the herd," Smallwolf called.

Cleve nodded, impressed by Smallwolf's instinct for responsibility. After such a night, many another hired hand would have lingered in camp near the food and the warmth.

Smallwolf rode off, and Cleve dismounted. Berry took his arm and walked with him as he led Ulysses to the old horse shed.

"Where's Alice?" Cleve asked.

"In the soddy, asleep in her cradle. Marigold is there. Cleve—I'm worried about Alice."

He stopped, and looked at her. "Tell me."

"She's got a fever—not a bad one, not yet, but there's some swelling under her jaw, and she's listless, Cleve. It presents as early symptoms of diphtheria!" Distressed, she reached out for him, and her hand fell on something cold and metallic pinned to his vest. She snatched her hand back as if from a scorpion. "Cleve— you're wearing a badge!"

"I was coming to that, my Berenice. Beaman appointed me Deputy United States Marshal. There's a salary. It's a limited territory, and I won't have to be gone much."

"My, you had that all rehearsed!"

He cleared his throat. "I do have a warrant to serve but it's not so far away, and I'll be back soon's I can."

Her mouth dropped open. "You're leaving here *now?*"

"Shortly. I've an obligation to fulfill, Berry. Let me get Ulysses into the shed . . ."

She walked alongside him, silent, chewing her lower

lip, as he saw to his horse. Not a word from Berenice, as he unsaddled Ulysses, dried him, saw that he had water and hay.

Then he heard the baby crying.

He turned from Berenice and strode to the soddy, heart thumping loudly with every step. Inside the air was close, a little smoky near the ceiling from the leaky stove.

Marigold was sitting on a rickety wooden chair, sweating in the hot stuffiness, rocking the baby slowly in her cradle. The outburst of crying had become a weak mewing sound. Cleve crossed the small room, his boots sloshing when they pressed the boards, making the water overflow.

He bent over the cradle and tried to catch Alice's eye. "Hullo, sweetheart!" The baby looked dreamily past him, her eyes half open.

"Is she bad?" he asked Marigold.

"Sometime, every child get sick. She is strong."

"Go and open the door, will you? Let some clean air in here."

"Yes."

Marigold went to the door, and as he put his fingers to Alice's forehead, he heard the women murmuring. Then Berenice crossed to look down at Alice. "I'll sit with her now."

"The fever—there's some but I've felt worse. Does not feel like a killing fever."

"You know what fever will kill an infant, do you, Cleve?" Her tone was flat.

"What do you want me to do, Berenice? Shall I get one of the men to take the badge back to the marshal?"

The baby whimpered. There was a paleness in her face; red spots on her cheeks. He could see the swelling under her jaw.

Berenice crossed her arms and said, "I don't know."

"I need the law behind me if I'm to face Hawthorn and the Paytons."

"You don't have to be the law to ask for its help."

"There's corruption in Sacramento. That came clear when I met with Marske."

She was silent for a long, pensive moment. "What did you learn in Independence?"

"Beaman is a good man and Sheriff Morse will do. I don't think he's crooked. But I hear the law in Sacramento is bent to help the big combines, like the Paytons. There's a powerful judge there, Jephthah Payton. Who do you think he finds for? It's not just about us, Berry. They want to steal the water rights for the whole valley—and farther west too."

"Your becoming a U.S. Marshal won't change that."

"It'll give me some leverage."

Berenice reached down and stroked Alice's wispy hair. "Beaman does not seem the sort of man who will tolerate your using your badge against enemies."

He looked at Berry. She seemed as pale as the baby, her eyes sunk in shadow as she bent over the cradle. "That's not what I meant by leverage. You think I'm that kind of man? To use the badge that way?"

"I think you'll take it right up to the edge, and I'm

afraid that you might cross that line, Cleve, if they push you. And they will push you. That's certain."

His heart sank. "Your opinion of me . . ." He shook his head. "I'm sorry you think that way."

"No man *always* does the right thing. Because it's impossible to always know what's right, Cleve." She straightened up and looked at him, and her face showed tenderness—but it was also pinched with worry. "Especially when there are so many . . . so many factors of *uncertainty.* People generally don't know they've made a mistake till it's all over."

He wondered if she were thinking of their marriage. He knew he hadn't made a mistake. But could be she thought it was a mistake, for her.

"That warrant I have to serve—it's about thirty-five miles away. I'll take a fresh horse, get it done. I'll have to take my prisoner to Independence. But there's a doctor there—I saw his board—and I'll talk to him about Alice. Try to get him to come back with me."

Berry frowned. "There are few physicians like Doctor Hull out in these settlements, Cleve. Most of them are little better than charlatans. Snake oil salesmen."

"We've no time to take her to Sacramento. The trip would be arduous and . . . she might not survive it. We need the closest physician we can find, Berenice."

"I have taken copious notes on Indian medicine. Certain herbal extracts are said to stave off disease. Marigold makes a syrup of echinacea. It seems to have saved one of the boys who was sick. There is elderberry. Mrs. Rinaldi has elderberry juice and—"

"You were not long ago speaking disparagingly of granny medicine!"

"But that is not what it is! Science has its experiments—and so does folk medicine, and native medicine. Some of it is mere superstition, but over centuries they must come across something useful."

"Berry—maybe I should send you and the baby with one of the men to Independence."

"The wagon would take a long time and to carry the baby on a horse, in this weather—" She shook her head firmly. "No!"

Alice began to cry again. Her voice sounded hoarse. "She needs some willow bark. We've got some in the wagon."

"I have already given her some, Cleve. She has a hard time keeping it down. I've sent for elderberry juice and some other things. If you want to help, Deputy United States Marshal Trewe, get me some fresh cold water and a clean rag. I'm going to hold her, and cool her with a damp cloth."

Cleve sloshed outside, muttering curses at the soddy floor. He hurried to the wagon, found a wooden bucket, filled it with water from the barrel, took a piece of gingham from a box of scrap fabric the women used for patching, and carried the bucket back to the soddy.

Berenice had the baby in her arms now, singing softly to her. Cleve set the bucket down beside her, soaked the cloth in it, wrung it out, and gave it to Berenice. She dabbed at Alice's forehead, whispering, "There you are. A little better and a little better still, my darling. Always a little better, I promise . . ."

Alice looks so small, he thought. *So fragile.*

"That Washoe baby who had diphtheria, Cleve," Berry said. "She died."

Cleve closed his eyes. "But the boy, you said . . ."

"He has come through it."

"Alice is strong. Marigold said it and I . . . we . . . have to believe it."

"You won't be of much help here, I don't suppose. Go and take your bad man, and bring back your doctor, if you must. Though I have little faith in such men."

Cleve bent over and stroked Alice's cheek. "I don't think you should ply her with Indian medicines, my Berenice," he said, trying to keep his voice gentle. "If they give her the wrong thing . . ."

"I shall consult my own judgment, thank you. Go now, if you're going."

Stung, he straightened up and turned away. He walked across the creaking, splashing floor—and stopped at the door. "I'll . . . I'll be back soon's I can." She didn't look up from the baby. "I'm going to get a bite to eat, in the chuckwagon, before I go. Shall I bring you something?"

She only shook her head.

Outside, the air seemed colder than he knew it to be. Leon hurried breathlessly up to him. "Cleve—I got some news!"

"And what is that."

"Well—I can't go with you, not right now. Maybe if you'll wait a day or two. Teresa needs me with her."

"She's sick?"

"She's . . . not so you'd say sick but . . . appears she's

with child." Leon seemed dazed. "She and Berry are sure of it."

"A child? That's a fine thing."

"Speaking of infants—how's your girl?"

"Low fever. Not sure if it's diphtheria or some manner of colic."

"How'd Berry take the sight of that badge?"

"She didn't warm to it. Truth is—the baby ailing's made her pretty short with me. Were it not for that . . ." He shook his head. "I've got to go. I need to get this horse thief and get him to Independence and I'm going to get some medicine for the baby."

"You can't take on those men on your lonesome!"

"I'll get Smallwolf to go with me. You keep a good watch on the ranch, Leon—there's still Hawthorn and his men. They'll be looking for us to let our guard down."

Leon nodded. "I'll keep a sharp watch."

"Be seeing you soon, I hope." Cleve strode off to the chuckwagon, found half a roast pheasant wrapped in wax paper. He sat on a crate and ate a good part of the pheasant, with bread, but scarcely tasted it. His mind was back in the soddy, with Berenice and Alice.

He finished his quick repast, pocketed a couple of wrinkled apples and some dried meat. All the time his mind was racing, yawing back and forth between Alice and the warrant—and Berenice's silent disapproval.

Drinking cold coffee, Cleve made up his mind. He would serve the warrant and then . . .

And then what?

His whirling mind sought an anchor and fixed on

getting the job done for Marshal Beaman. Deciding he needed Ulysses after all, Cleve turned and hurried to the horse shed. He saddled up and galloped into wet wind, heading for the cowboy camp at the herd.

But as he rode down the muddy trail, a thought shadowed him.

It just might be that when he came back from Independence, he'd find Alice had died while he was away.

Chapter 14

Cattle bawled as Guama chivvied bunch-quitters with a rope end, sending them back into the herd. Close by, Cleve was hunched in the saddle, feeling the thin rain on the back of his neck as he looked down at Luis Diaz who stood humbly before him, boot heels sunk in muddy, hoof-trampled sod.

"This time, *Jefe,* you must let me come with you!" Luis scowled up at him, hat in hand, his mustaches drooping in the rain.

Cleve shook his head. "I'll need a seasoned gunhand. I know you can shoot, but Smallwolf can keep his head under fire. There's at least four of them out there. We'll be outnumbered."

"Then take us both!"

"Can't. The herd . . ."

"And Jefe, Smallwolf is chasing strays, down by the river. Milt and Guama watch the herd." He revolved his hat brim in his hand as he spoke. "Smallwolf, he's three miles, maybe four. You say we must hurry!"

Cleve sighed. He didn't want to expose this young

man to gunfire if he didn't have to. His father would be heartbroken if Luis was cut down in his youth. "Where's Wovoka?"

"He is fishing."

Cleve nodded. He had given the Indian hands time off to handle tribal needs including hunting and fishing. It wouldn't be easy to find him. He thought about fetching Dave Kanaway to ride with him on this one. But Dave was in charge of the drovers' remuda. Was it good figuring to remove the watch on those horses when there was a gang of horse thieves about?

Cleve shook his head resignedly. He needed to deal with the warrant quick, get back to Berenice and Alice. "All right, Luis. Mount up."

They were soon cantering across the soggy valley, hooves churning mud. Cleve kept to high ground when he could, where the drier ground was more trustworthy.

An hour of riding, and then Cleve reined in where a thin, temporary stream swished down the slope. They let the horses drink, but it was the tracks that led him to stop. Deep, muddy tracks of three horses, shod, making their way southeast across the valley, heading toward the town of Sweet River.

Cleve led the way across the stream, and they followed the tracks a few miles toward the woods where the horse thieves were reported to be holed up. The clouds were breaking up in a stiff wind, and a beam of sunlight showed something dark lying on a hummock ahead. Cleve raised a hand and drew rein. A dead man lay near the tracks, face down. A muddy slouch hat lay nearby.

Cleve climbed down and went to the body. "Shot in the back."

"Who is it, Jefe?"

"Don't know yet." Cleve turned the body over. The man's bearded face was partly muddied, but Cleve could see enough he was sure he didn't know him. Nor did the face match the tintype of Carter Tucky that Marshal Beam had provided. The dead man was dressed rough, canvas trousers and farmer's boots and a rawhide jacket. His dead eyes were open, one coated in mud. His lower lip was bisected by a scar. The gun was missing from his holster and so were the cartridges.

Cleve went through the dead man's pockets, finding no papers and not a penny. Standing up, he looked along the tracks of the other riders. "Looks like he took a notion to turn off from the others, and somebody shot him in the back. They took his horse and guns and shells and anything else they wanted from him."

"It could be he tried to quit them, and they didn't like that idea."

Cleve nodded. "What I figured too." The leader of the horse theft gang was said to be ruthless. A man who murdered when he didn't have to. "They left their camp and headed toward town—and this man crossed Carter Tucky."

"Who is this Tucky?"

"Outlaw chief. The man named on my warrant."

"The others—no warrant? Then what do you do with them?"

"I'll arrest them, on suspicion. Maybe the court will

let them go." He made up his mind. "Let's follow the tracks."

"We take the body?"

Cleve remounted. "Slow us down too much. I'll hire someone to come back, bring it in for a burial."

Cleve hoped he was right about those tracks. If the Tucky gang was in Sweet River, he could get back to Berenice and Alice all the sooner. But a flipped coin had a tail side—what was Carter Tucky planning to do in Sweet River?

The sinking sun was behind them, casting dull red and gold across the scattering of buildings that made up Sweet River, California.

Cleve and Luis rode up the road, side by side, both watching for any man with a gun in his hands. He'd shown Luis the tintype of Tucky and they looked at the faces of the few men outside and saw no one but a couple of carpenters Cleve recognized and the blacksmith, who was closing up his shop.

Should get to know that big man, he thought. Might make a good ally. And a posse man.

Cleve reined in at the new building, where the two young carpenters were just finishing up the siding on a small house. They both wore blue jean coveralls and red undershirts. "Hiram and Eric, I think," he said.

The two slender, thinly bearded young men turned to squint at him. Then Hiram pointed. "You're that Cleve Trewe!"

Cleve smiled. "I am touched you remembered. Here

you are in Sweet River—last time I saw you was in Paradise, Nevada. You come a long way."

"We were looking for someplace more *peaceful,*" said Hiram, a trifle accusingly. He and his brother had seen Cleve bring in the bodies of several road agents.

"Has it been peaceful, up to now?"

"Well as to that . . ." Eric thoughtfully flipped his hammer in the air and caught it, then said, "There's talk of shootings, off across the valley. And one of the local farmers got shot in the leg."

"Drake Samuels," Cleve said. "He's relocated out by Independence. I bought his place."

"You?" Hiram blinked at him in disbelief. "A *farmer?*"

"A rancher and a farmer. My wife is skeptical too. Happens I'm also going to be working on the peace around here. Keeping it, I mean." Cleve leaned back, glanced around, and saw no one else about. Then he opened his coat and showed them the badge pinned to his vest. "Deputy U.S. Marshal. I mention it because I have this here . . ." He took the tintype from his pocket, leaned over, and handed it down to Hiram. "You seen that man?"

Hiram looked at it, shook his head, and showed it to his brother. Eric frowned and said, "Mebbe could be one of the men who rode in. Half hour ago. He's up in Mickal's saloon, with a few others."

"*Mickal's* saloon?" Luis asked, grinning. "That is what it's called now?"

"No, that's what we call it," Eric said. "Got some

funny name about Hell too. Run by a fiddle player. Says his boss is a rancher."

Luis hooked a thumb at Cleve. "This rancher."

"You don't mean it!" Hiram exclaimed. "The saloon too? Well, I never! You going to buy up the whole town?"

"What I've bought has already cost me dearly," Cleve said. He was looking up toward the Why the Hell Saloon. There were four horses tied up in front of it. "But in fact, I do have a need for a couple of carpenters." He looked at the house they were working on. "Keep an eye on that saloon, Luis. Call out, not too loud, if anyone comes out."

"*Bueno,* Jefe."

Cleve dismounted, patted Ulysses on the neck, and went to look through the open door into the new structure. The place looked to be neatly put together, everything foursquare and straight. He saw no rainwater leaking through the planked roof. "You building this for yourself?"

"No, sir," Eric said. "For the Gundersons. They're living in the back of his store and they're right tired of it. We're nearly done here—weather clears up a little, we'll put the tar shingles up, and that'll be it."

Cleve nodded. "Fact is, I need a power of building done, and you boys seem to be doing a good job. I'll make a deal right here and now and give you five hundred dollars to get started. The rest when you finish. You'd need to commence the morning after you drive the last nail on this one. I need it done before the winter sets in . . ."

The Royce boys were delighted. The deal was agreed on in two minutes. Then Cleve said, "Eric, Hiram—you say nothing to anybody about my being here, or what I asked you about, till I come back here for my horses, you hear?"

Both men nodded gravely.

"Luis, let's put our horses around back, if these boys don't mind, and we'll walk up to that saloon. Careful-like."

With the horses stowed out behind the new house, Cleve and Luis walked up along the grassy verge toward the saloon. Cleve wanted to approach the place quietly.

"Maybe," Luis said, clearing his throat, "we come from the back and front?"

"Seems sensible," Cleve said. "The back door would be you. I'll go in the front like I'm going to order. Those owlhoots aren't likely to know me." He took off his badge, put it in a coat pocket, and loosened his Colt in its holster.

"You are a man with ice in his blood," Luis said softly, shaking his head. "To make plans to buy a house when you have this to do!"

"You ever know a man after a long ride leave a saloon in under an hour?"

Luis chuckled. "Never have I known such a thing!"

"So I figured I had time. And the more time they have to drink, the better off we are. I sent off for some whiskey—did it come in?"

"Oh, sí, some good whiskey."

"Good. That'll slow them down, if the ball opens.

Wait a minute—how did you know it's good whiskey? Who said you could come over to the saloon? You're supposed to wait for me or Leon to give the nod on that."

Luis shrugged broadly. "Milt and me, we come, when you and Leon, you are with Samuels on the trail! No one here to ask!"

"I left Milt in charge."

"He told himself si! And me too!"

"I'll bet Pamahas wasn't happy with it."

"*Sí, eso es verdad* —when we come back, I hear her speaking some words in Indian—did not sound like words of love."

When they were within thirty strides of the saloon, Cleve could hear the violin playing. He whispered, "You go around back but don't go in unless you hear shots—or if you hear me call out, 'Where's Luis?'"

"'Where's Luis!' Yes!"

"These men—we're trying to get them alive, Luis. Don't get jumpy with your gun. If you start shooting— you're asking for them to shoot back. That's three men with guns."

"Yes, Jefe." Luis headed quietly around back.

Cleve approached the front door, stepping quietly. The door was open and he could see three men at the bar, two of them wearing cowboy duds. Their chaps were raggedy, their boots muddy. On their hips were low-slung, strapped-down revolvers. A shotgun was lying along the bar, beside a half empty bottle of whiskey. The man facing him, leaning back against the bar, was

Carter Tucky. Cleve recognized Tucky's badly-healed broken nose, his jutting lower jaw, from the tintype. Tucky even wore the same frock coat and buttoned-up white shirt. He had his back to the bar. He was hatless, his unbarbered hair damp from the rain; he had several days' growth of beard, and his bared teeth were crooked. The one on the end near the shotgun was turning toward Cleve.

Cleve had hoped to get the drop on the men, and call out for their surrender. But that simple tactic wasn't likely to work out, with two of them facing him.

Whistling "Darling Clementine" along with Mickal's fiddle, Cleve sauntered into the saloon.

Mickal was standing in a corner, playing the violin. He stopped playing and gave Cleve a desperate look—which Cleve returned with a smile.

Walking over to post himself at the opposite corner of the bar from the other men, Cleve said. "Is that whiskey I see back there?"

"Hey, fiddler!" barked Carter Tucky, looking up from his whiskey. "Did I tell you to stop playing?"

Cleve caught Mickal's eye and winked.

The fiddler resumed fiddling as Tucky and his men turned looks of whiskey-dulled suspicion at Cleve. Tucky's companions were long-haired, their beards matted with grease drippings; the one on the left had a droopy lower lip; the short one on the right had a skullish face pocked by smallpox.

Cleve had never seen a more unsavory group of men.

"Mister," said Tucky, "this here is now my saloon."

The fiddle was sawing away at "The Yellow Rose of Texas" now, but somewhat erratically, and out of tune. Without looking at the fiddler, Tucky raised a hand in one snapping motion, and the music cut off. "An' I don't let people just walk in my saloon without I know 'em."

Now Cleve saw something about Tucky's eyes he hadn't been able to see from the tintype. The outlaw's facial expression seemed frozen; his mouth hardly moving when he talked. But his eyes, reddened gray, fulminated with fury. There was a fierce desire in those eyes. The undiluted desire to hurt someone. Anyone.

Cleve just broadened his smile. "My name is Cleveland Trewe, gentlemen, and it appears there's a misapprehension about these proceedings, regarding the ownership of this establishment. It just happens this saloon belongs to me. I bought it not long ago, from the previous owner, you see."

The skull-faced man giggled. His eyes lit up so he seemed almost human. "It's *yorn?* But how thangs change! It's *our'n* now!"

"Tell you what," said Tucky. His face not changing. His eyes burning. "If you want a job, we need a bartender. We got us a fiddle player already." He dropped his hand to the butt of his gun. "How 'bout you take off your gunbelt, put on an apron, and pour us all a drink?"

"Boys, I fear I have a job already. Let me see now . . ." Cleve fished in his coat pocket, took out the U.S. Deputy Marshal's badge, and tossed it on the bar.

As Cleve had figured it, the eyes of the three horse thieves flicked to the badge as it rang on the wood—just long enough for Cleve to skin back his coat and draw his Colt.

As he drew, he called out, *"Where's Luis?"*

It happened fast.

Luis Diaz stepped through the open door behind the bar, shouting, *"Levanta t'manos!"* as Droopy-lip grabbed at the shotgun.

Tucky went for his Smith & Wesson revolver, and Skullface stumbled back, dragging at his gun, his face taut with panic as he turned to face Luis.

Cleve was already squeezing off a shot aimed at Tucky's hateful eyes—he was only a long two steps away and could scarcely miss. Tucky's gun cleared leather and fired spasmodically into the floor as his head snapped back, Cleve's bullet smashing through his forehead. Before Tucky fell, Cleve was tracking the Colt to Droopy-lip, firing twice as the outlaw swung the shotgun around. Droopy-lip spun under the impact and the shotgun blast punched a hole in the ceiling.

Luis and Skullface were firing at almost the same moment as Tucky slumped to the floor and Droopy-lip clutched at the bar and then fell over backward, coughing blood as he died, the shotgun clattering beside him.

Cleve saw Skullface on his knees, hugging his belly, gut-shot. Luis was standing there, behind the bar, looking dazed, blinking in the pall of gun smoke.

The man with the pockmarked face fell, tipping forward.

Mickal was standing as if frozen in the corner, bow trembling over his violin, his mouth open, his eyes wide.

A little rainwater struck Cleve's hand. He looked up.

"*Hellfire!* Got to have the roof fixed now. He blew a hole right on through." He looked at the floor. "Hole in the damned floor too. Why the hell did I ever buy a saloon?"

He holstered his gun, looked for Luis—and saw him collapse behind the bar.

Cleve hurried around the bar and found Luis lying in a puddle of blood.

Chapter 15

Cleve was kneeling beside Luis, using a clean kerchief to stanch Luis's wound. The bullet had struck under Luis's left shoulder, maybe low enough to injure the vaquero's lungs.

Luis's eyes were closed. His face was stiffened into a grimace.

"You still with us, Luis?" he asked softly.

"Sí." Little more than a grunt. "*Lento* . . . too slow . . ."

"You got your man, Luis. I was the one who was too slow. I should've nailed that son of a bitch before he shot you."

Mickal put the violin on the bar and came to look over Cleve's shoulder. "You have bandages, Mr. Trewe?"

"Field dressings, in my saddlebag. You know my horse? It's behind that new house they're building."

"Yes! I'll go!" Mickal ran out of the saloon.

Blood was seeping from under the handkerchief.

"You . . ." Luis winced at the pain and then went on. ". . . forget about taking them . . . alive?"

"Didn't work out that way."

"Like those men by the canyon . . ."

Cleve sighed. "Not having much luck taking folks alive lately. Now you just save your wind."

"Who . . . who's here?" called someone from the door of the saloon.

Cleve thought he knew that voice. "That you, Reverend?"

"Mr. Trewe!"

Oliver Blevin looked over the bar at them. "That's young Diaz, isn't it?"

"Anybody good at doctoring in this town?" Cleve asked. "Maybe a barber for pulling out lead?"

"Mrs. Rinaldi has more knowledge than many a physician. Who shot these men? Whose badge is this?"

"That's my badge. Just go get the woman, Blevin, if she's all we've got. Go on!"

Blevin scurried out. Cleve heard him say, "Oh, I am sorry!" as he collided with Mickal. Then more scuffling footsteps and Mickal rushed up with the small leather bag of field dressings.

"Hold him still!" Cleve ordered. Mickal hurried behind the bar and complied. Cleve reached to a shelf under the bar, drew out a bottle of Bolivar's Boston Bourbon, removed the handkerchief, and poured the spirits on the wound. Luis gasped with pain. He squirmed as Cleve drew out the field bandages, and tied them in place. "Hold still, boy, you'll do yourself a harm."

Cleve poured some whiskey into a beer cup and handed it to Mickal. "Get some water from that pump out back. Half water, half whiskey, and bring it back here."

Cleve folded his coat up, lifted Luis's head, and slid the coat under it. Luis groaned and Cleve decided he was going to have some whiskey himself, before long. The long ride, the gunfight. Luis shot badly. Cleve needed a drink.

Mickal returned with the cup. "Here it is, boss!"

Given water and whiskey, Luis eased a mite, and Cleve took a pull on the whiskey bottle and then passed it to Mickal.

Here I am tending Luis, he thought. *And Berenice is tending Alice. I should be there instead.*

Coming here, he'd had to kill three men—and maybe hadn't done all he could do for Alice. But what *could* he do?

Anyway, he had taken an oath. Berenice knew that you take an oath if they swear you in. An oath, a swearing-in, of such rituals was civilization bound together. A man had a responsibility . . .

To his family first, Berenice said. He heard her say it in his mind, clear as a bell.

Mickal passed Cleve the bottle. He had another swallow.

Strident footsteps, and then a woman was staring down at him. The widow, Catalina Rinaldi, in a long black dress. She was a thin, graceful woman, of perhaps forty; a woman of quick motions and long black hair. Her nose was Roman, her small red lips just now pressed primly; her large dark eyes emanated disapproval. "There are three men dead here! Do men never tire of killing? Always killing! And there—whiskey in your hand!" She had a slight Spanish accent. "You men drinking your strong spirits, it is no wonder you are always half mad to pull a trigger!"

"Well—ma'am," Cleve began, standing. He hastily put the bottle aside. "That is—I'm a U.S. Deputy Marshal." He picked up the badge and put it on. "Those men were murderers. Luis here is my deputy."

"And you could not find help, to surround these men, to take them in peacefully?"

Cleve grunted. He might have done it that way. But it would have taken time to get more men to surround the saloon. He had wanted to get this done with, so he could get a doctor for Alice. "Well, you see, my wife . . . our baby . . . I had to—"

"Enough!" She came around the bar and looked Luis over. "Bring me a door off its hinges, so we can carry this man to a bed. We shall take him to my cabin. I will remove the bullet there—I have many instruments. Bring the whiskey—it will do to cleanse my knives. But drink no more of it!"

On hearing the news, Delbert Hawthorn and his father just stared at Harl. Marske didn't react. He just stood at the window, looking out at the horses.

"You sure about this, Harl?" Hawthorn asked.

His nephew nodded, lowering his heavy body into the parlor chair so it creaked under the weight. "Yes sir. I was leaving Gunderson's, I heard a hatful of gunshots from the saloon. Out comes that bartender, running for help. He told me the U.S. Marshal's shot some horse thieves. I say, what U.S. Marshal? He says it's Cleve Trewe."

"But Beaman is the marshal for this territory!"

"Perhaps he meant deputy marshal," Delbert suggested.

Asa grunted. "Most likely. I wonder if those men were really horse thieves or was that Trewe's whim. Maybe he just didn't like their looks. What else did that fiddling bartender say?"

"He was impatient to do his errand, and he run off."

Marske turned to face them. There was a tautness in his slightly cockeyed face. "If Trewe says they're horse thieves, that's what they are."

Asa frowned at him. "You some kind of pardner of this interloper now?"

"I'm a good judge of character. He's that kind of man. I'm not like that. I wish I was." He took a tobacco pouch from his shirt pocket and set to making a smoke. "But howsomeever, first chance I get to face him, I'll kill him."

Harl snorted. "I had a look in that saloon. Those men had guns in their hands. There's a shotgun hole in the roof, and a bullet hole in the floor. Looked to me, he shot two of those men and face-on, too. Now if he can do that, why be such a fool as to face him? Dry-gulch him, that's the way."

Del felt a pang of shame for his cousin and he blurted, "Shouldn't the Hawthorns fight with honor?" The moment he said it, he cringed inside, knowing how his father would respond.

"Delbert," his father said, between gritted teeth. "Our honor stands as long as I say it does! I shall burn those damned *Faerie Queene* books of yours!"

"*Faerie Queene!*" Harl laughed. "What the hell is he reading?"

"Edmund Spenser," said Del in a low voice. "His allegory of the virtues of . . . of honorable men." He shrugged. "I rather prefer Malory's *Le Morte d'Arthur,* for, ah . . ." His voice trailed off as he noted the men staring at him.

"Remind me to burn that Malory too," Hawthorn said sourly. "You want to make yourself useful, boy, you'll scout the Trewe herd, get a good sense of who's guarding it. I have me an idea what to do about it . . ."

"What would that be?" Del asked, thinking of Mrs. Trewe.

"Never you mind. You're no good in a fight but you'll do for a spy." Hawthorn turned to Marske, who was lighting his quirly. "What's this about you facing off with Trewe, Marske? That your idea of a plan?"

"I'm good with this here," Marske said, slapping the gun tied down at his hip. "Better than any man I ever come across. I'll take care of Trewe my way. I'm healed up enough to ride. But I'll pick my time."

Hawthorn shrugged. "I'll tell you what it's time for—we got to set those Denk brothers to work."

"They been wailing on about being locked in that old barn," Harl said, chuckling.

"Marske—you take charge of those men. But don't turn your back on them."

"Foolish to hire a man you can't turn your back on," said Marske.

"You calling me a fool?" asked Del's father, his voice serrated.

Marske was unruffled. "What good am I if I don't tell you when you're making a mistake? The Denks aren't going to do what you tell them just because you took their damn chains off. You got to put a carrot in front of those donkeys."

Hawthorn considered. Then he gave a single nod. "I'll give them a taste of gold. A hundred dollars each in gold eagles. You tell them there'll be ten times that coming, if they stand by me all the way. Make them understand—we got to trust them, if they want that gold."

"What exactly will you be paying them for?" Del asked.

"Gun work. The smart kind."

"What I heard, they got a strange way to work, them Denk brothers," Harl said. "They kill *together*. The way coyotes do, coming from both sides. Always working together against one man. They killed seven men for money."

"Sounds like that method gets the job done," Marske allowed.

Hawthorn stretched and went to the liquor cabinet. "The time is coming for the Denks to earn their keep. But it's got to be set up shrewd and smart."

* * *

The baby coughed and her breathing came all raspy.

Berenice was sitting in the deepening darkness, holding Alice in her arms. They were in the Conestoga, Berry cross-legged on blankets laid over the wooden planks, her back against a keg of salt. The baby was swaddled warmly in thick cotton fabric, and Berry had a woolen comforter around her shoulders. She hugged Alice to her, and said, "Mama's here . . . Mama's here . . ."

The wind snapped the wagon's canvas. The darkness seemed to fill the covered wagon like rising water. Cradling the baby in her left arm, Berry reached to the empty crate beside her and lifted the chimney from the oil lamp.

Alice coughed and feebly kicked her feet.

Berry set the glass chimney carefully aside, felt around for the matches. She found one and struck it on the crate's top. The match flared like a mockery of hope, and she lit the lamp. She blew out the match, turned up the lamplight a trifle, and replaced the chimney. Now Berenice and Alice were in a little globe of dull gold light tinged with blue. Berry looked down at her infant daughter, seeing her more clearly in the lamplight, and what she saw made her heart plunge into a deeper darkness. Alice's lips were crusted; one of her eyes was cracked open, the other closed. The baby arched her back a little and whimpered.

Then Berry said, "If you leave this world, I shall go with you, my Alice, my love."

A cold, probing breeze whisked through the wagon, making Berry shiver. "Perhaps we should have stayed in the dugout. It's warmer there. Perhaps Mama made a foolish decision." She was speaking to comfort Alice with the sound of her voice. The baby yet lived, but Alice seemed in some distant place, locked in fever, her skin roughly dry, her neck swollen. Her eyes saw nothing. It was as if she were already halfway into the next world.

"You see, Alice, one so often hears that damp places give rise to sickness. One thinks of yellow fever. But it was warmer in the soddy, though dirty and damp, and perhaps that was better."

Forced to live in a hole dug in a hillside. What had she expected, out here? The frontier was a savage land. Berenice had gloried in its wildness, once. She hadn't seen it as savage then, but as another sort of order. But now she saw it as pitiless, chaotic, and eager for the kill.

"I don't think it was the damp that made you ail, my love," she said softly. "That was quite unempirical and irrational of me—as happens to people seized by emotion. I think you took sick when Mama carried you into the wickiups of our Washoe friends, and someone there was ailing. I left when I saw that child coughing. But it was too late."

Teresa and Marigold had gone out some time ago to look for certain herbs. Why were they not back?

"My sweet Alice, if you go, I will carry you into the soddy, knock down its beams, and pull it down on both of us. We shall be together, and sleep side by side . . . How I used to love to wake up and find you sleeping next to me . . . How often you made me wake up to feed you! I didn't mind at all . . . Yes, most assuredly, you and I will go into the great sleep together . . ."

But would that not be a great cruelty to wreak upon Cleve?

And yet—he had gone away from her, when she needed him here, had he not? Because Marshal Beaman had sworn him in. *And once Cleve takes an oath, he pursues it like a madman . . .*

No, she could not be so cruel to him. He would lose his wife and daughter at once. However, there was every possibility that she would die of the ailment herself. She felt weak and listless, and perhaps diphtheria was beginning to take hold of her. If she died of it, Cleve could not blame her . . .

It occurred to Berry that she was thinking like her brother Duncan in one of his black moods. "Alice, I'm afraid I'm becoming like Duncan. You have not had the pleasure of meeting your uncle. He works for your granddad, in Colorado now I believe. Duncan was prone to slide into a mire of melancholy. And yet he has always been wealthy, and comfortable. And had no sick little babes to weep for . . ."

She had wept only once since Alice had fallen sick, then she made herself stop.

"I mustn't . . . I mustn't . . ."

"Mustn't what?" someone said.

Berry looked up to see Teresa coming into the back of the wagon, carrying a little lunch pail in her hand.

"Oh, Berry—you look so pale, and your eyes . . . ! Have you eaten?"

"No, my stomach is quite closed against food. Teresa"

—Berenice steadied her voice and refused the tears that were burning her eyes—"she is dying."

"We'll just see about that." Teresa sat down beside Berry. "I have some chicken broth, and we found the echinacea. It may help. First, she shall take some and I shall insist you have some as well."

"But—she will not have it! She will not even take the breast, I can barely get a spoonful of water into her!"

"I have something . . ." She tugged a little cone of leather out of her dress pocket. "I use these when a patient is too sick to willingly take broth. It's like a funnel of leather. I squeeze the broth through here, you see. First I pinch it shut, then . . ."

Soon, she was able to force a little of the broth down Alice's tortured throat. But the baby coughed and squealed in pain and tried to draw back.

"She took a little," Teresa said. "We shall try again in a few minutes."

"Yes." She looked at Alice and thought her baby seemed so very close to death. Her only other child, with her previous husband, had been stillborn. And then her husband had died in a mining accident. "Your mama is a magnet for calamity, Alice," she murmured.

And Berenice thought, *Where is Cleve? Why isn't he here?*

Chapter 16

Cleve sat in a dark place, next to a wounded man with a bandage on his chest. Luis was stretched on a cot, dozing from the laudanum. The room was dimly lit and smelled sour. Against the walls of the big log shed were casks; some for fermenting wine, some for vinegar. Wooden boxes contained apples, elderberries, and blackberries.

Reaching to the lantern, Cleve turned the flame up brighter, then bent over Luis Diaz to have a closer look at him. Luis had some color in his cheeks, and he was breathing regularly. Good signs.

Cleve had been impressed by Mrs. Rinaldi's skill in cleanly removing the bullet and closing the wound. All the while, Cleve had pressed down on Luis's chest above the bullet hole, to hold blood back from escaping the broken veins. It took him back to the war, to his time volunteering in the surgical tents after a battle. The lives saved, and the lives lost.

"You know this work too, I see," Mrs. Rinaldi had said, as she began sewing the wound shut.

Cleve had said nothing. But now he thought, *I know it too well.*

He sat back on the keg of elderberry wine that served him as a seat. Cleve wished he could crack that keg and serve himself out a jar of wine. He was tired and felt the deep bitterness that came whenever he had to kill someone. Two men, this time. The world was better without them, but it always made him feel low afterward.

He should get up and get on with his mission. Sling Tucky's body over a horse, transport him to Independence, make his report. But it was a couple days to ride there, and the same to ride back to the ranch. To Berenice. To Alice. Maybe he couldn't do anything for Alice, but if he hurried, he could be there when the little one died. So Berenice wouldn't be alone.

But the cruel truth was, if Alice was going to die, it'd most like happen before he got home.

Hellfire. He'd gotten the job done. He hadn't had a chance to serve a warrant, exactly—but he'd dealt with Tucky and his gang. Bloodily—but legally. Maybe he could write a letter, gct some witnessing, and somehow—

"Cleve!" said the Reverend Blevin, coming to the door. He had his sleeves rolled up. His hands appeared to be dyed purple and he wore a long, stained purple apron.

"Keep your voice down," Cleve growled. "The boy's sleeping."

Blevin crossed his arms and spoke more softly. "How does he fare?"

"Good chance to pull through. How'd you come to

be here, Blevin? I thought you went off to Kerosene Corners."

"Ah! I did." His voice was laden with sadness. "I found my old friend in the bottom of an abandoned mining shaft. It seems he stumbled in, fell fifty feet, and broke his neck. The town, such as it be, teems with gunmen and claim jumpers and the like. No one was the least interested in my starting a church. So, I made my way here, and heard that Mrs. Rinaldi was looking for workers. That was two days ago . . ."

"Where'd she learn surgery?"

"Oh!" He stood up straighter. "Catalina Rinaldi— what a life she has had!" There was something in his voice when he said that name. Cleve smiled.

"When she was a very young woman," Blevin went on excitedly, "there was a rebellion in Spain led by a General Prim—she's from Andalusia in Spain, you see. Her brothers joined the uprising and came back sorely wounded. She assisted a surgeon who saved them, and went on to help others wounded in the fight. She became something of a nurse, often called upon by folk needing help. Her grandmother had taught her some folk medicine, and she began to learn more whenever she could. She sent medicine over to your friends the Indians! I heard it helped that Paiute boy who was sick. The prime ingredient in the tonic was a sort of mold—"

"Mold!" Cleve didn't like the sound of that. He knew of cases where mold could lead to dire lung diseases and hallucinations.

"I know it sounds like madness. But we got word the

boy survived. A baby died but it didn't receive this treatment."

"A baby!" Cleve went cold.

"Yes, the Washoe baby."

"Oh!" He could not help but feel relief it wasn't Alice, though it seemed churlish.

"Catalina reckons this is a particular mold kills bacteria. She cultures it on some particular grain. I can't recall which grain, but the mold is of the genus Penicillium."

"She is one of those healer grannies?"

"Why, she's rather more . . . more practical and precise than that. And she is *most* impressively learned! She has collected medicaments from distant places like Egypt and Persia. She's learned a good deal from the Indians too."

"She and Berenice would have much to talk about. The name Rinaldi—that's Italian, I believe, not Spanish."

"Yes—she fell in love with an Italian sailor, Giuseppe Rinaldi, the purser and ladings man, who was visiting Cádiz. She eloped with him, on the ship, and the captain married them. They left the ship in San Diego and came out to Kearsarge, for Rinaldi had dreams of striking it rich in silver and copper. But he had a tendency to overindulge in whiskey, which led to an argument in a saloon—whereupon he was shot dead."

"Explains her fierce dislike of strong spirits and drunken gun wielders. Yet she sells wine."

"Her father was a vintner, and she knows the trade. But she's quite firm on drink in moderation, and will not distill hard spirits." With a trace of sheepishness, he added, "She is teaching me how a man can drink in moderation!"

Cleve nodded. From his experience, some men could learn that, and other men couldn't. "She seems a rather, ah, *stern* woman . . ."

"Heavens, no! You should see her with the town children! She's like a second mother. And sometimes, she's a schoolmarm, quite unpaid, teaching reading and figures. She's a *saint,* truly, Cleve, if you only knew her better . . ." He trailed off, seeing the wry look on Cleve's face.

"A saint! You surely are smitten, for a man who's only known a lady for two days."

"*Smitten?*" He cleared his throat. "Don't be absurd. That is . . . well, I don't deserve her . . ."

"She's a bit older than you, is she not?"

Blevin scowled. "And what of it?"

Cleve snorted. "Yep. Smitten. You know, when I met Berenice, I knew then and there. So I do understand. But Oliver, you're a Protestant preacher. The lady is likely Catholic."

"Oh, well, you know, possibly I could . . . but of course, it's not really a matter of . . . that is to say . . ."

"Oliver!" called Mrs. Rinaldi, coming to the door. "Do move aside, please, I must examine our young vaquero."

"Yes, certainly, Catalina!" Blevin said breathlessly.

He stepped aside and she came in to bend over Luis, taking his pulse with one hand, touching his forehead with the other. "He does have a touch of fever."

Cleve nodded. "Man takes a bullet, often gets a bit

feverish from the shock of it. But I don't think he's in danger of gangrene. You did a good job."

"You were in the war?" she asked, standing up.

"Cleve was a major in the Army of the Republic, Catalina," Blevin said. "He was—"

"That's sufficient, Reverend," Cleve interrupted. "Ma'am . . . I have a little girl, just an infant. Alice is her name. My wife believes Alice has diphtheria."

She nodded gravely. "The Indians had two cases of it."

"The Reverend here tells me you've got some treatments that could be of help . . . A mold of some kind . . ."

"One flask remains. It is difficult to produce the right mold and even then it is not always strong enough to be effective."

Cleve recalled that the Egyptians had used a mold to fight infection. It hadn't hurt Cliffy the Paiute boy. "Ma'am, if you'll give me some of that tonic, I'll pay you anything you ask."

"I have some, yet. I will charge you only what I ask of the townsfolk. Some pay me in chickens. The child will need the tonic soon." She straightened and wagged a finger at Blevin. "Oliver, you really must get back to stirring. The pot must be stirred for half an hour longer."

"Yes, certainly, Catalina!" He scurried off.

"*Gracias, señora . . .*" said Luis huskily.

"Ah!" she said, taking his hand. "I'm afraid we have awakened you. How do you feel?"

"*Muy bueno. Me has salvado la vida, y estoy en deuda contigo.*"

Cleve snorted. "*Muy bueno?* That might be shining

it up some. But you'll do, I reckon. Luis—might you feel well enough to read a speck, and sign something for me? I need to write up what happened to Tucky. It requires you and Mickal to witness it."

"Sí, Jefe. This much I can do."

"And here is Javier," Mrs. Rinaldi said, giving a rare smile as another man appeared in the doorway holding his yellow and black sombrero in his hands. Javier was a stocky, bearded middle-aged man in a red serape, blue jeans, and laborer's heavy boots. He spoke rapidly and gently in Spanish to Luis too fast for Cleve to follow. Something about praying for Luis's health and salvation. Luis expressed his gratitude.

The older Mexican turned to Catalina Rinaldi. "Señora, the bodies are ready for the earth—but there is yet one more. Señor Giuntoli, out riding—he has found another man shot dead. He brings the body here on a mule. This man was shot in the back."

"The corpse is a white man in a rawhide jacket?" Cleve asked. "Scarred lip?"

Javier gave Cleve an unsettlingly deep look of appraisal. "Sí."

"Luis and I found his body, didn't have time to bring him along. One of the Tucky bunch, shot in the back by his own gang."

Luis confirmed it was so, and Mrs. Rinaldi said, "Then we will bury him with the others. Mr. Gunderson will pay you to dig the graves, Javier."

Cleve interposed, "One less grave to dig, ma'am. I've got to take Tucky's remains to Independence. Coroner there will have to see it, along with my paperwork and the tintype, to confirm this is the man—I have the warrant here."

"Very well, we will bury the others here. I will trust you on this warrant. You wear the badge." She turned to Javier, "Can you go to Independence tomorrow to get our supplies and the mail?"

"With pleasure, Señora."

This man was going to Independence in the morning? Cleve was very interested to hear that.

Mrs. Rinaldi realized she should introduce them. "Oh—Deputy Trewe, this is Javier Sanchez. He's our unofficial postman, our undertaker, and a very good orchardist. He's—what is it you ranchers say? He's a *good hand* at everything he does."

Cleve said, "Mr. Sanchez, I wonder if I could pay you something to take Tucky's body along to Independence. Say fifty dollars."

"Yes, sí, I can do that."

"I'm afraid you'll be spending the night with a dead man in your camp. But it can't be helped."

Javier shrugged. "The dead speak no foolishness. They give witness to the great silence, that is above all things."

Cleve was a bit taken aback by this. "I hadn't quite thought of it that way. Can't say I disagree."

Mrs. Rinaldi chuckled. "Javier is something of a philosopher, you see."

"And there's a letter to go, too," Cleve went on. "It'll be addressed to the U.S. Marshal and the town sheriff, explaining what happened to Tucky and the others. And there'll be a document from witnesses with it. If you could take those documents to Marshal Beaman, if he's still in town, I'd be obliged. I'll add in another twenty dollars for that. He'd be at The Owens River Hotel. If he's left town, give it to the sheriff, along with the body."

Javier nodded. *"No te preocupes, me agrada hacerlo."*

"Gracias. I have the new ranch, on what used to be Drake Samuels's land. You folks are all welcome to visit with us anytime."

"But you will not be going to Independence?" Mrs. Rinaldi asked.

"No, ma'am. It's true the law would probably prefer me to go right back, with the body and the documents. But I've got to get back to my wife. I want to bring the medicine, and see how the baby is."

"Yes, just so. I will get you the tonic . . . You should get it to the *nina* as soon as possible . . ."

A grand steamship plied the Sacramento River, chugging slowly through the night, the glow of many lanterns bejeweling its lines and laying gleams along its wake. The ship's two big chimneys glowed at the top with a diffused firelight that turned the black coal smoke hellish red.

Seated with his father in a window booth of the Gentleman's Club of Sacramento, Del admired the stately power of the steamship, and his engineer's mind went to envisioning its pistons pumping away, turning the great shaft that spun the paddle wheels. He had read a monograph suggesting that the oil of petroleum could be used with more efficiency than coal, providing a greater concentration of fuel to heat energy, and he wondered how that sticky black fluid could be made to burn evenly enough within the engine.

"Boy, what are you woolgathering about this time?" demanded Asa Hawthorn.

"Hmm? Just looking at the steamship, Papa."

"Now tell me this—do you recall the part you are to play when we meet with the Paytons? Grenville and Jephthah will be here any minute." He licked his lips and looked nervously at the door.

Del found his father's nervousness fascinating. It was not normal for the old man. Usually, Asa Hawthorn was the soul of confidence. Del found it strangely relaxing to learn that his father was afraid of the Paytons.

"*Do* you remember, Delbert?"

"Remember? Oh—about the riverine engineering. The diversion to the mines. All the rest. Yes. I have done as you've asked. I have it written up, in fact." He patted his coat pocket. "I have the plans with me."

"Here they come," Hawthorn said, sitting up straighter.

Grenville Payton and Jephthah Payton, the elder brother, did not seem especially imposing nor minatory. They both wore tailored suits, Grenville in light blue silk, Jephthah in snuff-colored tweed; Grenville in a blue-black homburg topper, his brother in a sulfur-colored top hat. Head of the Payton Land Consortium, Grenville looked to be a man in his thirties; Jephthah, a county judge, seemed in his forties, his neatly clipped beard and upcurled mustaches showing some gray.

In Jephthah's expression, as he tipped his hat and seated himself, was a smugness that seemed imprinted in the lines of his face, and settled in his pale blue eyes; Grenville's round face, with shaggy eyebrows and hooded eyes, seemed imprinted with impatience. But what of it?

Nothing to fear, surely, Del told himself.

After the greetings, the men engaged in polite banter about Jephthah's new carriage, and the Hawthorn ranch. The older men drank cognac; Del drank a little port. Hawthorn told them how his two thousand five hundred head of cattle fared; how he was experimenting with fifty head of black Angus, purchased from George Grant himself, to enhance his investment in longhorns.

Grenville was soon tapping his fingers with exasperation as Jephthah described a racing horse he'd just purchased.

At last, Grenville Payton turned with almost savage suddenness to Del and said, "But I am *most* curious to know what this quiet young gentleman has been up to!"

Del blanched. He swallowed and drew the folded papers from his pocket. "I do have this . . ."

"What have we here?" Jephthah asked, fixing reading spectacles to the bridge of his nose.

"Here, sir," said Del, with a growing understanding of his father's nervousness around the Paytons, "we have my copy of a map . . ." He unfolded it. "I will say that the county's charting of Sweet River Valley, the river's tributaries, attendant watersheds, and especially areas to the south beyond the fixed property line, is not entirely accurate. I would recommend a new survey."

They stared at him. Then Jephthah chuckled. "That's quite a mouthful for so young a fellow!"

"Get on with it, Delbert," Hawthorn grumbled.

Clearing his throat, Del said, "Here in yellow, I have added the first planned, ah, alterations my father has in mind."

"They are exactly what we spoke of, Grenville!" Hawthorn interposed hastily.

"Yes, yes, go on!" Grenville said, eyeing the map.

Del ran the tip of his finger along the yellow lines. "Here is the pipeline for hydraulic mining. You'll note five farms and three ranches in the area that would be affected. No doubt their property would have to be purchased . . ."

"Affected?" Grenville raised his shaggy eyebrows. "How do you mean?"

Del licked his lips and then plunged in. "Hydraulic mining would change the water drainage in the area, possibly directing mud and great clouds of dust on adjacent properties—in some cases the mining would be directly *on* their property and it would destroy pasturage and . . ." He noticed the three men were staring at him in stony hostility. ". . . and cropland."

"We will, of course, buy them out," said Grenville, shrugging.

"What about redirecting the river for the new townsites?" Jephthah asked. "Is it feasible?"

Ah yes, Del thought. *The townsites.*

"Diverting an entire river might take years," said

Del, warming to his subject. "You would probably do better with a series of canals upstream which would drain the water southwest, to the townsites, and to the farmlands that will serve them. Feasible pathways are here on the map, in blue. Perhaps the canals might be ready by the time you have the townships built. I assume . . . ah . . ."

"Yes?" asked Grenville impatiently.

"I assume that you have plans drawn up for those townships. Perhaps if I could see something more specific . . ."

"Have you ever worked up anything on this scale before?" asked Jephthah.

"I have not," Del admitted.

"We have plans, but they are not to be shown about as yet," said Grenville. "We envisage a herd of fifteen to twenty thousand head occupying most of Sweet River Valley. We will need *all* the grazeland for that. We further envisage a great center for slaughterhouses and leatherworks, which will need a multitude of employees. They will need somewhere to live, you see. And we intend to provide them that land, that housing, at a good price."

"It's . . . a conception on an, ah, ambitious scale," Del said, managing not to stutter. He was envisioning it himself—and he was appalled.

"I think we can buy up the rest of the land quite handily," said Hawthorn, "but this ranch of Trewe's occupies an awkward position. It straddles right across where we'll need the canals. And he has a good piece of the graze too. He refuses to sell. At any price, he claims."

"You said you had that matter handled," said Grenville in a low voice, glaring at Hawthorn.

"He proves to be not without allies. U.S. Marshal Beaman, for one. Cleveland Trewe, you see, has been made a United States Deputy Marshal."

Jephthah allowed a trace of alarm to invade his self-satisfaction. "Indeed! That is most awkward."

Hawthorn nodded. "It gives him pull. He is, well, quite a *formidable* man too. And he has well-armed cowboys. As well as a number of rather, ah, savage Indians who are loyal to him."

"If he is in the way," said Grenville in a low, acid voice, "then take him *out* of the way."

"There were three men sent to deal with the matter," Hawthorn said. "They're now lying in a morgue. But . . . I have other arrows in my quiver."

"Did Jephthah not see that those arrows were *released* from your quiver?" Grenville said. "Use them!"

He means the Denk brothers, Del realized. So, it was Judge Jephthah Payton who'd gotten them released into the custody of Asa Hawthorn.

"We're awaiting the right moment," said Del's father. "But they will be used."

"You are a partner in our great vision, Asa," said Grenville, "but only on sufferance. If you wish to be a full partner, see that this matter is taken care of."

"Certainly, yes, gentlemen. You may rest assured of it."

"There is a more elegant option," Jephthah said thoughtfully, signaling for another brandy. "These extreme measures might attract too much attention, seeing as the man is a deputy in the marshal service."

"What other option?" Hawthorn asked.

"You might *sue* Cleve Trewe. You can try to establish that both Drake Samuels and Trewe are in the wrong—that the land belongs to you after all. That the deed was not all it appeared to be."

"That might be difficult to prove," said Hawthorn. "For, in fact, the deed—"

Jephthah silenced him with a raised hand. "There are no facts established as yet—and we . . . *you* . . . can challenge the deed." He gave an unctuously self-satisfied smile. "And then . . ." He paused till the waitress had brought him his drink and departed. "And then you must see to it that litigation falls before the best *judge* in this matter."

Asa Hawthorn's eyes lit up. "I see! And that would be—"

Again, the raised hand. The silence. "No need to say it aloud," said Judge Jephthah Payton. He raised his glass. "Cheers, gentleman. To a great and grand undertaking!"

And Del saw Berenice Trewe in his mind's eye, asking, *What have you done, Delbert Hawthorn? What have you done?*

Chapter 17

Riding through the breezy, misty night, Cleve pushed Ulysses as hard as he could take it.

By the time Cleve cantered up to the Conestoga, Ulysses was sweating, panting, and missing his stride.

Cleve dismounted near the crackling campfire, patting the horse's wet neck, saying, "Sorry, old friend. It's all for Alice. She needs it quick."

Milt was kneeling by the fire, working up a pot of soup. He stood up, looking at the horse. "Boss, 'pears you were in some kind of a lather to get here!"

"Got my reasons," Cleve said, opening his saddlebag.

Then he stopped and turned to Milt. "The baby. You looked in on her?"

"Heard her crying just a minute ago."

Cleve let out a breath of relief. Alice was still alive. "Are they in the soddy?"

"Mrs. Trewe and the little one are in the wagon. Where's Luis?"

"We had a shooting affray with the Tucky bunch.

They're dead. Luis did his part but he caught a bullet. Going to pull through, looks like."

"Good God! Wasn't you just in a gunfight some handful of days ago?"

Cleve grimaced. First Wild Dog's bunch and then Tucky's. One after the other. It had the pace of war. Something he'd thought himself done with. Unconsciously, he touched the badge on his vest. "I guess I should have said no to Marshal Beaman. Where's Leon?"

"He's with the herd. No man ever took the job of foreman more serious-like. Sent me over here to watch over the ladies and Alice. Pamahas is cooking for the boys at the camp. What you got there?"

He was looking at the little leather bag Cleve had in his hand.

"Medicine for Alice. Least I hope so. Have you a clean pan over there, something not too big?"

"Sure, right here."

"Fill it halfway with some rainwater from the barrel, will you?"

"Sure will."

Cleve opened the bag, smelling the mold, the myrrh, the crystalline honey, the goldenseal. "She said about one-quarter of the bag would go in two cups of water . . ."

"Who said?" Milt asked, returning with the water in a small tin saucepan.

"Mrs. Rinaldi. There's a couple jars in that bag you can get for me." Cleve put the pan of water over the grill.

"Here you go. How about I put ol' Ulysses in the horse shed? Get that saddle off, give him some water and feed."

"I'd be obliged." Cleve tapped about a quarter of the powder into the pan of water and seethed it over the fire. "He's had scarce any rest today. Best damned horse in California, or anywhere else, by God."

"Come on, old fella," Milt said, leading Ulysses toward a comfortable stall.

"Is that you, Cleve Trewe?" said a woman's voice from the Conestoga.

Cleve didn't look up from the tonic makings. He knew Teresa's voice. "You can see it is," he said, using the tip of his knife to stir the tonic powder. Then he removed it from the fire, watched it steep. One full minute, Mrs. Rinaldi had said. Then add the juice and a couple teaspoons of elderberry wine.

"You making coffee?" Teresa asked, a tinge of accusation in her voice.

"Mrs. Rinaldi gave me a tonic for Alice. Makings of a brew."

"You've been to town?"

"I have."

Teresa came down from the Conestoga and looked over his shoulder. "It smells like . . ."

"Like mold. I know. She's got one that's restorative."

"I've heard of something like that."

"Now . . ." He opened one of the jars and poured in enough juice to dilute it and cool down the mixture. Then he added about two teaspoons from the other jar. The wine would help the baby rest.

"Is that—"

"I don't have time to answer your questions, Teresa,"

he said, knowing he was snappish and not giving a damn. "You can answer one for me. How's the little one?"

"Worse every hour. I've never seen Berenice so quiet."

Cleve stood up and carefully carried the little pan to the wagon. "I hope Alice can get this down."

"I've got a nurse's funnel, we'll get her to take it. Keeping it down is another matter. But if we do it slow . . ."

"Would you bring in those jars, Teresa?"

He carried the pan to the back of the wagon, went up the little retractable wooden steps, and ducked under the canvas.

The wagon smelled of sweat and the indecipherable whiff of sickness. Berenice sat on the floor, Alice in her arms.

"Cleve . . . you're here . . ." Berry said, her voice raspy.

Cleve was staring at Alice, whose eyes were half open; whose tiny lips were ulcerated, whose neck was swollen and purple. Who arched her back and made a croaking sound . . .

So this is what it feels like to be shot through the heart, he thought.

Teresa came over to touch Berry's forehead. "I don't think you're feverish, Berry, how do you feel?"

"Quite weak." Her eyes looked sunken; her lips were cracked. Her hair dirty, straggling.

"Because you haven't eaten. Does your throat hurt?"

"I suppose so. Cleve?"

"Yes, my Berenice?"

"She's dying, Cleve. Alice is dying."

"I . . . she's very sick. Still, I . . ."

"What have you there?"

"Mrs. Rinaldi made this tonic, for Alice."

"Truly? I sent Marigold to find her, been an hour or so . . ."

"She must have taken the road. I came cross-country. I've warmed this up."

"Alice must have it!" Her voice had a harsh edge.

"I thought I should tell you what is in it. You know these things so much better than I. It has myrrh in it, and goldenseal and elderberry essences and—it has mold in it, quite a lot. A special mold Mrs. Rinaldi cultivates. Perhaps, that's not a good idea? You would know better than I."

"But I *don't* know! Cleve . . . she's dying! Give it to her!"

Cleve nodded. "Teresa, where's that funnel for Alice? And then, my Berenice, you shall have some of this elderberry wine. I believe it's just the thing for you . . ."

Jim Crofton dragged Del out of bed around midnight. This filled Del with trepidation. The last time he'd been extracted so heartlessly from his sleep, they'd taken him to that dreadful jailhouse. What now?

"Come on, kid, the old man wants you to see this."

"To see what?" Del asked sleepily, putting on his spectacles.

"His notion of what a man's got to do in this world.

You'll have to figure it out. Get dressed and come right out to the barn. Hear me?"

"How could I not?"

It was a cold night, and Del was glad of his woolen overcoat when he got to the barn. Moonlight-edged clouds wheeled overhead, as he watched Crofton lead a saddled horse out to him. "Asa says you're to ride the pinto."

Del grimaced. The pinto was a spooky, nervous horse, which made Del nervous in turn. But it seemed he was going along on the ride no matter what, so he climbed into the saddle, and waited as Jim got himself a mount.

They rode out alongside the churning river, to the edge of the western edge of the property, finding Asa, Marske, Harl, and the Denk brothers, all on horseback, waiting under a cottonwood tree.

Autumnal cottonwood bolls lay like a drift of snow about them. "I'd be obliged to know what the emergency is," Del said. He was a tenuous sleeper at best, and they'd wakened him from his first good rest in days. He was feeling almost rebellious.

"Isn't an emergency, boy," said Del's father. "It's business. A man's got to be ready to take care of what needs taking care of, night or day. Just you remember that, Delbert!"

Del glanced over at the Denk brothers. In a swatch of moonlight spearing between tree limbs, the Denks looked more than ever like two possums, feral and beyond being understood.

"I reckon that's him," said Marske, pointing at a man

riding on a trail, to the south. The rider's silhouette was of a cowboy, complete with Stetson, Mexican boots, and chaps. He was riding a big buckskin quarter horse.

"What's he done?" Del asked in a whisper, leaning over to Harl.

"Stole that horse."

"You boys," Hawthorn said, turning to the Denks. "Head out and show us what you can do. We'll be right behind you."

As if connected by strings, the Denks turned their horses simultaneously and rode off after the rider. But almost immediately Chadley Denk cut from the course his brother was on, and veered into a stand of oaks alongside the southern side of the trail.

Watching the Denks, Marske said, "Like two hounds set after a boar."

"Let's go," Hawthorn said. Del hurried the pinto to keep up with his father, Crofton, and Marske. Harl cantered along close behind as they took the trail behind Monty Denk. Their hoofbeats pounded loudly on the packed dirt.

The cowboy turned in his saddle, looked back at his pursuers, then leaned forward, spurring his horse to greater exertions.

Monty Denk had a fast horse, and soon caught up, riding up to the cowboy's right side.

Drawing his sidearm, he aimed at the rider, who dodged his mount to the left, heading to the oaks.

Monty aimed at the horse—but Hawthorn shouted, "No, dammit, that's a good horse!"

Nodding, Monty lowered his aim, firing at the ground in front of the buckskin.

The horse shied, bucked the rider up. His Stetson went flying and the cowboy jumped away from the sun-fishing mount, skidding on his boots with the experience of a man who'd ridden broncos.

Monty fired at the cowboy and missed. His target dodged behind a thicket of sage.

Del and the others were reining in as Monty swung his horse to gallop past the fleeing buckskin. The cowboy was now sprinting into the cover of the woods. And the fugitive had his six-gun in hand.

"You see that?" Hawthorn said, breathlessly, as Harl caught up. "The bastard *ran!* He knows he's done wrong!"

"Wrong or right, most men would've rid off, seeing he was chased like that," Marske remarked.

Hawthorn glared at him and then grated, "Come on!"

He led them in a canter after Monty, who vanished into the woods.

Just when they'd reached the line of oaks, a shot and then two more banged from the underbrush. Del caught sight of muzzle flashes in the shadowy scrub.

"Whoa," Hawthorn said, raising a hand. They slowed to a trot, and heard another shot and a scream.

Del rode after the other men into the woods, ducking under branches.

They came upon a thin trail and followed it to a small, fern-grown clearing. Two horses were snorting after their exertion, nibbling at fiddleheads as the Denks, guns in hand, stood over the fallen man.

The cowboy was still alive. He was trying to crawl off into the ferns. His hat was gone now, Del noted, numbly. *Am I still asleep? Is this a dream?*

"Harl, you bring that lantern?" Hawthorn asked. "Get it lit!"

Harl dismounted, took a lantern from its loop on the saddle horn, and lit it with a lucifer. The light threw a quivering pool of yellow, showing the fugitive was shot three times. There were two bullet holes in his side and one in his lower back. He was crawling using his hands and one knee, grunting, cursing.

"Well, you going to let him crawl away, Denk?" Hawthorn demanded, as he climbed down off his horse. Del and Marske dismounted, holding their horses' reins.

Chadley grinned and shot the man in the back of the right leg. The cowboy yowled with pain and turned onto his back, waving his arms as if he could ward off bullets with his hands.

"I just wanted my pay!" he moaned.

"Then you should have waited for it!" Hawthorn growled.

"Said . . . said I could have the horse or my pay . . . The pay's so small . . ."

"Who said it?" Crofton asked.

"Mr. Hawthorn!"

"I said *maybe,*" Hawthorn said. "And I didn't mean right now, no-how!"

"My Lori, she wrote me, said she was in a terrible fix—oh God, I'm dying . . . who's to see to her?"

"Your girl's problems don't give you the right to steal my horses!" Hawthorn growled.

"He's got some good boots on him!" Monty said. "Look like they'll fit me!"

He set to tugging on one of the cowboy's boots, jerking hard on it, eliciting screams of agony.

"Not so much hunting dogs, as a couple of coyotes," observed Marske, in a low voice. "But they done what they know to do." He drew his sidearm, and fired, putting a bullet through the cowboy's forehead, blowing off the top of his head. The dying body kicked and twitched and went still.

"I was going to hang him, dammit!" Hawthorn complained.

"Wouldn't have lived that long," Marske said, holstering the gun.

The sight of the cowboy's shattered skull made Del feel sick, near to heaving.

And he recognized the dead cowboy. He'd seen him around the ranch, but he'd never known the man's name. He avoided socializing with the hands. They didn't seem to have much respect for him, and Del preferred to spend the time reading, or studying the hydrological landscape. Now he felt lost.

"Harl, you and Del find my quarter horse," Hawthorn said.

"Should we not . . . ah . . . bury this man?" Del asked, as Monty finished tugging the boots off the corpse.

"I'll send someone in the morning. They'll bury him right here."

"What was his name?" Del asked, watching as Monty sat down, and began tugging his broken-down boots off.

"His name?" Hawthorn looked at the cowboy, brows knitted. "Reggie Johnson."

"Jensen," Marske corrected, turning away to mount up.

"Never mind his goddamn boots, Monty," Hawthorn snarled. "You boys listen here."

Chadley and Monty turned to look at him, gaping. Monty had one boot on and one off. "I can't have the boots?" Monty asked.

"Yes, yes, but listen up! In the morning, you boys head out to Kerosene Corners. You know where that is?"

Staring, they shook their head, at exactly the same time.

"Marske knows his way there. He'll take you in the morning, he'll set you up there. Wouldn't take much for you to take it over."

"You said you'd pay us," Chadley said.

"When the job's finished. I'll need you for that high-bootin' son of a bitch, Trewe. And maybe for some others that don't want to sign on the dotted line."

"A dotted line?" Monty said, looking puzzled.

"Never you mind, just . . . head out there and wait for word."

"We'll need some pay," Chadley persisted.

"I *gave* you some pay. I'll give you fifty in gold for this Johnson here."

"Jensen," Marske murmured. Crofton chuckled but said nothing.

"Kerosene Corners," said Chadley nodding. "Sure. Why not."

"You'll wait for word out there. You understand? And it just might be I send some work out your way."

"Pa," Del said impulsively, "I would like to be one of the men's burying this man, in the morning."

Hawthorn looked at him in surprise. "Well! Suit yourself!"

"Come on, Delbert," Harl said, mounting up. "Let's look for that buckskin."

Grateful to leave the dead man and the chortling Denk brothers, Del mounted up. Harl led him back along the trail, away from the woods, and they followed the tracks of the buckskin east, as Del remembered Jensen saying, *"My Lori, she wrote me, said she was in a terrible fix . . . who's to see to her?"*

Del shook his head.

Nobody to take care of her now, Reggie Jensen. She's on her own.

Chapter 18

Stiff from sleeping on the wagon boards, Cleve woke a little after daybreak. He had to piss, and he went out in his socks to do it, not wanting to wake Berenice. Done with that, he went to the rain barrel and splashed water on his face. Somewhere in the brushy hilltop over the soddy, birds were singing. The dawn chorus, some called it. The morning air smelled sweet. The sky was cloudless.

But Cleve had a deep, powerful fear that Alice had passed away, during the night.

His heart seemed to stop for a moment when he heard Berry call out, "Cleve! Oh God, Cleve!"

He knew he had to face this. But it scared him more than any battle he'd been in.

Folks lose children every day, he told himself. But that thought didn't help.

Cleve climbed hurriedly back into the Conestoga, turned the lantern light up.

Berenice was sitting up, leaning forward so her hair draped to hide the still child in her arms.

The still child . . . stuck a tiny hand out to her mother's forelock, and tugged at it.

Berenice laughed. She looked up at Cleve, her eyes shining. "She's nursing! She's looking at me! She's pulling my hair! Alice is going to live, Cleve!"

And he saw then that Alice was taking mother's milk, the baby glancing over at him with recognition; with the light of life in those eyes . . .

Sixteen golden days.

No gunmen had showed themselves. No sign of Hawthorn. Instead, Indian summer had come. It was warm, with small clouds skating through a turquoise sky. Autumn leaves fell, since the trees know better than men, and drifted down to wreathe the roots of the cottonwoods and the live oaks. The green grasses began to yellow. Calves were sired, and the cattle grazed contentedly, bedding down quietly at night. Cleve could see the herd growing.

"You know, Leon," Cleve said, as they rode through the pasturage on a warm evening, "I have come to the conclusion that you have bribed Smallwolf, to get him to tell lies for you."

Leon looked at him askance, though he knew Cleve well and could tell he was being joshed. "Is that so? What lies are those?"

"Smallwolf says you've not lost one single cow, not one calf, not a steer or a bull. Almost like you've been doing a fine job as foreman!"

"He said that? Why the dirty liar! I lost *two!* But he brung 'em back."

They both laughed.

Cleve's mood improved every day, for Alice was now scarce showing the signs of having been sick. Her mouth and throat were mostly healed up. Berry was in good health, having taken the mold tonic herself.

Berry had spent hours poring over the procedure for making it. No mere recipe, it required that a kitchen become a mycological laboratory. She declared the proper cultivation of penicillium to be difficult and puzzling, with unpredictable outcomes. But she was determined to write a monograph on the penicillium applications for the *American Medical Association Journal.* She would proudly use her own daughter as a clinical example.

Cleve's outcome with the Tucky gang had been accepted by the law in Independence. Marshal Beaman had sent him notice, by way of Javier, of the outbreak of violence in Kerosene Corners. It appeared to be two gangs fighting for control, and Cleve was happy to let one bad bunch thin out another, for he had as yet received no warrant to serve, no request to investigate. He was content to settle into building up the ranch. Day after day of peace and good weather lifted everyone's spirits.

Tonight, Milt and Pamahas would cook barbacoa for all the hands, and for the Trewe Ranch's guests, including Mrs. Rinaldi, Oliver Blevin, Javier Sanchez, and Mickal Chocholak. It being Sunday, even the Gundersons were to come with their daughter. All the Washoe and the three Paiutes were invited as a matter of course. Cleve regarded them as extended family.

"You reckon Asa Hawthorn has given up?" Leon asked, as they drew up by the remuda. They sat in their saddles, watching Kanaway training two new young horses to be cattle ponies. "I mean—you being a U.S. deputy and all."

Cleve shook his head. "I've got to assume the enemy is merely regrouping." With that on his mind, he said, "You know, I'm thinking of asking a little more help from the Washoe braves. Maybe train 'em some for a coordinated response to an enemy action."

"I remember that sort of training. Only back then, it was *you* I was training against. You and yours anyhow. Round about nineteen years ago. Ain't time got wings!"

"You being trained by the enemy, you can help me train these men."

"Now you're mixed up. You was the enemy, not me."

"Well, we're in the same militia now, Leon."

"Teresa's right about you, Major. She says you're still in the army, you just don't know it."

Barbacoa could be made with just about any meat, but tonight they had a big old boar roasting up, in preparation for the sauce. Their Washoe and Paiute friends had gone on a hunting party and returned with the boar and a number of jackrabbits. The jackrabbits were cooked with vegetables for a stew. Cleve, Berenice, and Alice were watching Pamahas turning the boar over the spit on the big fire built over a knoll within site of the soddy and the covered wagon.

Milt's wife was smiling and talking the while with Berry in the Bannock dialect. Cleve held Alice in his arms and the baby watched and clucked as the big golden red sparks shot up from the log fire.

"It'll be a mite gamy, being boar," said Milt, stirring up his special "Texas sauce" in a pot. "I'll cook it some longer, and put in extry peppers."

The Indians were talking happily around the fire, describing the hunt. The other guests hadn't yet shown up.

Not able to understand most of the Washoe and Paiute spoken, Cleve decided to look in on Milt at the roaring cooking fire. He gently handed Alice to Berry. "Be right back."

He strolled over to Milt. "How long does she have to cook that pig?" Cleve asked. "You and Pamahas and Teresa and even Leon—you've been turning that thing out here for at least four hours. Folks will be coming soon."

"Oh it's a-gittin' there," said Milt. "Just you wait. I've got some taters and wild onions and carrots to go along. Gunderson done run out of store onions."

"I expect you know not all wild onions are edible," Cleve said.

"Pamahas finds them, she knows which is which. Says the ones with the white flowers are right. We eat 'em all the time and I'm still here. You know, she told me that you being a big chief around here, she was surprised you hadn't taken some extra wives."

"Berry has a liking for many Native American customs, but not that one. Does Pamahas expect you to get more wives—maybe to help with the work?"

"No, and I wouldn't want none. Anyway, Pammy says that's mostly for the big chiefs, and I'm not big chief enough."

Cleve laughed. "Me neither. Now as for onions and the like, in the spring, I'll be planting vegetables, we'll have our own garden over there . . ."

Cleve and Milt talked farming and ranching for a time, and then Berry came over, cradling Alice in her arms, and said, "I'm surprised no one from town's here yet!"

"I was told they were coming as a group." He took out his Waltham repeater pocket watch—a gift from General Sherman—and looked at its dial in the light from the fire. "They'll be here in about an hour. I thought you and Alice might want to see the new bunkhouse. I'm going to have to hire some more men, got to put them somewhere. Winter's coming."

"There's nothing I'd like more. You've had people hammering away for three weeks. Every time I thought to look at it, you put me off!"

"I was concerned to keep Alice quiet till we were sure she was fit to move around some. It's a bit of a walk. Tonight, both of you girls are invited." They ambled down the path, past the wagon and the soddy, toward the place where the road circled around the hill.

"The soddy is dry enough now," she said. "It's almost livable. But rain and snow will come and it will get soaked in there again. I envisage a drainage system! I've calculated the precise angularity and hydrological dispersal needed. And indeed, some of what we drain away can be used for bathing and cooking, if we strain it. We shall have to get some good piping, of course, wooden pipes won't last long . . ."

"That will be a great improvement," Cleve said. "We'll be far more comfortable in a dry soddy."

"Look at the stars!" she gasped.

He looked up and was startled by the blaze. Tonight, they seemed too many to fit into the sky. He thought of showing them to Alice, to see how she'd react—but saw she was peacefully asleep in her mother's arms.

"And the Milky Way, Cleve! It dons its best gown for us."

He nodded. "The air is special clear, this night. So many stars—looks like they're going to overflow on us."

"Oh, to go on an expedition to the stars!"

"We'll get there someday. Anyhow, somebody will. It's a long way. *De profundis ad astra.*"

"From the depths to the stars," she said, translating the Latin phrase.

He smiled and thought with pleasure, *I have a wife I can use my Latin on.* "You've barely looked up from Alice and that paper you're writing. Rocking a baby with one hand and scribbling away with the other. Deploying Latin, are you?"

"Certainly, medical men love Latin. What they don't like is medical women. Especially those without formal training. That's why I'm not optimistic that they'll heed us about researching penicillium."

"It sure worked for Alice. I'll be a witness to it! She's stronger every day."

"I'm not letting her out of my sight until she's the strongwoman in the circus."

"Are there strongwomen in circuses? I never noticed any."

"If there aren't, there should be. Look at Pamahas. I believe she could wrestle any of you men to the ground."

"I won't try it, couldn't bear the humiliation." They were walking into deeper shadow now, as pines crowded the road. They could hear the river swishing and purling as they got closer.

"What enormous bats!" Berry cried out.

Cleve looked up and glimpsed them flitting against the starry backdrop, swishing jaggedly about, pursuing insects. "I wonder how they winter?"

"They hibernate. I'd love to find their hibernacula, and have a closer look, if I can do it without disturbing them. You see how big they are? I really think they might be mastiff bats, like we saw in the Yosemite."

"Here's the river," Cleve said.

"You put the men's quarters over on the river?"

"The water's handy. Cowboys don't like to spend a lot of time carrying buckets."

"And there is the bunkhouse! Are they always so big?"

"Why, I intend to hire a great many more men. We'll triple the size of the herd next year. Come and have a closer look. Here's a lamp . . ." He took the kerosene lamp off the porch, lit it with the matches he'd left for that purpose, and led her into the house.

"Why—it has stone sidings! A fireplace! I'm beginning to envy your cowboys! Where are the bunks?

"The furnishings will be along. Couldn't get the sleeping arrangements in as yet. We do have one or two things." He lifted the lantern higher so she could see an article of furniture in the corner, near the door to the kitchen.

Berenice gasped. "That's a . . . that's for a . . ."

"That's for Alice, dear. A bassinet, made of wicker. Indian weavery. I'm afraid there's been something of a conspiracy . . ."

Berenice spun on her heel and pointed accusingly at him. "Why, you charlatan! You playacting fraud! You've been calling this a bunkhouse and it's . . ."

He bent and kissed her lightly, and said, "It's our house, my Berenice. Yours and mine and Alice's."

"And . . . you wanted to surprise me?" Tears glistened in her eyes.

"Have I done wrong?"

"Done *wrong?* If the baby wasn't in the way I'd ravish you right now, sir!"

Cleve laughed and kissed her again. Then he said, "Coincidentally, just down this little hall is our bedroom. It looks out on the river."

She laughed lightly in delight—then looked around, frowning. "What is that? That *sound?* Is that music?"

"Let us investigate," he said, though he knew full well what it was.

He lit the way to the front steps of the house. As pre-arranged, two fiddlers—Dave Kanaway and Mickal Chocholak—were emerging from the brush alongside the river, playing a duet of a rather upbeat version of "The California Trail." Berry's mouth dropped open as she saw they were followed by Javier and Blevin and Catalina Rinaldi, banging on pans with spoons to the rhythm. They were followed by Leon and Teresa, the Gundersons, the blacksmith Dan Ringus, the carpenters Hiram and Eric, and the farmers Harry and Shamus Tweedy, half a dozen town children; then the Indians, Wovoka, Smallwolf, Guama, Marigold, Cliffy, all the Washoes—all singing in the same rhythm, the housewarming party gathering around Berenice and Alice to serenade them.

Alice woke up, looked in alarm at the noisy display—and then giggled and waved her arms.

Everyone gathered around the bonfire on the knoll. More folks from town turned up at the barbacoa feast—people Cleve didn't know, drawn by the excitement—and they were not turned away. Cleve hadn't planned on liquor, but somehow kegs of beer turned up, brought by the latecomers, and a pewter carboy of elderberry wine. When he saw men growing drunk, Cleve put on his badge, in case it was needed.

Someone else arrived in a wagon driven by a Chinaman. Luis Diaz sat in the back of the wagon, waving his hat at them, looking hale if not quite hearty. The Chinaman identified himself as Aldo Cho, who did some freighting and worked as a farmhand. It seemed Luis had bribed him for the ride, an outing he had been forbidden by Catalina Rinaldi. Mr. Cho was promptly invited to join the festivities.

After Luis received a formal scolding from Mrs. Rinaldi, the cowboys were permitted to carry him to a comfortable spot by the bonfire, where he was propped up against a chuckwagon wheel. He ate a plate of barbacoa and spuds, pronouncing the repast "acceptable." His guitar was fetched from the cowboy camp, and he played enthusiastically along with the fiddlers, stopping only for a pull on a mug of elderberry wine.

Cleve chatted for a time with Hugo Gunderson and his wife, Lolly. Gunderson was a tall, broad-shouldered man with a red beard, who looked more like a teamster than a shopkeeper. He gazed about him with a proud air, as if he'd arranged the feast himself. Lolly was a short plump brunette, a Catholic crucifix about her neck. She spoke of Padre Ortiz, a priest who traveled on a circuit, coming to Sweet River once a month to perform mass. Perhaps, Mrs. Gunderson said sweetly, Mr. and Mrs. Trewe would like to have the baby baptized, for life is uncertain and an unbaptized child goes to Perdition if some misfortune falls.

Cleve's response was polite. "It can do no harm, ma'am. We shall consider it."

The Gundersons' daughter, a teenager named Bess, sat well apart, seeming to almost retreat into her blue bonnet, yet covertly watching the blacksmith, who sat on a stump, grinning, keeping time with the music by slapping a hand on his knee.

Cleve noticed Mrs. Rinaldi and Oliver Blevin sitting close, heads bent together, whispering intently. Both of them smiling shyly.

As Berenice remarked, "Someone spirited in some whiskey." And Leon obtained more than his share. Cleve noticed that Ringus the blacksmith was becoming annoyed with Leon's repeated demands that they wrestle to see who had the best "rassling smarts." Ringus stood up, dusted off his hands—and both Teresa and Cleve stepped in to gently but firmly drag Leon back to his seat on a stump . . .

Cleve returned to the fire, as Berenice came back from putting Alice to bed in the Conestoga.

"I'm so glad to see Luis looking well," Berry said, sitting on the grass beside Cleve. "I applaud him for defying Mrs. Rinaldi and making his way here."

Luis was striking up a new song and singing loudly in Spanish, as the fiddlers played along, and Ringus clapped his hands to the rhythm. Nearby, a group of Washoe men were boisterously playing the Hand Game with the bone of a fox.

"You think Alice will sleep through all this?" Cleve asked.

Berry glanced at the wagon. "She's just thirty feet away; I'll hear her if she wakes up, no matter the noise. I believe I'd know if she was crying, even if I was stone deaf." She leaned against her husband and spoke in his ear. "We'll see later if I can express my gratitude for the house, without waking her up."

"You earned that house, my Berenice," he whispered. "No gratitude is necessary. But I sure will not turn it down. Say you know that white silk shirt you gave me? The one with the French cuffs?"

"The one you wore but once or twice?"

"That's the one. I was thinking I might like to give it to you."

"But what would I wear it with?" she asked, pretending to be puzzled.

"Nothing at all."

"I shall pull it out of the trunk, directly after our guests depart!"

The next morning, Cleve, Berry, and Alice moved into the house. A few articles of furniture were brought in by wagon, including a bed frame with leather supports built by Hiram, and a mattress—late arriving—purchased from Gunderson's.

Another five days of peace ensued, though with the occasional blast of cold air sweeping down off the Sierras. Wovoka's son, Cliffy, came to ask Cleve for a job with the herd. He was young to be a drover, not quite thirteen, but Cleve found him work after checking with the boy's father, and made him a kind of assistant to Leon. Brokenwing and Datsa were trained as cowboys, too, and were soon helping to build fences.

On a Friday, Javier drove a buckboard to Cleve's

house just before suppertime. He had just come from Independence, and Cleve invited him in for supper—Leon and Teresa were already there, at the dining table in the front room. The pine fire was roaring and hissing on the river stone hearth, as Javier came in, smiling. *"Una casa amigable!"* he said, glancing around approvingly. "Señor Trewe, here is a post for you. A man I do not know gave it to me, in Independence. I did not trust this man, but . . ." He handed Cleve the envelope.

Opening it revealed a summons to court in Sacramento. Cleveland Trewe was required to appear at the state court in three weeks, by order of Judge Jephthah Payton.

Cleve was being sued for falsifying ownership of Trewe Ranch. The plaintiff, Asa Hawthorn, alleged that the land belonged to him.

Cleve handed the papers to Berenice and said, "Time to send a telegram to Caleb."

Chapter 19

Leon and Cleve were sitting on their mounts, gazing into the shady deeps of the woods. The wooded strip beneath the bluff was roughly a quarter-mile thick. It was here that Leon proposed to shelter the herd from winter storms. Winters in this part of the Sierras could be erratic. Most were fairly mild, but a quick change to bitter cold was not unknown. Caught by surprise, people and stock sometimes died. And today a biting wind was nosing out of the mountains, carrying flurries of light rain, and hints of snow.

"You think we can keep the herd contained in there?" Cleve asked. "I don't own the whole damn valley. And we were just reminiscing about the hell of chasing stock in deep brush."

"We'll need fences," Leon said. "Build em between the trees—where we can, use the trees for fence posts. Like we done along the Pecos."

"There's some forage in the brush, I suppose," Cleve said.

"It's not enough," Leon said. Feeding cattle through a winter was one of the challenges of keeping a herd till the spring drive. "You was wise to make the hay deal with Samuels."

Cleve had bought up Samuels's hay, and there were bales stacked up in the new barn. "Maybe not enough. There's so much grass out here, where it's high enough we can harvest it, store it up."

"Better do it quick, it's going to seed. Look ye— there come Luis and Javier."

The two men were riding briskly toward them. Javier had just come back from Independence. Javier had become like a *tío* to Luis. "How's Luis doing on the job, Leon?"

"He seems healed up enough to ride. I've got him on light duty. Spends a big patch of his time moaning there ain't enough señoritas in Sweet River. He was even sniffing 'round that Gunderson girl."

"Glad to see him with Javier. He needs the steadying influence."

"And I'm an *unsteadying* influence?"

"You got drunk at the barbacoa feast and told Ringus the blacksmith you could wrestle him down."

"Hankered for a friendly match, is all. I know some Texas twists."

"You were getting on his nerves, Leon. If me and your missus hadn't put a stop to the match, he'd have folded you up, put you in his back pocket, and sat on you."

Javier trotted up close and drew a striped envelope from his coat. "A telegram for you!"

As Cleve opened the telegram he asked, "Any mail for us?"

"There is. Books, magazines for the ladies. Some letters for Señora Trewe. She has one from Paris—in France!"

"Not surprised. She is in touch with the Sorbonne."

"Who's the telegram from?" Leon asked.

"Caleb," said Cleve, scanning it.

ARRIVING INDEPENDENCE FOUR DAYS.
HAVE SECURED CHANGE OF VENUE
FROM SACRAMENTO TO INDEPENDENCE.
NO JEPHTHAH PAYTON PRESIDING.
NEW JUDGE IS FAIR BUT PERSUASION
IS ALL. PREPARATION NEEDED.
SR TOWNSFOLK TO WITNESS FOR YOU.

Cleve passed the telegram to Leon. "Good news is, we won't get the hostile judge. And I think we've made friends in Sweet River. But testifying about land ownership—will folks here do it?"

Leon read the telegram and grunted. "I don't know. They're scared of Hawthorn. You've got the deed, anyhow."

"Look close at that deed, you see that Samuels bought the land from Indians. Miwuk tribe. They're scarce around here now. And not every court accepts tribal deeds."

"Jefe, you got some work for me?" Luis asked.

Cleve looked at him. He seemed steady enough. "You okay to keep riding today?"

"All day!" Luis declared.

Cleve pointed at the woods. "Head on in, look for places to put some fencing in, running north to south.

Mark the trees with your knife. We're going to winter the herd in there."

"In the forest? And if I'm eaten by a bear?" Luis asked, deadpan.

Leon said, "In that eventuation, we'll shoot the bear and eat it, and I guess you'll be some use to us that way. Go ahead on, you heard the boss."

"Sí, Leon. And after that?"

"After that, go on to the chuckwagon," Cleve said, "help Pammy with the supper."

"Oh, I love to be at the chuckwagon!"

"Don't serenade her with your guitar," Leon said. "Peel them taters."

"You are a cold-hearted hombre, Leon," Luis said, shaking his head. He trotted his mount off to the woods.

Javier said, "Señor Trewe—if you win in the court, what then?"

"Then we keep a close watch on Hawthorn. Say, Javier—I told you, call me Cleve. You are my elder."

Javier gave a slight bow. "You are good for this valley, Cleve. If you need possemen, call on me. I can shoot straight."

"You a fighting man?" Leon asked. He sounded dubious, and indeed they had never seen Javier carrying a gun.

Javier looked thoughtfully at the sky. A crow cried hoarsely from the woods; a hawk answered shrilly overhead. Then Javier said, "No, I am not a fighting man. I am *peaceful.*" He shrugged. "I am peaceful—until I have to kill a man."

Then he smiled, tipped his hat to them, and rode toward town.

Berenice heard a soft rattling, glanced up from her basketweaving, saw dry leaves from the cottonwoods skittering across the window glass. "Marigold," she said. "I believe we'll need a fire, before long. It's coming on to cold, as Teresa says it."

Marigold nodded. "Yes, I must build a fire at the lodge. Wovoka and my foolish boy will call for food."

"Thank you for the weaving lesson. I'm beginning to learn." She looked at her fingertips. "And I'm bleeding less too."

Alice was fussing in her bassinet. Berry picked her up, kissed her, and opened her blouse to nurse. "Enjoy it while you can, my love, you are soon to be weaned."

Marigold set her basket aside and went without ceremony to the door. "I go home to make the fire."

Berenice sat in the rocker as Marigold opened the door—and a man was standing on the porch, one hand raised to knock. It was Delbert Hawthorn, carrying a book and a large envelope. He gaped at Berry's bare bosom.

"You go in, mister, I go home," Marigold said, slipping past.

Berry was too amused by the shocked look on Del's face to be embarrassed. "You may as well come in now, Mr. Hawthorn. I shall draw down my shawl for more discretion."

"Oh—I am so very . . .. Truly, I did not mean to . . ."

"All is well. If you wish to make amends, you can get the fireplace logs started. The wood is already there, the matches on the mantel."

"If . . . if you don't think it's . . ."

"And please close the door, I don't wish to expose Alice to the draft. She is quite recovered but one becomes superstitious about such things, after such a . . . what would Cleve say? A close shave."

"Certainly!" Fumblingly, he closed the door and hurried to the fireplace, tripping on the braided rug but managing to stay upright. He found the matches, adjusted the kindling, and started the fire. "There you are . . ."

"Now have a seat on that bench if you please, Del, and do tell me what book you have there. I am starved for the sight of new books."

"Ah, yes!" He sat on the very edge of the bench. "It is . . ." He held the book up for her to see. "James Clerk Maxwell's *Treatise on Electricity and Magnetism*— with copious charts and illustrations! Perhaps you already have it?"

"Oh! I do not have it! I read a review of it—a very skeptical one. But I am of Maxwell's mind, at least based on a monograph I read. I believe that electric lighting will replace gas lighting one day—perhaps in our lifetimes!"

"Do you think so? I thought perhaps in a hundred years or so . . ."

"Not at all! You shall see! And I may borrow the book?"

He bowed to her. "It is my gift to you."

"That is most kind, but you may have it back, once I've absorbed it. I shall pore over it once the baby is . . . I think she's going back to sleep. She wanted comforting more than nourishment." Berry lifted a corner of her shawl to see the baby and only then remembered that her bosom was again partly exposed. She covered up, and turned to see that Del's cheeks had gone scarlet, he was staring fixedly at the floor and his hands were trembling.

She looked at him with a pitying fondness. But Berry was sharply aware that, despite his overtures of friendship, he was Asa Hawthorn's son, and she must take a care of what she said. "Delbert, what is in that envelope, pray?"

"The envelope?" He took a deep breath and recovered countenance. "It contains my monograph on the possibility of tapping underground rivers for irrigation. Rivers deeper than well water, you see."

"What a wonderful idea—and so ambitious! May I read it?"

"I had hoped—*yes!*" He handed it to her. "There is no hurry. I must go to Independence."

"That's a two-day journey, is it not?"

"It is. Jim Crofton volunteered to go along, supposedly to protect me—I suspect it's more to sample the delights of the saloons at the county seat."

She smiled. "You're probably right. What is your errand, in Independence? But perhaps I shouldn't ask. Your father and my husband will be meeting in court there soon."

"No, no—it isn't that." He gave a sad little laugh.

"My father was outraged when they changed the venue to Independence. An entirely different judge who has no connection to . . . Well, I shouldn't . . ."

"Quite so. No need to speak of it. I don't want you to run afoul of your father." Berenice got up and gently arranged Alice in the bassinet.

"I feel I must tell someone—Father and his partners wish to take control of Sweet River, to divert much of its flow to their own purposes—and they plan to force people from their homes. I provided the initial designs for the project but—I have removed myself from it. I cannot agree with Father in this."

Berry turned to him. "Really! How will they divert the river? Damming?"

"I shall leave it at that. I do not wish to be summoned to court as a witness . . ."

She nodded. "I understand. May I ask what takes you to Independence?" she asked, going to the fireplace to add another cut of wood.

"I am going to see a lady in Independence."

"What a delightful smell this wood has as it burns. I believe it is a variety of cedar." She turned to him and added. "I hope all goes well with the lady."

"Goes well? Oh, she is not . . . no. I'm on a mission of charity. The lady is the wife of one of our cowboys who died under rather unfortunate circumstances." He sighed. "Unfortunate and—questionable. Lori Jensen is her name. I wish to inform her of her husband's passing and give her a little money. And a few of her late husband's things. I helped bury the gentleman myself."

His downcast eyes told Berry he was hoping for

some commendation. He was telling her, *I am not the sort of man my father is.*

"That's very thoughtful of you—the burial, and going all that way to help the lady. You are a good man, Delbert."

He blushed. A whistle shrilled from outside. "That will be Crofton, calling me to the road. I should go."

"Speaking of the road—please don't take this wrongly, but I urge you not to wander from the road to Independence. You take a risk, visiting this property. Wovoka and some of the others might be inclined to shoot Mr. Crofton on sight. And possibly you with him."

His eyebrows lofted over his spectacles. "I hadn't thought . . . Good Lord . . ."

"Feelings about the Westcut massacre are still smoldering, and the others may wish to punish Hawthorn through you. Many a trigger is pulled in anger."

"We shall take your advice!" He handed Berenice his monograph. "As you have been so kind as to warn me—I will suggest that if Mr. Trewe wins his court case, he would best avoid the settlement of Kerosene Corners. If he must go, then let him bring along as many men as possible. I heard some discussion of a . . . a possible, an *ambuscade,* in that setting."

"What is the nature of this ambuscade?"

"There are certain men . . ." But he pursed his lips, and shook his head. "I am often at odds with my father. If I were to say any more, it would be dishonorable. He is the only father I have . . ."

He looked so agonized Berry felt a wave of pity for him. She crossed to him and took his hands in hers.

His fingers were delicate and cold. And now his eyes were wide. "I do appreciate your consideration, Del. I look forward to reading your monograph."

"Mrs. Trewe . . ."

"You may call me Berry."

"May I?" He moved a little closer, so that she quickly withdrew her hands, and stepped back.

"I know . . ." He stared at the floor. His fists clenched at his sides. Then he blurted, "I know you are married, and faithful, and . . . and yet you must know how I feel. You are the one woman in the world who . . . why, you are like Wordsworth's "Perfect Woman"—Her eyes as stars of Twilight fair; Like Twilight's, too, her dusky hair . . ."

"Oh, Del!" She could not help laughing. "I am far from a perfect woman!"

As if he hadn't heard her, his eyes shining with unshed tears, he said, "And yet you are above the simple woman Wordsworth admired! You have a warrior's courage and a celestial genius. There could be no other woman for me—"

"Delbert!" she said sharply.

He broke off, and turned away. Then with his back to her, he said, "Do . . . do forgive me. I know my place. And it is at your feet, not at your side."

Then he hurried through the door. After a few moments, Berenice heard the drumroll of horses' hooves.

Oh the poor boy, she thought. *The poor lonely boy.*

In his haste, Del had left the door open. She closed it, thinking she must tell Cleve of this conversation. Especially the warning about Kerosene Corners.

She went to her chair and opened the envelope he'd left her, absently glancing at his monograph, her mind on the hints he'd dropped—and then she came upon a diagram, laid out upon a rough map of Sweet Valley, the river, and close by. It was clearly not a part of the monograph. But Berry suspected Del had deliberately left it.

Looking at the markings on the map, she remembered what he'd said. *He and his partners purpose is to take control of Sweet River, to divert much of its flow to their own purposes, to force people from their homes . . .*

Chapter 20

Sunday morning was fair but nippy, as seventy-two people gathered by the riverside. Cleve and Berenice were at the edge of the crowd, Alice in Berry's arms. Teresa was there, in a pretty green dress, but Leon was with the herd. The crowd included the Gundersons in Sunday finery, Ringus the blacksmith, dressed in a rumpled suit, and Mrs. Rinaldi in a frilly blue and pink dress. Cleve spotted the Tweedy cousins and Javier standing with Luis. There were many others Cleve knew and some, from outlying farms, he hadn't met.

The Hawthorns had not been invited.

Padre Ortiz had just performed an open-air mass for about half those people. He was a cheerful priest, a very small, round-bellied man in full black cassock and broad black hat. He was shorter than everyone except the few children present and he had a face like a dried apple. But it was a smiling apple.

Reverend Blevin had listened carefully, though the mass was in a mix of Spanish and Latin, and had taken part in the eating of the wafer and the drinking of ritual wine. Afterward, Blevin had a very earnest colloquy with the little priest, just out of earshot.

Now the priest stood by, hands clasped, watching benignly as Blevin climbed up onto a riverside boulder.

"That will do for a podium," said Berenice, taking Cleve's arm.

"I hope I won't regret talking him into this," Cleve whispered.

Blevin stood with his back to the rushing water, as the crowd gathered around the riverside boulder. "My name is Oliver Blevin. Some of you folks know me, and some of you don't," declared Pastor Blevin, in a loud voice that somehow didn't sound like shouting. The expertise of a preacher, Cleve supposed. "Coming to Sweet River I feel like I have found the Promised Land! I have found my soul replenished and my hope renewed. I haven't been here long, but I promise you I will join you in bringing this land to fruitfulness and glory!"

Cleve snorted. *Fruitfulness and glory?* Yet, Blevin's voice resonated with belief, with the joy of someone bringing good news, and it carried a magnetism that Cleve could not deny. "I have been advised by U.S. Deputy Cleveland Trewe, and by others in our settlement, that a fearful danger—nay, a *catastrophe*—could be coming to Sweet River! And I do not mean merely this settlement—I mean to the river itself." He drew the plans Del had drawn from his inner coat pocket and held the paper up. "I have here a map and diagram drawn out for the Payton combine, showing how the river will be diverted away from your lands; how it will be separated into canals. How it will be used for hydro-logical mining, ending in the destruction of farmland and grazing. They intend to force you to sell out, and to ravage your lands with mining—they will take the river from you! From all of us!"

Looking around Cleve saw shocked faces. He saw doubt, fear, suspicion—but every face held rapt fascination.

"*Behold Sweet River*, ladies and gentlemen!" Blevin gestured grandly at the rushing, sparkling, emerald-hearted river. "We take our rivers for granted! We're sure they cannot be taken from us! But only consider— the great combines, the syndicates of greedy business-men, grown so big their bosses style themselves kings! Kings in America, land of the free! And these false gods wish to take this river from you! Consider the words of Longfellow, in his poem to a great river: *Through the meadows, bright and free, till at length thy rest thou findest, in the bosom of the sea! Four long years of mingled feeling, half in rest, and half in strife, I have seen thy waters stealing onward, like the stream of life!* Is it not so? The stream of life! This river gener-ously flows on, bright and free, giving us water to drink, and water for crops; it offers us fish and fowl, it offers us beauty and serenity. I tell you, it is against a hallowed tradition—for a river traditionally waters many lands, many people, shared by all! More than that, my friends"—and here his voice rose to a moving crescendo—"it is against the will of God! A river is a symbol of God's bounty! Recall to mind, the words of God, in Isaiah: *For I will pour water on the thirsty*

land, and streams on the dry ground; I will pour my
Spirit upon your offspring, and my blessing on your
descendants. They shall spring up among the grass,
like willows by flowing streams!"

There was a rising murmur of acclamation at this,
and a smattering of applause. Cleve glanced at Mrs.
Rinaldi and saw her clasping her hands to her bosom, as
tears glittered in her eyes. *Smitten.*

Padre Ortiz, standing beside her, was nodding too.
Even the priest seemed impressed by this Protestant
minister.

"We cannot allow this gift of God to be taken from
us!" Blevin went on. "We have a chance to fight for it!
Asa Hawthorn—a man who has bullied and threatened
many of you"—there was much nodding of heads at
this—"Hawthorn has filed a lawsuit against U.S. Deputy
Trewe, claiming that his land is Hawthorn's land! Yet
you all know Drake Samuels! I have here another
document—a letter from Drake witnessing that he had
the true deed to the land, and declaring that he legally
sold that land to Cleveland Trewe! And U.S. Deputy
Trewe has lawfully registered that land at the County
Courthouse in Independence. But now Hawthorn claims
the Indians had no right to sell that land to Drake
Samuels! I am assured by Deputy Trewe's attorney—
Caleb Drask, Esquire—that Drake's deed is legal. If we
want to make certain that the court accepts the deed's
legality, we must all join together to witness that
Drake's many years here in the valley established him
as the rightful owner, with full legality to sell that land
to Deputy Trewe! If some of you are willing to journey

to Independence to appear in court, it will help protect this river and this land from the ravening beasts who wish to steal it from you! If you cannot make the journey, documents will be drawn up and witnessed for you to sign, and we shall present them to the judiciary! My friends, gather round and look upon these documents, and then gaze upon the river itself and ask yourself— will I, or will I not . . . *defend my Sweet River!"*

Standing in front of the Blacksands Saloon, feeling queasy from his breakfast of rank sowbelly and bad coffee, Cullen Marske looked down the dusty main street of Kerosene Corners with a mounting discontent.

Had Asa Hawthorn sent him here because it was part of the grand design of the Paytons? Or was it because Marske was being pushed into these dry, drab boondocks, so Hawthorn could avoid paying Cullen Marske the rest of his fee? Maybe Hawthorn was hoping Marske would get killed in this gun-happy, half-deserted town, so he wouldn't have to be paid.

'Course, if Cleve Trewe showed up just as Hawthorn projected he would, Marske's cooling his heels in Kerosene Corners would finally pay off. He would settle matters between him and Trewe and get paid in the bargain.

Right now, it was hard to believe Trewe would show any interest in this Kerosene Corners. The place looked dead as a ghost town. It was almost noon, but only two people showed themselves on the rutted road. One of them was Tupper Bolton, the scrapper, riding in on his swaybacked nag, towing his pack mule with another load of metal junk. The other was one of the women from the KC Hotel, Prunie, mouth open as she slept in the porch chair with her legs extended, the breeze billowing her skirts.

About forty buildings still stood in Kerosene Corners. The silver mine had played out, the tin and copper mines, too, and the one-time boomtown was like an old man on his deathbed. Or so it seemed to Marske.

Kerosene Corners contained perhaps eight houses still occupied. Permanently shuttered shops lined the street. Still, there was a working combination of hostelry and general store—a store which contained damned few goods. And the town yet boasted a hotel turned miserable brothel. An oily smell hung about, a dull reek that never quite went away. That would be from the bitumen deposits, Marske figured. The place had got its name, according to Old Bergstrom, from the black and brackish oil sands. Old Bergstrom—who yet owned the Blacksands Saloon and Rooming House—had tried to turn the oil sands into a kerosene industry.

Too much work to refine it on his own and too few good men to hire, Bergstrom grumbled.

Looking down the street the other way, Marske saw the reason the town was still here. Prospectors, riding in on their horses, trailing pack mules. Bearded, tired young men, their shoulders slumped. Which meant they'd found nothing of worth out in the sere, scrubby hills around the old town.

Whenever possible, Bergstrom artfully fed the rumor that there was gold to be found here; that a wandering miner had found "a mine that would make a banker's eyes bulge." Only, this purported prospector "croaked of the brain fever" before he could tell anyone where his strike was. "Within an hour's ride of Kerosene Corners" was all he said. This ludicrous falsehood kept the town alive. It summoned just enough prospectors to support Scharre's Hostelry and General Store, and a couple of saloons.

True, there was a scrappy ranch or two in the area, to the north. Kerosene Corners was closer to them than Sweet River. From time to time, the ranch hands came for a few supplies, and a dalliance with the hotel ladies.

The ranch hands usually carried guns. But Marske didn't suppose they'd be any trouble. It was Griff Milligan's boys that concerned him. He'd had a fight with two of Milligan's men already. He and the Denks had killed those two, and now a tense standoff prevailed with the others.

And out of the Silver Lode Saloon, catty corner to the Blacksands, came Griff Milligan himself, and his shadow, a man known only as Indian Dutch. Milligan was clearly nursing a hangover. Wearing a yellowing white shirt, striped pants, and worn Spanish boots, he was a man broad in the beam, with thick arms, long, red hair, his droopy orange-red mustache completely covering his mouth. His bristly scarlet-brown eyebrows squirmed like caterpillars as he stood on the wooden sidewalk looking belligerently around as if expecting a fight, though none was on offer.

Indian Dutch was a man with thatchy blond hair,

blue eyes, but having been raised by the Kiowas, he wore buckskin and beaded boots, and his clean-shaven face was marked by a two blue tattoo stripes on each cheek. He had a big knife at his belt, an old Navy Colt, and in his right hand, as always, he carried a sawed-off ten-gauge shotgun. Prunie swore Dutch slept with that shotgun.

Across the street, Milligan's red-rimmed eyes fixed on Marske, who just smiled and called out, "Morning, Griff!"

Dutch looked at Marske with his usual absence of expression. A blankness, yet a sense that he saw you, and wasn't going to turn his back on you.

"Mornin' Dutch," Marske added, knowing he would get no response.

"You hunting for a fight, Marske, I'm just your man," called Milligan, in a voice that was almost indistinguishable from a bear's growl.

Marske shook his head and called out, "Now why would I want a gunfight directly after breakfast? No, thank you! I'm still hoping we can be friends, Griff. Tell you what—come on in the Blacksands, and I'll buy you an antifogmatic! Hair of the dog that bit you!"

Dutch whispered something to Milligan. That was the only talk anyone heard from Dutch—whispers. Mostly to Milligan. Marske had never heard what the whisper was, but reckoned it to be Dutch offering counsel.

Griff Milligan grunted in response to Dutch, and shook his head at Marske. Then winced at the pain that brought. And called, "Marske, you just watch your damned step! All this"—he waved his hands—"belongs to me!"

With that he and Dutch stalked toward the stables, probably planning to ride out to Milligan's shack in Los Buitres Canyon, north of town.

Marske watched him go and pondered how he was to unite the guns in the town behind him and the Denks. Hawthorn's plan might need some weeding.

And where were the Denks this morning? Sleeping it off in their room in the Blacksands, he supposed. They'd made a practice of drinking themselves into a stupor every single night they'd been here.

Marske decided he would go and see if the Denks were awake. He needed to get some coffee into them, and make plans.

He turned—and that's when Bufus Gwinn stepped out from the Silver Lode with a pistol in one hand and a bottle in the other. Gwinn aimed the six-gun at Milligan's back.

Milligan was about forty yards off. Gwinn was a rat-faced, churlish ridge-runner; a foul-tempered man always accusing someone. He'd accused Marske of cheating at cards. In that instance, Marske had not been cheating, and he'd nearly shot Gwinn over it, but he wasn't certain who the man might have backing him. Was he with Milligan or against him?

Hence, Marske refrained from pulling the trigger and instead forced Gwinn to apologize at gunpoint.

Gwinn bore Milligan a grudge, something about a

stolen horse. Now Marske saw a chance to get rid of one dangerous, irritating man, and make peace with another.

Gwinn extended his arm fully, cocked the pistol, closed one eye to aim at Milligan's back. Milligan was about thirty yards off.

"Milligan!" Marske shouted. "Behind you!"

Both Milligan and Indian Dutch spun around, Milligan clutching at his sidearm, Dutch raising the shotgun.

Dutch fired at the same time Bufus Gwinn did. Gwinn missed Milligan, and Dutch's sawed-off was too far off to do much damage. Gwinn cringed and bared his teeth as a few scattergun pellets struck him.

Marske had already drawn his pistol and now he shouted, "Hey, Bufus!"

Gwinn turned toward him and Marske shot him neatly in the chest, three times. Gwinn went down like a felled tree.

Marske spun his six-gun into his holster—adding that flourish in case anyone was watching. It was always good to strike a little awe into folks. Made them less likely to raise a hand against you.

He turned to look at Milligan, who was staring at Bufus Gwinn's body. Milligan had his unfired gun in his hand. He looked at Marske—and holstered the gun. Then he nodded to Marske and called out, "Let's get us that antifogmatic!"

Marske nodded, and struck off to join the two men. And he thought, *Well, that worked just fine.*

* * *

Berenice stood at the window, Alice in her arms, thinking that perhaps, just perhaps, Cleve was coming back today. Nine days had gone by since Oliver Blevin had worked his rhetorical miracle at the riverside. Forty-seven people had signed a document saying they fully recognized Drake Samuels as the previous owner of the property, and they were satisfied he had passed on the deed to Cleveland T. Trewe. Five townsfolk went with Cleve and Leon to Independence, to witness for Samuels and Cleve Trewe. The witnesses were Mrs. Rinaldi, Javier, Shamus Tweedy, Dan Ringus, and Padre Ortiz, who knew Samuels quite well. Samuels would testify, too, and Leon would assure the judge he had seen Cleve pay the money over to Drake Samuels. Gunderson refused to leave his store and his new house, but he wrote out a letter to the judge, assuring him that he and the other people of Sweet River had every confidence in the correctness of the deed.

Supposing that the court had found for Cleve Trewe, he still had two days on the open road to get to Sweet River. Today was the second day. Hawthorn might have ambushed the travelers on the way here.

Berenice told herself that Cleve was not alone on the road. The men with him were armed. Ringus was formidable, and known to be a good shot. Javier had taken a rifle along.

It would look bad if Hawthorn attacked Cleve just after the court ruling. But men were so often irrational. Cleve could be wounded right now. Or dead.

Berry put Alice in her new cradleboard, a gift from Marigold. Putting on a coat and a shawl and a hat, and taking the cradleboard on her back, Berry went out into the chilly day. She crossed to the newly completed barn. "What a nice snug barn you have, Suzie," she told her Arabian. "I hope you won't mind going out in the cold wind. I'm of a mind to ride a distance up the trail, and see what I can see . . ."

Suzie seemed full of zest, relieved to be free of the stall, tossing her head and softly whinnying as Berry saddled her, no mean feat with a baby strapped to her back, and they were soon riding down the road toward the cowboy camp.

She passed the new bunkhouse, made of logs and chinking, and rode within a hundred yards of the herd. Berry could see smoke rising in a corral, where Milt and Wovoka and Smallwolf were branding cattle.

She passed Leon and Teresa's unfinished house, a little beyond the soddy. It was more than a frame but not quite habitable. In a week or two, they would be moving in. None too soon, with Teresa's pregnancy showing.

Passing the soddy, Berry drew up, startled to see Leon's horse, Danny, tied to the Conestoga and Leon coming out of the dugout.

"Leon! You're here? Where is Cleve?"

Leon's face split with a grin. "He's like a tired-out turtle! Back along the trail is where he is. I wasn't going to trot along like Cleve. I galloped up like one of them armor knights of old, so's to see my Teresa!"

"Then he's all right? You weren't attacked on the way back?"

"No, 'course not! Go on along, he couldn't be more'n half a mile!"

She cantered on, Alice making trilling sounds, for the baby enjoyed the motion. "I should have asked Leon how it all went, Alice," Berry said. "But the look on his face was encouraging."

The wind tugged at her hat and stung her nose and ears. Then she came around a bend in the road and there was Cleve, coming steadily down the road, looking a little morose. The others straggled behind him.

He looked up and smiled. She drew up beside him, him facing south and her north. "You certainly took your time, Major Trewe."

"I apologize, ma'am. I do bear some news. Judge Peavy seemed impressed by the witnesses who assured him of the long establishment of Drake Samuels's ownership and their acceptance of my purchase. The witnessed declarations from the people of Sweet River helped too. Caleb spoke most eloquently. The lawyer for the plaintiff claimed that corruption was afoot, and hinted that Marshal Beaman had put his fingers on the scale."

"That is accusing Judge Peavy as well as Beaman!"

"The judge was sensible to that very implication, my Berenice. And he threw the case out of court, with some harsh words for the plaintiffs. It seems we are to keep our land!"

She was too happy to speak, and leaned over to kiss him; he kissed her back. A small cheer went up from the stragglers down the road, and some hooting.

Cleve straightened up, chuckling, but she could see in the set of his face, he was still worried. "What is it, Cleve? There's something . . ."

"Let's talk as we ride, Berry."

She swung Suzie around Ulysses—the two horses greeted one another with a quick nuzzling of muzzles—and trotted off toward the ranch. "I cannot think that it's truly over," Cleve said. "Hawthorn said after the ruling that it was not."

"He will appeal the ruling?"

"I think he has something else in mind. Some wily way to get at us, remove us from the land, and make it look like it was no fault of the Hawthorns."

"By what means?"

He shook his head. "I don't know. I'm going to have to leave the ranch for a few days tomorrow. That worries me too."

Berry couldn't keep down a groan. "Did Beaman give you another warrant to serve?"

"He did. And it's one we all want to see served. I cannot refuse. I must go to Kerosene Corners and serve a warrant to arrest Cullen Marske, for taking part in the massacre at the Westcut."

Chapter 21

"You asked for me, father?" said Del, coming into his father's library.

When informed his father wanted to speak to him alone, Del had considered riding out from the ranch. But someone would have been sent to drag him back.

"We are going to have us a talk, boy," said Asa Hawthorn. "Sit down."

Del perched on an armchair across from his father.

Sitting back on the buffalo skin settee, Asa had a glass of whiskey in one hand, and clearly, judging by the glaze of his eyes, it wasn't the first drink of the evening.

"Del," said Asa, "I sent you to Independence to send a telegram for me. And to pick up some mail."

"I did all of that, Father."

"But Crofton tells me you went off on some mission to give money to a woman for all the wrong reasons."

"The wrong reasons? Crofton went off to give money to ladies of the night. My aim was charitable."

"I'd rather seen you going to the pleasure palaces

with him, where you might at least gain some manhood! You ever even lain with a woman, boy?"

"Father!" Del was genuinely shocked.

"I let your mom raise you for too damned long," Asa said, shaking his head.

Del sat up straighter, in the mood to defend manhood—his own vision of manhood. "There is only one woman I would . . ." He gasped for the right words. ". . . that I would lie with. And then only in matrimony. But it will never be."

Asa snorted. "I have my suspicions as to who that would be. You're right—that'll never be. And one way or another, that woman and her husband . . ." He paused to take a long drink of the whiskey. Then he smacked his lips, and went on, "That woman and her husband are going to be clean gone from this land, and soon. Making land deals over an Indian deed! And they used that slicker from San Francisco to get 'round Jephthah! Found themselves Judge Peavy, who's a bosom buddy of Marshal Beaman! Well, I will not be cheated, boy! We will go after them—and you will take part!"

Del's mouth had gone dry as foolscap. "Take part in what exactly, Father?"

"I have found a means to get Trewe to Kerosene Corners."

Del frowned. He'd known of the plan to catch Trewe alone, away from his cowboys—but Del had thought they'd be unlikely to lure Trewe to their trap.

Del's father went on, "I've seen to it that certain . . . well, certain *claims* about Marske have found their way to Beaman . . ." He sipped more whiskey, and said,

"And Beaman has taken the bait and bit hard on the hook! He's sent Mr. U.S. Deputy Trewe to Kerosene Corners, where a fine reception awaits him. That will give us another opportunity, you see."

"Another opportunity?"

"We'll go directly after the ranch while he's out there. It won't be so well defended then. And once it's done, we'll make it look like them Indians of his done it."

"That's . . ." Del shook his head. "It'll never pass inspection."

"Oh, it will—we'll do it. And we'll see that Jephthah rules on the matter."

"A direct attack on Trewe Ranch?"

"That's right, Delbert. And you're going with us!"

Del stood up and said, "No, sir. I'm sorry. Not this time."

"Boy, this will be your hour of glory! As Uncle Rastas used to say, "'One crowded hour of glorious life is worth an age . . .'"

"If he said that, he was quoting Mordaunt," Del said. "And I still won't do it."

He turned to go—and found Harl blocking the doorway, arms crossed. With Harl was a man Del had never seen before. A sharp-eyed man with black hair, a neatly trimmed mustache, and a scrap of beard on his long chin. He wore a suit and vest of dove gray, in his hand was a gun. It was tilted at the ceiling. But Del knew what it meant.

"Sorry, kid," said Harl. "Uncle Pa decided you're not going anywhere till this business gets done. Oh, this fella here, he's Bret Nethercott. You maybe heard of him?"

"Yes," said Del, in a small voice. Even Del had heard of Bret Nethercott. A notoriously brutal hired gun.

Nethercott gave Del a big smile, showing a mouthful of teeth all covered in shining gold.

"Why you bring me?" Guama asked. He was wearing the dark sombrero and serape he'd bought at Gunderson's with money Cleve had paid him for ranch work.

Cleve stirred the campfire up a little, and tossed on another stick of deadwood. The flames leaped hungrily at it. Nearby, Ulysses and Guama's cayuse snorted and tore at the thin, dry grass. "I need a man to watch my back," Cleve said. "Why not you?"

"Leon is angry you don't take him."

"He's got a wife with child he has to watch over. Anyhow . . ." Cleve pulled off his boots and stood them by his gun and holster. "I didn't want to bring anyone at all. I need every man to stand watch over the ranch and Sweet River. But it just seemed right one of the Washoe should come along because we're going to arrest Cullen Marske. The last of the killers from Westcut Canyon."

They were camped in another canyon now, a nameless, boulder-strewn box canyon adjoining the trail to Kerosene Corners. Cleve looked up at the sky. Saw clouds crowding out most of the stars. At this hour, the heavy clouds looked charcoal-colored, and the air had the crisp tang that was a prelude to a snowstorm.

Sensing Guama's uncertainty about their undertaking, Cleve said, "You don't want to go with me, I'll

pay you half what we agreed on and you can go back to
Sweet River."

Guama looked as if he was considering it. "Marske,
you said?"

Cleve nodded. "Marske."

"I come with you."

"Better get some sleep then. We rise at daybreak.
Maybe get to town early enough to catch Marske still in
bed. A man sleeping off liquor hasn't got a lot of fight
in him."

"You shoot him in bed?"

"I'd rather see him hang."

The firelight reflected from the rocks. The night was
cold. Cleve stretched out on his bedroll, tugged his coat
over him for a cover, tilted his hat over his eyes, and
tried to will himself to sleep . . .

Berenice and Alice were safe, weren't they? Milt and
Pamahas were staying in the front room of the house.
Both of them armed. The Conestoga had been pulled in
out front, and Dave Kanaway was staying in it, keeping
watch. Wovoka and two other Indians and Leon kept a
night watch on the house and the soddy. Luis was there,
and Smallwolf and Javier too. Javier had a long gun, a
single-shot rifle that he swore was more accurate than
any carbine. Javier also had a pistol Cleve recognized
as a Spanish copy of the Smith &Wesson No. 3 Russian
revolver, a gun used by the revolutionaries in Mexico.
Had Javier ridden with them?

A burrowing owl called from a stand of manzanita.
The owl called again. What had Berenice called it?

He could almost hear her voice. "*Athene cunicularia,*

also called the shoco, or burrowing owl, my darling dear . . ."

Was that Alice stirring in her basket, or the wind whispering around the boulders? The firelight sank low . . . darkness moved closer . . .

Cleve's sleep was uneasy, riven with dreams of blazes in the night.

Gunfire. Cries of rage. A burning house suddenly collapsing in on itself, sending a plume of sparks up into the night sky.

Cleve woke, found he was staring up at the dimming stars. A faint predawn grayness showed in the eastern sky.

Guama was rolled up on the other side of the smoking remains of the fire, snoring softly. The horses were sleeping side by side. The threatened snowstorm hadn't come, not yet.

Cleve pulled on his boots, and stood, buckling on his gunbelt. Guama sat up suddenly, his rifle in his hand, staring.

"It's just me," Cleve said.

Guama looked around and said something in his own language. Then added, "Not just you. Ghosts."

"That right? Let's run up some coffee quick as we can and offer 'em some."

He used the night's embers to start a fire. The coffee was already in the pot with cold water, waiting to be boiled. They ate some dried pheasant and drank down two cups of Arbuckle's apiece, Guama pouring out a little on the ground for the ghosts.

Then they rolled up their blankets, roused and saddled their horses. Cleve gave Ulysses and the cayuse some grain, not too much, and a little water. He packed the coffeepot, kicked sand over the embers of the fire, and they mounted up.

They rode toward Kerosene Corners.

Berenice had just stepped out the door when Kanaway rode up on his steel-dust stallion, the horse's breath pluming in the biting morning air. "Berry—Leon sent me to find you. He said maybe you'd better take the baby to Sweet River."

"What's afoot, Dave?"

"Hawthorn's crossed a good part of his herd into Trewe land. He's got men running them this way. If he keeps pushing they'll stampede!"

"Hawthorn intends to run us down?"

"Looks that way to me and Milt."

"And our herd?"

"Javier said there's a storm coming, so we drove 'em into the woods, ma'am. Got 'em penned in there. But the Hawthorn herd is coming on fast!"

"Marshal Beaman has an unerring instinct for handing Cleve a warrant to serve when there's trouble right here at home. Have you told our Indian friends?"

"Wovoka's the one who told us what was coming! Their lodges aren't in the way—but Wovoka said they'll fight for us."

"Dave, will you saddle Suzie for me? I'll get Teresa to take Alice to town."

"Ma'am, it would be safer, if you went to town too—"

She raised a hand, "I'm going out to see for myself. But first, I will ask you to get something for me from the storage shed. Four somethings in fact . . ."

In a handful of minutes, Berry and Dave Kanaway were riding hard, down the valley to the west. They reined in as they saw the milling and thrusting of Hawthorn's herd, coming at them. Here the land sloped down and they could see the herd about a quarter-mile away. The herd was slowed by the incline, yet coming steadily on.

Berenice reached back into her saddlebag, found the Union Army field binoculars Cleve had given her. Till now she'd used them to watch wild birds and beasts, but today she raised them to look at cattle driven mad by thirteen men. It was hard to make out their faces but three seemed to be Hawthorns—Asa, Harl, and Delbert. Crofton wasn't there. The Hawthorns were side by side behind the other men, who were lashing at the cattle in the rear, driving them hard up the hill, whipping and shouting and whistling. Despite the slight incline, the big longhorns were picking up speed.

That's when the wind dropped for a moment—and thin snow swirled down.

"Lord, it's coming on to snow," said Kanaway. "I see Leon and Milt are riding up. Smallwolf too."

"Do get those bottles out, if you please," said Berenice, still gazing through the binoculars.

As she watched, one of the riders raised his gun and

grinned—there was a flash of gold at his mouth—and he fired the gun three times into the sky. The other men began to fire their weapons, and the spooked cattle surged forward with redoubled fury, jaws frothing, eyes alight with fear, as snow whirled down around them and gun smoke drifted into the sky.

"Berry!" Leon called out.

She lowered the binoculars and said, "Hello, Leon," as he rode up, his eyes almost as wild as the spooked cattle.

He reined in and gasped, "You need to get to town!"

"I will not scurry off like some shrieking damsel in the theater. This is my land every bit as much as Cleve's."

"I know that, Berry, but they intend to stampede us down and we're going to have to start shooting! And, by God, they'll shoot back!"

She patted her Winchester. "I can shoot back myself. But I have a bit of a plan. It comes from your saloon." Berry glanced at the cattle, now less than an eighth-mile away. "The bottles, Dave?"

"Right here, ma'am." In two gunny bags hanging from his saddle, Kanaway had six bottles of the homemade grain alcohol, which Noble had chosen to describe as "whiskey." He handed one of them to Berry.

"Gentlemen, we will pour out these highly flammable fluids in the herd's path. Even in the falling snow, they will burn if ignited."

Bullets zinged by, followed by the crack of the gunshot.

"They're shooting at us, damn them!" Milt shouted.

"I'll pour it out from horseback!" said Berry, struggling to hold Suzie as more bullets cut past.

"Berenice Trewe, you get behind us!" Leon bellowed.

But Berry was taking the cork out of the bottle. "Have your matches ready!"

Another bullet cut by and then she spurred Suzie to the north, ignoring Leon's furious shouts. Snow stung her in the face as she galloped.

Fifty yards—and Berry swung back and to the south, angling onto the lip of the slope. She saw Dave Kanaway following in her tracks, then Milt and Leon.

Here, the grass had been cropped back short. Berry pulled the cork from the liquor bottle with her teeth and leaned over hard to the right. Holding on to the saddle horn with her left hand she poured the colorless spirits thickly out. Then she straightened up, throwing the bottle so it shattered in the path of the oncoming cattle. A bullet sang by close under her jaw; she could feel the wind of it on her neck, and she thought, *Alice should not grow up without a mother.*

Then she swerved off to the east, trying to get out of effective firing range, so the enemy was at her back, and her mount would be harder to hit—for her greatest fear now was to have Suzie shot out from under her. The two of them falling together could end with broken necks . . .

"*Whoa,* Suzie girl!" she called, and reined in. Suzie skidded to a stop and Berenice turned in the saddle and saw the other men were following Kanaway's lead, Leon pouring a bottle just past where Berry had poured hers, and Milt poured out the last of another. Then Milt drew up, lighting a match—it took great courage, with gunfire cutting by him.

He flicked the burning lucifer at the ground and the potent liquor caught, flaring up blue and red, the roaring flames racing the path of the oncoming cattle just as they arrived at the lip of the hill. Snow hissed into mist as it struck the fire.

"Hold hard, Suzie!" she told the panting, shivering horse.

Smallwolf was throwing the last two bottles at the ground in the center of the wall of flames, and as they shattered their contents ignited. Two balls of fire rose— the big bull in the lead caught in the splashing, burning liquid—

And then most of the herd turned, panicking as the fire blinded their eyes and licked at their muzzles. Most of them veered off toward the woods to the north; others cut to the south, toward the river.

But the enormous lead bull was rushing through the curtain of fire, maddened by the burning liquor splashed on its face and horns. It was thundering right toward Berry, and for a moment, she was frozen with fascination at the sight of the massive black bull, its long sharp horns alight with flame, its jaws streaming fire, its eyes red with rage as it came bursting through a curtain of falling snow.

Berry drew her Winchester from its scabbard, chambered a round, and aimed as the bull got to within fifteen yards of her. She fired, the bullet striking the beast in its horned head. The bull stumbled but kept coming. It was coming as fast as its powerful legs could carry it, and she was afraid that if she tried to ride away from a dead stop it'd catch up with her, and gore Suzie—and down they'd go.

More gunfire, from her right and left, as the Trewe ranchmen fired at the bull. She chambered another round—and saw the bull stumble again, then regain its footing, coming at her once more. She fired at one of its furious red eyes . . .

The bull staggered. And fell, its head plowing into the ground. It lay there twitching but already dead, as flames licked up from its horns . . .

"Poor thing," she said. "Brave beast."

"Berry, dammit!" Leon called, riding hard up to her. His horse skidded as he pulled up short. "That crew down there's going to come up on this top land firing!"

"Then let's get to cover!" She started Suzie back toward the ranch, the men galloping up close behind her. She realized the cowboys ranged themselves close behind to give her cover.

Her heart wrung at that, and she felt tears start, but she forced her mind to focus on defending her home.

If Cleve were here, what would he do now?

Cleve drew his Colt and climbed the windblown backstairs of the Blacksands Saloon and Rooming House. He took every stair as quietly as possible, stepping carefully on the nailheads. But the outdoor stairs had been built for the cleaning woman and the piss-pot boy, who no longer worked there anymore, so they weren't kept in repair and they creaked and crackled with his every step.

Cleve reached the second-floor landing, glanced down the alley both ways. Nobody there, except a few chickens wandering out of a backyard coop. Cleve tried the door, found it was locked from the inside. He took out his knife, pressed the blade between the door and the jamb under the lock bolt, working it in. The wood was old and tired, and it wasn't hard to pop the door out enough to break the clasp free of the frame.

But it wasn't quiet either. The wood holding the lock broke with a loud crunching crack.

He glanced down the alley again, then pressed his ear to the door and heard nothing but a building creaking in the wind. He sheathed his knife, opened the door slightly, and peered at the dim hallway. There was just one flickering light, running low on lamp oil, over the inside steps that descended to the saloon.

Cleve opened the door a little wider, slipped through, tried to close it behind him, but the broken lock was in the way.

He moved on—and then stopped. It was awful quiet in here. He suddenly wondered if the report Beaman had forwarded with the warrant papers was accurate. Some source of the marshal's service reported Cullen Marske staying in the rear northeast side of the Blacksands Saloon.

The door to that room was up on Cleve's left, just four steps away.

Chapter 22

It wasn't snowing in Kerosene Corners. But a cold wind was nosing down the street.

Sitting on the front porch of the Blacksands, Guama peered up from under his sombrero, looking up and down the dirt road. Still early, no one was stirring yet.

Then a man came out the front door of the Blacksands. Guama closed his eyes, pretended to be asleep. But he could sense the man pausing to look at him. The man grunted, and stepped down onto the street. Guama opened his eyes and recognized the man instantly. Guama knew this man. He had seen him at the camp, close to Westcut Canyon. Where the killers had surprised them, had ridden in shooting . . .

The one who had led the murderers to kill Guama's people. Marske was looking around now, as if expecting to see someone. He put a hand rolled cigarette in his mouth, flicked a match alight with his thumbnail, and puffed smoke at the street.

Under the serape, Guama had his hand on the six-gun, the one he'd taken from the body of the patch-eyed man, after the gunfight, where he and Wovoka had taken a measure of revenge.

Now Guama must choose. Should he shoot this man now? Or find Cleve, and tell him what he'd seen? For that's what Cleve Trewe had said to do. *"Don't try to fight them alone. Because Marske won't be here alone."*

But Guama badly wanted to kill this man. To kill him right now.

His hand tightened on the gun.

Then someone called from inside the saloon. Marske turned and walked back into the saloon, before Guama, still slumped in the chair, could set himself to shoot.

I should have sung a song to kill my enemy, this morning, Guama thought.

But he got up from the chair, and looked through the saloon window. Marske and Milligan were alone there. It was early. Not even the man who tended bar could be seen. But Guama could see Marske talking to a squat man with long red hair and droopy red mustaches. The man had a pistol in his hand.

"So you're out of bed, Milligan," Marske was saying.

"Dutch told me someone's busted open that back door upstairs."

"That a fact? Then he's already here." Marske looked at the ceiling. "This ain't the way I wanted to do it. But we'll do it how we can. Where's Dutch?"

"He's watching the back."

"Well come on then."

They started toward the stairs . . .

* * *

Cleve was listening at the door of Marske's room. But it was a noise from across the hall that caught his attention. A creaking of boards. Someone near that other door, not quite directly across from this one. A man there—and maybe another in Marske's room.

Now there was the sound of someone coming up the stairs. Stealthy, slow steps.

A trap. So be it.

He flattened to the wall to one side of the door, banged on it with his gun butt, and shouted, "U.S. Deputy Marshal!"

Bullets smashed through the door, splinters flew, and the door across the hall crashed open. He caught a glimpse of a pale, small-eyed gunman with a Remington sixer in his hand. Cleve fired from the hip, could feel he'd missed even before the recoil. The gunman jumped back, fired through the half-open door so that a bullet cracked into the wall near Cleve's head.

Cleve backed down the hall, waiting for a shot at whoever was in those rooms. He was pretty sure neither one would be Marske.

Then he glimpsed a dim outline of two men coming up the stairway, one of them, coming into the light, with long red hair and mustaches. The other he couldn't see clearly but the hat made Cleve think of Marske. The stranger with the long red hair pointed his gun at Cleve—

But this time, Cleve had a better shot and when he fired from the hip, he caught the shooter square in the chest. The man stumbled backward, firing into the floor as he fell tumbling down the stairs—even as the darker figure on the stairs shouted, "Cleve Trewe!" and fired.

Cleve was firing and sidestepping. The gunman's round pierced Cleve's left side, clean through, and Cleve's round missed.

Then the door on the right opened and the hidden gunman fired through—as Cleve rushed to slam his shoulder into the door of the chamber near the back door.

The old door splintered and he was through. He found the room unoccupied—but his attention was swept up by a burning pain spreading from his left side. He pushed against the pain, moving to the wall beside the door, letting his practiced hands remove empty shells and reload. Within seconds, the gun was reloaded. He'd brought a field dressing with him—he'd learned to do that long ago—and, switching the gun to his left hand, Cleve dug the bandage from his coat pocket. Gritting his teeth at the stab of agony he pressed the bandage onto the blood-oozing wound. He switched the gun to his right hand, held the bandage in place with his left elbow, keeping his eyes on the doorway—where a shadow accompanied the creak of bootsteps.

Through the busted-open doorway he could see the back door, and stepping into it from the landing was a man in buckskins, with mussy blond hair, a clean-shaven face, icy-blue eyes. Cleve knew him—Indian Dutch. He'd passed through Axle Bust and Cleve had disarmed him and escorted him out of town, for Dutch had wounded a miner in a gunfight—a gunfight Dutch had prodded the man into.

And now Indian Dutch saw Cleve, remembering the humiliation—and snarling, he raised his gun and fired. A bullet cracked by Cleve and smashed a water jug on a dresser.

Cleve fired but he had a bad shooting angle and hit only the jamb of the back door. He flattened back—and someone in the hall fired right through the thin wood wall, just behind him.

Time to rush the enemy and hope for the best.

Cleve heard a Washoe war whoop, looked through the door, saw Indian Dutch turning to see who was behind him. Just in time for Dutch to get the top of his head blown off from the shooter, who could only be Guama.

Guama stepped up into view, firing down the hallway.

Despite the pain in his side, Cleve grinned. The odds were better now.

Gunfire cracked from down the hallway, hammering into the doorframe beside Guama, who darted through the doorway to join Cleve.

"Now we both in here," Guama said, grinning.

"Like two gophers in a rattlesnake hole," Cleve said—and another shot came through the wall, closer to him now. "Sure made these damned walls flimsy," he muttered, turning to fire three shots through the wall. Someone cussed and he could hear their boot steps as they moved back down the hall. Then there was whispering. They were calculating their next move.

Someone shouted, "Crofton! Where the hell is Crofton!"

"Guama," Cleve whispered. "Open that window . . ."

Delbert Hawthorn had his hands tucked under his armpits. He was feeling unbearably cold, and even his mount trembled with cutting wind. Del's father, in a long great coat, woolen scarf, and gloves, was not shivering, but he sat stiffly on his gray quarterhorse.

"Your stampede's done stampeded the wrong way," observed Bret Nethercott, riding up through the falling snow with Harl Hawthorn. He reined in alongside Harl.

"And she shot our best breedin' bull," said Harl.

Del was sitting on his mount beside his father, as the whole crew of cowboys joined them, looking for fresh orders. There was snow on their hats and shoulders— and worry on every face.

"She's a right clever gal," said Nethercott, chuckling, showing his gold teeth. "Setting that fire—you could see that was her, and them others just come along after. She was calling the shots, Asa."

"She!" snarled Asa Hawthorn. "That Trewe woman! From the first, she's dismissed me like she was queen and king of this valley! And now she's set the grazing on fire and burnt some of my cows!"

Del smiled at that. Berenice was indeed a queen. His queen. She was a Valkyrie, too, he thought, remembering her spreading a fire, with bullets flying about her. And then she'd shot down that boss bull.

"Only the bull was kilt," Harl said. "He's stone dead.

The others, they'll be okay. The fire sure ain't spreading in this snow. But what I want to know, Uncle, is what do we do now? Best do something before Trewe himself gets back here."

"That would sure be the question of the moment, Asa," put in Nethercott. He brushed snow off the shoulders of his suit coat.

On the job or not, Bret Nethercott was always dapper. *A well-dressed murderer,* Del thought. Nethercott had killed numerous sheepmen and sod squatters in the cattle wars. He was notorious for killing three young boys along with their daddy. He'd also gunned down a deputy in San Antonio, Texas, and was still wanted in Texas. And he'd killed a faro dealer in Arizona, on a whim. Had even that discouraged Asa Hawthorn?

Del shook his head. *Not a speck.*

But now Del's father was glaring at Nethercott. "Nethercott—you were paid. You know what to do."

"I was paid *half,*" Nethercott returned, looking at the sky. "Be good if the damn snow would let up."

"You want the other half," Asa said, "you'd better get these men rallied and take on those squatters! That's all they are—squatters on my land! I don't care about some judge mooning after the U.S. Marshal. This is my land!"

Del growled in his throat. He had satisfied himself that his father had no claim on the land. But he kept quiet about it because Bret Nethercott had been watching him. Nethercott with his gold-plated grin and his hand always near his gun. Nethercott overflowing with contempt for everyone but himself.

"Maybe we should hold off, Asa," Harl said. "Till after Marske takes care of that Cleve Trewe. Then Marske and Crofton and the Denks, they can ride up with us."

Asa spat at the ground. "You're scared of some woman and a few Indians and a couple of loafers with rifles?"

"I expect we can take 'em," said Nethercott. "We can do it today if we move in right soon. Now it seems to me this snow could help us. They can't see us so well, with this mess a-falling. They're out there afoot in this cold. We could take them on cavalry style."

"Like the Confederates did at Shiloh?" Del said, barely aware he was saying it aloud. It hadn't worked so well in Shiloh.

Asa glowered at him. "We *will* do it—today! And you will help, Delbert! You're taking that rifle into your hand and you're riding into battle!"

Amazed at himself, Del took the rifle out of its scabbard—and tossed it on the ground. He looked at his father's cowboys, bunched together, shivering in the cold, faces tight with fear. They were ranch hands, not killers. "Was I you," Del told the cowboys. "I'd toss in my weapon too. It's sheer madness to get yourself killed today."

"Nethercott!" Hawthorn growled.

"Boys," said Nethercott, a false amiability in his voice, "I'll shoot the first man who rides off."

Asa nodded and turned to his cowboys. "You men are getting extra pay today—three hundred dollars a man! You're paid to be here and don't you forget it! But

I'll tell you what—I'll make it *five hundred* a man! Now get your pants unbunched and get out there!"

Nethercott pointed a finger at Hawthorn. "Just one thing—you want me to do this, Asa, I got to do it my way, without being roped up! And I need these men to follow my play!"

"That's the way it'll be!" Hawthorn declared. "You men do as he tells you! And Harl—you have them lamps?"

"I do," said Harl. He had two full kerosene lamps hanging from his saddle horn.

"You get close, light 'em and do as I told you. Berenice Trewe wants to play with fire—now she'll get burnt!" He pointed at Del's Winchester. "Now—get me that damn rifle!"

Harl dismounted, picked up the rifle, dusted snow off the barrel, and handed it butt-first to his uncle.

Asa Hawthorn leaned over and shoved the gun back in Del's saddle scabbard. "You will use that, Del! You're goin' with them. Now, Nethercott—lead the way!"

Bret Nethercott flashed his gold teeth, took off his hat, waved it in the air. "Let's get it done, boys! But damn you—do it how I call it!"

Then he rode off. Harl quickly followed—and less eagerly, so did the cowboys.

"Go on, boy!" Hawthorn snarled. "Get that gun out and go with 'em!"

Del shook his head and tossed the reins away. "I'm staying right here. I'll have no part in this."

"Oh, you will," declared Asa Hawthorn. "Because once the killing starts—you'll find your loyalty. Not even you could be so low as to turn his back on his own father."

Del just watched the men riding up toward the Trewe Ranch. He could tell that Bret Nethercott was shouting orders, but he couldn't make them out. Then he saw the cowboys ride out in front of Nethercott.

Nethercott kept going—but it was clear he wasn't going to be the first to ride into the fight.

A thought struck Del like a hard slap in the face.

Who will be the one to kill Berenice Trewe?

Her own Winchester in her hands, Berenice was just crawling up under the chuckwagon as the riders came at them.

The snowfall was thickening, and the sun was hidden behind clotted clouds. The snowfall and the dimness made cover for the raiders, and they came on, silhouettes behind the lace curtain of frosty precipitation.

Berry thought about Alice, and hoped it was possible to keep these men focused here instead of at the ranch house. Datsa was posted at the house, to protect Teresa and Alice. Teresa was armed, and formidable herself. And Marigold, with her son, was looking after Alice— Marigold was no pushover, and neither was young Raincatcher, who'd been given a shotgun.

Ten yards on her left, Dave Kanaway was hunkered half behind the wheel of the Conestoga, which they'd turned north-south, sideways to the oncoming men. On his left at the other end of the wagon, was Milt, armed with a Sharps rifle, and hunched down a little behind him was Pamahas, clutching a pistol. He had been unable to convince her to go to the comparative safety of the ranch house. Luis and Javier were posted at the tackle house by the corral. Smallwolf and Wovoka and Leon were crouched behind a freight wagon, rifles in hand. On Berry's suggestion, the rest of the Indians had taken shelter in the soddy, but Brokenwing was posted at its door, rifle in hand, ready to fight. The stock had been put away and there was a bullet chambered in Berry's rifle and the Trewe Ranch was as ready as it would ever be without Cleve there.

And then the riders loomed out of the snowfall, firing at the wagons. Berenice picked a target coming her way, aimed at the center of the man's torso, and squeezed the trigger, and he sagged in the saddle, his horse veering wildly off.

Her gut wrenched at having shot a man, likely killing him, but Berenice made herself lever another round into the chamber and pick a new target—and then Kanaway's big Austro-Hungarian Gasser boomed, and a horse screamed and fell heavily. Its rider leapt free of the saddle.

Kanaway shouted "Dammit!" and Berry knew it was because he'd been aiming at the rider, not the horse— Dave Kanaway was fond of horses—and now the fallen rider, one of Hawthorn's cowboys, was getting up, aiming at Kanaway.

Dave shot the man at close range, right through the middle, the big powerfully propelled bullet blasting a shower of the man's entrails and bones out to hideously decorate the snow.

Looking away, Berry saw another rider coming right at her. She fired, and he twitched but stayed in the saddle and fired back, the bullet ricocheting from the metal rim of the wheel close by, as she chambered another round. But now he rode up, and pointed his six-gun right at her—then Pamahas was there, running up with pistol clutched in both hands, firing over and over, and the raider fell from his horse and lay clutching handfuls of snow, dying.

Milt fired several times at someone Berry couldn't see. A rider screamed in pain.

Brokenwing fired from the soddy, and another raider fell from his horse.

Bullets from a pair of riders struck the freight wagon, and Smallwolf stood up and shot at a cowboy, who seemed to peel slowly from his horse and slip lifeless to the ground.

Leon fired from the side of the wagon, and the other rider slumped in his saddle, the horse veering off. There was a big man, farther away, shouting something at the others. Wovoka stood up and fired at him. The man jerked a little, then turned his horse, and bolted out of range.

She saw Harl Hawthorn, beside a man she didn't know, the two of them riding hard past her, galloping toward Leon and Teresa's house. Berenice had no shot from under the wagon.

As they swung by the house both men tossed lit kerosene lamps through the glassless windows, and fire bloomed inside. They kept riding, angling toward the corral, drawing their pistols and firing at Javier and Luis. The bullets kicked up little sprays of snow near Luis. Javier stood up, calmly aimed, and fired, shooting Harl off his horse; Luis shot the other man with a pistol; the cowboy wheeled his horse and rode off toward town, clutching a wounded shoulder.

Berenice fired at another raider, farther off, who was riding at Smallwolf and the Washoe men. She missed.

Gunfire flicked back and forth, red against the falling whiteness, and then the big rider swung off to the west, calling out, "Back up, boys! Regroup!"

Berenice had made a suggestion to Smallwolf about Hawthorn and she wondered if he'd take it. She was not sure it was the morally right thing to do. But she had to think about Alice.

What would Cleve come back to, she wondered . . .

Cleve stepped to the door, reached around, and fired two shots down the hallway. Someone cursed him and returned fire.

"Come and get it, boys!" he shouted. He reloaded and then followed Guama through the window onto the windy roof—it was a flat-topped roof of the one-story kitchen and storage extension of the big saloon.

Guama was flattened against the wall of the second story, between two windows, pistol in one hand and knife in the other. Cleve eased over to him. Nodding at the window they'd climbed through, Cleve whispered, "Keep an eye on that one."

Guama pointed his gun toward the window and waited. But no one made a move to come out that way.

Cleve sidled toward the other window. The wind soughed, tugging at his hat. He decided to oblige the wind—he took the hat off, and flung it past the window. Someone fired through the window toward it, sending glass flying, likely not even clear on what they were seeing.

Before the glass had fallen, Cleve stepped out and swung his pistol to the window, guessing the shooter was distracted enough he could catch him out . . .

There he was—two dark deep-set button eyes, a hatchet face, his gun swiveling toward Cleve.

And Cleve shot him between those button eyes. The gunman's eyes rolled back and he vanished from the window frame.

"Cleve!" Someone shouted.

Cleve spun, looking for a target, and saw a man standing on the ground below. A man who looked like the one he'd just killed was aiming a rifle up at him. Cleve tried to get a bead on the outlaw but knew he'd be too late—the gunman's head snapped to one side, blood spitting from his left ear. He crumbled, getting off a shot as he fell back. The bullet soared into the sky, its report echoing the shot that had killed him.

"Hold your fire, Cleve!" called a familiar voice. Same voice that had called out the warning.

James Crofton stepped out into view, his hands raised. His right hand had a smoking pistol in it.

"Who'd you shoot, Jim?" Cleve called, stepping

away from the window. Marske was somewhere around, and he didn't want to give anyone another chance to backshoot him.

"That was Monty Denk," said Crofton. "Hired by the feller I used to work for."

"When you stop working for Hawthorn?" Cleve asked.

"When I saw you was about to get shot in the back."

"I'm obliged," Cleve said. "Where's Marske?"

"I'm in here!" Marske called, from the other window. "You can try to get the drop on me here or you can meet me out front!"

Cleve still had that wound in his left side. But he gave it no thought at all. "I'll be there!"

"You tell your friend and that turncoat there to hold their fire," Marske said. "You'll get your chance at me. I give you my word!"

"Your word any good, Marske?"

"Hell, yeah, it is! About the only thing I got worth keeping."

Cleve nodded. "Then we meet, just you and me."

And Cleve Trewe holstered his gun.

The snow had stopped, but as the clouds broke, it was a six-inch blanket of white, sparkling on the ground around them.

"I can't see much from here, lost sight of our boys," Asa muttered.

And then a man rode toward them from the east.

Not one of the Hawthorn hands. Del knew his name. Smallwolf.

"That's one of the Trewe men!" Hawthorn burst out. "Get your rifle out, boy!"

"I told you, Father. I won't do it."

Del was cold, and sick to his stomach. Watching through a spyglass, he'd seen what'd had happened to Ike Springer. His guts shot out with that big Gasser gun. Half a dozen others killed. And the Hawthorns had accomplished nothing.

Smallwolf rode up slowly, one hand on the reins, the other on a holstered six-gun. He was looking right at Asa Hawthorn.

"You come to try for some kind of truce?" demanded Hawthorn.

Smallwolf reined in about fifteen feet away, and shook his head. "No, Hawthorn. All but two of your men are dead, dying, or run off."

"Harl?" asked Del.

"Shot off his horse. Dead."

"Harl!" Del's father blurted. "Killed!"

"He came in shooting. All your men did, and all the living at the ranch are witnesses to that. Mrs. Trewe, she asks me to say this: You can throw down your guns, and go away, and let the law decide. Me, I think they'll put you in jail, Hawthorn. I knew Nethercott when I saw him. He's a coward, and they will send him to Texas, where he'll be hung. Now, speak your piece, old man."

"I will just say"—Hawthorn put his hand on his own sidearm and showed his teeth in an ugly smile—"that

Nethercott and another of my boys are riding up right behind you."

It was true, Del saw. They'd just ridden into sight around a tree-tussled knoll about thirty yards away. Bret Nethercott and a young, bucktoothed cowboy, Checkers Shaw. They'd circled round to get here, Del supposed, to avoid the guns of the Trewe Ranch. Looked like Nethercott had been wounded in the upper left arm. He'd tied a kerchief around it, now bloodstained.

Smallwolf turned to look. In that instant, Hawthorn bared his teeth, pulled his sidearm, and pointed it at Smallwolf.

"No!" Del shouted, leaning to slap his father's gun upward. The gun discharged into the sky. Hawthorn pushed his son angrily away and pointed the gun at Smallwolf again.

Smallwolf drew and fired.

Asa Hawthorn bent over, clutching at his chest, gasping. He stared at the blood on his hand in amazement . . . and then his eyes glazed over and he slumped in the saddle. His mount trotted nervously away . . .

He's dead, Del thought. *He's truly gone. I did that, when I stopped him killing Smallwolf. Am I a patricide?*

A bullet cut by, along with the crack of the gun, and Del turned to see Nethercott riding up, smoking pistol in his hand, aiming it with a golden grin at Smallwolf.

Smallwolf turned in the saddle and fired, and Nethercott twisted in his saddle, the grin becoming a grimace, as the shot caught up right below the heart. He fired back—and Smallwolf grunted, clenching his teeth.

Smallwolf fired twice more, and Nethercott fell, sliding from the saddle.

Swaying, blood dripping onto his saddle, Smallwolf aimed at young Checkers—who threw his gun at the ground, and raised his hands.

"I got no fight here, mister!" the young cowboy said, in a high-pitched voice, his face pent with terror.

Smallwolf waved a hand dismissively. The cowboy turned his mount and galloped off toward the Hawthorn ranch.

Holstering his gun, Smallwolf clutched at a wound just under his ribs.

Del looked at his father's limp body, carried off by his horse as if by the spirit of death. Del didn't feel the cold now. He felt nothing but numb emptiness. His voice came out as a croak. "How bad are you hit, Mr. Smallwolf?"

"Maybe not so bad."

"I'm going to get my father . . . his horse . . . take them to town. If you think you can ride, I'll take you to Mrs. Rinaldi. They say she can work wonders."

"I can ride. Maybe. Yes. I ride."

"Then . . ." Del swallowed a lump in his throat. "Sweet River it is."

"Too bad I bleed so," Smallwolf said. "But for that, I would pry out Nethercott's gold teeth. Make a necklace . . ."

Chapter 23

They'd been waiting in front of the Blacksands for at least ten minutes. The bartender, awakened by all the shooting, had come out to ask if they wanted to order drinks. Cleve, Crofton, and Guama all shook their heads no to that.

Cleve's wound was tied down with another dressing. The bullet had cut clean through, and done little damage so far as he could tell. It hurt—but he knew from experience that wouldn't slow his draw. Pain could put a sharp edge on it.

Now, the wind swirled street dirt into dust devils, and Cleve looked both ways, to the north and south . . . but no Cullen Marske.

"He's got the coward feather," said Guama.

Crofton shook his head. "Don't seem like him. He swore up and down he wanted to duel you down face-to-face, Cleve. Seemed like he meant it."

Cleve was surprised Marske hadn't shown up. Maybe he was setting them up for a rifle kill. Could be Marske was getting a bead right now from a rooftop.

Cleve was standing under the porch roof with his back to the wall. Guama and Crofton were both sitting in porch chairs, Guama holding the shackles Cleve had brought from his saddlebag. He clinked them from one hand to the other, back and forth. They sat there, Cleve thought, like spectators waiting for a bout.

Then he heard the clop of horse's hooves, down to the left.

It was Marske, trotting his horse up to a hitching post at the next building down, a closed-down hardware and tackle store. Marske tied the horse up, and loosened his gun in its holster. Then he looked over, and nodded to Cleve.

Cleve nodded back.

Marske turned and walked to the middle of the street.

"He wants to do this like Wild Bill and Davis Tutt, it seems," Crofton remarked.

Cleve grunted. "Seems so."

Keeping his hands clear of his holstered Colt Army, Cleve walked to the center of the street, stopping about fifty feet from Marske.

"You took your time," Cleve said. "Trying to make me nervous?"

"Wanted to get my horse so I can ride out of here quick, once it's done," Marske said. "Your friends going to stay out of this, afterward?"

"In the unlikely event you survive the encounter," Cleve said, "they are to let you walk away."

Marske nodded. "Fair deal."

"You want to come closer, Cullen, it might be to

your advantage," Cleve said. "I can give you another ten paces nearer."

Marske frowned. His uneven eyes seemed to pull down even more cockeyed with the frown. "Why would you think I'd need to be closer?"

"Can you hit a silver dollar tossed in the air at a distance of fifty feet?"

"I . . ." Marske puzzled for a moment. "I doubt it. Never tried. Can you?"

"Yes, I can. Used to raise money on a bet that way, when I was broke."

Marske nodded. "I believe you. I'll take the ten paces."

He walked slowly closer, exactly ten paces, and stopped. "Say when, Cleve Trewe."

"When," Cleve said, casually.

Marske pulled, and so did Cleve—and Marske stopped, his crooked eyes staring, his gun only halfway out of the holster.

The Colt Army was pointed directly at Marske's heart. Cocked.

But Cleve made no move to fire. He didn't have to—he had the drop on Marske.

Marske licked his lips. "I . . . I didn't see it."

"You were too busy worrying about getting your gun out to see it," Cleve said. "You want to try it again?"

Marske swallowed. A small cloud of dust blew by. "Sure." He holstered his gun.

Cleve holstered his. "Anytime you want."

Marske drew—and again stopped halfway, staring into the muzzle of Cleve's gun.

"No reason to die today," Cleve said. "Tell me this, Marske. Did you kill that little boy?"

"Nope." Marske shoved the gun angrily back into his holster. "I'd have killed the man who did it but the Injuns got him first."

"Maybe you could talk the judge into giving you, say, twenty years. Blame it all on your men. Could be you wouldn't hang, Cullen. Unbuckle the belt, and let it drop, or next time I'll trigger the cartridge."

Marske closed his eyes. Then his shoulders sagged. He unbuckled the gunbelt and let it fall to the street.

"Guama!" Cleve called, still keeping an eye on Marske. He could have a derringer. "Come over here and pick up the gunbelt, if you please, and bring along those shackles."

The shackles dangling in one hand, Guama walked over, singing something in Washoe as he came. There was a ritualistic sound to it.

He stood in front of Marske, dropped the shackles, picked up the gunbelt, and—still singing—drew the gun and shot Marske twice through the body. Marske fell, shouting with pain—and, still singing, Guama shot him in the head.

Crofton gave out a dry, barking laugh.

Cleve holstered his gun, growling, "Goddammit, I wanted to bring one back alive."

Guama tossed the gun aside. He turned to Cleve and asked, "You going to hang me?"

"Nope." Cleve walked over to look at the body. "I can't blame you any."

"He shot my uncle, and my brother. I heard you say he would not hang!"

"I'll write it up that he was trying to escape and got hold of your gun, so you stabbed him. I do hate to lie to the law." Cleve shrugged. "The marshal will guess, anyhow. But he won't mind. Let's tie him over his horse . . ."

Two days later. Five p.m.

It had warmed up just enough for the snow to mostly melt away. It lay in patches here and there, as Cleve rode Ulysses at a canter up to the Trewe Ranch house. Crofton and Guama were riding a ways behind him.

The house seemed untouched. He'd had visions of returning to find it burning down. When he'd stopped in Sweet River, to arrange for Marske's body to be taken to Independence, Javier had told him about the fight at the ranch.

Cleve dismounted and strode up to the door—and it opened for him. His wife stood there looking at him, with a kind of mute wonder.

Cleve's heart lifted but his mouth seemed to stumble. "My Berenice! I heard about—well, I'm sorry, I truly never thought—are you okay? And Alice? Is—"

She put a hand over his mouth. "Do stop babbling, darling. It does not become you." She removed her hand and kissed him.

Leon came to the door, grinning. "This man of yours,

I never see him lose his calm till it's something to do with you, Berry. Then he turns into a worried old lady!"

Teresa was there too—and she laughed at that. She was holding Alice in her arms and the baby seemed to smile at Cleve.

Cleve shrugged—all he really cared about was seeing them all alive and well.

"As you see, we are in rosy health, Cleve," Berry said, reaching to grip his shoulders—it was as if she had to feel the solid reality of him. "You were not to have known Hawthorn would make his move so soon." She put her hands around his waist, and then stepped back at his involuntary gasp of pain. "You're wounded!"

"It's all right, my Berenice. Went right through, all bandaged up—it's a trifle touchy is all."

"Come in this instant, Cleve, take off your hat and I shall pour you a comforting libation . . . Oh! Here are Guama and Crofton!"

They were riding up, and now they dismounted, Crofton taking off his hat. "Ma'am. Appears I'm to work for y'all now."

"Will you? Very well. Come in, both of you."

Chairs and benches were found and arranged, and everyone was soon sitting about the fire in the parlor, except Guama, who sat on the floor near the fire.

"You find Marske out there?" Leon asked.

"Him and his crew. Worked out that Guama had to kill Marske himself. There was a general fight with Marske's crew. Guama killed Indian Dutch too."

"I remember him," said Leon. "Shifty bastard."

"One of Hawthorn's boys got the drop on me and

Jim Crofton here decided it was time to change sides, and cut the man down."

"He was the lowest sort, was Monty Denk," said Crofton. "I had no hesitation. Cleve got the other Denk and Griff Milligan." He turned his hat nervously in his hands and looked at Leon. "Cleve says you're the man I'm to ask about a job."

"I thought you fancied yourself a 'gunny for money,'" Leon said dourly.

Crofton gave a rueful smile. "I've come to think I'm better with a lasso than a gun."

"And better served by that trade," said Berenice.

Crofton ducked his head in a sort of bow to her. "Yes, ma'am."

"Can you rope, or are you just talkin'?" Leon asked.

"I can," said Crofton. "I know ranching and farming and scant else."

"We'll see what we can find for you," Leon said. "Cleve, you heard what happened here?"

"I did. I heard that Smallwolf was wounded, and in Mrs. Rinaldi's care. He was asleep, so I didn't speak to him, but he seems well. She expects him to come through. But hellfire, she gave me an earful! 'Why, Cleve Trewe, do those who work for you catch bullets in your employ?' I tried to say that most of them don't, but she would not hear of it."

There was some laughter at that, but it was subdued, for everyone was thinking of the fight—and the dead.

Cleve drank his brandy as Berry and Leon gave him a full account of the fight; the turning of Hawthorn's herd, the short, brutal battle, the death of Asa Hawthorn.

This last they'd heard from Ringus, who'd gotten it from Smallwolf.

Leon finished off with, "The bodies of Hawthorn's raiders are wrapped up, in a wagon, on its way right now to his ranch. Dave is taking them there, him and Luis."

"I understand Del Hawthorn is now running the place."

"I had a note from him," Berry put in. "He's placing the blame for the deaths entirely on his father's shoulders."

"That eases my mind," Cleve said. "I've sent my account of the affray in Kerosene Corners to Sheriff Morse, along with Marske's body. I'll ask everyone here to sign witnessed affidavits of what happened at the ranch. With so many witnesses here, and with that note from Del, I expect the law will come down clear on our side." After a moment he glanced over at Teresa. "Sorry to hear your house burnt down, Teresa."

"We'll build another," she said. Leon nodded.

There was a silence, except for the crackling of the fire, and Alice's burbling as she tugged at one of Teresa's earlobes.

Then, his voice husky with emotion, Cleve said, "We all came through it. I'm not much for religion. But— that's a blessing."

Still, he wondered about the Paytons. They were behind the attack on the ranch. Hawthorn had been their man. According to what Del Hawthorn had told

Berenice, they'd anticipated making mountainous profits from Sweet Valley. Robber baron profits.

Would they really give it all up?

Fifteen days later. Eight-thirty p.m. Sacramento.

A scornful wind was dashing cold rain at Delbert Hawthorn as he strode up to the front door of the mansion of Jephthah Payton. He ignored the wind and the rain. He didn't feel the cold much now.

An oil lamp glowed over the stone doorstep, making a cone of light in the darkness.

Del lifted the brass knocker and banged four times.

Something more than a minute passed. The rain hissed down. The wind soughed. Del waited, a knot in his stomach.

I could still leave here, he told himself.

But Del stayed right there, waiting. He just wanted to get matters settled. He had scarcely slept since his father's death.

An elderly man in a black suit and tails answered the door. He had rheumy blue eyes that regarded Del with instinctive disapproval. "Yes?"

"I have arranged to visit Judge Payton."

"Indeed?"

"And Grenville Payton. I am Delbert Hawthorn. I fear I'm a little behind my time."

The elderly man looked disappointed. He had hoped to send Del away. "You are expected. Come this way, if you please."

He was escorted to an overwarm library, much larger and finer than his father's. The warm air coming from ornate vents along the floor smelled of heavy heating oil. Somewhere was a furnace. Sitting in a big, black leather chair facing the enormous mahogany desk, Del tried to keep his mind busy imagining the convection system for bringing heat through this imposing house. But his mind returned to the real matter at hand.

I should be afraid, he thought. *But I'm not. Most curious.*

The door opened, and Grenville Payton stalked into the room with his usual urgency, and Jephthah Payton followed, smiling with his usual smugness. Jephthah was in shirtsleeves and a gold-sewn scarlet vest, Grenville in the same suit he'd worn at the gentleman's club that day.

"You're half an hour late!" Grenville snapped. He leaned on the edge of the desk, so he was looming vulture-like over Del.

"I had some last-minute business to attend to," said Del. "Sending some telegrams. Most crucial."

"'Sakes, Gren, it's all right," Jephthah said, chuckling as he lowered himself into the desk chair. "We'll not starve! Why, I shall invite Hawthorn to join us—don't forget, this young man has recently lost his father."

Del winced at that.

Jephthah took a cigar from the desk humidor and offered it to Del, who shook his head. "All the same," the judge went on, "we had better get our business cleared up." He lit the cigar and settled back in his seat. "I understand you've got a proposal, dealing with the

Trewe Ranch." He blew a meditative plume of smoke at the ceiling and went on, "I hope it's better than what poor Asa attempted."

Del smiled sadly at that. "Oh, I think it will be."

Grenville gave Del a look of disgust. "And I heard a rumor that you blame your *father* for that . . . that gun-battle out there!"

"Very good tactics, too, blaming Asa," Jephthah said, pointing his cigar at his brother. "Thus, Delbert separates himself from that dreadful fiasco!" He turned a look of oozing benevolence on Del. "What's your proposal, son?"

Del sat up a little straighter. "I have been busy settling my father's will. He did not approve of me, you know, but I am his only son. He left everything to me, except for a portion meant for Harl. But Harl is dead, so that's mine too."

Jephthah furrowed his brow, managed a look of sympathy. "Tragic, the loss of your father and your cousin too."

"Get on with it, boy!" Grenville snarled, leaning closer.

"The Hawthorn land being now my property," Del went on, "I have arranged to sell it for a marginal sum— to Cleve Trewe."

"What!" Grenville rocked back a little. "Wait—you don't mean you're going into business with Trewe! He's willing to partner with us? Is that it?"

"That is *not* it." Del enjoyed saying it. "He will do with the land, the herd, the house, the stock *exactly as he pleases*. He will get it all. Trewe's payment will go to my estate, which is being handled by Caleb Drask. Drask will see that the money Trewe is to pay is for a schoolhouse in Sweet River, and for a year's pay in the hiring of a teacher. I think a thousand five hundred dollars will cover that. The rest of the Hawthorn cash goes to Trewe."

Grenville looked as if he doubted his own hearing. "You cannot mean . . . a thousand five hundred . . . for all that . . . no!"

"I do mean it. Trewe will own it all for just that sum. Indeed—it's already been done. I got a telegram of confirmation today from Caleb Drask."

"The man is insane, Jephthah!"

"I was thinking the same thing," the judge said calmly, opening a drawer of his desk.

It seemed to Del then that the expression now on Jephthah's face expressed something of his true nature. Snake-like. Venomous.

Jephthah pulled papers and a pen and ink from his drawer. "See that he does not leave, Grenville. The key is there, in that cup. I shall draw up papers to have him committed to an asylum. It will be a simple matter, then, to have the will voided . . ."

Grenville snatched up the key, strode to the door, and locked it. He returned to the desk, showily stowing the key in his pocket. Now his eyes glittered and his mouth was drawn into a rictus grin. "Folks sometimes don't live long in those asylums. Madmen there, you know."

Del nodded, marveling at how little he felt about all this. Just simple, undiluted determination. That's what he felt. It was all clear as a bell. "I rather thought you would play that card, as my father liked to say. Committing me to a madhouse. Well, perhaps I *am* a bit mad now. But it won't matter. I won't be going to a madhouse."

Jephthah looked at him narrowly. "I recall . . . you said that your estate would receive the money from Trewe?"

"They will." Del unbuttoned his coat as he said, "A bank will transfer it tomorrow to the executor of my estate."

"What do you mean, your estate?" Grenville demanded.

"I will be dead, you see." Del stood up, clawing the gun from his pants pocket, and he stepped back from the two men. It was small, a .32, but it would do the job at this range.

They gaped at the pistol as Del went on, "I'll be dead but so will you gentlemen. I cannot let you pursue the Trewe Ranch—and I know you would. I saw it in your faces when I showed you that map. The lust for money, unbridled, is a *true* madness—far worse than mine. You will not stop till you have the land to see your project through. And Berenice Trewe would not come out of it unscathed. You would kill her if it helped your cause."

"So that's it!" Jephthah said, laughing as he opened another drawer. "A woman!"

The judge plucked up a .45 revolver from the drawer, raised it—and Del shot him, without hesitation, right in the breastbone. Jephthah gasped, and his trembling hand dropped the gun on the desk as Del fired again.

The judge collapsed into his chair.

Del pivoted to bring the gun to Grenville—who was scooping up the gun on the desk.

Del fired. But so did Grenville.

Del fired the .32 again as he stumbled backward, slammed by the bullet from the .45. He bumped into the wall and sank down, sitting heavily on the carpeted floor. He felt life draining out, hot and red and wet, through a burning hole in his chest.

Grenville swayed, shot close to the heart. He went to his knees. He tried to raise the .45 again . . . but it was too heavy for his hand now. He licked his lips, then his eyes opened wide and he stared into Del's face. "You have *killed* me. You!"

"I . . ." Del coughed and tasted the blood filling his lungs. "I wish to thank you for allowing me to die . . . to die thus." He spat a mouthful of blood on the carpet. "I had thought to shoot myself, when . . . but this . . . It is better . . ."

Grenville wavered on his knees, his mouth going slack, his face gone to puzzlement.

The two dying men looked into each other's eyes. Del saw Grenville anew. He seemed to see him as a worried, anxious boy, a young man bullied by some tyrannical father into the twisted thing he had become.

And, as it became much harder to breathe, he felt that Grenville glimpsed something in him too.

Just for a moment, two dying men saw each other as they really were . . .

And then Grenville tipped forward, falling onto his face. And Del's vision darkened. He wished he could see someone else, one more time.

Yes—there she was, luminous, glowing against the all-encompassing night. And his last thought was . . .

Berenice.

Chapter 24

Summer. 1876.

"Mr. Watson, come here, I want to see you."

"So that's what he said, my Berenice? The first words on that telephonic instrument—one would think they'd be of more moment."

"It's not important what he said, dear. Only that Mr. Bell's assistant was able to hear them."

"I don't know if I'd want such a device in my house, might be like a guest you can't get rid of. It'd wear out its welcome. Though I could see its use on the battlefield."

They were relaxing in padded high-backed wicker chairs, enjoying the warm evening on the broad porch of the Hawthorn house. The sprawling two-story home was now primarily occupied by Leon and Teresa and their new baby, Nathaniel, named after one of Leon's many relatives. Naturally, the infant was already called Nate, and just now he was sleeping peacefully in a cradle near Berenice. Teresa was in the kitchen, and as she had often looked after Alice, now sometimes Berenice looked after Nate.

Alice was sitting on the porch at Cleve's feet, playing in the lamplight with a wooden horse artfully carved for her by Javier. "Horse . . . jump!" she chirped, making the horse jump.

"What's that horse's name, Alice?" Cleve asked.

"It's Poly Lita," she said somberly.

"You mean Hippolyta?"

"Yes, Poly Lita. My horse."

Cleve smiled, glad to be talking with Alice and not worrying about the announcement he had to make tonight. He was a little unsettled about how it might be taken by the guests coming to this dinner party. He was of a mind to wait till they all got there.

Teresa was making dinner with Pamahas and Javier, the three of them making an extravagant Mexican dinner under the critical eye of Luis Diaz, and aided by Luis's young *amaguita,* Mariana. Every so often Cleve could hear fragments of argument in rapid-fire Spanish coming from the kitchen.

He listened to the crickets sawing away like tuneless fiddlers, and watched the fireflies darting like runaway stars. He stretched and took a deep breath of the fragrant night. Berenice and Teresa had planted roses in the spring, while he was away with the drovers taking the herd to market. The market for beef was up this season, and Cleve and Leon had fattened their bank accounts considerably on the original herd. Another set of drovers had been hired to take Asa Hawthorn's cattle to auction. Cleve and Berry donated their share of that herd to the Occidental Mission House, for the benefit of distressed Chinese women.

The big house was in sight of the river, rippling with moonlight, and Cleve wondered if he should have kept it for his own family. But it hadn't felt right, and Berenice was reluctant to move from the house nestled against the foothills of the Sierras. She had insisted, however, on having three rooms added to it.

"It's a pity the Blevins couldn't come. I'd like to talk to Catalina about the correspondence from Professor Hydebank—his doubts regarding penicillium."

"Kind of discouraging correspondence, from those old medical mummies."

"An apt description of them, but we must keep trying. Oliver and Catalina will be back from Spain shortly and we must have them over. Oliver having dutifully converted to the Holy Roman Church, he would see Alice baptized . . . Do you think we should?"

"Mrs. Gunderson asks me about baptism every time I'm in the store, with many a hint of calamity in the afterworld. It'd be worth it just to put a stopper on that. It'll make the Blevins happy too."

"Cleve—it was so sweet of you to pay for their wedding trip."

"Me? The town paid for it! A hat was passed!"

"A hat indeed! You try to hide these things, but I know perfectly well you paid almost all of it. And you paid for a second room in the schoolhouse. Then there was the money you *suppose* you secretly gave to Javier for that Mexican family living in the cabin down by the cemetery."

Cleve scowled. "Who are the spies you keep in this gossip-ridden place?"

"Never you mind. My intelligence service is vast and loyal."

He spread his hands. "I don't know what to do with all this munificence from the Hawthorn estate. All this land—and the house. It doesn't seem quite right, how it came to us. In fact—well, we'll discuss that a little later." Wanting to change the subject and knowing just how to do it with Berenice, he said, "Now how do you suppose those fireflies came to glow like lamps?"

"There are theories, but it's yet a mystery. Biological fluorescence is perplexing—almost miraculous."

"As a boy, I captured fireflies in a jar, to try to make a light in my bedroom."

"There are numerous species of firefly—yet they are all *Lampyridae,* order *Coleoptera,* a form of beetle, feeding on snails and slugs. I think our friends here are the species *Ellychnia californica.* Some have supposed the glow helps them to see their prey at night but it's more likely courtship behavior, and in fact, patterns of lighting passing betwixt male and female are quite apparent to me . . ."

And she was off, speculating, marveling, making plans to capture some fireflies for scrutiny with the Hawkins and Wale compound microscope, brought all the way from New York, that he'd given her for Christmas. Cleve had ordered it via telegram when they'd come through Sacramento. It had taken four months to arrive. She'd rewarded him with especial passion.

The Washoe and Paiute were having some sort of a midsummer powwow tonight, off at their property adjacent the Trewe Ranch—the wickiup camp had become a lodge and log cabins. But Smallwolf was here, coming now from the barn, lantern in hand, accompanied by Leon, Milt, and Jim Crofton. They'd been inspecting Hippolyta, who was now a young horse. "That filly's a lady now, Berry," Milt said.

"She's no lady," Berry said, "she's a suffragette, just like me and her mother."

Milt stopped in his tracks and looked at her critically to see if he was being made fun of. "A suffragette! Not votes for horses now!"

"Careful, Milt," Cleve said. "Berry keeps a derringer near to hand."

Berry smiled—a smile that, for Cleve, outshone firefly glow and the rising moon.

She shook her head demurely. "I was referring to the fact that a herd of horses is a matriarchal society. There are males who protect the herd, but the real leadership comes from the women."

Milt frowned—then nodded. "It's true enough, of horses. But—"

"Quit before she shoots you, Milt," Leon said.

Cleve heard the jangle of an approaching buggy. Kanaway was arriving, bringing Mickal with him, and both their fiddles.

Cleve figured it was just about time to tell them all what he had in mind . . .

Once the babies were put to bed upstairs, the dinner unfolded in numerous courses. Numerous toasts were drunk, and there was a general discussion about plans to move the ranch to new, larger quarters on the Hawthorn land. Berry spoke about her enthusiasm for the small herd of Brahma bulls she'd purchased, extolling the resistance to disease in the hardy breed from India.

Leon was sitting on Cleve's left, talking intently with Dave Kanaway about horse breeding.

Cleve poured himself another brandy, and Leon turned to him, and said, "I don't think I told you, there was a feller looking for you in Sweet River yesterday, when I was there buying supplies."

"What feller was that?"

"Turns out he was a reporter from Sacramento, looking to talk to you about the fight at Kerosene Corners, and the raid on Trewe Ranch."

"I wasn't even here for that."

"I told him so. He insisted on seeing you, going to write you up big."

"And you told him what?"

Leon elbowed him. "That you was long gone to the Yukon, looking for gold! Your poor wife was like to be a gold dust widow! Y'all are wasting your time here, I said. And if you go out to the ranch, those Indians will stake you to an anthill! They hate newspapermen!"

"Quick thinking, Leon. Where's he now?"

"I told him I didn't like newspapermen, neither, and I strongly hinted that if he didn't want his hide nailed to a wall, he should clear out. Well, he got in his buggy and drove lickety-split for parts unknown!"

Cleve raised a glass to Leon. "To absent newspapermen!"

They drank to that. Then Cleve decided it was time. He took a deep breath, and said, somewhat loudly, "There's something I'd like to discuss with all you folks . . ."

The room quieted. They looked at him, wondering if this was something good—or something bad.

"Firstly, if Berenice is in agreement, I'm thinking I'll sell off my part of the Hawthorn Ranch." There was stunned silence. He turned to Berry. "I'm sorry to be so sudden. I didn't make up my mind till we got here—and decided to just lay it in front of everybody all at once."

Berry looked more interested than alarmed. "Sell it to whom, Cleve?"

"Most of the folks who wanted it are dead," Crofton said. This dry observation drew frowns among the other guests.

"Plenty of buyers out there for land like that," said Leon. "But like Berry said . . . Who?"

"Why—*you,* Leon," said Cleve. "You're already living here. You got a good payout for your share of the herd. Now, I won't sell it for a foolish price like the one I got it for—that was just poor Delbert's way of making a point. But it'll be a reasonable price. You'll go from foreman and part-owner to full-on cattle baron!"

Leon blinked. "Are you funning me?"

"Nope. I don't feel I should own the Hawthorn land. Might get used to it—but I don't want that much responsibility. I'm already Deputy U.S. Marshal. It didn't feel right, when I quit being Deputy of Elko County so soon after taking that oath. I'll see this one out for a year or two. But with what it takes to run a big spread like that, I don't think I can be working for the U.S. Marshals at the same time. Not and be a good husband—and a father. And as for that . . . if Berenice is okay with telling folks now . . ."

She nodded. "I am with child again!"

Congratulations poured forth, with the men pounding on the table and everyone raising glasses to Berenice.

"So you see," Cleve went on, "I want to stay around the ranch as much as I can. We'll still be raising Brahma bulls, and we'll get some Angus in, too. Not a big herd. And I intend to start a vineyard, with the partnership of Mr. and Mrs. Blevin."

"A fine idea!" called Luis. "Put me in charge of the wine barrels!"

They laughed, and then Cleve continued, "Like my father before me, I'll be using a good deal of my land for raising vegetables. I believe that Sweet River will grow. A telegraph is to come here next year. And a stagecoach line!"

"What!" cried Leon. "When you hear of this?"

"From me, this morning," said Javier. "I have come

from Independence last night. It is true. And a railroad is coming to Independence."

"A splendid time for an ambitious farm," said Berenice.

"Ha! Farmer Cleve!" snorted Milt.

Cleve smiled ruefully. "I grew up with it. I know more about that business than I let on. But all this is depending on"—He turned to Berenice—"Mrs. Trewe. For she and I"—He took her hand—"Are partners in everything. If Mrs. Trewe says *no* . . . Then I'll keep the Hawthorn ranch and have another think about what to do with it."

Berenice put a crafty look on her face. "I have been corresponding with the botanist Gregor Mendel."

Cleve blinked in confusion. "And the bearing of that, my Berenice?"

"Can we use part of our own land for botanical research? Say, ten percent?"

"Certainly we can!"

"*And*—can I ask Gregor Mendel himself to voyage here from Austria, all expenses paid, to carry out certain experiments?"

The expression on Cleve's face made some of his friends laugh. "Why . . . I suppose so."

"Then by all means—full steam ahead, Mr. Trewe!" With that, she kissed him.

After another round of hooting and table pounding, Cleve called for quiet, and said, "But there is another consideration—I have decided that my top hands can have ten acres of good Hawthorn land along the river. Call it a bonus for their hard work. All they need do is agree to stay for at least ten years, and improve that land. Smallwolf there, Dave Kanaway, Milt, Wovoka, and Guama—and Crofton, too, because he saved my bacon in Kerosene Corners."

Smallwolf nodded. Crofton and Milt stared at Cleve, then looked at one another. And grinned.

"That's mighty generous, Cleve," Kanaway said, looking dazed. "Ten acres along the river!"

"We're going to need good men close by," said Cleve. "Now, Leon—if those grants are good with you . . . all the rest of the Hawthorn land is yours for . . ." He bent over and whispered a price to Leon. Not a small price—but more than reasonable.

Leon's eyes lit up.

Cleve said, "Mr. Studge—do we have a deal?"

Leon looked at Teresa, who nodded excitedly. Then Leon said, "Dammit, Major—we have a deal!"

Cleve and Leon shook hands. There was applause and foot-stomping at this too.

Then Cleve called out, "Just one more thing!"

Groans and nervous laughter from the assemblage. "Now what, Cleve?" Leon demanded.

Cleve drew a small folder from his inside coat pocket. "I have here a document sent to me by Marshal Beaman this morning . . ."

"Oh no," said Berry, sighing. "How soon?"

"Tomorrow," Cleve said. "The Cutter Gang, over on the Humboldt River. Dead or alive. But . . ." He put an arm around Berenice. "I'll be back, quick as I can. You have my oath on that, my Berenice. And now . . ."

He tossed the warrant onto the table and turned to the others. "We got two fiddlers and a guitar player just sitting here, eating and drinking and giving nothing in return. What say we have some music?"

So everyone went to the parlor, where two fiddles and a guitar played on and on, well into the night.

Did you miss the previous book
in the Cleve Trewe Western series?

Keep reading for an excerpt.

GUNMETAL MOUNTAIN

John Shirley

Civil War veteran Cleveland Trewe stumbles onto
a bizarre cult in the Sierra Nevada mountains—
where the faithful are healed and fates are sealed . . .
in blood.

They say the road to Hell is paved with good
intentions. But it's hard to know what's going on
inside the twisted mind of Magnus Lamb, the
charismatic leader of an isolated logging town known
for its healing hot springs. Some might say he's
created a peaceful utopia here on Gunmetal Mountain.
But for Cleveland Trewe and his lovely traveling
companion, Berry, this little piece of Heaven
is more like Hell on Earth . . .

Cleve and Berry first discover the town after an
encounter with a dangerous band of Indians.
Cleve vows to find "the Coyote," a young brave last
seen headed for the strange settlement of Lambsville.
At first, Cleve and Berry are charmed by the town's
natural beauty and simple way of life.
But soon they see the community for what it really is:
a brainwashed cult with some oddball beliefs,
a rigid caste system, and a leader who thinks
he's the new Messiah.
This not-so-innocent Lamb has heard about Cleve's
legendary gunfighting skills and wants him to lead
an army to expand his power across the West.
It's bound to be a blood-soaked mission,
and Cleve wants no part of it.
But if he refuses, there'll be hell to pay . . .

Look for *Gunmetal Mountain*. On sale now!

Chapter 1

Northern Nevada. November 1874.

Chance Breen was just sitting in the saddle, he and his mustang half hidden by the gnarled bristlecone pines fringing the top of the bluff, when he spotted a man and a woman riding together far below. The riders were alone, looking small in the broad basin of windblown yellow grass below the limestone bluff. Breen took a spyglass from his saddlebag, his horse stirring nervously under him. "Hold still, you," Breen muttered.

Circled in the spyglass, the man and woman were a scruffy pair. The fellow in the charcoal Stetson was bearded, his long gray coat battered; the woman a little slumped, wiping dust from her eyes, her bonnet hanging behind on its tie. Both looked trail worn. The man rode a sorrel stallion, the woman a dappled Arabian mare. They had scarcely anything packed on their lean, weary mounts. But Breen did see that each had a saddle gun, maybe Winchesters. He could just make out an

ammunition belt on the man. Likely there was a revolver
to go with it.

Riding from that direction, they must have been
traveling alone for a powerful long distance. There
wasn't much out that way. After such a long, parched
ride they'd be just about worn-out, and wondering if
they were lost.

Yep, Breen figured, they'd be ready to talk to folks.
Might be happy for someone to guide them along . . .

Breen grinned, put away his spyglass, and drew his
horse slowly back from the edge of the bluff. Then he
turned and rode back toward the camp in the small
grove of locust trees.

Berenice Conroy Tucker and Cleveland Trewe were
indeed saddle weary.

Cleve glanced appraisingly over at Berenice. She'd
worn that same black riding habit most of the way. Her
jacket was lined but not warm enough. Though tired,
underfed, and dusty, Berenice Conroy Tucker never lost
her wide-eyed pleasure in the countryside. A natural
philosopher—what some called a "scientist"—Berry
observed the world more closely than most. *She's not
naive*, Cleve thought, *just recklessly brave*. She had
grown up in a wealthy family and for the greater part of
her life she had lived in luxury. But she had a wild
streak, a fervent interest in nature, and a fierce determination.

Looking barren from a distance, northern Nevada's
rough landscape teemed with life if you watched for it.

Berry delighted in the snakes and lizards; in bighorn sheep clambering impossible routes across sheer cliff faces, where no track should be. Her gaze trailed hawks and eagles across the sky. She was fascinated by the instinctive strategy of coyotes in the gullies, cooperating to take a fat grouse. Passing through a dry wash, Berry and Cleve had cooly observed a wolverine driving off a puma. When they camped, Cleve sat quietly beside her, watching her make pencil sketches and notes.

He was forever keeping watch over Berenice. Cleve knew how perilous this country could be. Sometimes his watchfulness and warnings exasperated her and she would sigh and give him a wry look. But she never really complained.

Seven days back in the foothills of the Santa Rosa Range they'd run into rough weather. They kept on, riding head on into cold, bone-dry winds. When they found the trail ahead collapsed into a ravine, they were forced to detour northeast and then south, through sere, nearly waterless country. It had taken them four days to get out of the hills and down into the grasslands of Paradise Valley.

Berry didn't grumble after they were forced twenty-one miles out of their way to search for another trail, not even when they went two days without water. She was concerned for the horses when their water ran dry, but said nary a word about being thirsty herself.

Before they set out from Axle Bust, Cleve thought he couldn't admire her more. He was mistaken.

One day when the thirst got especially bad, Cleve noticed Ulysses and Suzie snuffling the air and whickering as they looked northwest. He decided to give them their head. Cleve and Berry both felt a childlike joy when the horses found a clear, deep waterhole—and the trail that ran northwest beside it.

Now they trotted their horses along a sketch of a road—merely dirt ruts in the grass. The sun was easing down before them. Their overlapping shadows stretched out behind.

Cleve pulled the brim of his hat down in front, and Berenice put her bonnet on to shade her eyes.

"There is no doubt at all we're going due west," she said, watching a slender green coachwhip snake sliding sinuously off through the grass.

He gave an exaggerated frown, pretending to be perplexed. "Now just how do you figure that?"

Berry smiled. "My hypothesis is based on this fact: the sun is sinking low and we're riding straight for it. Thus—west."

He nodded sagely. "I concur, Doctor Tucker. I'm pleased to ratify your observation."

"That is the crux of the scientific method in a nutshell—one's observations tested by peers."

"That's what I am to you, your peer?"

"Why, you're another kind of *hypothesis* being tested," she said pertly. "I *theorize* that you are suitable for mating purposes."

"Seems to me we've already mated a number of times on the way here."

"The tests must continue," she declared. She lifted her chin and put on a pedagogical tone. "A great many such experiments will be necessary."

"I sure as hell hope I confirm your hypothesis," he said. "Already made up my mind, on my end of things."

"So far, the results are encouraging." Done teasing him, she reached over and took his hand. "Are we really back on track to the trading post, Cleve?"

"I reckon we're no more than fifteen miles away."

She sighed, and unconsciously reached up to pat her windblown chestnut hair into place, tucking stray locks under her bonnet. "I must look like a scarecrow," she said. "The town women will stare and shake their heads."

"Won't be many women there to judge you. Mostly men. The men will be agog to see a pretty woman ride in at all. Those men would be pleased to see you even if you were dressed in an old feed sack."

She laughed. They rode on, and in a few minutes, she asked, "Should we not rest the horses?"

"Oh, they'll be all right. They'll be just as happy to get to town as we will. Once there, we'd best stake them well apart . . ." They'd had to work at keeping the horses from mating in the last two days, the mare having come into heat a bit late in the season. They would have a long journey, and a mare in foal shouldn't undergo such rigors.

"Suzie is looking to confirm her mate, too—with your Ulysses—but on a more temporary basis," Berry observed. "Horses, perhaps wisely, do not mate for life."

"Does Berenice Conroy Tucker mate for life?"

"She mates for life or not at all."

Cleve smiled. He hadn't proposed marriage—"mating

for life" might have to be enough. Berry had told him that her only experience with marriage, ending when Mr. Tucker had died, had put her off the institution. She had come to regard it as "a ritual devised by ancient patriarchs to make serfs of women." But he already felt married to Berry, and he hoped that in time she'd accept the legalities. Convincing her might not be easy, she being as forward-thinking a woman as he'd ever heard of: a suffragist, a scientist, a social reformer. He'd dallied with many a woman in his travels. But Berenice was a woman of empathy, strength, intellect, and beauty—and the only woman he'd ever truly fallen for. Settling down didn't come easily to Cleveland Trewe . . .

After serving as a Union officer in the war, Cleve had traveled extensively in Europe and England. When he ran short of funds, he returned to the States and tried working on his father's estate and clerking for his uncle. But when he wasn't traveling—afoot somewhere new—the darkest memories of the war would plague him.

So Cleve headed west. He took work as an itinerant scout, mostly for the cavalry. He found that if he kept traveling, the war receded to the back of his mind. He put in his time as a cowboy for a long drive with Charles Goodnight. After that he'd tried his hand gambling in Colorado—and when his luck ran dry, he hired on as assistant town marshal in Denver.

A few years of lawing were quite enough. He caught the gold fever and took up prospecting. He traveled from mining claim to mining claim, working feverishly but futilely around Virginia City—and then he got a letter from his uncle.

Threatened by claim jumpers, Uncle Terrence summoned him to the lawless northern Nevada town of Axle Bust. There, Cleve met Berry. And there, too, he reluctantly accepted the job of Elko County sheriff's deputy.

In time, Cleve left Axle partly to get away from his own growing reputation as a gunman, but mostly because he'd supposed Berenice, the daughter of a mining magnate, was taking up with a certain former beau.

In reality, Berenice had no such union in mind. All alone, she tracked Cleve down on the trail north, and insisted—against all propriety and common sense—on riding out to California with him. They were headed to San Francisco, and maybe farther. There was a certain valley he'd found near the California Sierras . . .

"Let's get on and see if there's room at the inn," he said. "A little canter won't hurt these two."

Cleve and Berry picked up their pace, both wanting to get to shelter, fresh water, food supplies, and the possibility of barbering and baths.

As they rode, Cleve scanned the valley: the grassy basin stretching on to the west ahead, the distant blue hills to the north, the tree-topped bluff, rising in red clay to the south. A quarter mile to the south, the bluff ended in a precipice.

Beneath the cliff, a rider swung into view, heading northwest.

"Now who could that be?" Berry asked, shading her eyes with her hand.

"Just a drifter on his way to the trading post, I expect," Cleve said.

"It appears he's coming our way."

"Could be he figured maybe it's safer to ride with us. The Bannock might be stirred up."

Cleve and Berry hadn't seen any Indians since leaving Axle Bust, though in the hills they'd noticed the tracks of unshod ponies likely belonging to the Paiute.

The rider seemed to notice them and halted his dun mustang about four hundred yards distant. He peered at them, then took off his hat and waved it. Berry waved back. The rider turned his horse, coming toward them at a casual lope.

They all reined in at the edge of an old buffalo wallow, and there the rider trotted up with a grin and a wave. He was a thickset man, dressed in beaded buckskins. He had long, uncombed brown hair and a spade beard, and wore the sort of floppy, oiled-leather hat protecting against hard weather. His bronzed, sun-etched face was round, and his gap-toothed grin jolly. On his left hip was a Remington Army revolver. A shotgun waited in a scabbard by the cantle of his saddle.

Cleve kept his expression genial, but he'd let his right hand fall to the butt of his Colt. He knew how to lay his hand loosely on his gun to let folks know it could be easily drawn, without quite making a threat.

"How do!" the stranger said, giving a mock salute. "Well say, you folks are coming from the far country. Headed for the Overland railroad? You're a long fetch from Winnemucca." The nearest leg of the Transcontinental railroad was the Central Pacific, with a station at

Winnemucca, maybe sixty or seventy miles south from where they were. Cleve and Berry were both much attached to their mounts and reluctant to ship them by rail, having heard of many a horse getting a broken leg with the pitching of stock cars. Still, Cleve had suggested they head to Winnemucca for the train, since it might be safer for Berry. She refused to risk Suzie, and pointed out that the train would keep her "a considerable remove from the living abundance of the land." And she treasured a desire to meet Indians up close.

"You two goin' to Paradise?" the stranger asked.

Cleve thought of a facetious reply to that, but he said, "The trading post. They call it Paradise now?"

"They sure do, this being Paradise Valley. I'm headin' there. Mind if I ride along? Safety in numbers."

"You're welcome to," said Berry, more quickly than Cleve would have liked.

"What do they call you?" Cleve asked it mildly but kept a close watch on the man.

"My name's Breen. And you folks?"

"The lady is Mrs. Berenice Tucker," Cleve said. Still *Mrs.* because she was widowed. Her husband, a mining engineer, had died in a flooded shaft several years earlier.

Breen touched his hat brim to her. "Miz Tucker."

Cleve decided not to give his own name unless pressed. His notoriety might have spread to Paradise Valley. "You can tag along, if you choose, Breen."

He gestured to indicate Breen should start off first. The drifter hesitated, then started out.

Cleve rode after him, keeping a few paces back.

Berry caught up to Cleve and gave him a puzzled look, wondering about his coldness to a harmless stranger.

He shrugged. He was just taking commonsense precautions, a procedure Berry often set aside as uninteresting.

"Going to get cold out here," Breen said, raising his head to sniff the wind. "T'was mighty hot, and I cussed it too. Another fortnight or so comes a sharp wind from the north—Indians call it the Ice Wing. You'll feel it flyin' down through this valley. Won't snow much, but that wind's enough to make a man's nose fall off. Was me, did I have money for the fare, I'd take the train to somewhere easier."

Instinctively wanting to change the subject, Cleve said, "Last time I was through here, I saw a good many herds. Cowboys watching the beef. We've seen no one in this valley so far."

"It's the season. They get fat enough, they take them down to the Little Humboldt River, not so cold there and plenty of water. Fatten 'em up some more along the riverbanks, then drive 'em to Winnemucca for freighting." Breen looked over his shoulder at Cleve. "Where you folks headed to after Paradise? Up to Oregon?"

When Cleve didn't answer, Berry said, "Cleve wanted a look at California." She took up her canteen. "He's only seen a small part of it." She drank from the canteen, with the reins wound around the saddle horn, knowing Suzie would stay on the road. "I'm eager to see California myself. We hope to spend most of the winter in San Francisco. In the spring, we plan to see the

Yosemite. I read about it in *Hutchings' Magazine*. A wondrous place! Then there's a valley Cleve wishes to see in southeastern California . . ."

Breen was looking at her openmouthed. He wasn't used to a woman answering for a man and speaking out so boldly. He closed his mouth, chuckled, and asked, "Going to buy some land, are you?"

"We just might," Berry said airily. "There are matters yet unsettled. Life is more exciting, is it not, Mr. Breen, when things aren't quite settled?"

"Ha-*ha!* That it is!" Breen shook his head. "But it seems to me there's easier ways to get to San Francisco than what you took. 'Course, those ways cost a mite . . ."

"We did it our own way," said Cleve shortly, nettled by this prodding into their business. It seemed to Cleve that Breen wanted to know how much money they might be carrying.

Breen slowed his mustang, dropping back a little. "Ha-*ha!* Why sure! Don't mean to pry. Just talking to try out my tongue. Been so long out here with no one to jaw with but Bart here." He patted the horse and glanced sidelong at Suzie. "That's a fine mare you're riding, ma'am. She an A-rab?"

"She is a purebred Arabian, yes, and a very spirited girl too." Berry used her hand to brush dust from Suzie's mane. "One who needs a good brushing."

"How'd you come to be out here, yourself?" Cleve asked. "Business up on that bluff?"

"You could say so. I went to see a prospector friend, he's got hisself a cabin out that way. Pays me to bring him whiskey. His woman sets a good table too. But it's no more'n an excuse for the ride, you see. Then I heads out to do some prospecting, all on my lonesome. Found nothing but a piece of silver no bigger'n a booger. Run out of supplies, so I'm off to the trader. But a man like me, what keeps him going is his curiosity. And I cannot calculate how it come, you two riding out of that wilderness alone. Maybe you had a Conestoga, back along the trail? Lost a wheel?"

"Nope." Cleve said. "We rode from Axle Bust on these mounts."

"Axle Bust! Why a man would take that route at all, I don't know, if he ain't prospecting. And you ain't got the look of prospectors. Could be you needed to get out of Axle Bust right quick?"

Cleve nudged Ulysses up a little and gave Breen a cold look. "You wouldn't understand our reasons, Mr. Breen. Your *curiosity* will have to be satisfied with that."

"Why sure, sure . . . ha-*ha!*"

Cleve slowed Ulysses, to keep Breen ahead, and the three rode on in silence, except for Breen humming a drover song, sometimes throwing in a phrase or two. "When she see me comin' . . ." *Hum, hum-hum.* ". . . is you a cowboy'n has you been paid . . ." *Hum, hum-hum.*

Another three miles of the same song with many repetitions. Now orange outcroppings of dull red sandstone humped out from the grass. The wind picked up, not yet the Ice Wing, but cold enough to make Cleve shiver. It blew at them in gusts, so the grass rippled like a yellow sea.

A mile more and the outcroppings became boulders. Some were big enough to hide a man and his horse. Cleve noticed Ulysses pricking up his ears, neighing softly, head lifted, eyes searching ahead. He could feel the tension in the horse's body.

Breen reined in, and muttered something about, "I believe ol' Bart has a durn rock in his shoe . . ." He dismounted and went down on one knee, frowning at the mustang's right front horseshoe.

Ulysses stepped past Breen and a gust of wind brought the smell of horses from up ahead. Quite near. Cleve realized he'd let Breen get behind him. He drew Ulysses up short—

"Cleve!" Berry said sharply.

Cleve turned in his saddle to see Breen going for his revolver.

Berry had already drawn her rifle from its scabbard, and she shouted, "Drop it, mister!"

Surprised, Breen turned to her, his hand dropping from the pistol butt, as Cleve drew his Colt Army. Then a shot cracked past him—and he swiveled in the saddle, drawing his gun. A man was crouched by a boulder on the left. Floppy hat slanted low over his face, the shooter was aiming a rifle at Cleve's brisket.

Ulysses held just steady enough—as Cleve dropped the muzzle of the revolver and returned fire.

The outlaw jerked backward, Cleve's round cutting a deep groove through his forehead.

Breen shouted, "Davy!" and jumped on his horse, rode toward the boulder. He paused to stare a moment at the dead man. Ulysses was shifting nervously and Cleve was trying to get him back under control so he could aim at Breen . . .

The outlaw cursed and spurred his horse, riding off hard to the south.

Cleve aimed—then Breen was around the boulder, hooves thumping as he rode away south.

Berry fired her Winchester—but not at Breen. Cleve looked up in time to see a bearded man in a plug hat ducking under cover at the top of the boulder.

Spurring Ulysses, Cleve called out, "Take cover, Berry!" He rode at a canter around the big rock, past the dead man. He saw no sign of Breen, but the bush-whacker in the plug hat was just jumping down to the grassy turf. The outlaw landed heavily on his feet, grunting, his hat falling off. He turned a dragoon pistol toward Cleve.

Ulysses was still cantering, which made the shot harder, so Cleve fired three times in under two seconds, the first shot grazing the man, the next taking him in the right shoulder, the third catching him under the chin.

The dragoon dropped from the man's shaking fingers as the outlaw tipped onto his back. Cleve drew up, glancing around, seeing no one else.

The outlaw gurgled, spat blood, tried to rise—and then went limp.

Cleve noticed two horses—a mustang and a paint pony—about thirty yards back, staked out in a cleft between boulders. There were saddles on the ground back there and a few tin cans—signs of a cold camp. The men had been waiting here for a while; Breen had set the trap, and tried to herd Cleve and Berry into it.

Cleve smiled grimly, then turned Ulysses around, patting the horse's neck with one hand. "You're a good man in a fight, Ulysses." He'd trained the stallion to steadiness around gunfire, but it couldn't hurt to praise him.

He rode back to Berry; she was down on one knee, in a shooting position, rifle in her hands, looking off to the south, the way Breen had gone.

"You think he's close by, Cleve?" Just the faintest tremble in her voice.

"He's probably gone out of range. And if I chase him, he'll set up to ambush me."

"Then please refrain."

Cleve nodded. "I was wondering about that shotgun. Most anyone with honest business out here, they're going to have a rifle. Shotgun's more something carried by road agents. I didn't give him a chance to use it, so he set up for the six shooter."

He shaded his eyes, stood up in the saddle but saw no sign of Breen—except maybe a little dust rising, a good distance off. "I don't think we'll see him again today."

Berry looked sheepish. "I was foolish to trust him, I guess."

Cleve dismounted and went to Berry. She stood up and stepped into his arms.

"You did fine," he said softly. "You're a wonder, Berry."

"The other two men?" whispering into his shoulder.

"They're dead. We'll put the bodies on their horses, and take them . . ." He shrugged.

". . . to Paradise."

Visit our website at
KensingtonBooks.com
to sign up for our newsletters, read
more from your favorite authors, see
books by series, view reading group
guides, and more!

Become a Part of Our
Between the Chapters Book Club
Community and Join the Conversation

Betweenthechapters.net

Submit your book review for a chance to win exclusive
Between the Chapters swag you can't get anywhere else!
https://www.kensingtonbooks.com/pages/review/